The Voyage of
Ilse Witch

"*The Voyage of the* Jerle Shannara should help fill the void Harry Potter fans feel in the pits of their stomachs, and they might even find themselves waiting for the next Shannara novel with the same thirst they have for Harry."
—*Rocky Mountain News*

"If you were delighted and entranced by Michael Ende's *The Never Ending Story*, you will definitely want to sample one or more of Terry Brooks's books."
—*Santa Cruz Sentinel*

"This lively new adventure, set a generation later, combines the familiar quest format used in *The Sword of Shannara* with an array of well-defined characters and malevolent beings. . . . Fans familiar with the Shannara series, and new readers as well, will enjoy this first Shannara tale in four years."
—*Publishers Weekly*

"The myriad Shannara fans will relish the adventure, the mystery, the magic, and the well-developed characters . . . The ending is a gripping cliff-hanger."
—*Booklist*

"The Shannara mythology gains a new level of history and depth in a tale that should appeal to the series' legions of fans."
—*Library Journal*

THE VOYAGE OF THE JERLE SHANNARA

BOOK ONE

ILSE WITCH

Terry Brooks

A Del Rey® Book
THE BALLANTINE PUBLISHING GROUP • NEW YORK

A Del Rey® Book
Published by The Ballantine Publishing Group
Copyright © 2000 by Terry Brooks

www.delreydigital.com

ISBN 0-345-39655-3

Manufactured in the United States of America

First Hardcover Edition: September 2000
First Mass Market Edition: August 2001

OPM   10   9   8   7   6

TO CAROL AND DON MCQUINN

For redefining the word *friends* in more ways
than I can count

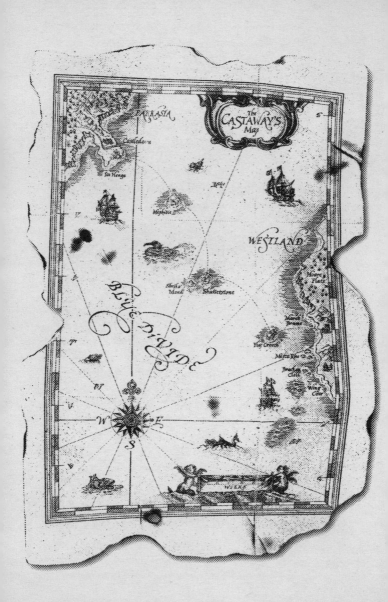

NORTHLAND
Mile Swamp
Kierlak Desert
Skull Kingdom
Skull Mt.
Charnal Mts.
Knife Edge Mts.
River Lethe
STRELEHEIM PLAINS
Jannison Pass
WESTLAND
Valley of Rhenn
Druids Keep
RABB PLAINS
EAST LAND
Rabb River
Hall of Kings
Upper Anar
Dragons Teeth
Valley of Shale
Kennon Pass
Kern
Mountains of Runne
Varfleet
Sterlock
Tyrsis
CALLAHORN
Anar Forest
Rainbow Lake
Silver River
Culhaven
SOUTHLAND
Mist Marsh
Duln Forests
Battle Mound Lowlands
Leah
Lower Anar
Shady Vale
Lowlands of Clete
N

ONE

Hunter Predd was patrolling the waters of the Blue Divide north of the island of Mesca Rho, a Wing Hove outpost at the western edge of Elven territorial waters, when he saw the man clinging to the spar. The man was draped over the length of wood as if a cloth doll, his head laid on the spar so that his face was barely out of the water, one arm wrapped loosely about his narrow float to keep him from sliding away. His skin was burned and ravaged from sun, wind, and weather, and his clothing was in tatters. He was so still it was impossible to tell if he was alive. It was the odd rolling movement of his body within the gentle swells, in fact, that first caught Hunter Predd's eye.

Obsidian was already banking smoothly toward the castaway, not needing the touch of his master's hands and knees to know what to do. His eyes sharper than those of the Elf, he had spotted the man in the water before Hunter and shifted course to effect a rescue. It was a large part of the work he was trained to do, locating and rescuing those whose ships had been lost at sea. The Roc could tell a man from a piece of wood or a fish a thousand yards away.

He swung around slowly, great wings stretched wide, dipping toward the surface and plucking the man from the waters with a sure and delicate touch. Great claws wrapped securely, but gently, about the limp form, the Roc lifted away again. Depthless and clear, the late spring sky spread away in a brilliant blue dome brightened by sunlight that infused the warm air and reflected in flashes of silver off the waves. Hunter Predd guided his mount back toward the closest piece of land available, a small atoll some miles from Mesca Rho. There he would see what, if anything, could be done.

They reached the atoll in less than half an hour, Hunter Predd keeping Obsidian low and steady in his flight the entire way. Black as ink and in the prime of his life, the Roc was his third as a Wing Rider and arguably the best. Besides being big and strong, Obsidian had excellent instincts and had learned to anticipate what Hunter wished of him before the Wing Rider had need to signal it. They had been together five years, not long for a Rider and his mount, but sufficiently long in this instance that they performed as if linked in mind and body.

Lowering to the leeward side of the atoll in a slow flapping of wings, Obsidian deposited his burden on a sandy strip of beach and settled down on the rocks nearby. Hunter Predd jumped off and hurried over to the motionless form. The man did not respond when the Wing Rider turned him on his back and began to check for signs of life. There was a pulse, and a heartbeat. His breathing was slow and shallow. But when Hunter Predd checked his face, he found his eyes had been removed and his tongue cut out.

He was an Elf, the Wing Rider saw. Not a member of the Wing Hove, however. The lack of harness scars on his wrists and hands marked him so. Hunter examined his body carefully for broken bones and found none. The only obvious physical damage seemed to be to his face. Mostly, he was suffering from exposure and lack of nourishment. Hunter placed a little fresh water from his pouch on the man's lips and let it trickle down his throat. The man's lips moved slightly.

Hunter considered his options and decided to take the man to the seaport of Bracken Clell, the closest settlement where he could find an Elven Healer to provide the care that was needed. He could take the man to Mesca Rho, but the island was only an outpost. Another Wing Rider and himself were its only inhabitants. No healing help could be found there. If he wanted to save the man's life, he would have to risk carrying him east to the mainland.

The Wing Rider bathed the man's skin in fresh water and applied a healing salve that would protect it from further damage. Hunter carried no extra clothing; the man would have to travel in the rags he wore. He tried again to give the man fresh water, and this time the man's mouth worked more eagerly in response, and he moaned softly. For an instant his ruined eyes tried to open, and he mumbled unintelligibly.

As a matter of course and in response to his training, the Wing Rider searched the man and took from his person the only two items he found. Both surprised and perplexed him. He studied each carefully, and the frown on his lips deepened.

Unwilling to delay his departure any longer, Hunter picked up the man and, with Obsidian's help, eased him into place on the Roc's broad back. A pad cushioned and restraining straps secured him. After a final check, Hunter climbed back aboard his mount, and Obsidian lifted away.

They flew east toward the coming darkness for three hours, and sunset was approaching when they sighted Bracken Clell. The seaport's population was a mixture of races, predominantly Elven, and the inhabitants were used to seeing Wing Riders and their Rocs come and go. Hunter Predd took Obsidian upland to a clearing marked for landings, and the big Roc swung smoothly down into the trees. A messenger was sent into town from among the curious who quickly gathered, and the Elven Healer appeared with a clutch of litter bearers.

"What's happened to him?" the Healer asked of Hunter Predd, on discovering the man's empty eye sockets and ruined mouth.

Hunter shook his head. "That's how I found him."

"Identification? Who is he?"

"I don't know," the Wing Rider lied.

He waited until the Healer and his attendants had picked

up the man and begun carrying him toward the Healer's home, where the man would be placed in one of the sick bays in the healing center, before dispatching Obsidian to a more remote perch, then following after the crowd. What he knew was not to be shared with the Healer or anyone else in Bracken Clell. What he knew was meant for one man only.

He sat on the Healer's porch and smoked his pipe, his long-bow and hunting knife by his side as he waited for the Healer to reemerge. The sun had set, and the last of the light lay across the waters of the bay in splashes of scarlet and gold. Hunter Predd was small and slight for a Wing Rider, but tough as knotted cord. He was neither young nor old, but comfortably settled in the middle and content to be there. Sun-browned and windburned, his face seamed and his eyes gray beneath a thick thatch of brown hair, he had the look of what he was—an Elf who had lived all of his life in the outdoors.

Once, while he was waiting, he took out the bracelet and held it up to the light, reassuring himself that he had not been mistaken about the crest it bore. The map he left in his pocket.

One of the Healer's attendants brought him a plate of food, which he devoured silently. When he was finished eating, the attendant reappeared and took the plate away, all without speaking. The Healer still hadn't emerged.

It was late when he finally did, and he looked haggard and unnerved as he settled himself next to Hunter. They had known each other for some time, the Healer having come to the seaport only a year after Hunter had returned from the border wars and settled into Wing Rider service off the coast. They had shared in more than one rescue effort and, while of different backgrounds and callings, were of similar persuasion regarding the foolishness of the world's progress. Here, in an outback of the broader civilization that was designated the Four Lands, they had found they could escape a little of the madness.

"How is he?" Hunter Predd asked.

The Healer sighed. "Not good. He may live. If you can call it that. He's lost his eyes and his tongue. Both were removed forcibly. Exposure and malnutrition have eroded his strength so severely he will probably never recover entirely. He came awake several times and tried to communicate, but couldn't."

"Maybe with time—"

"Time isn't the problem," the Healer interrupted, drawing his gaze and holding it. "He cannot speak or write. It isn't just the damage to his tongue or his lack of strength. It is his mind. His mind is gone. Whatever he has been through has damaged him irreparably. I don't think he knows where he is or even who he is."

Hunter Predd looked off into the night. "Not even his name?"

"Not even that. I don't think he remembers anything of what's happened to him."

The Wing Rider was silent a moment, thinking. "Will you keep him here for a while longer, care for him, watch over him? I want to look into this more closely."

The Healer nodded. "Where will you start?"

"Arborlon, perhaps."

A soft scrape of a boot brought him about sharply. An attendant appeared with hot tea and food for the Healer. He nodded to them without speaking and disappeared again. Hunter Predd stood, walked to the door to be certain they were alone, then reseated himself beside the Healer.

"Watch this damaged man closely, Dorne. No visitors. Nothing until you hear back from me."

The Healer sipped at his tea. "You know something about him that you're not telling me, don't you?"

"I suspect something. There's a difference. But I need time to make certain. Can you give me that time?"

The Healer shrugged. "I can try. The man inside will have something to say about whether he will still be here when you return. He is very weak. You should move swiftly."

Hunter Predd nodded. "As swift as Obsidian's wings can fly," he replied softly.

Behind him, in the near darkness of the open doorway, a shadow detached itself from behind a wall and moved silently away.

The attendant who had served dinner to the Wing Rider and the Healer waited until after midnight, when the people of Bracken Clell were mostly asleep, to slip from his rooms in the village into the surrounding forest. He moved quickly and without the benefit of light, knowing his path well from having traveled it many times before. He was a small, wizened man who had spent the whole of his life in the village and was seldom given a second glance. He lived alone and had few friends. He had served in the Healer's household for better than thirteen years, a quiet, uncomplaining sort who lacked imagination but could be depended on. His qualities suited him well in his work as a Healer's attendant, but even better as a spy.

He reached the cages he kept concealed in a darkened pen behind the old cabin in which he had been born. When his father and mother had died, possession had passed to him as the eldest male. It was a poor inheritance, and he had never accepted that it was all to which he was entitled. When the opportunity had been offered to him, he snatched at it eagerly. A few words overheard here and there, a face or a name recognized from tales told in taverns and ale houses, bits and pieces of information tossed his way by those rescued from the ocean and brought to the center to heal—they were all worth something to the right people.

And to one person in particular, make no mistake about it.

The attendant understood what was expected of him. She had made it clear from the beginning. She was to be his Mistress, to whom he must answer most strongly should he step from between the lines of obedience she had charted for him. Whoever passed through the Healer's doors and whatever they said, if they or it mattered at all, she was to know. She told him the decision to summon her was his, always his. He must be prepared to answer for his summons, of course. But it would be better to act boldly than belatedly. A chance missed was much less acceptable to her than time wasted.

He had guessed wrongly a few times, but she had not been angry or critical. A few mistakes were to be expected. Mostly, he knew what was worth something and what was not. Patience and perseverance were necessary.

He'd developed both, and they had served him well. This time, he knew, he had something of real value.

He unfastened the cage door and took out one of the strange birds she had given him. They were wicked-looking things with sharp eyes and beaks, swept-back wings, and narrow bodies. They watched him whenever he came in sight, or took them out of the cages, or fastened a message to their legs, as he was doing now. They watched him as if marking his efficiency for a report they would make later. He didn't like the way they looked at him, and he seldom looked back.

When the message was in place, he tossed the bird into the air, and it rose into the darkness and disappeared. They flew only at night, these birds. Sometimes, they returned with messages from her. Sometimes, they simply reappeared, waiting to be placed back in their cages. He never questioned their origins. It was better, he sensed, simply to accept their usefulness.

He stared into the night sky. He had done what he could. There was nothing to do now, but wait. She would tell him what was needed next. She always did.

Closing the doors to the pen so that the cages were hidden once more, he crept silently back the way he had come.

Two days later, Allardon Elessedil had just emerged from a long session with the Elven High Council centered on the renewal of trade agreements with the cities of Callahorn and on the seemingly endless war they fought as allies with the

Dwarves against the Federation, when he was advised that a
Wing Rider was waiting to speak to him. It was late in the day,
and he was tired, but the Wing Rider had flown all the way
to Arborlon from the southern seaport of Bracken Clell, a
two-day journey, and was refusing to deliver his message to
anyone but the King. The aide who advised Allardon of the
Wing Rider's presence conveyed quite clearly the other's determination not to be swayed on this issue.

The Elf King nodded and followed his aide to where the
Wing Rider waited. His arrangement with the Wing Hove demanded that he accede to any request for privacy in the con-
veyance of messages. Pursuant to a contract drawn up in the
early years of Wren Elessedil's rule, the Wing Riders had
been serving the Land Elves as scouts and messengers along
the coast of the Blue Divide for more than 130 years. They
were provided with goods and coin in exchange for their services, and it was an arrangement that the Elven Kings and
Queens had found useful on more than one occasion. If the
Wing Rider who waited had asked to speak with Allardon
personally, then there was good reason for the request, and he
was not about to ignore it.

With Home Guards Perin and Wye flanking him protectively, he trailed after his aide as they departed the High
Council and walked back through the gardens to the Elessedil
palace home. Allardon Elessedil had been King for more than
twenty years, since the death of his mother, the Queen Aine.
He was of medium height and build, still fit and trim in spite
of his years, his mind sharp and his body strong. Only his
graying hair and the lines on his face gave evidence of his advanced years. He was a direct descendant of the great Queen
Wren Elessedil, who had brought the Elves and their city out
of the island wilderness of Morrowindl into which the Federation and the hated Shadowen had driven them. He was her
great-great-grandson, and he had lived the whole of his life as
if measuring it against hers.

It was difficult to do so in these times. The war with the

Federation had been raging for ten years and showed no signs of ending anytime soon. The Southland coalition of Bordermen, Dwarves, and Elves had halted the Federation advance below the Duln two years earlier on the Prekkendorran Heights. Now the armies were stalemated in a front that had failed to shift one way or the other in all that time and continued to consume lives and waste energy at an alarming rate. There was no question that the war was necessary. The Federation's attempt at reclaiming the Borderlands it had lost in the time of Wren Elessedil was invasive and predatory and could not be tolerated. But the King couldn't help thinking that his ancestor would have found a way to put an end to it by now, where he had failed to do so.

None of which had anything to do with the matter at hand, he chided himself. The war with the Federation was centered at the crossroads of the Four Lands and had not yet spilled over onto the coast. For now, at least, it was contained.

He walked into the reception room where the Wing Rider was waiting and immediately dismissed those who accompanied him. A member of the Home Guard would already be concealed within striking distance, although Allardon had never personally heard of a Wing Rider turned assassin.

As the door closed behind his small entourage, he extended his hand to the Rider. "I'm sorry you had to wait. I was sitting with the High Council, and my aide didn't want to disturb me." He shook the other's corded hand and scanned the weathered face. "I know you, don't I? You've brought me a message once or maybe twice before."

"Once, only," the other advised. "It was a long time ago. You wouldn't have reason to remember me. My name is Hunter Predd."

The Elven King nodded, failing to recognize the other's name, but smiling anyway. Wing Riders cared nothing for formalities, and he didn't bother relying on them here. "What do you have for me, Hunter?"

The Wing Rider reached inside his tunic and produced a

short, slender length of metal chain and a scrap of hide. He held on to both as he spoke. "Three days ago, I was patrolling the waters north off the island of Mesca Rho, a Wing Hove outpost. I found a man floating on a ship spar. He was barely alive, suffering from exposure and dehydration. I don't know how long he was out there, but it must have been some time. His eyes and his tongue had been cut out before he had been cast adrift. He was wearing this."

He held out the length of metal chain first, which turned out to be a bracelet. Allardon accepted it, studied it, and went pale. The bracelet bore the Elessedil crest, the spreading boughs of the sacred Ellcrys surrounded by a ring of Bloodfire. It had been more than thirty years since he had seen the bracelet, but he recognized it immediately.

His gaze shifted from the bracelet to the Wing Rider. "The man you found wore this?" he asked quietly.

"It was on his wrist."

"Did you recognize him?"

"I recognized the bracelet's crest, not the man."

"There was no other identification?"

"Only this. I searched him carefully."

He handed the piece of softened hide to Allardon. It was frayed about the edges, water stained and worn. The Elf King opened it carefully. It was a map, its symbols and writing etched in faded ink and in places smudged. He studied it carefully, making sure of what he had. He recognized the Westland coast along the Blue Divide. A dotted line ran from island to island, traveling west and north and ending at a peculiar collection of blocky spikes. There were names beneath each of the islands and the cluster of spikes, but he did not recognize them. The writing in the margins of the map was indecipherable. The symbols that decorated and perhaps identified certain places on the map were of strange and frightening creatures he had never seen.

"Do you recognize any of these markings?" he asked Hunter Predd.

The Wing Rider shook his head. "Most of what the map shows is outside the territory we patrol. The islands are beyond the reach of our Rocs, and the names are not familiar."

Allardon walked to the tall, curtained windows that opened onto the garden, and stood looking out at the flower beds. "Where is the man you found, Hunter? Is he still alive?"

"I left him with the Healer who serves Bracken Clell. He was alive when I left."

"Have you told anyone else of this bracelet and map?"

"No one knows but you. Not even the Healer. He is a friend, but I know enough to keep silent when silence is called for."

Allardon nodded his approval. "You do, indeed."

He called for cold glasses of ale and a full pitcher from which to refill them. His mind raced as he waited with the Wing Rider for the beverage and containers to be brought. He was stunned by the salvaged articles and by what he had been told, and he wasn't certain, even knowing what he did, what course of action to take. He recognized the bracelet and, thereby, he must assume, the identity of the man from whom it had been taken. He had not seen either in thirty years nor had he expected to see them ever again. He had never seen the map, but even without being able to decipher its language or read its symbols, he could guess at what it was meant to show.

He thought suddenly of his mother, Aine, dead for twenty-five years, and the memory of her anguish during the last years of her life brought tears to his eyes.

He fingered the bracelet absently, remembering.

Thirty years earlier, his mother, as Queen, had authorized an Elven sailing expedition to undertake a search for a treasure of great value purported to have survived the Great Wars that had destroyed the Old World. The impetus for the expedition had been a dream visited on his mother's seer, an Elven mystic of great power and widespread acclaim. The dream had foretold of a land of ice, of a ruined city within the land, and of a safehold in which a treasure of immeasurable worth lay protected and concealed. This treasure, if recovered, had the power to change the course of history and the lives of all who came in contact with it.

The seer had been wary of the dream, for she understood the power of dreams to deceive. The nature of the treasure sought was unclear, and its source was vague and uncharted. The land in which the treasure could be found lay somewhere across the Blue Divide in territory that no one had ever seen. There were no directions for reaching it, no instructions for locating it, and little more than a series of images to describe it. Perhaps, the seer advised, it was a dream best left alone.

But Allardon's elder brother, Kael Elessedil, had been intrigued by the possibilities the dream suggested and by the challenge of searching for an unexplored land. He had embraced the dream as his destiny, and he had begged his mother to let him go. In the end, she had relented. Kael Elessedil had been granted his expedition, and with three sailing ships and their crews under his command, he had departed.

Just before leaving, his mother had given him the famous blue Elfstones that had once belonged to Queen Wren. The Elfstones would guide them to their destination and protect them from harm. Their magic would bring the Elves safely back home again.

When he left Arborlon to travel to the coast, where the ships his mother had commissioned were waiting, Kael Elessedil was wearing the bracelet his brother now held. It was the last time Allardon saw him. The expedition had never returned. The ships, their crews, his brother, everything and everyone, had simply vanished. Search parties had been dispatched, one after the other, but not a trace of the missing Elves had ever been found.

Allardon exhaled softly. Until now. He stared at the bracelet in his hand. Until this.

Kael's disappearance had changed everything in the lives of his family. His mother had never recovered from her eldest son's disappearance, and the last years of her life were spent in a slow wasting away of health and hope as one rescue effort after another failed and all were finally abandoned. When she died, Allardon became the King his brother was meant to be and he had never expected to become.

He thought of the ruined man lying wasted, voiceless, and blind in the Healer's rooms in Bracken Clell and wondered if his brother had come home at last.

The ale arrived, and Allardon sat with Hunter Predd on a bench in the gardens and questioned the Wing Rider again and again, covering the same ground several times over, approaching the matter from different points of view, making certain he had learned everything there was to know. Perhaps understanding in part at least, the trauma he had visited upon the Elven King by his coming, Hunter was cooperative. He did not presume to ask questions of his own, for which Allardon was grateful, but simply responded to the questions he was asked, keeping company with the King for as long as it was required.

When the interview was ended, Allardon asked the Wing Rider to stay the night so that the King could have time to consider what further need he might have of him. He did not make it a command, but a request. Food and lodging would be provided for rider and mount, and his staying would be a favor. Hunter Predd agreed.

Alone again, in his study now, where he did most of his thinking on matters that required a balancing of possibilities and choices, Allardon Elessedil considered what he must do. After thirty years and considerable damage, he might not be able to recognize his brother, even if it was Kael whom the Bracken Clell Healer attended. He had to assume that it was, for the bracelet was genuine. It was the map that was troubling. What was he to do with it? He could guess at its worth, but he could not read enough of it to measure the extent of its information. If he were to mount a new expedition, an event he was already seriously considering, he could not afford to do so without making every possible effort to discover what he was up against.

He needed someone to translate the phrases on the map. He needed someone who could tell him what they said.

There was only one person who could do that, he suspected. Certainly, only one of whom he knew.

It was dark outside by now, the night settled comfortably down about the Westland forests, the walls and roofs of the city's buildings faded away and replaced by clusters of lights that marked their continued presence. In the Elessedil family home, it was quiet. His wife was busy with their daughters, working on a quilt for his birthday that he was not supposed to know about. His eldest son, Kylen, commanded a regiment on the Prekkendorran front. His youngest, Ahren, hunted the forests north with Ard Patrinell, Captain of the Home Guard. Considering the size of his family and the scope of his authority as King, he felt surprisingly alone and helpless in the face of what he knew he must do.

But how to do it? How, so that it would achieve what was needed?

The dinner hour had come and gone, and he remained where he was, thinking the matter through. It was difficult even to consider doing what was needed, because the man he must deal with was in many ways anathema to him. But deal with him he must, putting aside his own reservations and their shared history of antagonism and spite. He could do that because that was part of what being a King required, and he had made similar concessions before in other situations. It was finding a way to persuade the other to do likewise that was difficult. It was conceiving of an approach that would not meet with instant rejection that was tricky.

In the end, he found what he needed right under his nose. He would send Hunter Predd, the Wing Rider, as his emissary. The Wing Rider would go because he understood the importance and implications of his discovery and because Allardon would grant the Wing Hove a concession they coveted as a further enticement. The man whose services he required would respond favorably because he had no quarrel with the Wing Riders as he did with the Land Elves, and because Hunter Predd's direct, no-nonsense approach would appeal to him.

There were no guarantees, of course. His gambit might fail, and he might be forced to try again—perhaps even to go there himself. He would have to, he knew, if all else failed. But he was counting on his adversary's inquisitive mind and curious nature to win him over; he would not be able to resist the challenge of the map's puzzle. He would not be able to ignore the lure of its secrets. His life did not allow for that. Whatever else he might be, and he was many things, he was a scholar first.

The Elf King brought out the scrap of map the Wing Rider had carried to him and placed it on his writing desk. He would have it copied, so that he might protect against its unforeseen loss. But copied accurately, with all symbols and words included, for any hint of treachery would sink the whole venture in a second. A scribe could accomplish what was needed without being told of the map's origins or worth. Discretion was possible.

Nevertheless, he would stay with the scribe until the job was completed. His decision made, he dispatched an aide to summon the one who was needed and sat back to await his arrival. Dinner would have to keep a little while longer.

Two

On the same night Allardon Elessedil awaited the arrival of his scribe to make a copy of the map delivered by Hunter Predd, the spy in the household of the Bracken Clell Healer received a response to the message he had dispatched to his Mistress two days earlier. It was not the kind of response he had anticipated.

She was waiting for him when he came to his rooms at nightfall, his day's work finished, his mind on other things. Perhaps he was thinking of slipping out later to his cages to see if one of her winged couriers had arrived with a message. Perhaps he was thinking only of a hot meal and a warm bed. Whatever the case, he was not expecting to find her. Surprised and frightened by her appearance, he flinched and cried out when she detached herself from the shadows. She soothed him with a soft word, quieted him, and waited patiently for him to recover himself enough to acknowledge her properly.

"Mistress," he whispered, dropping to one knee and bowing deeply. She was pleased to discover he had not forgotten his manners. Although she had not come to him in many years, he remembered his place.

She left him bowed and on his knee a moment longer, standing before him, her whisper of reassurance and subtle pressure soft and light upon the air. Gray robes cloaked her from head to foot, and a hood concealed her face. Her spy had never seen her in the light or caught even the barest glimpse of her features. She was an enigma, a shadow exuding presence rather than identity. She kept herself at one with the darkness, a creature to be felt rather than viewed, keeping watch even when not seen.

"Mistress, I have important information," her spy murmured without looking up, waiting to be told he might rise.

The Ilse Witch left him where he was, considering. She knew more than he imagined, more than he could guess, for she possessed power that was beyond his understanding. From the message he had sent—his words, his handwriting, his scent upon the paper—she could measure the urgency he was feeling. From the way he presented himself now—his demeanor, his tone of voice, his carriage—she could decipher his need. It was her gift always to know more than those with whom she came in contact wished her to know. Her magic laid them bare and left them as transparent as still waters.

The Ilse Witch stretched out her robed arm. "Rise," she commanded.

The spy did so, keeping his head lowered, his eyes cast down. "I did not think you would come . . ."

"For you, for information of such importance, I could do no less." She shifted her stance and bent forward slightly. "Speak, now, of what you know."

The spy shivered, excitement coursing through him, anxious to be of service. Within the shadows of her hood, she smiled.

"A Wing Rider rescued an Elf from the sea and brought him to the Healer who serves this community," the spy advised, daring now to lift his eyes as far as the hem of her robes. "The man's eyes and tongue were removed, and the Healer says he is half-mad. I don't doubt it, from the look of him. The Healer cannot determine his identity, and the Wing Rider claims not to know it either, but he suspects something. And the Wing Rider took something from the man before bringing him here. I caught a glimpse of it—a bracelet that bears the crest of the Elessedils."

The spy's gaze lifted now to seek out her own. "The Wing Rider left for Arborlon two days ago. I heard him tell the Healer where he was going. He took the bracelet with him."

She regarded him in silence for a moment, her cloaked form as still as the shadows it mirrored. A bracelet bearing the crest of the Elessedils, she mused. The Wing Rider would have taken it to Allardon Elessedil to identify. Whose bracelet was it? What did it mean that it was found on this castaway Elf who was blind and voiceless and believed mad?

The answers to her questions were locked inside the castaway's head. He must be made to give them up.

"Where is the man now?" she asked.

The spy hunched forward eagerly, the fingers of his hands knotted together beneath his chin as if in prayer. "He lies in the Healer's infirmary, cared for but kept isolated until the Wing Rider's return. No one is allowed to speak with him." He snorted softly. "As if anyone could. He has no tongue with which to answer, has he?"

She gestured him away and to the side, and he moved as if a puppet in response. "Wait here for me," she said. "Wait, until I return."

She went out the door into the night, a spectral figure sliding effortlessly and soundlessly through the shadows. The Ilse Witch liked the darkness, found comfort in it she could never find in daylight. The darkness soothed and shaded, softening edges and points, reducing clarity. Vision lost importance because the eyes could be deceived. A shift of movement here changed the look of something there. What was certain in the light became suspect in the dark. It mirrored her life, a collage of images and voices, of memories that had shaped her growing, not all fitting tightly in sequence, not all linked together in ways that made sense. Like the shadows with which she so closely identified, her life was a patchwork of frayed ends and loose threads that invited refitting and mending. Her past was not carved of stone, but drawn on water. Reinvent yourself, she had been told by the Morgawr a long time ago. Reinvent yourself, and you will become more inscrutable to those who might try to unravel who you really are.

In the night, in darkness and shadows, she could do so more easily. She could keep what she looked like to herself and conceal who she really was. She could let them imagine her, and by doing so keep them forever deceived.

She moved through the village without challenge, encountering almost no one, those few she did unaware of her presence as they passed. It was late, the village mostly asleep, the ones who preferred the night busy in the ale houses and pleasure dens, caught up in their own wants and needs, uncaring of what transpired without. She could forgive them their weaknesses, these men and women, but she could never accept them as equals. Long since, she had abandoned any pretense that she believed their common origins linked them in any meaningful way. She was a creature of fire and iron. She was born to magic and power. It was her destiny to shape and alter the lives of others and never to be altered by them. It was her passion to rise above the fate that others had cast for her as a child and to visit revenge on them for daring to do so. She would be so much more than they, and they would be forever less.

When she let them speak her name again, when she chose to speak it herself, it would be remembered. It would not be buried in the ashes of her childhood, as it had once been. It would not be cast aside, a fragment of her lost past. It would soar with a hawk's smooth glide and shine with the milky brightness of the moon. It would linger on the minds of the people of her world forever.

The Healer's house lay ahead, close by the trees of the surrounding forest. She had flown in from the Wilderun late that afternoon, come out of her safehold in response to the spy's message, sensing its importance, wanting to discover for herself what secrets it held. She had left her War Shrike in the old growth below the bluffs, its fierce head hooded and its taloned feet hobbled. It would bolt otherwise, so wild that even her magic could not hold it when she was absent. But as a fighting bird, it was without equal. Even the giant Rocs were wary of it, for the Shrike fought to the death with little thought to protecting itself. No one would see it, for she had cast a spell of forbidding about it to keep the unwanted away. By sunrise, she would have returned. By sunrise, she would be gone again, even given the dictates of what she must do now.

She slipped through the door of the Healer's home on cat's paws, moving through the central rooms to the sick bays, humming softly as she passed the attendants on duty, turning their minds inward and eyes elsewhere as she passed so they would not see her. The ones who kept watch outside the castaway's curtained entry, she put to sleep. They sank into their chairs and leaned against walls and tables, eyes going closed, breathing slowing and deepening. It was quiet and peaceful in the Healer's home, and her song fit snugly into place. She layered the air with her music, a tender blanket tucking in around the cautions and uneasiness that might otherwise have been triggered. Soon, she was all alone and free to work.

In his bay, with a light covering over his feverish body and the window curtains drawn close to keep out the light, the castaway lay dozing on the pallet that had been provided for him. His skin was blistered and raw, and the mending salve the Healer had applied glistened in a damp sheen. His body was wasted from lack of nourishment, his heart beat weakly in his chest, and his bruised and ravaged face was skeletal, the eyelids sunken in where the eyes themselves had been gouged out, the mouth a scarred red wound behind cracked lips.

The Ilse Witch studied him carefully for a time, letting her eyes tell her as much as they could, noting the man's distinctly Elven features, the graying hair that marked him as no longer young, and the rigid crook of fingers and neck that screamed silently of tortures endured. She did not like the feel of the man; he had been made to suffer purposely and used for things she did not care to guess at. She did not like the scent he gave off or the small sounds he made. He was living in another place and time, unable to forget what he had suffered, and it was not pleasant.

When she touched him, ever so softly on his chest with her slim, cool fingers, he convulsed as if struck. Quickly, she employed her magic, singing softly to calm him, lending peace and reassurance. The arched back relaxed slowly, and the clawed fingers released their death grip on the bed covering. A sigh escaped the cracked lips. Relief in any form was welcome to this one, she thought, continuing to sing, to work her way past his defenses and into his mind.

When he was at rest again, given over to her ministrations and become her dependent, she placed her hands upon his fevered body so that she might draw from him his thoughts and feelings. She must unlock what lay hidden in his mind— his experiences, his travails, his secrets. She must do so through his senses, but primarily through his voice. He could no longer speak as ordinary men, but he could still communicate. It required only that she find a way to make him want to do so.

In the end, it was not all that hard. She bound him to her through her singing, probing gently as she did so, and he began to make what small and unintelligible sounds he could. She drew him out one grunt, one murmur, one gasp at a time. From each sound, she gained an image of what he knew, stored it away, and made it her own. The sounds were inhuman and rife with pain, but she absorbed them without flinching, bathing him in a wash of compassion, of reassurance and pity, of gentleness and the promise of healing.

Speak to me. Live again through me. Give me everything you hide, and I will give you peace.

He did so, and the images were brightly colored and stunning. There was an ocean, vast and blue and uncharted. There were islands, one after the other, some green and lush, some barren and rocky, each of a different feel, each hiding something monstrous. There were frantic, desperate battles in which weapons clashed and men died. There were feelings of such intensity, such raw power, that they eclipsed the events that triggered them and revealed the scars they had left on their bearer.

Finally, there were pillars of ice that reached to the misted, cool skies, their massive forms shifting and grinding like giant's teeth as a thin beam of blue fire born of Elfstone magic shone through to something that lay beyond. There was a city, all in ruins, ancient and alive with monstrous protectors. And there was a keep, buried in the earth, warded by smooth metal and bright red eyes, containing magic . . .

The Ilse Witch gasped in spite of herself as the last image registered, an image of the magic the castaway had found within the buried keep. It was a magic of spells invoked by words—but so many! The number seemed endless, stretching away into shadows from soft pools of light, their power poised to rise into the air in a canopy so vast it might cover the whole of the earth!

The castaway was writhing beneath her, and the hold she kept on him slipped away momentarily as she lost focus. She brought her song to bear again, layering it over him, embedding herself more deeply within his mind to keep him under control.

Who are you? Speak your name!

His body lurched and the sounds he made were terrifying. *Tell me!*

He answered her, and when he did, she understood at once the importance of the bracelet.

What else were you carrying? What else, that speaks to this?

He fought her, not realizing what it was he was fighting,

only knowing that he must. She sensed it was not entirely his idea to fight her, that either someone had implanted within his mind the need to do so or something had happened to persuade him it was necessary. But she was strong and certain in her magic, and he lacked the defenses necessary to resist her.

A map, she saw. Drawn on an old skin, inked in his own hand. A map, she surmised at once, that was no longer his, but was on its way to Arborlon and the Elven King.

She tried to determine what was on the map, and for a moment she was able to reconstruct a vague image from his grunts and moans. She caught a glimpse of names written and symbols drawn here and there, saw a dotted line connecting islands off the coast of the Westland and out into the Blue Divide. She traced the line to the pillars of ice and to the land in which the safehold lay. But the writings and drawings were lost to her when he convulsed a final time and lay back, his voice spent, his mind emptied, and his body limp and unmoving beneath her touch.

She stilled her song and stepped away from him. She had all she was going to get, but what she had was enough to tell her what was needed. She listened to the silence for a moment, making sure her presence had not yet been detected. The castaway Elf lay motionless on his raised pallet, gone so deeply inside himself he would never come out again. He would live perhaps, but he would never recover.

She shook her head. It was pointless to leave him so.

Kael Elessedil, son of Queen Aine, once destined to be King of the Elves. It was before her time, but she knew the story. Lost for thirty years, and this was his sorry fate.

The Ilse Witch stepped close and drew back her hood to reveal the face that few ever saw. Within her concealing garments, she was nothing of what she seemed. She was very young, barely a grown woman, her hair long and dark, her eyes a startling blue, and her features smooth and lovely. As a child, when she had the name she no longer spoke, she would look at herself in the mirror of the waters of a little cove that pooled off the stream that ran not far from her home and try to imagine how she would look when grown. She had not thought herself pretty then, when it mattered to her. She did not think herself pretty now, when it did not.

There was warmth and tenderness in her face and eyes as she bent to kiss the ruined man on his lips. She held the kiss long enough to draw the breath from his lungs, and then he died.

"Be at peace, Kael Elessedil," she whispered in his ear.

She went from the Healer's home as she had come, hooded once more, a shadowy presence that drew no notice by its passing. The attendants would come awake after she was gone, unaware that anything had transpired, not sensing they had slept or that time had passed.

The Ilse Witch was already sifting through the images she had culled, weighing her options. The magic Kael Elessedil had discovered was priceless. Even without knowing exactly what it was, she could sense that much. It must be hers, of course. She must do what he had failed to do—find it, claim it, and retrieve it. It was protected in some way, as such magic necessarily would be, but there were no defenses she could not overcome. Her course of action was already decided, and only a settling of the particulars remained.

What she coveted, even if she did not require it in order to succeed, was the map.

Sliding through the darkness of Bracken Clell, she gave consideration to how she might gain possession of it. The Wing Rider had taken it to Allardon Elessedil in Arborlon, along with Kael Elessedil's bracelet. The Elven King would recognize the importance of both, but he would not be able to translate the writings on the map. Nor would he have the benefit of his now dead brother's thoughts, as she did. He would seek help from another in deciphering the mysterious symbols to determine what his brother had found.

Who would he turn to?

She knew the answer to her question almost before she had

finished asking it. There was only one he could ask. One, who would be sure to know. Her enemy, one-armed and dark-browed, crippled of body and soul. Her nemesis, but her equal in the nuanced wielding of magic's raw power.

Her thinking changed instantly with recognition of what this meant. Now there would be competition in her quest, and time would become precious. She would not have the luxuries of long deliberation and careful planning to sustain her effort. She would be faced with a challenge that would test her as nothing else could.

Even the Morgawr might choose to involve himself in a struggle of this magnitude.

She had slowed perceptibly, but now she picked up her pace once more. She was getting ahead of herself. Before she could return to the Wilderun with her news, she must conclude matters here. She must tie up loose ends. Her spy was still waiting to learn the value of his information. He would expect to be complimented on his diligence and well paid for his efforts. She must see to both.

Still, as she moved silently through the village and nearer to her spy's rooms, her thoughts kept returning to the confrontation that lay ahead, in a time too distant yet to fix upon, in a place perhaps far removed from the lands she traveled now—a confrontation of wills, of magics, and of destinies. She and her adversary, locked in a final struggle for supremacy, just as she had dreamed they would one day be— the image burned in her thoughts like a hot coal and fired her imagination.

Her spy was waiting for her when she entered his rooms.

"Mistress," he acknowledged, dropping obediently to one knee.

"Rise," she told him.

He did so, keeping his gaze lowered, his head bent.

"You have done well. What you told me has opened doors that I had only dreamed about."

She watched him beam with pride and clasp his hands

in anticipation of the reward she would bestow upon him. "Thank you, Mistress."

"It is for me to thank you," she replied. She reached into her robes and withdrew a leather pouch that clinked enticingly. "Open it when I am gone," she said quietly. "Be at peace."

She left without delay, her business almost finished. She went from the village to the decaying cottage that belonged to her spy, uncaged her birds, and sent them winging back into the Wilderun. She would find them waiting within her safehold when she returned. The spy would have no further use for them. Within the bag of gold she had given him nested a tiny snake whose bite was so lethal that even the smallest nick from a single fang was fatal. Her spy would not wait until morning to count his coins; he would do so tonight. He would be found, of course, but by then the snake would be gone. She guessed that the money would be gone almost as fast. In quarters of the sort where her spy lived, it was well known that dead men had no need for gold.

She gave the matter little thought as she made her way back to where she had hobbled and hooded her War Shrike. Although they were many and were positioned in large numbers throughout the Four Lands, she did not give up her spies easily. She was fiercely protective of them when they were as useful and reliable as this one had been.

But even the best spy could be found out and made to betray her, and she could not chance that happening here. Better to cut her losses than to take such an obvious risk. A life was a small price to pay for an edge on her greatest enemy.

But how was she to gain possession of that map? She thought momentarily of going after it herself. But to steal it from Allardon Elessedil, who would have it by now, in the heart of Elven country, was too dangerous a task for her to undertake without careful planning. She could try to intercept it on its inevitable way to her enemy, but how was she to determine the means by which it would be conveyed? Besides, she might already be too late, even for that.

No, she must bide her time. She must consider. She must find a more subtle way to get what she wanted.

She reached her mount, removed the stays and hood while keeping him in check with her magic, then mounted him behind his thick, feathered neck and above the place where his wings joined to his body, and together they lifted away. Time and cunning would reward her best, she thought contentedly, the wind rushing past her face, the smells of the forest giving way to the pure cold of the high night air that swept the clouds and circled the stars.

Time and cunning, and the power of the magic she was born to, would yield her a world.

THREE

Typical of Wing Riders in general, Hunter Predd was a pragmatic sort. Whatever unwelcome cards life dealt him he accepted as gracefully as he could and went on about his business. Journeys into the interior of the Four Lands that stretched beyond Elven territory fell into that category. He was uncomfortable with traveling anywhere inland, but especially uncomfortable with traveling to places he hadn't been before.

Paranor was such a place.

He was surprised when Allardon Elessedil requested that he carry the map there. Surprised, because it seemed more appropriate that a Land Elf make the journey on behalf of the King than a rider from the Wing Hove. He was a blunt, straightforward man, and he asked the King's reason for making such a choice. The Elf King explained that the individual to whom Hunter was taking the map might have questions about it that only he could answer. Another Elf could accompany him on his journey if he wished, but another Elf could add nothing that Hunter did not already know, so what was the point?

What was needed was simple. The map must be carried to this certain individual to examine. Hunter should convey Allardon Elessedil's respects and request that the map's recipient come to Arborlon to discuss with the Elf King any usable translation of the writings and symbols.

There was a catch to all this, of course. Hunter Predd, who

was no one's fool, could see it coming. The Elf King saved it for last. The individual to whom the Wing Rider was to deliver the map was the Druid they called Walker, and the Rider's destination was the Druid's Keep at Paranor.

Walker. Even Hunter Predd, who seldom ventured off the coast of the Blue Divide, knew something of him. He was purported to be the last of the Druids. A dark figure in the history of the Four Lands, he was said to have lived for more than 150 years and to still be young. He had fought against the Shadowen in the time of Wren Elessedil. He had disappeared afterwards for decades, then resurfaced some thirty years ago. The rest of what the Wing Rider knew was even more shadowy. There was talk of Walker being a sorcerer possessed of great magic. There was talk that he had tried and failed to establish a coven. It was said he wandered the Four Lands still, gathering information and soliciting disciples. Everyone feared and mistrusted him.

Except, it seemed, Allardon Elessedil, who insisted that there was nothing to fear or mistrust, that Walker was a historian and academician, and that the Druid, of all men, might possess the ability to decipher the drawings and words on the map.

After thinking it over, Hunter Predd accepted the charge to take the map east, not out of duty or concern or anything remotely connected to his feelings for the Elf King, which in general bordered on disinterest. He accepted the charge because the King promised him that in reward for his efforts, he would bestow upon the Wing Hove possession of an island just below and west of the Irrybis that the Wing Riders had long coveted. Fair enough, Hunter decided on hearing the offer. Opportunity had knocked, the prize was a worthwhile one, and the risks were not prohibitive.

In truth, he did not see all that much in the way of risk no matter how closely he looked at the matter. There was the very good possibility that the Elf King wasn't telling him everything; in fact, Hunter Predd was almost certain of it.

That was the way rulers and politicians operated. But there was nothing to be gained by sending him off to die, either. Clearly, Allardon Elessedil wanted to know what information the map concealed—especially if the castaway on whom it had been found was his brother. A Druid might be able to learn that, if he was as well schooled as the Elf King believed. Hunter Predd did not know of any Wing Riders who'd had personal dealings with this one. Nor had he heard any of his people speak harshly of the Druids. Balancing the risks and rewards as he understood them, which was really the best he could manage, he was inclined to take his chances.

So off he went, flying Obsidian out of Arborlon at midday and traveling east toward the Streleheim. He crossed the plains without incident and flew into the Dragon's Teeth well above Callahorn, choosing a narrow, twisting gap in the jagged peaks that would have been impassable on foot but offered just enough space for the Roc to maneuver. He navigated his way through the mountains quickly and was soon soaring above the treetops of Paranor. Once over the woodlands, he took Obsidian down to a small lake for a cold drink and a rest. As he waited on his bird, he looked out across the lake to where the trees locked together in a dark wall, a twisted and forbidding mass. He felt sorry, as he always did, for those who were forced to live their lives on the ground.

It was nearing sunset when the Druid's Keep came in sight. It wasn't all that hard to find from the air. It sat on a promontory deep in the woodlands, its spires and battlements etched in sharp relief by the setting sun against the horizon. The fortress could be seen for miles, stone walls and peaked roofs jutting skyward, a dark and massive presence. Allardon Elessedil had described the Keep in detail to Hunter Predd before he left, but the Wing Rider would have known it anyway. It couldn't be anything other than what it was, a place where dark rumors could take flight, a haunt for the last of a coven so mistrusted and feared that even their shades were warded against.

Hunter Predd guided Obsidian to a smooth landing close by the base of the promontory on which the Keep rested. Shadows layered the surrounding land, sliding from the ancient trees as the sun lowered west, stretching out into strange, unrecognizable shapes. Lifting out of the woods, out of the shadows, rising above it all, silent and frozen in time, only the Keep was still bathed in sunlight. The Wing Rider regarded it doubtfully. It would be easier to fly Obsidian to the top of the rise than to leave him here and walk up himself, but he was loath to risk landing so close to the walls. Here, at least, the trees offered a protective perch and there was room for a swift escape. For a Wing Rider, his mount's safety was always foremost in his mind.

He did not hobble or hood the great bird; Rocs were trained to stay where they were put and come when they were called. Leaving Obsidian at the base of the rise and the edge of the trees, Hunter Predd began the short walk up. He arrived at the towering walls as the sunlight slid away completely, leaving the Keep bathed in shadows. He stared upward, searching for signs of life. Finding none, he walked to the closest gate, which was closed and barred. There were smaller doors set on either side. He tried them, but they were locked. He stepped back again and looked up at the walls once more.

"Hello, inside!" he shouted.

There was no response. The echo of his voice faded into silence. He waited patiently. It was growing increasingly dark. He glanced around. If he didn't rouse someone soon, he would have to retreat back down the rise and make camp for the night.

He looked up again, scanning the parapets and towers. "Hello! I have a message from Allardon Elessedil!"

He stood listening to the silence that followed, feeling small and insignificant in the shadow of the Keep's huge wall. Maybe the Druid was traveling. Maybe he was somewhere else, away from the Keep, and this was all a big waste of time. The Wing Rider frowned. How could anyone even know if the Druid was there?

His question was cut short by a sudden movement at his side. He turned swiftly and found himself face-to-face with the biggest moor cat he had ever seen. The huge black beast stared at him with lantern eyes in the manner of a hungry bird eyeing a tasty bug. Hunter Predd stayed perfectly still. There was little else he could do. The big cat was right on top of him, and any weapons he might call upon to defend himself were woefully inadequate. The moor cat did not move either but simply studied him, head lowered slightly between powerful front shoulders, tail switching faintly in the darkness behind.

It took Hunter a moment to realize that there was something not quite right about this particular moor cat. In spite of its size and obvious power, it was vaguely transparent, appearing and disappearing in large patches as the seconds passed, first a leg, then a shoulder, then a midsection, and so forth. It was the strangest thing he had ever seen, but it did not prompt him to change his mind about trying to move.

Finally, the moor cat seemed satisfied with his inspection and turned away. He advanced a few paces, then turned back. Hunter Predd did not move. The moor cat walked on a few paces more, then looked back again.

To one side of the main gates, a small, iron-bound door swung open soundlessly. The cat moved toward it, then stopped and looked back. It took a few more tries, but finally the Wing Rider got the message. The moor cat was waiting on him. He was supposed to follow—through the open door and into the Druid's Keep.

Hunter Predd was not inclined to argue the matter. Taking a deep breath, he passed from the bluff face through the entry and into the Keep.

*   *   *

The man who had once been Walker Boh and was now simply Walker had seen the Wing Rider coming from a long way off. His warding lines of magic had alerted him to the other's approach, and he had stood on the walls where he could not be seen and watched the Rider land his Roc and walk up the rise to the gates. Black robes gathered close about his tall, broad-shouldered frame, Walker had watched the Wing Rider scan the Keep's walls. The Wing Rider had called up, but Walker had not answered. Instead, he had waited to see what the other would do. He had waited, because waiting until he was sure was an advisable precaution.

But when the Wing Rider called up a second time, saying that he carried a message from Allardon Elessedil, Walker sent Rumor down to bring him in. The big moor cat went obediently, silently, knowing what he must do. Walker trailed after him, wondering why the King of the Land Elves would send a message with a Wing Rider. He could think of two reasons. First, the King knew how Walker would respond to an Elf from Arborlon and to her King in particular, and he was hoping a Wing Rider would do better. Second, the Wing Rider had special insight into what the message concerned. Descending the stairs from his perch on the battlements, Walker shrugged the matter away. He would find out soon enough.

When he reached the bottom of the stairs and moved out into the courtyard, the Wing Rider and Rumor were already waiting. He drew back his hood and left his head and face bare as he crossed to give greeting. There was nothing to be gained by trying to intimidate this man. Clearly the Wing Rider was a tough, seasoned veteran, and he had come because he had chosen to do so and not because he had been commanded. He owed no allegiance to the Elessedils. Wing Riders were notoriously independent, almost as much so as Rovers, and if this one was here, so far from his home and people, there was good reason for it. Walker was curious to learn what that reason was.

"I am Walker," he said, offering his hand to the Wing Rider.

The other accepted it with a nod. His gray eyes took in Walker's dark face, black beard and long hair, strong features, high forehead, and piercing eyes. He did not seem to notice the Druid's missing arm. "Hunter Predd."

"You've come a long way, Wing Rider," Walker observed. "Not many come here without a reason."

The other grunted. "Not any, I should think." He glanced around, and his eyes settled on Rumor. "Is he yours?"

"As much as a moor cat can belong to anyone." Walker's gaze shifted. "His name is Rumor. The joke is, wherever I go, I am preceded by Rumor. It fits well with the way things have turned out for me. But I expect you already know that."

The Wing Rider nodded noncommittally. "Does he always show up like that—in bits and pieces, sort of coming and going?"

"Mostly. You called up that you had a message from Allardon Elessedil. I gather the message is for me?"

"It is." Hunter Predd wiped at his mouth with the back of his hand. "Do you have any ale you can spare?"

Walker smiled. Blunt and to the point, a Wing Rider to the core. "Come inside."

He led the way across the courtyard to a doorway into the main keep. In a room he used for storing foodstuffs and drink and for taking his solitary meals, he produced two glasses and a pitcher and set them on a small wooden table to one side. Gesturing the Wing Rider to one seat, he took the other and filled their glasses. They drank deeply, silently. Rumor had disappeared. He seldom came inside these days unless called.

Hunter Predd put down his glass and leaned back. "Four days ago, I was patrolling the Blue Divide above the island of Mesca Rho, and I found a man in the water."

He went on to tell his story—of finding the castaway Elf, of determining his condition, of discovering the bracelet he wore and the map he carried, of conveying him to the Healer in Bracken Clell, and of continuing on to Arborlon and Allardon Elessedil. The bracelet, he explained, had belonged to the King's brother, Kael, who had disappeared on an expedition in search of a magic revealed in a dream to Queen Aine's seer thirty years earlier.

"I know of the expedition," Walker advised quietly, and bid him continue.

There wasn't much more to tell. Having determined that the bracelet was Kael's, Allardon Elessedil had examined the map and been unable to decipher it. That it traced his brother's route to the sought-after magic was apparent. But there was little else he could determine. He had asked Hunter to convey it here, to Walker, whom he believed might be able to help.

Walker almost laughed aloud. It was typical of the Elf King that he would seek help from the Druid as if his own refusal to supply it in turn counted for nothing. But he kept silent. Instead, he accepted the folded piece of weathered skin when it was offered and set it on the table between them, unopened.

"Have you provided sufficiently for your mount?" he inquired, his gaze shifting from the map to the other's face. "Do you need to go outside again tonight?"

"No," Hunter Predd said. "Obsidian will be fine for now."

"Why don't you have something to eat, a hot bath afterwards, and then some sleep. You've done much traveling over the past few days, and you must be tired. I will study the map, and we will talk again in the morning."

He prepared a soup for the Wing Rider, tossed in a little dried fish, added a side portion of bread, and watched in satisfaction as the other ate it all and drank several more glasses of ale in the bargain. He left the map where he had put it, on the table between them, showing no interest in it. He was not sure yet what he had, and he wanted to be very sure before he conveyed to the Wing Rider a reaction that might be carried back to the Elf King. The uneasy relationship he shared with Allardon Elessedil did not permit giving anything away in their dealings. It was bad enough that he must pretend at civility with a man who had done so little to deserve it. But in a world in which alliances were necessary and, in his case, tended to be few and infrequent, he must play at games he would otherwise forgo.

When Hunter Predd was fed, bathed, and asleep, Walker returned to the table and picked up the map. He carried it from that room down musty halls and up winding stairs to the library, which had served the Druids since the time of Galaphile. Various inconsequential books filled with Druid recordings of weather and farming and lists of surnames and the births and deaths of noted families lined the ancient shelves. But behind those shelves, in a room protected by a magic that no one could penetrate save himself, lay the Druid Histories, the fabled books that recorded the entire history of the order and the magic its members had conceived and employed in the passage of more than a thousand years.

Settling himself comfortably in place amid the trappings of his predecessors, Walker unfolded the map and began to study it.

He took a long time doing so, much longer than he had supposed would be necessary. What he found astonished him. The map was intriguing and rife with possibilities. Inarguably, it was valuable, but he could not make a firm determination of how valuable until after he had translated the writings in the margins, most of which were scripted in a language with which he was unfamiliar.

But he had books of translations of languages to which he could turn, and he did so finally, walking to the shelving that concealed the Histories and their secrets of power. He reached back behind a row of books and touched a series of iron studs in sequence. A catch released, and a section of the shelving swung outward. Walker slipped through the opening behind and stood in a room of granite walls, floor, and ceiling, empty of everything but a long table and four chairs set against it. He lit the smokeless torches set in iron wall racks and pulled the shelving unit back into place behind him.

Then he placed his hand against a section of the granite wall, palm flat and fingers spread, and lowered his head in concentration. All the lore of all the Druids since the beginning of their order belonged now to him, given when he recovered lost Paranor and became a Druid himself those many years ago. He brought a small part of it to bear, recalling the Druid Histories from their concealment. Blue light emanated from his fingertips and spread through the stone beneath like veins through flesh.

A moment later, the wall disappeared, and the books of his order lay revealed, shelved in long rows and in numbered sequence, their covers bound in leather and etched in gold.

He spent a long time with the books that night, reading through many of them in his search for a key to the language on the map. When he found it, he was surprised and confounded. It was a derivation of a language spoken in the Old World, before the Great Wars, a language that had been dead for two thousand years. It was a language of symbols rather than of words. How, Walker wondered, would an Elf from his era have learned such a language? Why would he have used it to draw the map?

The answers to his questions, once he thought them through, were disturbing.

He worked on the translation almost until dawn, being careful not to misinterpret or assume. The more he deciphered, the more excited he became. The map was a key to a magic of such worth, of such power, that it left him breathless. He could barely manage to sit still as he imagined the possibilities. For the first time in years he saw a way in which he could secure what had been denied him for so long—a Druid Council, a body independent of all nations, working to unlock the secrets of life's most difficult and challenging problems and to improve the lives of all the peoples of the Four Lands.

That dream had eluded him for thirty years, ever since he had come awake from the Druid Sleep and gone out into the world to fulfill the promise he had made to himself when he had become what he was. What he had envisioned was a council of delegates from each of the lands and races, from each of the governments and provinces, all dedicated to study, learning, and discovery. But from the very beginning there had been resistance—not just from quarters where resistance might be expected, but from everywhere. Even from the Elves, and especially from Allardon Elessedil and his mother before him. No one wanted to give Walker the autonomy he believed necessary. No one wanted anyone else to gain an advantage. Everyone was cautious and suspicious and fearful of what a strong Druid Council might mean to an already precarious balance of power. No one wanted to take the kind of chance that the Druid was asking of them.

Walker sighed. Their demands were ridiculous and unacceptable. If the nations and the peoples were unwilling to let go of their delegates, to give up control over them so that they could dedicate themselves to the Druid life, the whole exercise was pointless. He had been unable to convince anyone that what he was doing would, given enough time, benefit them all. Druids, they believed, were not to be trusted. Druids, they believed, would visit problems on them they could do without. History demonstrated that Druids had been responsible for every war fought since the time of the First Council at Paranor. It was their own magic, the magic they had wielded in such secrecy, that had finally destroyed them. This was not an experience anyone wanted to repeat. The magic belonged to everyone now. It was a new age, with new rules. Control over the Druids, should they be permitted to re-form, was necessary. Nothing less would suffice.

In the end, the effort fell apart, and Walker was made outcast everywhere. Petty feuds, selfish interests, and short-

sighted personalities stymied him completely. He was left enraged and stunned. He had counted heavily on the Elves
to lead the way, and the Elves had spurned him as surely as
the others. After the death of Queen Aine, Allardon Elessedil
had been his best hope, but the Elf King had announced he
would follow his mother's wishes. No Elves would be sent to
study at Paranor. No new Druid Council would be approved.
Walker must make his way alone.

But now, Walker thought with something bordering on euphoria, he had found a way to change everything. The map
gave him the kind of leverage that nothing else could. This
time, when he asked for help, he would not be refused.

If, of course, he cautioned himself quickly, he could find
and retrieve the magic that had eluded the Elven expedition
under Kael Elessedil. If he could recover it from the safehold
that hid and protected it. If he could survive the long, dangerous journey such an effort would require.

He would need help.

He replaced the Druid Histories on their shelves, made a
quick circular motion with his hand, and closed the wall
away. When the room was restored to blank walls and snuffed
torches, he went back out into the library and pushed the
shelving unit securely into place again. He looked around
momentarily to be certain that all was as it had been. Then,
with the map tucked into his robes, he went up onto the battlements to watch the sunrise.

As he stood looking out over the treetops to the first faint
silvery lightening of the eastern sky, Rumor padded up to join
him. The big cat sat beside him, as if seeking his companionship. Walker smiled. Each was all the other could turn to for
comfort, he mused. Ever since the shade of Allanon had appeared. Ever since they had been locked in limbo in lost
Paranor. Ever since he had brought the Druid's Keep back
into the world of men by becoming the newest member of the
order. Ever since Cogline had died.

All the rest were gone, too, from that earlier time—the

Ohmsfords, Morgan Leah, Wren Elessedil, Damson Rhee, all of them. Rumor and he alone survived. They were outcasts in more ways than one, solitary wanderers in a world that had changed considerably during the time of his sleep. But it wasn't the changes in the Four Lands that worried him this morning. It was his sense that the events that would transpire because of his reading of the map and his search for the magic it detailed would require him to become what he had always worked so hard to avoid—a Druid in the old sense, a manipulator and schemer, a trader in information who would sacrifice who and what he must to get what he believed necessary. Allanon, of old. It was what he had always despised about the Druids. He knew he would despise it in himself when it surfaced.

And surface it would, perhaps changing him forever.

The sun crested the horizon in a splash of brilliant gold. The day would be clear and bright and warm. Walker felt the first rays of sunlight on his face. Such a small thing, but so welcome. His world had shrunk to almost nothing in the past few years. Now it was about to expand in ways he had barely imagined possible.

"Well," he said softly, as if to put the matter to rest.

He knew what he must do. He must go to Arborlon and speak with Allardon Elessedil. He must convince the Elven King they could work together in an effort to discover the secret of the map. He must persuade him to mount an expedition to go in search of the magic of which the map spoke, with Walker in command. He must find a way to make the Elven King his ally without letting him see that it was the Druid's idea.

He must reveal just enough of what he knew and not too much. He must be cautious.

He blinked away his weariness. He was Walker, the last of the Druids, the last hope for the higher ideals his order had espoused so strongly when it had been formed. If the Four Lands were to be united in peace, the magic must be controlled by a Druid Council answerable to no single government or people, but to all. Only he could achieve that. Only he knew the way.

He bent to Rumor and placed his hand gently on the broad head. "You must stay here, old friend," he whispered. "You must keep watch for me until I return."

He rose and stretched. Hunter Predd slept in a darkened room and would not wake for a while yet. Time enough for Walker to catch an hour's sleep before they departed. It would have to be enough.

With the moor cat trailing after him, fading and reappearing like a mirage in the new light, he abandoned his watch and descended the stairs into the Keep.

FOUR

His worn black flight leathers creaking softly, Redden Alt Mer strode through the Federation war camp on his way to the airfield, and heads turned. For some it was the mane of red hair streaming down past his shoulders like fiery threads that drew attention. For some it was the way he carried himself, fluid, relaxed, and self-assured, a big man who exuded strength and quickness.

For most, it was the legend. Seventy-eight confirmed kills in 192 missions, all flown in the same airship, all completed without serious mishap.

It was good luck to fly with Redden Alt Mer, the old boots swore. In a place and time where an airman's life expectancy was rated at about six months, Alt Mer had survived for three years with barely a scratch. He had the right ship, sure enough. But it took more than that to stay alive over the front. It took skill, courage, experience, and a whole basketful of that most precious of commodities, luck. The Captain had all of them. He was steeped in them. He'd lived almost his whole life in the air, a cabin boy at seven, a First Officer by fifteen, a Captain by twenty. When the winds of fortune shifted, the old boots said, Redden Alt Mer knew best how to ride them.

The Rover didn't think about it. It was bad luck to think about good luck in a war. It was worse luck to think about why you were different from everyone else. Being an exception to the rule was all well and good, but you didn't want to dwell on the reasons you were still alive when so many others were dead. It wasn't conducive to clear thinking. It wasn't helpful in getting a good night's sleep.

Walking through the camp, he joked and waved to those who acknowledged him, a light, easy banter that kept everyone relaxed. He knew what they thought of him, and he played off it the way an old friend might. What harm did it do? You could never have too many friends in a war.

He'd been three years now in this one, two of them stuck here on the broad expanse of the Prekkendorran Heights while Federation and Free-born ground forces hammered each other to bloody pulps day after day after day. A Rover out of the seaport of March Brume, west and south on the Blue Divide, he was a seasoned veteran of countless conflicts even before he signed on. It was no exaggeration to say that he had spent his whole life on warships. He'd almost been born at sea, but his father, a Captain himself, had managed to reach port with his mother just before she gave birth. But from the time he'd taken that first commission as a cabin boy, he'd lived in the air. He couldn't explain why he loved it so; he just did. It felt right when he was flying, as if a net of invisible constraints and bonds had been slipped and he had been set free. When he was on the ground, he was always thinking about being in the air. When he was in the air, he was never thinking about anything else.

"Hey, Cap!" A foot soldier with his arm tied against his body and a bandage over one side of his face hobbled into view. "Blow me a little of your luck!"

Redden Alt Mer grinned and blew him a kiss. The soldier laughed and waved with his good arm. The Rover kept walking, smelling the air, tasting it, thinking as he did that he missed the sea. Most of his time in the air had been spent west, over the Blue Divide. He was a mercenary, as most Rovers were, taking jobs where the money was best, giving allegiance to those who paid for it. Right now, the Federation offered the best pay, so he fought for them. But he was growing restless for a change, for something new. The war with the

Free-born had been going on for more than ten years. It wasn't his war to begin with, and it wasn't a war that made much sense to him. Money could carry you only so far when your heart lay somewhere else.

Besides, no matter who you were, sooner or later your luck ran out. It was best to be somewhere else when it did.

He passed out of the sprawling clutter of tents and cooking fires onto the airfield. The warships were tethered in place by their stays, floating just off the ground, ambient-light sails tilted toward the sun off twin masts. Most were Federation built and showed it. Big, ugly, cumbersome brutes, sheathed in metal armor and painted with the insignia and colors of their regiments, in flight they lumbered about the skies like errant sloths. As troop transports and battering rams, they were a howling success. As fighting vessels that could tack smoothly and quickly, they left something to be desired. If they were ably commanded, which most weren't, their life expectancy on the front was about the same as that of their Captains and crews.

He walked on, barely giving them a glance. The banter that had passed between himself and the foot soldiers was absent here. The officers and crews of the Federation airships despised him. Rovers were mercenaries, not career soldiers. Rovers fought only for money and left when they chose. Rovers cared nothing for the Federation cause or the lives of the men that had been expended on its behalf. But the worst of it was the knowledge that the Rover officers and crews were so much better than the Federation crews were. In the air, faith in a cause did little to keep you alive.

A few taunting remarks were tossed at him from behind the anonymity of metal-clad hulls, but he ignored them. No one would make those same remarks to his face. Not these days. Not since he had killed the last man who'd dared to do so.

The sleeker, trimmer Rover airships came into view as he neared the far end of the field. *Black Moclips* sat foremost,

polished wood-and-metal hull gleaming in the sunlight. She
was the best ship he had ever flown, a cruiser built for battle,
quick and responsive to the tack of her ambient-light sails
and the tightening and loosening of her radian draws. Just a
shade under 110 feet long and 35 feet wide, she resembled
a big black ray. Her low, flat fighting cabin sat amidships on a
decking braced by cross beams and warded by twin pontoons
curved into battering rams fore and aft. Twin sets of diapson
crystals converted to raw energy the light funneled from the
collector sails through the radian draws. Parse tubes expelled
the converted energy to propel the ship. The bridge sat aft
with the pilot box front and center on the decking, its controls
carefully shielded from harm. Three masts flew the ambient-
light sails, one each fore, aft, and center. The sails themselves
were strangely shaped, broad and straight at the lower end,
where they were fastened to the booms, but curved where
spars drew them high above to a triangle's point. The design
allowed for minimal slack in a retack and minimal drag from
the wind. Speed and power kept you alive in the air, and both
were measured in seconds.

Furl Hawken came racing down the field from the ship,
long blond beard whipping from side to side. "We're ready
to lift off, Captain," he shouted, slowing as he reached
Alt Mer and swung into step beside him. "Got a good day for
it, don't we?"

"Smooth sailing ahead." Redden Alt Mer put his hand
on his Second Officer's broad shoulder. "Any sign of Little
Red?"

Furl Hawken's mouth worked on whatever it was he
was chewing, his eyes cast down. "Sick in bed, Captain. Flu,
maybe. You know her. She'd come if she was able."

"I know you're the worst liar for a hundred miles in any direction. She's in a tavern somewhere, or worse."

The big man looked hurt. "Well, maybe that's so, but you'd
better let it pass for now, 'cause we got a more immediate problem." He shook his head. "Like we don't have one

every time we turn around these days. Like every single oink doesn't come from the same pig's house."

"Ah, our friends in Federation Command?"

"A full line Commander is aboard for the flight with two of his flunkies. Observation purposes, he tells me. Reconnaissance. A day in the skies. Shades! I nod and smile like a sailor's wife at news of his plans to give up sailing."

Redden Alt Mer nodded absently. "Best thing to do with these people, Hawk."

They had reached *Black Moclips*, and he swung onto the rope ladder and climbed to the bridge where the Federation Commander and his adjutants were waiting.

"Commander," he greeted pleasantly. "Welcome aboard."

"My compliments, Captain Alt Mer," the other replied. He did not offer his own name, which told the Rover something right away about how he viewed their relationship. He was a thin, pinch-faced man with sallow skin. If he'd spent a day on the line in the last twelve months, it would come as a surprise to the Rover. "Are we ready to go?"

"Ready and able, Commander."

"Your First Officer?"

"Indisposed." Or she would wish as much once he got his hands on her. "Mr. Hawken can take up the slack. Gentlemen, is this your first time in the air?"

The look that passed between the adjutants gave him his answer.

"It is our first," the Commander confirmed with a dismissive shrug. "Your job is to make the experience educational. Ours is to learn whatever it is you have to teach."

"Run 'em up, Hawk." He gestured his Second Officer forward to oversee lofting the sails. "We'll be seeing action today, Commander," he cautioned. "It could get a little rough."

The Commander smiled condescendingly. "We're soldiers, Captain. We'll be fine."

Pompous fathead, Alt Mer thought. You'll be fine if I keep you that way and not otherwise.

He watched his Rover crew scramble up the masts, lofting the sails and fastening the radian draws in place. Airships were marvelous things, but operating them required a mind-set that was sorely lacking in most Federation soldiers. The Southlanders were fine on solid ground executing infantry tactics. They were comfortable with throwing bodies into breaches, like sandbags, and relying on the sheer weight of their numbers to crush an enemy. But put them in the air and they couldn't seem to decide what to do next. Their intuition vanished. Everything they knew about warfare dried up and blew away with the first breath of wind to fill the sails.

Rovers, on the other hand, were born to the life. It was in their blood, in their history, and in the way they had lived their lives for two thousand years. Rovers did not respond well to regimentation and drill. They responded to freedom. Flying the big airships gave them that. Migratory by nature and tradition, they were always on the move anyway. Staying put was unthinkable. The Federation was still trying to figure that out, and they were constantly sending observers aloft with the Rover crews to discover what it was their merce-naries knew that they didn't.

Trouble was, it wasn't something that could be taught. The Bordermen who fought for the Free-born weren't any better. Or the Dwarves. Only the Elves seemed to have mastered sailing the wind currents with the same ease as the Rovers.

One day, that would change. Airships were still new to the Four Lands. The first had been built and flown barely two dozen years earlier. They had been in service as fighting ves-sels for less than five years. Only a handful of shipwrights understood the mechanics of ambient-light sails, radian draws, and diapson crystals well enough to build the vessels that could utilize them. Using light as energy was an old dream, only occasionally realized, as in the case of airships. It was one thing to build them, another to make them fly. It took skill and intelligence and instinct to keep them in the air.

More were lost through poor navigation, loss of control, and panic than through damage from battle.

Rovers had sailed the seas in trading ships and pirate vessels longer than anyone had, and the jump to airships was easier for them. As mercenaries, they were invaluable to the Federation. But the Southlanders continued to believe that if they could just learn how the Rovers managed to make it all look so easy, they wouldn't need them as Captains and crews.

Hence, his passengers, three more in a long line of Federation hopefuls.

Resigned, he sighed. There was nothing he could do about it. Hawk would fuss enough for the both of them. He took his station in the pilot box, watching his men as they finished tying down the draws and securing the sails. Other ships were preparing to lift off, as well, their crews performing similar tasks in preparation. On the airfield, ground crews were preparing to release the mooring lines.

The old, familiar excitement was humming in his blood, and the clarity of his vision sharpened.

"Unhood the crystals, Hawk!" he shouted to his Second Officer.

Furl Hawken relayed the instructions to the men stationed at the front and rear parse tubes, where the crystals were fed light from the radian draws. Unhooding freed the mechanisms that allowed Alt Mer to fly the ship. Canvas coverings and linchpins securing the metal hoods that shielded the crystals were released, giving control over the vessel to the pilot box.

Alt Mer tested the levers, drawing down power from the sails in small increments. *Black Moclips* strained against her tethers in response, shifting slightly as light converted to energy was expelled through the parse tubes.

"Cast off!" he ordered.

The ground crew freed the restraining lines, and *Black Moclips* lifted away in a smooth, upward swing. Alt Mer spun the wheel that guided the rudders off the parse tubes and fed power down the radian draws to the crystals in steadily increasing increments. Behind him, he heard the hurried shift of the Federation officers toward pieces of decking they could hold on to.

"There are securing lines and harnesses coiled on those railing stays," he called back to them. "Fasten one about your waist, just in case it gets bumpy."

He didn't bother checking to see if they did as he suggested. If they didn't, it was their own skins they risked.

In moments, they were flying out over the flats of the Prekkendorran, several hundred feet in the air, *Black Moclips* in the lead, another seven ships following in loose formation. Airships could fly comfortably at more than a thousand feet, but he preferred to stay down where the winds were less severe. He watched the twin rams slice through the air to either side of the decking, black horns curving upward against the green of the earth. Low and flat, *Black Moclips* had the look of a hawk at hunt, soaring smooth and silent against the midday sky.

Wind filled the sails, and the Rover crew moved quickly to take advantage of the additional power. Alt Mer hooded the diapson crystals in response, slowing the power fed by the radian draws, giving the ship over to the wind. Furl Hawken was shouting out instructions, exhorting in that big, booming voice, keeping everyone moving smoothly from station to station. Accustomed to the movements of a ship in flight, the crew wore no restraining lines. That would change when they engaged in battle.

Alt Mer risked a quick glance over his shoulder at the Federation officers—risked, because if he started laughing at what he found, he would find himself in trouble he didn't need. It wasn't as bad as it might have been. The Commander and his adjutants were gripping the rail with white-knuckled determination, but no one was sick yet and no one was hiding his eyes. The Rover gave them a reassuring wave and dismissed them from his thoughts.

When *Black Moclips* was well away from the Federation camp and approaching the forward lines of the Free-born, he gave the order to unlock the ship's weapons. *Black Moclips* carried several sets, all of them carefully stacked and stored amidships. Bows and arrows and slings and javelins were used mostly for long-range attacks against opposing crews and fighters. Spears and blades were used in close combat. Long, jagged-edge pikes and grappling hooks attached to throwing ropes were used to draw an enemy ship close enough to tear apart her sails or sever her radian draws.

The two dozen Federation soldiers who rode belowdecks during embarkation climbed up the ladder through the hatchway amidships and moved to arm themselves. Some took up positions behind shielding at the rails. Some moved to man the catapults that launched buckets of metal shards or burning balls of pitch. All were veterans of countless airship battles aboard *Black Moclips*. Alt Mer and his crew of Rovers left the fighting to them. Their responsibility was to the ship. It took all of their concentration to hold her steady in the heat of battle, to position her so that the soldiers could bring their weapons to bear, and to employ her when necessary as a battering ram. The crew was not expected to fight unless the ship was in danger of being boarded.

Watching the soldiers take up their weapons and move eagerly into position, the Rover Captain was struck by the amount of energy men could summon for the purpose of killing one another.

Furl Hawken appeared suddenly at his side. "Everything's at the ready, Captain. Crew, weapons, and ship." He shifted his eyes sideways. "How's our stouthearted passengers holding up?"

Alt Mer glanced briefly over his shoulder. One adjutant had freed himself from his safety line and had buried his head in the slop bucket. The other, white faced, was grimly forcing himself not to look over at his companion. The pinch-faced

Commander was scribbling in a notebook, his black-clad body wedged into a corner of the decking.

"They'd prefer it if we just stayed on the ground, I think," he offered mildly.

"Wonder if they've got anything to report regarding the functions of their insides?" Hawk chuckled and moved away.

Black Moclips passed over the Free-born lines headed toward their airfields, the other seven airships spread out to either side. Two were Rover ships, the other five Federation. He knew their Captains. Both Rover Captains and one of the Federation Captains were reliable and skilled. The rest were marking time until one mistake or another caught up with them. Redden Alt Mer's approach to the situation was to try to keep out of their way.

Ahead, Free-born airships were lifting off to meet them. The Rover Captain produced his spyglass and studied the markings. Ten, eleven, twelve—he counted them as they rose, one after the other. Five were Elven, the rest Free-born. Not the kind of odds he liked. Ostensibly, he was to engage and destroy any enemy airships he encountered, without sustaining damage to his own. As if doing so could possibly make a difference in the outcome of the war. He brushed the thought aside. He would engage the Elven airships and let the others bang up against themselves.

"Safety lines in place, gentlemen!" he called to his Federation passengers and crew, gripping the controls as the enemy ships drew near.

At two hundred yards and with an airspeed approaching twenty knots, he sideslipped *Black Moclips* out of formation and dipped sharply toward the ground. Leveling out again, then increasing his speed, he brought the airship out of her dive and into a climb beneath the Free-born. As he sailed upward on their lee side, his catapults began launching scrap metal and fireballs into the exposed hulls and sails. One ship exploded into flame and began drifting away. A second responded to the attack by launching its own catapults. Jagged bits of metal screamed overhead as Alt Mer spun the wheel sharply to carry *Black Moclips* out of the line of fire.

In seconds, all the airships were engaged in battle, and on the ground, the men of the opposing armies paused to look skyward. Back and forth the warring vessels glided, rising and falling in sudden tackings, fireballs cutting bright red paths across the blue, metal shards and arrows whistling through their deadly trajectories. Two of the Federation ships collided and went down in a twisted, locked heap, steering gone, hoods shattered, crystals drawing down so much power they exploded in midair. Another of the ships spun away from an encounter in a maneuver that lacked explanation and suggested panic. A Free-born vessel skidded into a Rover ship with a sharp screech of metal plates. Radian draws snapped loudly, sending both into slides that carried them away from each other. Everywhere, men were shouting and screaming in anger and fear and pain.

Black Moclips rose through the center of the maelstrom, breaching like a leviathan out of turbulent waters. Redden Alt Mer took her sideways and out from the pack in pursuit of a lone Elven ship that was maneuvering for position. Fireballs sizzled through the air in front of Alt Mer, but he slid underneath, tilting to bring his own weapons to bear. The Elf ship swung about and came at him. No coward, this Captain, the Rover thought with admiration. He banked left and rose sharply, the curved tip of his right battering ram taking off the top of the Elf's mainmast and dropping her mainsail. The Elf vessel lurched in response, fought to stay level.

Black Moclips swung about, readying an attack. "Steady, now!" Alt Mer yelled, red hair flying behind him in the wind like a crimson flag.

But a second ship lumbered into view from his right, a Federation vessel with her bridge in ruins, her Captain nowhere in sight, and her crew frantically trying to regain control. Flames leapt from her decking amidships and climbed her mainmast with feathery steps. Alt Mer held *Black Mo-*

clips steady, but all at once the Federation ship swung around, slewing sideways toward a collision. The Rover Captain hauled back on the steering, opened the hoods, and fed power through the parse tubes. *Black Moclips* surged upward, barely missing the Federation vessel as it passed underneath, pontoons scraping mast tips and tearing sails.

Alt Mer swore under his breath; it was bad enough that he had to worry about the enemy's ships. Expecting to find the partially disabled Elven ship, he brought *Black Moclips* about and found the Federation ship he had just avoided instead. Somehow it had come back around and was sweeping right in front of him. He hauled back on the hooding controls, lifting away on the ship's nose, trying to avoid it. But the Federation vessel was still slewing left and right. A burning brand, its captainless crew was desperately trying to tie off the radian draws before power to the crystals spilled her sideways. Sails were aflame and crystals were exploding and the Federation crew was screaming in fear.

Alt Mer couldn't get out of the way in time. "Brace!" he roared to everyone who could listen. "Brace, brace, brace!"

Black Moclips struck the Federation ship just below her foresail decking, shuddered and rocked violently, and absorbed the blow through her rams. Even so, the force of the collision threw him into the controls. Behind him, he caught a glimpse of the Federation Commander and his adjutants flying sideways across the decking. The restraining harnesses brought the Commander and one adjutant up short, but the line securing the second adjutant snapped, and the unfortunate man pinwheeled across the deck, flew over the railing, and was gone. Alt Mer could hear him screaming all the way down.

"Captain!" he heard the Federation Commander howl in anger and terror.

But there was no time to respond. Two more of the Elven ships were closing fast, sensing that they had a chance to destroy their greatest enemy. Alt Mer shouted to brace for evasive maneuvers, and took the ship into a sudden, slewing dive that sent the Federation Commander and his remaining adjutant flying back across the deck in the other direction. One Elf ship dropped after him, and when it did, he took it back under the second, *Black Moclips* twisting and dipping in smooth response to his hands on her controls.

The Federation Commander was still screaming at him from behind, but he paid no attention. He took *Black Moclips* around and up in a tight spiral, missiles from his catapults firing into the Elf ships, which were firing back. Scrap metal took out the foresail of one and, in one of the luckiest shots Alt Mer had ever seen, damaged the steering rudders, as well. The ship lurched and fought to regain power. Alt Mer ignored it, wheeling on the other. Metal shards hammered into *Black Moclips'* pontoons and upper decking, knocking her sideways. But her armor held, and Alt Mer swung right into the enemy.

"Brace!" he yelled down, jamming the controls forward to feed power to the crystals.

Black Moclips collided with the second Elf ship about halfway up its mainmast. The mast snapped as if caught in a high wind and toppled to the deck, bringing down sails and radian draws alike. Bereft of more than a third of his ship's power, her Captain was forced to hood his crystals and take her down. Alt Mer held *Black Moclips* away, watching as both Elf vessels began to descend, rolling and slewing as they fought to stay upright, crews scrambling madly to reposition the draws. All around them, Free-born ships were descending, giving up the hunt. Four Federation ships were down, burning on the plains. Two of those still airborne were damaged, one badly. Alt Mer glanced earthward at the crippled Free-born ships and gave the order to withdraw.

Suddenly the Federation Commander was shouting in his ear, his pinched face red and sweating. He had freed himself from his safety line and dragged himself across the decking. One hand gripped the railing of the pilot box and the other gestured furiously. "What do you think you're doing, Captain?"

Alt Mer had no idea what he was talking about and didn't care for his tone of voice. "Heading home, Commander. Put your safety line back on."

"You're letting them get away!" the other snapped, ignoring him. "You're letting them escape!"

Alt Mer glanced over the side of *Black Moclips* at the Free-born vessels. He shrugged. "Forget about them. They won't fly again for a while."

"But when they do, they'll be back in the skies, hunting our airships! I'm ordering you to destroy them, Captain!"

The Rover shook his head. "You don't give the orders aboard this vessel, Commander. Get back in place."

The Federation Commander seized his jacket. "I'm a superior officer, Captain Alt Mer, and I'm giving you a direct order!"

Redden Alt Mer had put up with enough. "Hawk!" he yelled. His Second Officer was beside him in a heartbeat. "Help the Commander back into his safety harness, please. Make sure it's securely fastened. Commander, we'll discuss it later."

Furl Hawken removed the almost incoherent officer from the pilot box, muscled him over to the aft railing, and snapped him back into his harness, pulling out the release pin in the process. He passed by Alt Mer on his way forward with a wink, tossing the Captain the pin. "Wish Little Red were here to see this," he whispered with a grin.

Well and good to say so now, the Rover thought darkly, his hands steady on the ship's controls, but it would be a different story when they landed. This wasn't something the Commander was likely to overlook, and he doubted that a board of inquiry would back a mercenary against a regular. Even the appearance of insubordination was enough to have you brought up on charges in this army. The right or wrong of it wouldn't matter, nor even the fact that on board any airship, like any sailing ship, the Captain's was the final word. The Federation would back its own, and he would be reduced in rank or dismissed from service.

His green eyes scanned the horizon, west to where the mountains rose against the blue of the sky. The one good thing about being a flyer was that you could always be somewhere else by nightfall.

He thought momentarily of taking *Black Moclips* and heading out, not even bothering to go back. But she wasn't his ship, and he wasn't a thief—not just then, anyway—and he couldn't leave Little Red behind. It was best to go back, pack up, and be out of there by dark.

Before he knew it, he was smelling the Blue Divide and remembering the colors of spring in March Brume.

He brought the ship down carefully, letting the ground crew haul her in and secure her, then walked back to free the Commander and his aide. Neither of them said a word or even looked at him. As soon as they were unhooked, they bolted from the ship as if scalded. Alt Mer let them go, turning his attention to checking the damage to *Black Moclips*, making certain steps would be taken to complete the necessary repairs. Already he was thinking of her as someone else's ship. Already, he was saying good-bye.

As it turned out, he was a little too slow doing so. He was just coming down off the rope ladder onto the airfield when the Commander reappeared with a squad of Federation regulars.

"Captain Alt Mer, you are under arrest for disobeying a superior officer while engaged in battle. A hanging offense, I think. Let's see who's in charge now, shall we?" He attempted a menacing smile, but it failed, and he flushed angrily. "Take him away!"

Furl Hawken and his crew started off the ship, weapons already in hand, but Redden Alt Mer motioned for them to stay where they were. Slipping free his weapons, he deliberately walked past the Commander and handed them to the grizzled squad leader, a man with whom he had shared more than a few glasses of ale and knew well enough to call by his first name.

"I'll see you tonight, Hawk," he called back over his shoulder.

He paused suddenly to look at *Black Moclips*. He would never see her again, he knew. She was the best ship he had ever captained, maybe the best he ever would. He hoped her new Captain would prove worthy of her, but he doubted it. Whatever the case, he would miss her more than he cared to imagine.

"Lady," he whispered to her. "It was grand."

Then, looking past the Commander to the squad leader, he shrugged his indifference to the whole business. "Lead the way, Cap. I put myself in your capable hands."

Whatever his thoughts might have been on the matter, the squad leader was smart enough to keep them to himself.

FIVE

The flat-faced, burly line sergeant had been drinking at the bar in the back room of the company blacksmith's for over an hour before he got up the nerve to walk over to Little Red. She was sitting alone at a table in the rear, clouded by shadow and the kind of studied disinterest in her surroundings that made it clear she was not to be approached. The line sergeant might have recognized as much five tankards of ale earlier, when his judgment was still clear enough to warn him against foolish behavior. But his anger at the way that she had humiliated him the night before, coupled with false bravado fueled by the quantity of his drink, finally won out.

He squared himself away in front of her, a big man, using his size as an implied threat.

"You and me got something to settle, Little Red," he declared loudly.

Heads turned. A few soldiers rose and quietly moved for the doors leading out. The blacksmith's wife, who tended bar for her husband in the midday, glanced over with a frown. Outside, in the sweltering heat of the forge, iron clanged on iron, and hot metal thrust into water hissed and steamed.

Rue Meridian did not look up. She kept her gaze steady and direct, staring off into space, her hands cupped loosely around her tankard of ale. She was there because she wanted to be alone. She should have been flying, but her heart wasn't in it anymore and her thoughts were constantly on the coast and home.

"You listening to me?" he snapped.

She could smell the line sergeant, his breath, unwashed body and hair, soiled uniform. She wondered if he noticed how foul he had become while living in the field, but guessed he hadn't.

"You think you're something, don't you?" Perhaps because of her silence, he was growing braver. He shifted his weight closer. "You look at me when I talk to you, Rover girl!"

She sighed. "Isn't it enough that I have to listen to you and smell you? Do I have to look at you, too? That seems like a lot to ask of me."

For a moment he just stared at her, vaguely confused. Then he knocked the tankard of ale from between her hands and drew his short sword. "You cheated me, Little Red! No one does that! I want my money back!"

She leaned back in her chair, her gaze lifting. She gave him a cursory glance and looked away again. "I didn't cheat you, Sergeant." She smiled pleasantly. "I didn't have to. You were so bad that it wasn't necessary. When you get better, which you might one day manage to do, then I might have to cheat you."

His bearded face clouded with fresh anger. "Give me back my money!"

Like magic, a throwing knife appeared in her hand. At once, he backed away.

"I spent it, all of it, every last cent. There wasn't that much to begin with." She looked at him once more. "What's your problem, Sergeant? You've been drinking at the bar for the last hour, so you're not broke."

He worked his mouth as if he was having trouble getting words out. "Just give me my money."

Last night she had bested him in a knife-throwing contest, although that would be using the word *contest* rather loosely since he was the worst knife thrower she could remember competing against. The cost to him had been his pride and his purse, and evidently it was a price he had not been prepared to pay.

"Get away from me," she said wearily.

"You're nothing, Little Red!" he exploded. "Just a cheating little witch!"

She thought momentarily about killing him, but she didn't feel like dealing with the consequences of doing so, so she abandoned the idea. "You want a rematch, Sergeant?" she asked instead. "One throw. You win, I give you back your money. I win, you buy me a fresh tankard of ale and leave me in peace. Done?"

He studied her suspiciously, as if trying to determine what the catch was. She waited him out patiently, watching his eyes, the throwing knife balanced loosely in her palm.

"Done," he agreed finally.

She rose, loose and easy in her dark Rover clothing, decorative bright scarves and sashes wrapped about her waist and shoulders, the ends trailing down in silken streamers, her long red hair shimmering in the lamplight. Rue Meridian was a beautiful woman by any standard, and more than a few men had been attracted to her when she had first joined the Federation army. But the number had dwindled after the first two who had tried unsuccessfully to force their affections on her had spent weeks in the hospital recovering from their wounds. Men still found her attractive, but they were more careful now about how they approached her. There was nothing "little" about Little Red. She was tall and broad-shouldered, lean and fit. She was called Little Red in deference to Big Red, her half brother, Redden Alt Mer. They had the same red hair and rangy frame, the same green eyes, the same quick smile and explosive temper. They had the same mother, as well, but different fathers. In theirs, as in many Rover clans, the men came and went while the women remained.

The line sergeant was casting about for a target. Last night, they had used a black circle the size of a thumbnail drawn on a support beam. They had thrown their knives in turn, two throws each. The sergeant had missed the mark both times; she had not. The sergeant complained, but paid up, cowed perhaps by the presence of so many other Rovers and fellow soldiers. There had been no mention of cheating then, no mention of getting his money back. He must have been stewing about it all night.

"There," he said, pointing at the same black circle on the beam, stepping to the same line they had drawn on the board flooring the night before.

"Here, here," the smith's wife complained at once. "You busted up a whole row of glasses throwing past the beam last night. Your aim's as poor as your judgment, Blenud Trock! You throw your knives somewhere else this time!"

The sergeant glared at her. "You'll get your money when I get mine!"

Trock. It was the first time Rue Meridian had heard his name spoken. "Let's move over here, Sergeant," she suggested.

She led him away from the bar and deeper into the room. The makeshift building was backed into a hill, and a stain from runoff had darkened the rear wall in a distinctive V. Just above and to the right, water droplets hung from a beam, falling every now and then onto the floor.

She stopped twenty feet away and drew a line with her toe in the dust and grime. Not the cleanest establishment she had ever frequented, but not the dirtiest either. These sorts of places came and went with the movement of the army. This one had endured because the army hadn't gone anywhere in some time. It was illegal, but it was left alone because the soldiers required some sort of escape out in the middle of nowhere, miles from any city.

She brushed back her fiery hair and looked at the sergeant.

"We'll stand together at the line. Once set, when the next drop of water falls from that beam, we throw at the V. Closest and quickest to the crease wins."

"Huh!" he grunted, taking his place. He muttered something else, but she couldn't hear. Throwing knife in hand, he set his stance. "Ready," he said.

She took a deep, slow breath and let her arms hang loose at her sides, the throwing knife resting comfortably in the palm of her right hand, the blade cool and smooth against the skin of her wrist and forearm. A small crowd had gathered behind them, soldiers from the front on leave and off duty, anxious for a little fresh entertainment. She was aware of others drifting in from outside, but the room remained oddly hushed. She grew languid and vaguely ethereal, as if her mind had separated from her body. Her eyes remained fixed, however, on the beam with its water droplets suspended in a long row, tiny pinpricks of reflective light against the shadows.

When the droplet of water finally fell, her arm whipped up in a dark blur and the throwing knife streaked out of her hand so fast that it was buried in the exact center of the V before the line sergeant had completed his throwing motion. The sergeant's knife was wide of the mark by six inches.

There was a smattering of applause and a few cheers from the spectators. Rue Meridian retrieved her knife and walked over to the bar to collect on her wager. The smith's wife already had the tankard of ale on the counter. "This one's yours, Sergeant Trock," she said in a loud voice, giving Rue a broad smile. "Pay up before you leave."

The line sergeant stalked over to the wall and pulled his heavy throwing knife free. For a moment he held it balanced in his hand as he gave Rue Meridian a venomous look. Then he sheathed the knife beneath his tunic and swaggered over to where she stood. "I'm not paying," he announced, planting himself at her side.

"Up to you," she replied, sipping at the ale.

"If you don't, you won't be coming back in here again," the smith's wife advised pointedly. "Stop being so troublesome."

"I'm not paying because you cheated!" he snapped, his response directed at Rue. "You threw before the water drop left the beam. It was plain as day."

There was a general murmur of dissent and a shaking of heads from the assembled, but no one called him on it. Emboldened, he leaned close enough that she could feel the heat of his breath and smell its stink. "You know what your problem is, Little Red? You need someone to teach you some manners. Then you wouldn't be so stuck—"

The rest of what he was going to say caught in his throat as he felt the tip of her throwing knife pressed against the soft underside of his bearded chin.

"You should think carefully before you speak again, Sergeant," she hissed. "You've already said enough to persuade me that it might be just as well if I cut your throat and have done with it."

The room had gone silent. No one was moving, not even the smith's wife, who stood watching with a dishrag in one hand and her mouth open.

The line sergeant gasped as Rue Meridian pressed upward with the knife tip, lifting his chin a little higher. The knife had appeared so suddenly that his hands still hung loose at his sides and his weapons remained sheathed. "I didn't mean—"

"You didn't mean," she cut him short, "that I needed to learn new manners, am I right?"

"Yes." He swallowed thickly.

"You didn't mean that someone as crude and stupid as yourself could teach them to me in any case, right?"

"Yes."

"You wish to tell me that you are sorry for saying I cheated and for spoiling my midday contemplation of things far away and dear to me, right?"

"Yes, yes!"

She backed him away, the knife tip still pressed against his neck. When he was standing clear of the bar, she reached down with her free hand and stripped him of his weapons. Then she shoved him backwards into a chair.

"I've changed my mind," she said, her own knife disappearing into her dark clothing. "I don't want you paying for my drink, wager or no. I want you sitting quietly right where you are until I decide you can leave. If I see you move a muscle, I'll pretend the V of your crotch is the V on the back wall and try my luck with a fresh throw."

The big man's eyes dropped involuntarily and then lifted. The rage reflected in his eyes was tempered only by his fear. He believed she would do what she said.

She was reaching for her tankard of ale when the door to the smith's shop burst open and Furl Hawken lumbered into view. Everyone in the room turned to look, and he slowed at once, aware of the unnatural silence, his eyes darting right and left.

Then he caught sight of her. "Little Red, something's come up. We have to go."

She stayed where she was, taking the tankard of ale in hand, lifting it to her lips, and drinking down the contents as if she had all the time in the world. Everyone watched in silence. No one moved. When she was finished, she set the tankard on the counter and walked over to the line sergeant. She bent close, as if daring him to do something about it. When he didn't, she said softly, "If I see you again, I'll kill you."

She dropped a coin on the counter as she passed the smith's wife, giving her a wink as she did so. Then she was through the door and surrounded by the clamor and fire of the forge, Furl Hawken at her back as he followed her out.

They moved swiftly through the maze of anvils, furnaces, and scrap heaps to the cluster of makeshift buildings beyond— kitchen, armory, surgery, command center, stables, supply depots, and the like, all bustling with activity in the midday heat. The sky was cloudless and blue, the sun a ball of white fire burning down on the dusty heights and the encamped army. Rue Meridian shook her head. It was the first daylight she had seen since yesterday, and it made her head pound.

"Is Big Red upset with me?" she asked as they moved away from the buildings and into the tented encampment, where she slowed her walk.

"Big Red is in irons and looking at twenty years' hard labor or worse," her companion growled, moving closer, keeping his voice low. "We had some company on our outing this morning, a couple of Federation officers. One went over the side during an attack, an accident, but he's just as dead. The ranking officer was furious. He was even madder when your brother refused to go after a couple of disabled Freeborn ships, knock 'em out of the sky instead of letting them descend. When we set down again, he had Big Red arrested and taken away, promising him that he would soon be experiencing an abrupt career change."

She shook her head. "Nothing we can do about it, is there? I mean, nothing that involves words and official procedure?"

Furl Hawken grunted. "We're Rovers, Little Red. What do you think?"

She put her hand on his massive shoulder. "I think I'm sick of this place, these people, this war, the whole business. I think we need a change of employment. What do we care about any of this? It was only the money that brought us here in the first place, and we have more than enough of that to last us for a while."

Furl Hawken shook his head. "Can't ever have enough money, Little Red."

"True," she admitted.

"Besides, it's not so bad here." His voice took on a wistful tone. "I've kind of gotten used to it. Grows on you, all this flatness and space, dust and grit—"

She shoved him playfully. "Don't you play that game with me! You hate it here as much as I do!"

His bluff face broke into a wide grin. "Well, maybe so."

"Time to go home, Hawk," she declared firmly. "Gather up the men, equipment, our pay, supplies, horses for everyone, and meet me on the south ridge in one hour." She shoved him anew, laughing. "Go on, you great blowhard!"

She waited until he was on his way, then turned toward the stockade where Federation convicts and miscreants were housed, chained in the open or in barred wooden boxes that on a hot day could cook the brain. Just thinking of her brother in one of those set her teeth on edge. The Federation's attitude toward Rovers hadn't changed a whit in the three years of their service. Rovers were mercenaries, and mercenaries were a necessary evil. It didn't matter how faithfully they served. It didn't matter how many of them died in the Federation cause. It didn't matter that they had proved themselves the better flyers and, for the most part, the better fighters. In the eyes of most Southlanders, Rovers were inferior solely because of who they were, and nothing of their abilities or accomplishments could ever change that.

Of course, Rovers were at the bottom of almost everyone's list because they were nomadic. If you lacked homelands, a central government, and an army, you lacked power. Without power, you had difficulty commanding respect. Rovers had survived in the same way for two thousand years, in mobile encampments and by clans. Rovers believed the land belonged to everyone, but especially to those who traveled it. The land was their mother, and they shared the Elven concept that it should be protected and nurtured. As a consequence, the Elves were the most tolerant and allowed the Rovers to make their way through the forests of the Westland, functioning as traders inland and sailors along the coast.

Elsewhere, they were less welcome and lived in constant danger of being driven out or worse. Except when they were taken on as mercenaries to fight in wars that never had much of anything to do with them.

Rue Meridian and her brother, along with several dozen others, had come east from the area around the coastal village of March Brume to serve the Federation in this one. The money was good and the risks acceptable. The Free-born weren't much better than the Federation at handling airships. There were regular battles, but they were viewed by the Rovers largely as exercises in trying to stay out of the way of incompetents.

Still, she concluded, it had grown boring, and it was time to move on. Especially now. She had been looking for an excuse to make a break for weeks, but her brother had insisted on sticking out the term of their enlistment. She shook her head. As if the Federation deserved their loyalty while treating them as subhuman. Now this. Clapping Big Red in irons over something as silly as ignoring an order from an officer of the Federation who ought to have known better than to try to give one. On an airship, the Captain's word was law. It was just another excuse to try to bring the Rovers into line, to put their collective necks under the Federation boot. Stupid, stupid people, she seethed. It would be interesting to see how successful they were with their airships once they lost the Rover crews who manned them.

She kicked at the dusty trail as she wound her way through the encampment, ignoring the inevitable catcalls and whistles, shouts and crude invitations, giving a wave or an unmistakable gesture where appropriate. She checked her weapons—slender rapier, brace of throwing knives strapped about her waist, dirk hidden in her boot, and sling looped through her shoulder strap and hanging down her back amid the scarves. Any one of them would be enough for this effort.

She could already smell the sea, the salt-laden pungency of the air, the raw damp of wooden docks and timbers, the fish-soaked reek of coastal shores, and the smoke from fireplaces lit at sunset to drive out the night's chill from homes and ale houses. Inland smells were of dust and dryness, of hard-packed earth and torrential rainwater that flooded and seeped away in a matter of hours. Three years of grit and dehydration, of men and animals who smelled alike, and of never seeing the blue of the ocean were enough.

Detouring momentarily at a campsite she recognized, she begged a meal off one of the cooks she was friendly with,

wrapped it in paper, and took it with her. Big Red would be
hungry.

Striding down through the outer stretches of the encampment, she approached the flat wooden walls of the stockade
as if she were out for a midday stroll.

"Hey, Little Red," one of the two guards standing watch at
the gates greeted cheerfully. "Come to see your brother?"

"Come to get him out," she replied, smiling.

The other guard grunted. "Huh, that'll take some doing."

"Oh, not all that much," she said. "Stockade commander in?"

"Having lunch or an afternoon snooze, take your choice."
The first guard chuckled. "What's that you're carrying?"

"Lunch for Big Red. Can I see him?"

"Sure. We put him in the shade by the back wall, under the
catwalk overhang. Might as well make him as comfortable as
we can while this business gets settled, though I don't like his
chances from the look of that officer that hauled him in. Mean
face on that one." He shook his head. "Sorry about this, Little
Red. We like your brother."

"Oh, you like him, but not me?"

The guard flushed. "You know what I mean. Here, hand
over your weapons, let me check your food package, and then
you can go in and see him."

She handed over her belt with the knives and rapier, then
unhooked the sling. She kept the dirk in her boot. Compliance got you only so far in this world. She smiled cheerfully
and passed through the gates.

She found her brother sitting under the overhang against
the back wall, right where the guards had told her she would.
He watched her approach without moving, weighted down in
irons that were clamped to his wrists, ankles, and waist and
chained to iron rings bolted tightly to the walls. Guards pa-
trolled the catwalks and stood idly in the roofed shade of
watchtowers at the stockade's corners. No one seemed much
interested in expending any energy.

She squatted in front of her brother and cocked a critical eyebrow. "You don't look so good, big brother."

Redden Alt Mer cocked an eyebrow back at her. "I thought you were sick in bed."

"I was sick at heart," she advised. "But I'm feeling much better now that we're about to experience a change of scenery. I think we've given the Federation army just about all of our time it deserves."

He brushed at a fly buzzing past his face, and the chains clanked furiously. "You won't get an argument out of me. My future as a mercenary doesn't look promising."

She glanced around. The stockade was filled with the sounds of men grumbling and cursing, of chains clanking, and of booted feet passing on the catwalk overhead. The air was dry and hot and still, and the smell of unwashed bodies, sweat, and excrement permeated everything.

She adjusted her stance to sit cross-legged before him, setting the food package on the ground between them. "How about something to eat?"

She unwrapped the food, and her brother began to devour it hungrily. "This is good," he told her. "But what are we doing, exactly? I thought you might have thought of a way to get me out of here."

She brushed back her thick red hair and smirked. "You mean you haven't figured that out for yourself? You got yourself in, didn't you?"

"No, I had help with that." He chewed thoughtfully on a piece of bread. "Do you have anything to drink?"

She reached inside her robes and produced a flask. He took it from her and drank deeply. "Ale," he announced approvingly. "What's going on? Is this my last meal?"

She picked at a cut of roast pheasant. "Let's hope not."

"So?"

"So we're killing time until Hawk gets things ready for our departure." She took the flask back from him and drank.

"Besides, we may not have time to eat again once we set out. I don't expect we'll be stopping until after dark."

He nodded. "I suppose not. So you do have a plan."

She grinned. "What do you think?"

They finished the meal, drank the rest of the ale, and sat quietly until Rue Meridian was satisfied that enough time had passed for Furl Hawken to be ready and waiting. Then she rose, brushed herself off, gathered up the remains of their feast, and walked toward the shack that served as the stockade commander's office. On the way, she dropped their leftovers in the stockade compost heap. You did what you could to care for Mother Earth, even here.

She walked into the commander's office without knocking, closing the door behind her. The commander was leaning back in his chair against the wall behind his desk, dozing. He was a red-faced, corpulent man, his face and hands scarred and worn. Without slowing, she walked around the desk, the dirk in her hand, and hit him as hard as she could behind the ear. He slumped to the floor without a sound.

Racks of keys lined the wall. She selected the set with her brother's name tagged to the peg and walked back to the door. When she caught sight of a guard passing across the compound, she called him over. "The commander wants to see my brother. Bring him over, please."

The guard, used to obeying orders from almost everyone, didn't question her. He took the keys and set off. A few minutes later he was back, herding Big Red at a slow shuffle, the wrist and ankle irons still attached. She stood aside to let them enter, closed the door, and flattened the guard with a blow to the neck.

Her brother glanced at her. "Very efficient. Do you plan to dispatch the entire garrison this way?"

"I don't think that will be necessary." She worked the keys into the wrist and ankle locks, and the chains dropped away. He rubbed his wrists appreciatively and looked around for a weapon. "Never mind that," she said, gesturing impatiently.

She took a sheet of paper from the commander's desk, one embossed with the Federation insignia, and wrote a brief note on it with a quill pen and ink. When she was finished, she eyed it critically, then nodded. "Good enough. You're a free man. Let's go."

She slipped the dirk back in her boot, and they walked out of the command shack and across the yard toward the gates. Her brother's eyes shifted about nervously. Prisoners and guards alike were watching them. "Are you sure about this?"

She laughed and shoved him playfully. "Just watch."

When they reached the gates, the two guards she had given her weapons to on entering were waiting. She waved the insignia-embossed paper at them. "What did I tell you?" she asked brightly, handing the paper to the first guard.

"Let me have a look at that," he replied suspiciously, squinting hard at the paper.

"You can see for yourself," she declared, pointing at the writing. "He's released to my custody until all this gets straightened out. I told you it wouldn't be that hard."

The second guard moved closer to the first, peering over his shoulder. Neither seemed entirely certain what to do.

"Don't you understand?" she pressed, crowding them now, jamming her finger at the paper. "The army can't afford to keep its best airship pilot locked up in the stockade with a war going on. Not because of one Federation officer who thinks it's a good idea. Come on! Give me back my weapons! You've looked at the order long enough! What's the matter, can't you read?"

She glared at them now. Neither guard said a word.

"Do you want me to wake up the commander again? He was mad enough the first time."

"Okay, okay," the first guard said hastily, shoving the piece of paper at her.

He handed back her knives, rapier, and sling and shooed them out the gates and back into the encampment. They walked in silence for several dozen paces before Redden Alt Mer said, "I don't believe it."

She shrugged. "They can't read. Even if they could, it wouldn't matter. No one could make out what I wrote. When they're asked about it, they'll claim I had a release order signed by the commander. Who's to say I didn't? This is the army, big brother. Soldiers don't admit to anything that might get them in trouble. They'll fuss for a day or two and then decide they're well rid of us."

Her brother rubbed his arms to restore the circulation and glanced at the cloudless sky. "Three years in this forsaken place. Money or no, that's a long time." He sighed wearily and slapped his thighs. "I hate leaving *Black Moclips*, though. I hate that."

She nodded. "I know. I thought about taking her. But stealing her would be hard, Big Red. Too many people keeping watch."

"We'll get another ship," he declared, brushing the matter aside, a bit of the old spring returning to his step. "Somewhere."

They walked through the camp's south fringe to where the passes led downward out of the heights toward the city of Dechtera and the grasslands west. Once across the Rappahalladran and the plains beyond, they were home.

Ahead, Furl Hawken stood waiting in a draw with a dozen more Rovers and the horses and supplies.

"Hawk!" Redden Alt Mer called, and gave him a wave. Then he glanced over his shoulder at the fading outline of the camp. "Well, it was fun for a time. Not as much fun as we'll have where we're going, of course, wherever that turns out to be, but it had its moments."

Rue Meridian smirked. "My brother, the eternal optimist." She brushed stray strands of her long hair from her face. "Let's hope this time you're right."

Ten minutes later, they had left the Federation army behind and were riding west for the coast of the Blue Divide.

SIX

At first light, the Druid known as Walker slipped from the sleeping room he had been given in the summer house on his arrival the night before. Arborlon was still sleeping, the Elven city at rest, and only the night watch and those whose work required an early rising were awake. A tall, spare, shadowy figure in his black robes, hair, and beard, he glided soundlessly from the palace grounds and through the streets and byways of the city to the broad sweep of the Carolan. He was aware of the Home Guard who trailed him, an Elven Hunter assigned to him by the King. Allardon Elessedil was not a man who took chances, so the presence of a watchdog was not unexpected, and Walker let the matter be.

On the heights, where the Carolan fronted the sprawl of the Westland forests, visible all the way to the ragged jut of the Rock Spur south and the Kensrowe north, he paused. The first glimmer of sunlight had crested the trees behind him, but night still enfolded the land west, purple and gray shadows clinging to treetops and mountain peaks like veils. In the earthen bowl of the Sarandanon, small lakes and rivers reflected the early light in silvery flashes amid the patchwork quilt of farms and fields. Farther out, the waters of the Innisbore shimmered in a rough, metallic sheen, their surface coated with broken layers of mist. Somewhere beyond that lay the vast expanse of the Blue Divide, and it was there that he must eventually go.

He looked all about the land, a slow, careful perusal, a drinking in of colors and shapes. He thought about the history of the city. Of the stand it had made in the time of Eventine Elessedil against the assault of the demons freed from the Forbidding by the failure of the Ellcrys. Of its journey out of the Westland in the Ruhk staff and the magic-riven Loden to the island of Morrowindl—buildings, people, and history disappeared as if they had never been. Of its journey back again, returned to the Four Lands by Wren Elessedil, where it would withstand the onslaught of the Shadowen. Always, the Elves and the Druids had been allies, bound by a common desire to see the lands and their peoples kept free.

What, he asked himself in dark contemplation, had become of that bond?

Below the heights, swollen with snowmelt off the mountains and spring's rainfall, the Rill Song churned noisily within its banks. He listened to the soothing, distant sound of the water's heavy flow as it echoed out of the trees. He stood motionless in the enfolding silence, not wanting to disturb it. It felt strange to be back here, but right, as well. He had not come to Arborlon in more than twenty years. He had not thought he would come again while Allardon Elessedil lived. His last visit had opened a rift between them he did not think anything could close. Yet here he was, and the rift that had seemed so insurmountable now seemed all but inconsequential.

His thoughts drifted as he turned away. He had come to Arborlon and the Elven King out of desperation. All of his efforts at brokering an agreement with the races to bring representatives to Paranor to study in the Druid way had failed. Since then, he had lived alone at Paranor, reverting to the work of recording the history of the Four Lands. There was little else he could do. His bitterness was acute. He was trapped in a life he had never wanted. He was a reluctant Druid, recruited by the shade of Allanon in a time when there were no Druids and the presence of at least one was vital to the survival of the races. He had accepted the blood trust bestowed by the dying Allanon hundreds of years earlier on his ancestor Brin Ohmsford, not because he coveted it in any way, but because fate and circumstance conspired to place him in a position where only he could fulfill its mandate. He had done so out of a sense of responsibility. He had done so hoping that he might change the image and work of the Druids, that he might find a way for the order to oversee civilization's advancement through cooperative study and democratic participation by all of the peoples of the Four Lands.

He shook his head. How foolish he had been, how naive his thinking. The disparities between nations and races were too great for any single body to overcome, let alone any single man. His predecessors had realized that and acted on it accordingly. First bring strength to bear, then reason. Power commanded respect, and respect provided a platform from which to enjoin reason. He had neither. He was an outcast, solitary and anachronistic in the eyes of almost everyone. The Druids had been gone from the Four Lands since the time of Allanon. Too long for anyone to remember them as they once were. Too long to command respect. Too long to serve as a catalyst for change in a world in which change most often came slowly, grudgingly, and in tiny increments.

He exhaled sharply, as if to expel the bitter memory. All that was in the past. Perhaps now it could be buried there. Perhaps now, unwittingly, he had been given the key to accomplishing what had been denied him for so long.

The Gardens of Life rose ahead of him, sun-streaked and vibrant with springtime color. Members of the Black Watch stood at their entrances, rigid and aloof, and he passed them by without a glance. Within the gardens grew the Ellcrys, the most sacred of the Elven talismans, the tree that kept in place the Forbidding, the wall conjured in ancient times to close away the demons and monsters that had once threatened to overrun the world. He walked to where she rooted on a small rise, set apart from the rest of the plantings, strikingly beautiful with her silver limbs and crimson leaves, wrapped in serenity and legend. She had been human once. When her life cycle was complete and she passed away, her successor would come from among the Chosen who tended her. It was a strange and miraculous transition, and it required sacrifice and commitment of a sort with which he was intimately familiar.

A voice spoke at his elbow. "I always wonder if she is watching me, if by virtue of having been given responsibility over all of her people I require her constant vigilance. I always wonder if I am living up to her expectations."

Walker turned to find Allardon Elessedil standing beside him. It had been many years since he had seen him last, yet he recognized him at once. Allardon Elessedil was older and grayer, more weathered and careworn, and the robes he wore were pale and nondescript. But he carried himself in the same regal manner and exuded the same rocklike presence. Allardon Elessedil was not one of the great Elven Kings; he had been denied that legacy by a history that had not given him reason or need to be so and by a temperament that was neither restless nor inquisitive. He was a caretaker King, a ruler who felt his principal duty was to keep things as they were. Risk-taking was for other men and other races, and the Elves in his time had not been at the forefront of civilization's evolution in the Four Lands.

The Elven King did not offer his hand in greeting or speak any words of welcome. It remained to be seen, Walker judged, how their meeting would conclude.

Walker looked back at the Ellcrys. "We cannot hope to know what she expects of us, Elven King. It would be presumptuous even to try."

If the other man was offended, he did not show it. "Are you rested?" he asked.

"I am. I slept undisturbed. But at first light, I felt the need to walk here. Is this a problem?"

Allardon Elessedil brushed the question off with a wave of his hand. "Hardly. You are free to walk where you choose."

Yes, but not to do as I please, Walker thought. How bitter he had been on leaving all those years ago. How despairing. But time's passing had blunted the edges of those once sharp feelings, and now they were mostly memory. It was a new age, and the Elven King was growing old now and in need of him. Walker could achieve the result that had been denied him for so long if he proceeded carefully. It was a strange, exhilarating feeling, and he had to be cautious to keep it from showing in his voice and eyes.

"Your family is well?" he asked, making an effort at being cordial.

The other shrugged. "The children grow and take roads of their own choosing. They listen to me less and less. I have their respect, but not their obedience. I am more a father and less a King to them, and they feel free to ignore me."

"What is it you would have them do?"

"Oh, what fathers would usually have children do." The Elven King chuckled. "Stay closer to home, take fewer chances, be content with the known world. Kylen fights with the Free-born in a struggle I do not support. Ahren wanders the north in search of a future. My sons think I will live forever, and they leave me to be ruler alone." He shrugged. "I suppose they are no different than the sons of other fathers."

Walker said nothing. His views would not have been welcomed. If Allardon Elessedil's sons grew up to be different men than their father, so much the better.

"I am pleased you decided to come," the King ventured after a moment.

Walker sighed. "You knew I would. The castaway elf—is he Kael?"

"I assume as much. He wore the bracelet. Another elf would have carried it. Anyway, we'll know tomorrow. I hoped the map would intrigue you sufficiently that you would be persuaded. Have you studied it?"

Walker nodded. "All night before flying here yesterday."

"Is it genuine?" Allardon Elessedil asked.

"That's difficult to say. It depends on what you mean. If you are asking me whether it might tell us what happened to your brother, the answer is yes. It might be a map of the voyage on which he disappeared. His name appears nowhere in the writings, but the condition and nature of the hide and ink suggest it was drawn within the last thirty years, so that it might have been his work. Is the handwriting his?"

The Elven King shook his head. "I can't tell."

"The language is archaic, a language not used since the Great Wars changed the Old World forever. Would your brother have learned that language?"

The other man considered this for a moment, then shrugged. "I don't know. How much of what it says were you able to decipher?"

Walker shifted within his dark robes, looking out again toward the Carolan. "Can we walk a bit? I am cramped and sore from yesterday's journey, and I think it would help to stretch my legs."

He began moving slowly down the pathway, and the Elf King fell into step beside him wordlessly. They walked in silence through the gardens for a time, the Druid content to let matters stay as they were until he was ready to speak to them. Let Allardon Elessedil wait as he had waited. He turned his attention to other things, observing the way in which the gardens' plantings flowed into one another with intricate symmetry, listening to the soft warble of the resident birds, and gazing up at the clouds that drifted like silk throws across the clear blue of the spring sky. Life in balance. Everything as it should be.

Walker glanced over. "The guard you assigned to watch me appears to have lost interest in the job."

The Elven King smiled reassuringly. "He wasn't there to watch you. He was there to let me know when you awoke so that we could have this talk."

"Ah. You sought privacy in our dealings. Because your own guards are absent, as well. We are all alone." He paused. "Do you feel safe with me, then?"

The other's smile was uneasy. "No one would dare to attack me while I was with you."

"You have more faith in me than I deserve."

"Do I?"

"Yes, if you consider that I wasn't referring to an attack that might come from a third party."

The conversation was clearly making the King uncomfortable. Good, Walker thought. I want you to remember how you left things between us. I want you to wonder if I might be a greater threat to you than the enemies you more readily fear.

They emerged from the gardens onto the Carolan, the sunlight illuminating the green expanse of the heights in bright trailers that spilled over into the forests below. Walker led the way to a bench placed under an aging maple whose boughs canopied out in a vast umbrella. They sat together, Druid and King, looking out over the heights to the purple and gold mix of shadow and light that colored the horizon west.

"I have no reason to want to help you, Allardon Elessedil," Walker said after a moment.

The Elven King nodded. "Perhaps you have better reason than you think. I am not the man I was when last we spoke. I regret deeply how that meeting ended."

"Your regret can be no greater than my own," Walker replied darkly, keeping his gaze averted, staring off into the distance.

"We can dwell on the regret and the loss or turn our attention to what we might accomplish if we relegate both to the past." The Elven King's voice was tight and worried, but there was a hint of determination behind it, as well. "I would like to make a new beginning."

Now Walker looked at him. "What do you propose?"

"A chance for you to build the Druid Council you desire, to

begin the work you have sought to do for so long, with my support and blessing."

"Money and men would count for more than your support and blessing," the Druid remarked dryly.

The Elven King's face went taut. "You shall have both. You shall have whatever you need if you are able to give me what I need in return. Now tell me of the map. Were you able to decipher its writings?"

Walker took a long moment to consider his answer before he spoke. "Enough so that I can tell you that they purport to show the way to the treasure of which your mother's seer dreamed thirty years ago. As I said, the writing is archaic and obscure. Some symbols suggest more than one thing. But there are names and courses and descriptions of sufficient clarity to reveal the nature of the map. Travel west off the coast of the Blue Divide to three islands, each a bit farther than the one before. Each hides a key that, when all are used together, will unlock a door. The door leads to an underground keep that lies beneath the ruins of a city called Castledown. The ruins can be found on a mountainous spit of land far west and north of here called Ice Henge. Within the ruins lies a treasure of life-altering power. It is a magic of words, a magic that has survived the destruction of the Old World and the Great Wars by being kept hidden in its safehold. The magic's origins are obscure, but the map's writings say it surpasses all others."

He paused. "Because it was found on the blind and voiceless Elven castaway together with your brother's bracelet, I would be inclined to believe that if followed, it would reveal your brother's fate and perhaps the nature of the magic it conceals."

He waited, letting the King collect his thoughts. On the heights, the Elves were beginning to appear in clusters for the start of the workday. Guards were exchanging shifts. Tradesmen and trappers were arriving from the west, crossing the Rill Song on ferries and rafts bearing wagons and carts laden with goods, then climbing the ramps of the Elfitch. Gardeners were at work in the Gardens of Life, weeding and pruning, planting and fertilizing. Here and there, a white-robed Chosen wandered into view. Children played as teachers led them to their study areas for lessons on becoming Healers in the Four Lands.

"So you support a quest of the sort my brother undertook all those years ago?" the King asked finally.

Walker smiled faintly. "As do you, or you would not have asked me to come here."

Allardon Elessedil nodded slowly. "If we are to learn the truth, we must follow the route the map chronicles and see where it leads. I will never know what happened to Kael otherwise. I will never know what became of the Elfstones he carried. Their loss is perhaps the more significant of the two. This is not easy to admit, but I can't pretend otherwise. The stones are an Elven heritage, passed down from Queen Wren, and the last of their kind. We are a lesser people without them, and I want them back."

Walker's dark face was inscrutable. "Who will lead this expedition, Allardon?"

There was no hesitation in his answer. "You will. If you agree to. I am too old. I can admit it to you if to no one else. My children are too young and inexperienced. Even Kylen. He is strong and fierce, but he is not seasoned enough to lead an expedition of this sort. My brother carried the Elfstones, and even that was not enough to save him. Perhaps a Druid's powers will prove more formidable."

"And if I agree to do this, you give me your word that the Elves will support an independent Druid Council, free to study, explore, and develop all forms of magic?"

"I do."

"A Druid Council that will answer to no one nation or people or ruler, but only to its own conscience and the dictates of the order?"

"Yes."

"A Druid Council that will share its findings equally with all people, when and if those findings can be implemented peacefully and for the betterment of all races?"

"Yes, yes!" The King made an impatient, dismissive gesture. "All that you sought before and I denied. All. Understand, though," he added hurriedly, "I cannot speak for other nations and rulers, only for the Elves."

Walker nodded. "Where the Elves lead, others follow."

"And if you disappear as my brother did, then the matter ends there. I will not be bound to an agreement with a dead man—not an agreement of this sort."

Walker's gaze wandered across the Carolan to the Gardens of Life and settled on the men and women working there, bent to their tasks. It spoke to him of his own work, of the need to care for the lives of the people of the races the Druids had sworn long ago to protect and advance. Why had their goals been so difficult to achieve when their cause was so obviously right? If plants were sentient in the way of humans, would they prove as difficult and obstructive to the efforts of their tenders?

"We understand each other, Allardon," he said softly. His eyes found the King's face. He waited for the lines of irritation to soften. "One more thing. Any treasure I discover on this journey, be it magic or otherwise, belongs to the Druids."

The Elven King was already shaking his head in disagreement. "You know I will not agree to that. Of money or precious metals, I care nothing. But what you find of magic, whatever its form, belongs to the Elves. I am the one who has sanctioned and commissioned this quest. I am the one whose cause requires it. I am entitled to the ownership of whatever you recover."

"On behalf of your people," Walker amended casually.

"Of course!"

"Suggesting that the cause and ownership rights of the Elven people are greater than those of the other races, even if the magic recovered might benefit them, as well?"

The King flushed anew, stiffening within his robes. He leaned forward combatively. "Do not try to make me feel guilt or remorse for the protections I seek to give to my own people, Walker! It is my duty to do so! Let others do so, as well, and perhaps a balance will be struck!"

"I have trouble understanding why, on the one hand, you support a Druid Council giving equal rights to all nations and peoples while, on the other, you seek to withhold what might benefit them most. Should I undertake a quest only for you, when what I would most covet at its end is forbidden me?" He paused, reflecting. "Magic belongs to everyone, Elven King, especially when it impacts all. A sharing of magic must begin somewhere. Let it begin here."

Allardon Elessedil stared hard at him, but the Druid held his gaze and kept his expression neutral. The seconds dragged past with neither man speaking further, eyes locked.

"I cannot agree," the Elven King repeated firmly.

Walker's brow creased thoughtfully. "I will make a bargain with you," he said. "A compromise of our positions. You will share fully in what I find, magic or no. But we shall make an agreement as to the nature of that sharing. That which you can use without my help, I will give to you freely. That which only I can use belongs to me."

The King studied him. "The advantage is yours in this bargain. You are better able to command the use of magic than I or my people."

"Magic that is Elven in nature will be readily understood by Elves and should belong to them. The Elfstones, for example, if found, belong to you. But magic that has another source, whatever its nature, cannot be claimed by Elves alone, especially if they cannot wield it."

"There is no magic in the world except that which was handed down by the Elves out of the world of Faerie! You know that!"

"Then you have nothing to worry about."

The King shook his head helplessly. "There is a trick in all this."

"Describe it, then."

"All right, all right!" The Elf sighed. "This matter has to be resolved. I'll accept your compromise. That magic that is Elven in nature and can be commanded by us is ours. The rest stays with the Druid Council. I don't like this bargain, but I can live with it."

They shook hands wordlessly. Walker rose, squinting against the sharp glare of the sunrise as he looked east over the trees. His black robes rippled softly in the breeze. Allardon Elessedil stood up with him. The sharp features looked pinched and tired despite the early hour. "What do you intend to do now?"

The Druid shifted his gaze back to the King. "I'll need the use of the Wing Rider and his Roc."

"Hunter Predd? I'll speak with him. Will you fly to Bracken Clell?"

"Will you go with me, if I do?" the Druid countered. "Or have you done so already?"

Allardon Elessedil shook his head. "I've been waiting on you."

"It is your brother, perhaps, who lies dying in the Healer's home, Elven King."

"Perhaps. But it's been thirty years, and he's been dead to me a long time already." The King sighed. "It complicates things if I go with you. Home Guard will insist on going as well, to protect me. Another Roc will be needed. It might be better if I remain here."

Walker nodded. "I'll go alone then, and afterwards farther on to find a ship and crew."

"I could help you with that."

"You could, but I would prefer that you helped me in another way if you choose to remain here. There are certain things I want from a ship and crew that will take us in search of the map's treasure, things that I must determine for myself. But I will rely on you to select those who would defend us.

Elven Hunters, of course, but perhaps a handful of others as well. Bordermen and Dwarves, I should think. Are you willing to find them for me?"

The Elven King nodded. "How many do you wish?"

"Two dozen to choose from, no more."

They began to walk back across the heights, moving toward the gardens once more, taking their time. All around them, the city of Arborlon was waking.

"Two dozen is a small number of blades and bows on which to depend," the King observed.

"Three ships with full crews and dozens of Elven Hunters were apparently too few, as well," Walker pointed out. "I prefer to rely on speed and stealth and on the heart and courage of a few rather than on sheer numbers."

"One ship is all you will take, then?"

"One will suffice."

Allardon Elessedil hunched his shoulders, his eyes lowered. "Very well. I will not go with you myself, as I have said, but I will want to send someone in my place."

"Send anyone you like, only . . ."

Walker was shading his eyes against the sun's brightness as he spoke or he would have missed the flash of the metal blade as it was hurled. The assassin was one of the gardeners, inconspicuous in his working clothes, just another worker at his job. He had come to his feet as if to move his tools, and suddenly the knife appeared.

Walker's swift gesture sent the blade spinning harmlessly, knocked aside as if it had struck a wall.

By now, the second assassin was attacking, this one with a blowgun. Another of the seeming gardeners, he knelt in a patch of bright yellow daffodils and fired three darts in rapid succession. Walker yanked the King aside and blocked that attack as well. A third assassin came at them with a rapier and a knife. All of the assassins were Elves, their features unmistakable. But their eyes were fixed and unseeing, and the

Druid knew at once that they had been mind-altered to assure their compliance in making the attack.

Screams rose across the Carolan as the other Elves realized what was happening. Black Watch soldiers charged to the King's defense, massive pikes lowered. Elven Hunters appeared, as well, lean, swift forms bolting from the trees. All were too far away.

Walker gestured toward the assassin with the rapier and knife, and a massive, ethereal form materialized before the man, a giant moor cat lunging out of nowhere to intercept him. The man screamed and went down, weapons flying as the beast sailed into him and vanished, leaving him huddled and cringing against the earth. The remaining two assassins charged, as well, silent and determined, skirting the third man, madness in their empty eyes. They barreled into the Druid and were cast aside as if made of paper. Black robes flaring like shadows released, Walker turned from one to the other, stripping them of weapons and blunting their attacks.

But the Home Guard and Black Watch were close enough now to respond as well. Frightened for their king, they acted instinctively and unwisely to protect him. A hail of spears and arrows took down the assassins, leaving them sprawled on blood-soaked earth, their lives draining away. Even the third man was caught in the barrage, come back to his feet too quickly to be spared. Walker yelled at the Elves to stop, to leave the assassins to him, but he was too late to save them.

Too late, as well, to save Allardon Elessedil. An arrow meant for the assassins struck the Elf King squarely in the chest. He gasped at the impact, lurched backwards, and went down in a heap. Walker had no chance to save him. Focused on stopping the assassins, he could not react to the King's guards in time.

The Druid knelt at the King's side, lifted his shoulders, and cradled his head in his lap. "Elven King?" he whispered. "Can you hear me?"

Allardon Elessedil's eyes were open, and his gaze shifted at the sound of the Druid's voice. "I'm still here."

Elven Hunters had surrounded them, and there were calls for a Healer and medicines. The heights were a maelstrom of activity as Elves pushed forward from every quarter to see what had happened. Black Watch formed a ring about their stricken ruler and pushed the crowds back. The assassins lay dead in their own blood, their lifeless forms bathed in sunlight and bedded in deep grasses.

Allardon Elessedil was coughing blood. "Call a scribe," he gasped. "Do it now."

One was found almost at once, a young man, barely grown, his face white and his eyes frightened as he knelt next to the king.

"Move everyone back but this boy, the Druid, and two witnesses," Allardon Elessedil ordered.

"High Lord, I cannot . . . ," a Captain of the Home Guard began softly, but the King motioned him away.

When an area had been cleared around them, the Elven King nodded to the scribe. "Copy down what I say," he whispered, keeping his eyes on Walker as he spoke. "Everything."

Carefully, detail by detail, he repeated the agreement that he had reached with the Druid moments earlier. A voyage was to be undertaken with Walker as its leader. The purpose of the voyage was to follow the route described on a map carried by the Druid, a copy of which was held by the King's scribe at the palace. A search for the missing blue Elfstones was to be undertaken. And on and on. Slowly, painstakingly, he repeated it all, including the bargain struck regarding the recovery of magic. A Healer appeared and began work on the injury, but the King kept talking, grimacing through his pain, his breathing raspy and thick and his eyes blinking as if he was fighting to see.

"There," he said, when he was finished. "They have killed me for nothing. See this through, Walker. Promise me."

"He's bleeding to death," the Healer announced. "I have to take him to my surgery and remove the arrow at once."

Walker lifted the Elven King as if he weighed nothing, cradling him in the crook of his good left arm and with the stump of his right, and carried him from the plains. All the while, he talked to him, telling him to stay strong, not to give up, to fight for his life, for it had worth and meaning beyond what he knew. Surrounded by Home Guard, he bore the King as he might a sleeping child, holding him gently within his arms, head cushioned against his shoulder.

Several times, the King spoke, but the words were so soft that only Walker could hear them. Each time the Druid replied firmly, "You have my promise. Rest, now."

But sometimes even a Druid's exhortations are not enough. By the time they reached the surgery, Allardon Elessedil was dead.

SEVEN

It took Walker until well after noon to secure a copy of the young scribe's notes and carry it to Ebben Bonner, who was First Minister of the Elven High Council and nominal leader of the Elves pending the formal succession of Allardon Elessedil's eldest son. There, in an extraordinary concession to the circumstances surrounding the King's death, the First Minister approved Walker's request to depart for Bracken Clell so that he might act on the terms of the dead King's agreement. Walker successfully argued that there was reason to believe that the mind-altered Elves who were behind the death of Allardon Elessedil had been sent by someone intent on preventing an expedition to retrace the route detailed on the castaway's map. It was entirely too coincidental that the attack had come just as King and Druid had agreed to mount such an expedition, especially since it was their first meeting in twenty-three years. Certainly the King had believed it was more than coincidence or he would not have spent the last moments of his life dictating instructions for carrying out the expedition to his scribe. Clearly, someone had found out about the map and the treasure it revealed. It took a leap of faith to accept that there was a connection between the King's death and the map's appearance, but it would be better to make that leap than do nothing. Walker was concerned that if the King's enemies were bold enough to strike in the Elven capital city, they would be equally quick to strike in Bracken Clell. The castaway who

was under care in the healing center would be at great risk.
Perhaps Walker could still reach him in time. Perhaps he
could discover yet if he was Kael Elessedil.

He recruited Hunter Predd and Obsidian for the journey.
The Wing Rider was anxious to depart the chaos unfolding
around him and frankly curious to know more about where
this business of the castaway and the map was leading. With
barely a word of encouragement from Walker or question of
his own, he had Obsidian saddled and ready for flight. They
rose into the afternoon sun while the people of Arborlon were
still trying to come to terms with the news of their King's
death. Some were just learning, returned from journeys of
their own or preoccupied with the demands and difficulties
of their own lives. Some still didn't believe it was true.
Walker wasn't sure what he believed. The suddenness of the
King's death was shocking. Walker was no less affected than
the Elves. To not have seen or spoken to the man in so many
years and then to watch him die, on their first morning, was
difficult to accept. It was bad enough that he had been hostile
toward the King in their final meeting and almost intolerable
that he had all but wished him dead. He did not feel guilt for
his behavior, but he did feel shame.

Allardon Elessedil already lay in state, awaiting his funeral
and burial. Messengers had been sent to his children, east to
the front where Kylen fought with the Free-born, north into
the wilderness where Ahren hunted. Across the length and
breadth of the Four Lands, word of the Elven King's death
had gone out.

But Walker could give no further thought to any of it. His
concern now was for the safety of the castaway and the initial
preparations for the voyage chronicled on the map he carried
within his robes. He strongly believed that whoever arranged
for the King's assassination had done so to keep him from
underwriting the voyage. Until a new King sat upon the
throne, the Elven High Council would be unlikely to do much
more than tread water. What saved Walker from being blocked

entirely was the old King's quick action in recording, almost literally with his last breath, the agreement they had struck regarding the map so that the Druid could act on it without having to wait around.

And, if the Druid's suspicions were correct, whoever had recruited the Elven assassins had probably determined to make the voyage, as well.

Steady and unflagging, Obsidian flew his master and Walker south for the remainder of the afternoon over the dense tangle of Drey Wood and the watery mire of the Matted Brakes. As sunset neared, they passed the Pykon's solitary spires and crossed the silver thread of the Rill Song into the deep woods that fronted the Rock Spur. The light was beginning to fail badly as Hunter Predd guided his mount to a good-size clearing. There, he sent the Roc back into the trees to roost, while he and the Druid made camp. They lit a fire in a shallow pit, laid out their bedrolls on a carpet of soft needles beneath an ancient pine, and cooked their meal. Druid and Wing Rider, they sat as if a part of the forest shadows, dark figures in the deepening gloom, eating in silence and listening to the sounds of the night.

"Strange day," the Elf remarked, sipping at the ale he shared with his traveling companion. "Makes you wonder about the way life works. Makes you wonder why anyone would want to be King."

Walker nodded, straight-backed within his black robes, eyes distant. "The Wing Hove must have thought the same thing a long time ago."

"It's true. It's one reason we have a council to make our laws and decisions for us, not just one man." The Wing Rider shook his head. "Killed by his own people. He wasn't a bad man, Walker. Why would they do it?"

Walker's gaze fixed on him. "They didn't. I saw their eyes. Whatever their motives in acting against the King, they were not the men they had been even a few days ago. They had been mind-altered in some permanent way. They were meant to attack the King, to kill him however they could manage it, and then to die."

Hunter Predd frowned. "How could a man be made to do that?"

"Magic."

"Elven?"

Walker shook his head. "I'm not sure yet. If they had lived, I might have been able to tell. Dead, they could give me nothing."

"Who were they? Not gardeners, surely?"

"No one could identify them. Elves, but not of Arborlon. Hard men, who had led hard lives, from the look of their hands and faces. They would have killed other men before this."

"Still."

"Still, they would have needed some incentive to kill an Elven King. Whoever recruited them provided that incentive using magic." Walker held the other's gaze. "I'm sorry to drag you out again so suddenly, but there wasn't time to wait. I think our castaway is in danger. And it won't stop there. I'm going to need you to fly me a few more places in the next week or two, Hunter Predd. I'm going to need your help."

The Wing Rider drained the rest of the ale from his cup and poured himself another serving from the skin pouch beside him. "Tell you the truth, I was ready to leave anyway. Not just because of the King's dying, but because cities and me don't much agree. A few days are more than enough. I'm better off flying, whatever the risk."

The Druid gave him a wry smile. "Nevertheless, it appears you are knee-deep in something more than you bargained for when you decided to carry that map and bracelet to Arborlon."

The Elf nodded. "That's fine. I want to see where all this is going." He grinned suddenly. "Wouldn't it be a shame if I didn't give myself the chance?"

*　　　*　　　*

They slept undisturbed and by sunrise were winging their way south once more. The weather had changed during the night, with heavy clouds rolling inland off the coast and blanketing the skies from horizon to horizon. The air was warm and still, smelling of new rain, and in the distance, farther west, the sound of thunder echoed ominously. Shadows draped the land they passed over, a cloaking of movement and light that whispered in their thoughts of secrets and concealments not meant to be revealed.

Walker was already beginning to suspect the identity of the enemy who was trying to undermine his efforts. There were few in the Four Lands who could command magic strong enough to alter minds—fewer still with a sufficient number of well-placed eyes to know what was happening from Bracken Clell to Arborlon. He was afraid that he had acted too slowly in this matter, though he accepted at the same time that he could not have acted any faster. He was only one man, and his adversary, if his suspicions were correct, commanded a small army.

Obsidian flew them through the jagged defiles and down the deep canyons of the Rock Spur Mountains, angling to keep low enough for cover, high enough to clear the ridges. They passed over the dark bowl of the Wilderun, home to castoffs and outcasts who had come from everywhere to that final refuge. At its center, the Hollows was a pool of shadows, dark and forbidding, a quagmire that might swallow them up should they fly too low. Beyond, at the south end of the wilderness, they passed through the deeper maze of the Irrybis Mountains and came in sight of the Blue Divide.

Rain had begun to fall in a slow drizzle, soon soaking their clothing through, and it was approaching nightfall when they arrived at the seaport of Bracken Clell. In darkness unbroken by the light of moon or stars, they proceeded slowly along muddied, rain-slicked pathways, hooded and cloaked, wraiths in the night.

"Not much farther," the Wing Rider advised from the darkness of his cowl, when the lights of the seaport came in view.

They came to the healing center where Hunter had left the castaway less than a week earlier. They mounted the steps of the covered porch, shaking the rain from their cloaks, and knocked on the door. Waiting, they could hear a low murmur of voices from inside and see shadows move across the lighted, curtained windows.

The door opened on a lean, graying Elf with kind, tired eyes and a questioning look. He smiled on seeing Hunter Predd and extended his hand to invite them in.

"My friend, Dorne," the Wing Rider said to Walker. "This man," he advised the Healer in turn, gesturing in a deliberately offhanded way toward the Druid, "is an emissary sent by Allardon Elessedil to have a look at our castaway."

He offered no further explanation and said nothing of the King's death. The healer seemed to accept this. He shook Walker's hand solemnly. "I have some bad news for you. I did my best, but it wasn't enough. The man Hunter left in my care is dead. He died in his sleep several days ago."

Walker took the news calmly. He was not surprised. It merely confirmed his suspicions. Whoever had sent the assassins to kill Allardon Elessedil had disposed of the castaway, as well. "Have you buried him?"

"No." The Healer shook his head quickly. "I've put him in the cold house, waiting to see what news Hunter brought from Arborlon."

"And his room? The room in which he died? Is it occupied?"

"Vacant. We've cleaned it, but it services no new patient yet." The Healer glanced from face to face. "Come in by the fire and dry off. I'll have some hot soup brought. It's turning nasty out there."

He placed them in chairs before the fire burning in the great room, took their cloaks, and gave them blankets with which to dry. Assistants to the Healer came and went in pur-

suit of their tasks, glancing over at the travelers, but saying nothing. Walker paid them no attention, his thoughts
on the dead man. All chance was lost to learn anything from
him in life. Could he find a way to learn something from him
in death?

The Healer returned with bowls of soup and cups of ale,
gave them a moment to begin eating, then pulled up a chair
beside them. He seemed tired and nervous, but both were to
be expected. Walker sensed no dissembling or bad intention
in him; he was not an evil man.

The Healer asked after their journey, and they exchanged
small talk with him as they ate. Outside, the rain was falling
harder, the sound of the drops on the roof and windowpanes a
constant, dull thrum. Lights burning in the windows of the
surrounding houses turned watery and blurred through the
gloom.

"The man you cared for, Dorne—did he ever communicate with anyone?" Walker asked finally.

The Healer shook his head. "No one."

"Did anyone ever come to see him, even for a few
moments?"

"No, never."

"Did his condition change in any way before he died?"

"No."

"Was there anything different about him after he died?"

The Healer thought about it for a moment. "Well, I may be
reading more into this than I should, but he seemed somehow
at peace." He shrugged. "But death is a form of release from
suffering, and this man was suffering greatly."

Walker considered the matter silently for a moment. In the
hearth, the burning wood snapped and popped in the flames.
"Has anyone else died in the village in the past two days, unexpectedly perhaps?"

The Healer's eyes widened. "Yes, as a matter of fact. A
man who worked for me as an attendant—not in healing,
but in caretaking—was found dead in the woods not far from

his cottage. It was lucky he was found at all, really. A remote spot, not often visited. A snake bit him, a very poisonous variety—unusual for around here, really. Something you might better expect to find in the Wilderun."

Walker put aside his bowl and cup and stood up. "Could you show me the room in which the man died?" he asked the Healer. "Hunter, finish your dinner. I can do this alone."

He followed Dorne down a hallway to a room at the rear of the healing center. Then he sent Dorne back out to keep Hunter company, saying he would be along shortly. The Healer tried to give him a light for the wall candles, but Walker said the darkness was better suited for what he intended.

When he was alone, he stood in the middle of the room, cloaked in its gloom, listening to the sound of the rain and watching the movement of the shadows. He closed his eyes after a time, tasting the air, smelling it, making himself a part of his surroundings. He let his thoughts settle within him and his body relax. Down the hall, he could hear the soft murmur of voices. Carefully, he shut them out.

Time slipped away. Slowly, he began to find fragments of what he was looking for, the leavings and discards of a powerful magic employed not long ago. They came to him in different ways, some as small sounds, some as flickers of movement that reached him even behind his closed eyelids, and some as scents of the magic's wielder. There was not enough to form an entire image, but enough to determine small truths that could allow him to make educated guesses.

He opened his eyes finally, satisfied. Magic's use could never be disguised entirely from those who knew how to look for it. A residue always remained to testify.

He went back out into the main room, where Hunter Predd and Dorne were visiting. Both looked up quickly at his appearance. "Can you take me to the cold house?" he asked the Healer. "I need to see the castaway's body."

The Healer said he could, although he informed the Druid

that the cold house was some distance away from the healing center. "It's not much of a night to be out in the weather,"
he said.

"I'll go alone," Walker advised. "Just show me the way."

The Druid wrapped himself in his damp cloak and went
out the front door. Following the Healer's instructions, he
worked his way around the house, first along the porch and
under the veranda, then under the eaves along one side, and
slipped through the shadows in the rain. The forest began
twenty yards from the back of the center, and the cold house
was a hundred more beyond. Cowled head dipped against
the rainfall and low-hanging branches, Walker made his way
down a footpath widened from usage by the Healer and his
attendants. Thunder rumbled in the distance, and whistling
fiercely, a wind off the ocean blew steadily through the sodden
limbs.

At the end of the footpath, the cold-house door opened into
an embankment buttressed by huge boulders and covered
thickly with sod and plants. Runoff cascaded down a sluice to
one side and disappeared into a stream. The handle on the
door was slippery and cold beneath the Druid's fingers, and it
took him a moment to release the catch.

Inside, the sounds of the storm faded into silence. There
were torches set in brackets on the wall, and tinder with
which to light them. Walker lit one in its bracket, then lit a
second to carry. He looked around. The room was large and
square and laid floor to ceiling with slabs of rock. Niches in
the wall contained wooden sleds for the bodies, and runnels
chiseled in the stone floor carried away excess moisture and
body fluids. A metal-sheathed wood table sat in the center of
the room, empty now, but used by the Healer for his examina-
tion of the dead. In the deep shadows, glinting like predators'
eyes, sharp instruments hung from pegs on the wall.

The room smelled of blood and death, and the Druid
moved quickly to do what was needed and get out of there.
The castaway was in the lower niche to the far left of the

entry, and Walker slid the body free of its casing and turned down the covering sheet. The man's face was bloodless and white in the torchlight, his body rigid and his skin waxy. Walker looked upon him without recognition. If he had been Kael Elessedil, he no longer looked so.

"Who were you?" Walker whispered to the dead man.

He jammed the torch he was carrying into the nearest wall bracket. Carefully, he placed his fingertips on the man's chest, moving them slowly down his torso and then up again to his shoulders. He felt along the man's throat and skull, probing gently, carefully. All around the man's face he worked his fingers, searching.

"Tell me something," he whispered.

Outside, a burst of thunder shook the earth, but the Druid did not look up from his work. He placed his fingers against the dead man's ruined eyes, the unsupported lids giving beneath his touch, then probed slowly down to his nose and cheeks.

When he reached the man's bloodless lips, he jerked away as if stung. Here, he mused silently, this was where the man's life had been taken from him! The magic lingered still, and even two days later it was potent enough to burn. He brushed the lips quickly, testing. No force had been used. Death had come gently, but with a swift and certain rendering.

Walker stepped away. He knew the man's identity now, knew it with certainty. What fragments remained of the magic used against him confirmed that he was Kael Elessedil.

Questions flooded Walker's mind. Had the dead man's killer probed his memory before giving him over to his death? He had to believe so. The killer would have looked there for what Walker had found in the map. A dark certainty began to grow in the turmoil of the Druid's thinking. Only one person had the ability to do that. His enemy was one to whom he felt no hostility himself, but for whom he was anathema. He had feared for a long time that one day there must be a resolution of their antagonism, but he would have preferred that it wait awhile longer.

She, of course, would be most pleased and eager to have it happen now.

His eyes lifted to the darkness of the room, and for the first time he felt the cold. He must change his plans. Any other enemy but this one would not require the adjustments he was now forced to make. But a confrontation with her—a confrontation that must surely come—would be resolved only if he could blunt her rage by revealing a truth that had been hidden for many years. It pained him anew to think that he had not been present to prevent that truth from being concealed when it might have had a more immediate impact. But there was no help for it now; the events of the past were irreversible. What was given to him to do was to alter the future, and even that might be possible only at great cost.

He placed Kael Elessedil's body back in its niche, extinguished the torches, and went out into the night once more. Darkness and rain closed about him as he threaded his way through the forest trees towards the center. He must act quickly. He had thought to go next in search of a ship and crew, but that would have to wait. There was a more pressing need, and he must see to it at once.

By midnight tomorrow, he must speak with the dead.

EIGHT

By sunrise of the following day, Walker had left Bracken Clell behind. Back aboard Obsidian and seated just behind Hunter Predd, he watched through a curtain of rain as the eastern sky slowly brightened to the color of hammered tin. The rains had lessened from the night before, but not abated altogether. The skies remained clouded and dark, pressing down upon a sodden earth with a mix of shadows and mist. Hunched within his travel cloak, cold and damp already, he retreated deep inside himself to help pass the time. There, he worked his way carefully through the details of the tasks he faced. He knew what was needed, but he found himself wishing again and again that there could be others with whom to share his responsibilities. That he felt so alone was disheartening. It lessened to almost nothing the margin of error he was permitted. He thought of how he had disdained the work of the Druids in his youth, of Allanon in particular, and he chided himself anew for his foolishness.

They flew through the morning with only a single stop to rest Obsidian and to give themselves a chance to eat and drink. By midday, they had crossed the Tirfing and left the Westland behind. The Duln Forests passed beneath, then the slender ribbon of the Rappahalladran. The rains began to lessen, the storm clouds to move south, and snatches of blue sky to appear on the horizon. They were flying east and slightly north now, the Wing Rider taking them along the southern edge of the Borderlands below Tyrsis and across the

Rainbow Lake. Lunch was consumed on the lake's western shores, the day clear and bright by then, their clothing beginning to warm in the sun, their interest in their mission beginning to sharpen once more.

"The castaway, Walker—was he Kael Elessedil?" Hunter Predd asked as they finished the last of the cold grouse Dorne had provided them on leaving that morning.

Walker nodded. "He was. I couldn't tell at first. I haven't seen him since he was not much more than a boy and don't remember him all that well in any case. Even if I had remembered how he looked then, it would have been difficult to recognize him after what he had been through. But there were other signs, scattered traces, that revealed his identity."

"He didn't die in his sleep, did he? Not of natural causes. Someone helped end his life."

The Druid paused. "Someone did. How did you know that?"

The Wing Rider shrugged, his whipcord-tough body lengthening as he stretched. "Dorne is a talented Healer and a careful man. The castaway had survived days at sea before I found him. He should have survived a couple more in a Healer's bed." He glanced at Walker questioningly. "Our assassins' employer?"

The Druid nodded. "I would guess so. Magic was used to kill the man, to steal his life. Not so different from what was done to those men sent to kill Allardon Elessedil."

For a moment the Wing Rider was silent, sipping at his cup of ale and looking off into the distance. Then he said, "Do you know yet who your enemy is?"

My enemy. Implacable and deadly. Walker's smile was ironic. "I'll know better by tonight."

The Wing Rider cleaned and packed their gear, made certain his mount was fed and watered sufficiently, then motioned Walker back aboard. They flew east across the Rainbow Lake, passing below the mouth of the Mermidon and the broad, rumpled humps of the Runne Mountains. A handful of fishing boats floated on the lake below but, absorbed in their work, the fishermen did not glance up. The day wore on, the sun dropped toward the western horizon, and the light began to fade. The moon brightened in the skies ahead, and a single star appeared close by. Shadows lengthened across the land below, stretching out like fingers to claim it for nighttime's coming.

It was twilight by the time they started up the south end of the Rabb Plains for the Dragon's Teeth. By then, the huge jagged peaks were dark and shadowy and stripped of definition, a forbidding wall that stretched all the way across the northern skyline. The temperature was dropping, and Walker pulled his cloak closer about his body for warmth. Hunter Predd seemed unaffected. Walker marveled at how little the Wing Rider seemed to mind the weather, aware of, but untroubled by it. He supposed that to be a Wing Rider, one had to be so.

It was fully dark when they reached the foothills leading up to where he would go this night. Guided by the light of moon and stars, Obsidian landed on an open rise, safely away from rocks and brush that might hide enemies or hinder a quick escape. After seeing to the needs of the Roc, the Wing Rider and the Druid set camp, built a fire, and cooked and ate their dinner. In the distance, they could hear the hunting cries of night herons and the strident wail of wolves. Moonlight bathed the plains south and east, and through the pale brightening, furtive shadows moved.

"I've been thinking about the castaway," Hunter Predd declared after a period of silence. They were almost finished with their meal, and he was digging at the hard ground with the heel of his boot, sitting back from the fire with his cup of ale. "How could a blind man have escaped his captors unaided?"

Walker looked up.

"How could he have made his way from wherever he was imprisoned to come back across the Divide to us?" The Wing

Rider's frown deepened. "Assuming he was returning from the voyage Kael Elessedil made thirty years ago, he'd have had to travel a long way. A blind man couldn't have managed it without help."

"No," Walker agreed, "he couldn't."

The Elf hunched forward. "Something else's been bothering me. How did he get his hands on the map? Unless he drew it himself, he either stole it or it was given to him. If he drew it himself, he must have done so before he was blinded. How did he hide it from his captors? If someone else drew it, they must have given it to him. Either way, he must have had help. Even to escape. What became of that other person?"

Walker nodded approvingly. "You've asked all the right questions, Hunter Predd. Questions I have been asking myself for several days. Your mind is as sharp as your instincts, Wing Rider."

"Have you answers to give?" Hunter pressed, ignoring the compliment.

"None I care to share just yet." He stood up, setting his plate and cup aside. "It's time for me to go. I won't be back before morning, so you might as well get some sleep. Do not come looking for me, no matter how tempted you might be. Do you understand?"

The Wing Rider nodded. "I don't need to be told to stay out of those mountains. I've heard the stories of what lives there. I'll be content to stay right where I am." He wrapped his cloak more tightly about him. "Good luck to you."

It grew colder on the walk up from the foothills and into the Dragon's Teeth, the temperature dropping steadily as the Druid climbed. Within the massive rock walls, the night was silent and empty feeling. The moon disappeared behind the peaks, and there was only starlight to guide the way, though that was sufficient for the Druid. He proceeded along a narrow pebble-strewn trail that angled through clusters of

massive boulders. The jumble of crushed and broken rock
suggested that an upheaval in some long-forgotten time
had changed the landscape dramatically. Once another peak
might have occupied the place. Now there was only ruin.

It took him almost two hours to make the climb, and it
was nearing midnight when he reached his destination.
Cresting a rise, he found himself looking down on the Valley
of Shale and the fabled Hadeshorn. The lake sat squarely in
the valley's center, its smooth waters dull and lifeless within
the bowl of polished black rock that littered the walls and
floor. Starlight reflected brightly off the stone, but was absorbed by the Hadeshorn and turned to shadow. Within the
valley, nothing moved. Cupped by the high, lonesome peaks
of the Dragon's Teeth, it had the look and feel of a tomb.

Not far from wrong, Walker thought to himself, staring out
across its lifeless expanse.

Faced toward the Valley of Shale, he seated himself with
his back against a huge slab of rock and dozed. Time slipped
away without seeming to do so, and before he knew it, the
night was almost gone. He rose and walked, moving steadily
but cautiously over the loose rock, picking his way down the
valley's slope to its floor. He was careful not to trip and fall;
the edges of the polished rock were razor sharp. Only the
crunching of the rubble beneath his boots broke the silence of
his descent. Starlight flooded the valley, and he made his way
without difficulty to the edge of the lake by the hour before
dawn, when the spirits of the dead might be summoned to reveal secrets hidden from the living.

There, a solitary figure silhouetted against the flat terrain,
he stilled himself within to prepare for what would come next.

The waters of the Hadeshorn had taken on a different
cast with his approach, shimmering now from just beneath
the surface with light that did not reflect from the stars but
emanated from some inner source. There was a sense of
something stirring, coming awake and taking notice of his
presence. He could feel it more than see it. He kept his focus

on the lake, disdaining all else, knowing that any break in concentration once he began would doom his efforts and possibly cause him harm.

When he was at peace within and fully concentrated, he began the process of calling to the dead. He spoke softly, for it was not necessary that his voice carry, and gestured slowly, for precision counted more than speed. He spoke his name and of his history and need, motioning for the dead to respond, for the lake to give them up. As he did, the waters stirred visibly, swirling slowly in a clockwise motion, then churning more violently. Small cries rose from their depths, calling out in tiny, ethereal voices, whispers that turned to screams as thin as paper. The Hadeshorn hissed and boiled, releasing the cries in small fountains of spray, then in geysers that plumed hundreds of feet into the air. Light beneath the lake's surface brightened and pulsed, and the valley shuddered.

Then a rumbling sounded from deep within the earth, and out of the roiling waters rose the spirits, white and transparent forms that climbed slowly into the air, linked by thin trailers of vapor, freed from their afterlife for a few precious moments to return to the earth they had left in dying. Their voices intertwined in a rising wail that made the Druid's skin crawl and chilled the bones of his body. He held his ground against their advance, fighting down the part of him that screamed at him to back away, to turn aside, and to be afraid. They spiraled into the night sky, reaching for what was lost, seeking to recover what was denied. More and more of them appeared, filling the empty bowl of the valley until there was no space left.

Who calls? Who dares?

Then a huge, black shadow lifted from the waters and scattered the spirits like leaves, a cloaked form that took shape as it ascended, one arm stretching out to sweep aside the swarms of ghosts who lingered too close. The Hadeshorn churned and boiled in response to its coming, spray jetting everywhere, droplets falling on the Druid's exposed face and hand. Walker lifted his arm in a warding gesture, and the cloaked figure turned toward him at once. Suspended in space, it began to lose some of its blackness, becoming more transparent, its human form showing through its dark coverings like bones exposed through flesh. Across the wave-swept surface it glided, taking up all the space about it as it came, drawing all the light to itself until there was nothing else.

When it was right on top of Walker, it stopped and hung motionless above him, cowled head inclining slightly, shadows obscuring its features. Flat and dispassionate, its voice flooded the momentary silence.

—What would you know of me—

Walker knelt before him, not in fear, but out of respect.

"Allanon," he said, and waited for the shade to invite him to speak.

Farther west where the deep woods shrouded and sheltered the lives of its denizens as an ocean does its sea life, dawn approached in the Wilderun, as well. Within the old-growth trees, the light remained pale and insubstantial, even at high noon and on the brightest summer day. Shadows cloaked the world of the forest dwellers, and for the most part there was little difference between day and night. Long a wilderness to which few outsiders came, in which only those born to the life remained, and by which all other hardships were measured, the Wilderun was a haven for creatures for whom the absence of light was desirable.

The Ilse Witch was one such. Though born in another part of the Four Lands, where her past was bright with sunlight, she had long since adapted to and become comfortable with the twilight existence of her present. She had lived here nearly all of her life, which was to say since she was six. The Morgawr had brought her here when the Druid's minions had killed her parents and tried to steal her away for their own use. He had given her his home, his protection, and his knowledge of magic's uses so that she might grow to adulthood and discover who she was destined to be. The darkness in which she was raised suited her, but she never let herself become a slave to it.

Sometimes, she knew, you became dependent on the things that gave you comfort. She would never be one of those. Dependency on anything was for fools and weaklings.

On this night, working through the rudimentary drawings she had stolen from Kael Elessedil's memories before dispatching him, she felt a stirring in the air that signaled the Morgawr's return. He had been gone from their safehold for more than a week, saying little of his plans on departing, leaving her to her own devices pending his return. She was grown now, in his eyes as well as her own, and he did not feel the need to watch over her as he once had. He had never confided in her; that would have gone against his nature in so fundamental a way as to be unthinkable. He was a warlock, and therefore solitary and independent by nature. He had been alive for a very long time, living in his Hollows safehold deep within the heart of the Wilderun, not far from the promontory known as Spire's Reach. Once, it was rumored, these same caverns had been occupied by the witch sisters, Mallenroh and Morag, before they destroyed each other. Once, it was rumored, the Morgawr had claimed them as his sisters. The Ilse Witch did not know if this was true; the Morgawr never spoke of it, and she knew better than to ask.

Dark magic thrived within the Wilderun, born of other times and peoples, of a world that flourished before the Great Wars. Magic rooted in the earth here, and the Morgawr drew his strength from its presence. He was not like her; he had not been born to the magic. He had gained his mastery through leeching it away and building it up, through study and experimentation, and through slow, torturous exposure to side effects that had changed him irrevocably from what he had been born.

Looking up from her work, the Ilse Witch saw the solitary

candles set in opposite holders by the entry to the room flicker slightly. Shadows wavered and settled anew on the worn stone floor. She set aside the map and rose to greet him. Her gray robes fell about her slender form in a soft rustle, and she shook back her long dark hair from her childlike face and startling blue eyes. Just a girl, a visitor come upon her unexpectedly might have thought. Just a girl approaching womanhood. But she was nothing of that and hadn't been for a long time. The Morgawr would not make such a mistake, although he had once. It took her only a heartbeat to set him straight, to let him know that she was a girl no longer, an apprentice no more, but a grown woman and his equal.

Things had not been the same between them since, and she sensed that they never would be again.

He appeared in the entry, all size and darkness within his long black cloak. His body was huge and muscular and still human in shape, but he was looking more and more like the Mwellrets with whom he spent so much of his time. His skin was scaly and gray and hairless. His features were blunt and unremarkable, and his eyes were reptilian. He could shape-shift like the rets, but far better and with greater versatility, for he had the magic to aid him. Numerous once, the rets had been reduced over the past five hundred years to a small community. They were secretive and manipulative of others, and perhaps that was why the Morgawr admired them so.

He looked at her from out of the cowl's darkness, the green slits of his eyes empty and cold. Once, she would have been terrified to have him regard her so. Once, she would have done anything to make him look away. Now, she returned his gaze, her own colder and emptier still.

"Allardon Elessedil is dead," he said softly. "Killed by mistake by his own guards in an assassination attempt by Elves who had been mind-altered. Who do we know who has the ability to use magic in that way?"

It was not a question that required an answer, and so she ignored it. "While you were gone," she replied calmly, "a castaway was found floating in the Blue Divide. He carried with him an Elessedil bracelet and a map. A Wing Rider bore him to the village of Bracken Clell. One of my spies told me of him. When I went to have a look, I discovered who he was. Kael Elessedil. The map he carried was already on its way to his brother, but I extracted much of its writings from the memories in his head."

"It is not your place to decide to take the life of a King!" the Morgawr hissed angrily. "You should have consulted with me before acting!"

She went very still. "I do not need your permission to do what I deem necessary. Ever. The taking of a life—of anyone's life—is my province and mine alone!"

She might as well have told him the sun would rise in less than an hour. His reaction to her words was indifferent, his response unreadable, and his body posture unchanged. "What of this map?" he asked.

"The map is of a treasure, one of magic formed of words, come out of the Old World from before the Great Wars." She used her voice to draw him close, to bind him to her own sense of urgency and need. He would sense what she was doing, but he was vulnerable still. "The magic is hidden in a safehold in a land across the Blue Divide. Kael Elessedil has been there and seen the magic. It exists, and it is very powerful. Unfortunately, his brother knew of it as well. Until I stopped him, he intended to act on the matter."

The Morgawr came into the room, not toward her, but away, sidling along the far wall, as if to retrieve something from the cases that lined it. A potion, perhaps? A recording of some discovery? Then he slowed and turned, and his voice was like ice. "You intend to go in his place, little witch?"

"The magic should be ours."

"You mean yours, don't you?" He laughed softly. "But that's as it should be."

"You could go with me," she said, hoping as she said it he would not.

He cocked his reptilian head, considering. "This is your discovery and your cause. Pursue it if you wish, but without me. If the magic will belong to both of us, I am content."

She waited, knowing there would be more. "But?" she said finally.

His eyes glimmered. "You will go alone?"

"Across the Blue Divide? No. I will need a ship and crew to take me." She paused. "And there is a complication."

The Morgawr laughed again, slow and faintly mocking. "I sensed as much from the way you approached this business. What sort of complication?"

She walked toward him a few steps and stopped, showing she was not afraid, that she was in command of what she intended. Presence was of great importance with Mwellrets and with the Morgawr in particular. If they thought someone confident, they were less likely to challenge. The Morgawr was a powerful warlock, and he had spent a lifetime learning to command magic that could destroy his enemies in a heartbeat. She was his equal now, but she had to be careful of him.

"Before he died, Allardon Elessedil sent the map to Paranor and summoned Walker to Arborlon."

"The Druid!" the warlock said, loathing in his voice.

"The Druid. He arrived in time to agree upon the terms of a search for the map's treasure before witnessing the King's death. If luck had favored us, he would have died, as well. As it was, he lived. He will lead an Elven expedition in quest of the magic."

The Morgawr studied her wordlessly for a moment. "A contest with your greatest enemy. How keen your anticipation must be."

"He is a formidable opponent."

"One you have sworn you would one day destroy." The warlock nodded. "Perhaps that day has arrived."

"Perhaps. But it is the magic I covet more than the Druid's death."

The Morgawr shifted within his cloak, and one clawed

hand gestured at the air. "A Druid, some Elven Hunters, and a Captain and crew. A few others, as well, if I know Walker. He will draw a strong company to support his quest, particularly since he knows that Kael Elessedil has failed already. Even with the Elfstones to protect him, he failed."

He glanced sideways at her. "And what of them, little witch? What of the precious Elfstones?"

She shook her head. "Nothing. He did not bring them back with him. His memories did not reveal what had become of them. Perhaps they are lost."

"Perhaps." His rough voice had lost its edge and taken on a contemplative tone. "Where is the Druid now?"

"He was in Bracken Clell a day ago. He left and has not yet resurfaced. My spies watch for him."

The warlock nodded. "I leave him to you. I know you will find a way to deal with him. It is left to me to give you the rest of what you need to undertake your search—a ship, Captain, and crew, and a handful of suitable protectors. I shall supply them all, little witch. You shall have everything you need."

She did not like the way he said it, and she knew that by doing her this favor he intended to keep close watch and perhaps even control over her while she was away from him. He did not trust her anymore. Where once he had been the teacher and she the student, now they were equals. Worse still, she knew, they were rivals—not yet at odds, but headed there. But she could not refuse his help. To do so would be to acknowledge her fear of his intentions. She would never do that.

"Whatever assistance you can give me will be welcome," she told him, inclining her head slightly as if in gratitude. It was better to keep him appeased for now. "Where do we begin?"

"With the details of the map you reconstructed from Kael Elessedil's memories." He glanced past her to the table at which she had been seated and the drawings that lay there. "Do I see the beginnings of your work?"

Without waiting for her response, he walked over for a closer look.

It was well after dawn when Walker departed from the Valley of Shale. His meeting with the shade of Allanon had sapped him of strength and energy in a way he hadn't expected. It had been a long time since he had come to the Hadeshorn, a long time since he had needed to, and he had forgotten how draining the experience could be. So much concentration was required. So much intuition had to be applied to interpretation of the shade's words. Even though the Druid knew as much as he did and was prepared for the rest, it was necessary to be careful while he listened and not to make false assumptions or to forget any of what he was told.

When the spirits of the dead were gone and the sun had crested the horizon, he had looked at himself in the now still waters, and his face seemed weathered and lined beyond his years. For just an instant, he imagined himself an old, old man.

This day was sunny and bright, the clouds and rain of the past two had disappeared east, and the air carried the smell of living things once more. Over the course of the next several hours, he retraced his steps, too weary to complete the journey more quickly, using the time to contemplate what he had learned. The shade of Allanon had spoken to him of a past he already knew, of a present he suspected, and of a future he did not understand. There were people and places with whom he was familiar and ones with whom he was not. There were riddles and strange visions, and the whole was a jumble in his mind that would not straighten itself out until he was better rested and had time to consider the information more thoroughly.

But his course of action was determined, and his mind was focused on where he must go.

When he reached the encampment in the foothills where he had left Hunter Predd, the Wing Rider was waiting. He had struck camp, repacked their gear, and was grooming Obsidian's ebony feathers so that they gleamed. The Roc saw the Druid first and dipped his fierce head in warning. Hunter Predd turned, put down the curry brush, and watched the Druid approach. He handed Walker a thick slice of bread with jam spread over it and a cup of cold water and went back to grooming his mount.

Walker moved to a patch of grass, seated himself, and began to devour the bread hungrily. Images roiled in his mind as the Hadeshorn had with the coming of the spirits of the dead. Allanon's shade loomed over him, blacking out the starlight, eyes bright within shadows, voice deep and commanding, an echo of the rumbling earth. Walker could see him still, could feel his dark presence, could hear him speak. When Allanon's shade departed finally at first light, it was as if the world was coming to an end, the air swirling with shadows, shimmering with spirit bodies, and filling with the keening of the dead. The waters of the Hadeshorn geysered anew, as if some leviathan were breaching, and the dead were drawn back again from the world of the living to their own domain. Walker had felt as if his soul was being torn from him, as if a part of him had gone with them. In a way, he supposed, it had.

He paused in his eating and stared into space. If he thought too long and hard on what was required of him, if he dwelled on the demands the shade of Allanon had made, he would begin to question himself in ways that were harmful. What would keep him sane and whole was remembering what was at stake—the lives of people who depended on him, the safety of the Four Lands, and his dream of seeing a Druid Council become a reality in his lifetime. This last drove him more strongly than the others, for if it came to pass, it would vindicate his still-troubling decision to become the very thing he had abhorred for so long. If he must be a Druid, let him be one on his own terms and of a sort that would not require him to live with shame.

When he had finished eating the bread and jam and drinking the water from the cup, he rose again. Hunter Predd glanced over his shoulder at the movement and ceased his grooming.

"Where do we go now, Walker?" he asked.

The Druid took a moment to study a flight of egrets as they passed overhead toward the Rainbow Lake. "South," he answered finally, eyes distant and fixed, "to find someone whose magic is the equal of my own."

NINE

Bek Rowe crept through the tall grasses at the edge of a clearing just below a heavily wooded line of hills, listening to the sound of the boar as it rooted in the tangle of thicket across the way. He paused as the wind shifted, mindful of staying downwind of his quarry, listening to its movements, judging its progress. Somewhere to his left, Quentin Leah waited in the deep woods. Time was running out for them; the sun was descending toward the western horizon, and only another hour of good light remained. They had been hunting the boar all day, trailing it through the rough up-country scrub and deep woods, waiting for a chance to bring it down. Their chances of doing so were negligible under the best of conditions; boar hunting afoot with bow and arrow was risky and difficult. But as with most things that interested them, it was the challenge that mattered.

The soft scent of new leaves and fresh grasses mixed with the pungent smell of earth and wood, and Bek took a deep breath to steady himself. He could not see the boar, and the boar, having exceptionally poor eyesight, certainly could not see him. But the boar's sense of smell was the sharper, and once he got a whiff of Bek, he might do anything. Boars were short-tempered and fierce, and what they didn't understand they were as likely to attack as to flee.

The wind shifted again, and Bek dropped into a hurried crouch. The boar had begun moving his way, grunts and coughs marking his progress. A boy still, though approaching manhood rapidly, Bek was small and wiry, but made up for his size with agility and speed and surprising strength. Quentin, who was five years his senior and already considered grown, was always telling people that they shouldn't be fooled, that Bek was a lot tougher than he looked. If there was a fight, the Highlander would insist, he wanted Bek Rowe at his back. It was an overstatement, of course, but it always made Bek feel good. Especially since it was his cousin saying it, and nobody would even think of challenging Quentin Leah.

Putting an arrow to his bow in readiness, Bek crept forward once again. He was close enough to the boar to smell it, not a pleasant experience, but it meant he would likely have a shot at it soon. He drifted right, following the boar's sounds, wondering if Quentin was still up on the forested slope or had come down to approach from the boar's rear. Shadows stretched from the trees at Bek's back, lengthening into the clearing like elongated fingers as the day waned. A bristly dark form moved in the grasses ahead—the boar coming into view—and Bek froze where he was. Slowly, he brought up his bow, nocked his arrow, and drew back the string.

But in the next instant a huge shadow passed overhead, sliding across the clearing like liquid night. The boar, startled by its appearance, bolted away in a tearing of earth and a cacophony of squeals. Bek straightened and sighted, but all he caught was a quick glimpse of the boar's ridged back as it disappeared into the thicket and then into the woods beyond. In seconds, the clearing was empty and quiet again.

"Shades!" Bek muttered, lowering his bow and brushing back his close-cropped dark hair. He stood up and looked across the empty clearing toward the woods. "Quentin?"

The tall Highlander emerged from the trees. "Did you see it?"

"I got a glimpse of its backside after that shadow spooked it. Did you see what that was?"

Quentin was already wandering down into the clearing and through the heavy grasses. "Some kind of bird, wasn't it?"

"No birds around here are that big." Bek watched him come, glancing away long enough to scan the empty skies. He shouldered his bow and shoved his arrow back into its quiver. "Birds that big live on the coast."

"Maybe it's lost." Quentin shrugged nonchalantly. He slipped in a patch of mud and muttered a few choice words as he righted himself. "Maybe we should go back to hunting grouse."

Bek laughed. "Maybe we should go back to hunting earthworms and stick to fishing."

Quentin reached him with a flourish of bow and arrows, arms widespread as he dropped both in disgust. "All day, and what do we have to show for it? An empty meadow. You'd think we could have gotten off at least one shot between us. That boar was making enough noise to wake the dead. It wasn't as if we couldn't find it, for cat's sake!"

Then he grinned cheerfully. "At least we've got that grouse from yesterday to ease our hunger and a cold aleskin to soothe our wounded pride. Best part of hunting, Bek lad. Eating and drinking at the end of the day!"

Bek smiled in response, and after Quentin retrieved his castoff weapons, they swung into step beside each other and headed back toward their camp. Quentin was tall and broadshouldered, and he wore his red hair long and tied back in the manner of Highlanders. Bek, his lowland cousin, had never adopted the Highland style, though he had lived with Quentin and his family for most of his life. That his origins were cloudy had fostered a strong streak of independence in him. He might not know who he was, but he knew who he wasn't.

His father had been a distant cousin of Coran Leah, Quentin's father, but had lived in the Silver River country. Bek remembered little more than a shadowy figure with a dark, strong face. He died when Bek was still tiny, barely two years of age. He contracted a fatal disease and, knowing he was dying, brought Bek to his cousin Coran to raise. There was no one else to turn to. Bek's mother was gone, and there were no siblings, no aunts and uncles, no one closer than Coran. Coran Leah told Bek later, when he was older, that Bek's father had done a great favor for him once, and he had never thought twice about taking Bek in to repay the favor.

All of which was to say that although Bek had been raised a Highlander, he wasn't really one and had never been persuaded to think of himself in those terms. Quentin told him it was the right attitude. Why try to be something you know you're not? If you have to pretend to be something, be something no one else is. Bek liked the idea, but he hadn't a clue what that something else might be. Since he never talked of the matter with anyone but Quentin, he kept his thoughts to himself. Sooner or later, he imagined, probably when it mattered enough that he must do something, he would figure it out.

"I'm starved," Quentin announced as they walked through the deep woods. "Hungry enough to eat that boar all by myself, should it choose to fall dead at my feet just now!"

His broad, strong face was cheerful and open, a reflection of his personality. With Quentin Leah, what you saw was what you got. There was no dissembling, no pretense, and no guile. Quentin was the sort who came right at you, speaking his mind and venting his emotions openly. Bek was more inclined to tread carefully in his use of words and displays of temperament, a part of him always an outsider and accustomed to the value of an outsider's caution. Not Quentin. He opened himself up and laid himself bare, and if you liked him, fine, and if you didn't, that was all right, too.

"Are you sure about that bird?" Bek asked him, thinking back to that huge shadow, still puzzled by its appearance.

Quentin shrugged. "I only caught a glimpse of it, not enough to be certain of anything much. Like you said, it looked like one of those big coastal birds, black and sleek and fierce." He paused thoughtfully. "I'd like to ride one of those someday."

Bek snorted. "You'd like to do lots of things. Everything, if you could manage it."

Quentin nodded. "True. But some things more than others. This one, I'd like to do more."

"I'd just settle for another crack at the boar." Bek brushed a hanging limb away as he ducked beneath. "Another two seconds . . ."

"Forget it!" Quentin grabbed Bek's shoulders playfully. "We'll go out again tomorrow. We have all the rest of the week. We'll find one sooner or later. How can we fail?"

Well, Bek wanted to say, because boars are quicker, faster, and stronger, and much better at hiding than we are at finding them. But he let the matter drop, because the truth was that if they'd bagged the boar today, they'd have had to figure out what to do with the rest of the week. Bek didn't even want to speculate on what Quentin might have come up with if that had happened.

Shadows were layering the woodlands in ever-darkening pools, the light failing quickly as the sun slipped below the horizon and the night began its silent advance. Serpentine trailers of mist already had begun to appear in the valleys and ravines, those darker, cooler havens were the sun had been absent longer and the dampness was rooted deeper. Crickets were beginning to chirp and night birds to call. Bek hunched his shoulders against a chilly breeze come up off the Rappa-halladran. Maybe he would suggest they fish tomorrow as a change of pace. It wasn't as exciting or demanding as boar hunting, but the chances of success were greater.

Besides, he mused, he could nap in the afternoon sun when he was fishing. He could dream and indulge his imagination and take small journeys in his mind. He could spend a little time thinking about his future, which was a good exercise since he really didn't have one figured out yet.

"There it is again," Quentin announced almost casually, pointing ahead through the trees.

Bek looked, and as sharp as his eyes were, he didn't see anything. "There *what* is again?" he asked.

"That bird I saw, the one that flew over the meadow. A Roc—that's what it's called. It was right above the ridge for a moment, then dropped away."

"Rocs don't travel inland," Bek pointed out once more. Not unless they're in thrall to a Wing Rider, he thought. That was different. But what would a Wing Rider be doing out here? "This late-afternoon light plays tricks with your eyes," he added.

Quentin didn't seem to hear him. "That's close to where we're camped, Bek. I hope it doesn't raid our stash."

They descended the slope they were on, crossed the valley below, and began to climb toward the crest of the next hill, on which their camp was set. They'd quit talking to each other, concentrating on the climb, eyes beginning to search the deepening shadows more carefully. The sun was below the horizon, and twilight cloaked the forest in a gloom that shifted and teased with small movements. A day's-end silence had descended, a hush that gave the odd impression that everything living in the woods was waiting to see who would make the first sound. Though not conscious of the effort, both Bek and his cousin began to walk more softly.

When it got dark in the Highland forests, it got very dark, especially when the moon wasn't up, as on this night, and there was only starlight to illuminate the shadows. Bek found himself growing uneasy for reasons he couldn't define, his instincts telling him that something was wrong even when his eyes could not discover what it was. They reached their camp without incident but, as if possessed of a single mind, stopped at the edge of the clearing and peered about in silence.

After a moment, Quentin touched his cousin's shoulder and shrugged. Nothing looked out of place. Bek nodded.

They entered the clearing, walked to where their stash was strung up in a tree, found it undisturbed, checked their camping gear where it was bundled in the crotch of a broad-rooted maple, and found it intact, as well. They dragged out their bedrolls and laid them out next to the cold fire pit they'd dug on their arrival two days earlier. Then they released the rope that secured their provisions and lowered them to the ground. Quentin began sorting foodstuffs and cooking implements in preparation for making their dinner. Bek produced tinder to strike a flame to the wood set in place that morning for the evening's meal.

Somewhere close, out in the darkness, a night bird cried shrilly as it flew in search of prey or a mate. Bek looked up, studied the shadows again, and then lit the fire. Once the wood was burning, he walked to the edge of the clearing and bent down to gather more.

When he straightened up again, he found himself face-to-face with a black-cloaked stranger. The stranger was no more than two feet away, right on top of him really, and Bek hadn't heard his approach at all. The boy froze, arms wrapped about the load of deadwood, his heart in his throat. All sorts of messages screamed at him from his brain, but he couldn't make himself respond to any of them.

"Bek Rowe?" the stranger asked softly.

Bek nodded. The stranger's cowl concealed his face, but his deep, rough voice was somehow reassuring. Bek's panic lessened just a hair.

Something about the unexpected encounter caught Quentin Leah's notice. He walked out of the firelight and peered into the darkness where Bek and the stranger stood facing each other. "Bek? Are you all right?" He came closer. "Who's there?"

"Quentin Leah?" the stranger asked him.

The Highlander continued to advance, but his hand had dropped to the long knife at his waist. "Who are you?"

The stranger let the Highlander come up beside Bek. "I'm called Walker," he answered. "Do you know of me?"

"The Druid?" Quentin's hand was still on the handle of his long knife.

"The same." His bearded face came into the light as he pulled back the cowl of his cloak. "I've come to ask a favor of you."

"A favor?" Quentin sounded openly skeptical, and frown lines creased his brow. "From us?"

"Well, from you in particular, but since Bek is here, as well, I'll ask it of you both." He glanced past them to the fire. "Can we sit while we talk? Do you have something to eat? I've come a long way today."

As if arrived at a truce, they left the darkness and moved into the light, taking seats on the ground around the fire. Bek studied the Druid carefully, trying to take his measure. Physically, he was forbidding—tall and dark-featured, with long black hair and beard, and a narrow, angular face that was seamed by sun and weather. He looked neither young nor old, but somewhere in between. His right arm was missing from just above the elbow, leaving only a stump within a pinned-up tunic sleeve. Even so, he radiated power and self-assurance, and his strange eyes registered an unmistakable warning to stand clear. Although he said he had come to find them, he did not seem particularly interested now that he had. His gaze was directed toward the darkness beyond the fire, as if he was watching for something.

But it was his history that intrigued Bek more than his appearance, and the boy found himself digging through his memory for bits and pieces of what he knew. The Druid lived in the Keep at ancient Paranor with the ghosts of his ancestors and companions dead and gone. He was rumored to be Allanon's successor and direct descendant. It was said he had been alive in the time of Quentin's great-great-grandfather, Morgan Leah, and the most famous of all the Elf Queens, Wren Elessedil, and that he had fought with them in the war against the Shadowen. If that was true, then the Druid was more than 130 years old. No one else from that time was still alive, and it seemed strange and vaguely chilling that the Druid should have survived what no ordinary man could.

Bek knew a lot about the Druids. He had made it his business to know about them because of their long-standing connection to the Leah family. There had been a Leah involved in almost every great Druid undertaking since the time of the Warlock Lord. Most people were frightened of the Druids and their legacy of magic, but the Highlanders had always been their advocates. Without the Druids, they believed, the people of the Four Lands would be living much different lives at a cost they would not have cared to pay.

"You said you came far today?" Quentin broke the momentary silence. "Where did you come from?"

Walker's dark gaze shifted. "The Dragon's Teeth originally. Then from Leah."

"That was your Roc," Bek blurted out, suddenly able to speak again.

Walker glanced at him. "Not mine. Obsidian belongs to a Wing Rider named Hunter Predd. He should be along in a minute. He's bedding down his bird first." He paused. "You saw us, did you?"

"Saw your shadow, actually," Quentin said as he worked on laying out strips of smoked fish in a pan. He had coated them with flour and seasonings, and was adding a bit of ale for flavor. "We were boar hunting."

The Druid nodded. "Your father told me so."

Quentin looked up quickly. "My father?"

Walker stretched his legs and braced himself with his good arm as he leaned back. "We know each other. Tell me, did you have any luck with the boar?"

Quentin went back to his fish, shaking his head to himself. "No, he was frightened off by you. The Roc's shadow spooked him."

"Well, my apologies for that. On the other hand, getting

you back here to speak with me was of more consequence than seeing you bag that boar."

Bek stared. Was he saying that he had spooked the boar deliberately, that the Roc's passing hadn't been by chance? He glanced quickly at Quentin to catch his cousin's reaction, but Quentin's attention had shifted at the sound of someone else's approach.

"Ah, here is our friend, the Wing Rider," Walker said, rising.

Hunter Predd trooped into the firelight, a lean, wiry Elf with gnarled hands and sharp eyes. He nodded to the Highlander and his cousin as they were introduced. He took a seat across from the Druid. Walker spent a few minutes talking about Wing Riders and Rocs, explaining their importance to the Elves of the Westland, then asked Quentin for news of his family. The conversation continued as the Highlander prepared the fish, some fry bread, and a clutch of greens. All the while, Bek watched Walker carefully, wondering what the meeting was all about, what sort of favor the Druid could want of them, how he knew Coran Leah, what he was doing with a Wing Rider, and on and on.

They had eaten their meal, washed it down with cold stream water, and cleaned up the dishes before Walker provided Bek with the answers he was seeking.

"I want you to come with me on a journey," the Druid began, sipping at the ale Quentin had poured into his cup. "Both of you. It will be long and dangerous. It may be months before we return, maybe longer. We have to travel across the Blue Divide to a land none of us has ever seen. When we get there, we have to find a treasure. We have a map, and we have instructions written on the map about what we need to do to find this treasure. But someone else is after it, as well, someone very dangerous, and she will do everything she can to prevent us from reaching it first."

There were no preliminaries, no buildups, and no small talk to lead into all this. The explanation was casual; they might have been talking about taking a rafting trip down the Rappahalladran. Bek Rowe had never ventured outside the Highlands, and now someone had appeared who wanted him to travel halfway around the world. He could scarcely believe what he was hearing.

Hunter Predd was the first to speak. "She?" he asked curiously.

Walker nodded. "Our nemesis is a very powerful sorceress who calls herself the Ilse Witch. She is the protégé of a warlock known as the Morgawr. The names derive from a language used in the world of Faerie, most of it lost. Hers means *singer*. His means *wraith* or something like it. They reside in the Westland, down in the Wilderun, and seldom venture far from there. How the Ilse Witch found out about the map and our journey, I don't know. But she is responsible for the death of at least two people because of it." He paused. "Do you know of her?"

Bek and Quentin glanced at each other blankly, but the Wing Rider was shaking his head in dismay. "Enough to keep clear," he snapped.

"We don't have that option." Walker crossed his legs in front of him and leaned forward. "One of the dead men is Allardon Elessedil, the Elven King. If the Ilse Witch was willing to kill him to prevent us from seeking out the treasure described by the map, she will certainly not hesitate to kill us, as well. Forewarned is forearmed, I'm afraid."

His eyes shifted to Quentin and Bek. "The other dead man is the map's bearer, a castaway Hunter found floating in the Blue Divide a little more than a week ago. The hunt I'm proposing begins with him. He was Allardon Elessedil's older brother, Kael, one of a company of Elves that undertook a search similar to ours thirty years ago. All of them disappeared. No trace of them or their ships was ever found. The map our castaway carried suggests their search might have yielded something of great importance. It is up to us to find out what that something is."

"So you intend to sail all the way across the Blue Divide to search out this treasure?" Quentin asked dubiously.

"Not sail, Highlander," the Druid replied. "Fly."

There was a moment's silence. The wood burning in the fire pit crackled sharply. "On Rocs?" Quentin pressed.

"On an airship."

The silence resumed. Even Hunter Predd seemed surprised. "But why do you want us to come?" Bek asked finally.

"Several reasons." Walker fixed the boy with his dark gaze. "Bear with me for a moment. Aside from the three of you, I have told this to no one. Most of it, I have determined only very recently, and I am still in the process of deciphering quite a bit more. I need to have someone with whom I can discuss my thinking, someone I can trust and in whom I can confide. I need someone of sharp mind and willing spirit, of ability and courage. Hunter Predd is one such. I think you and your cousin are two more."

Bek felt his excitement growing by leaps and bounds. He leaned forward in response to the Druid's words.

"Hunter's usefulness is obvious," Walker continued. "He is a seasoned veteran of the skies, and I intend to take a small number of Wing Riders as escorts for our airship. Hunter will be their leader, if he agrees to accept the position. But in doing so, he needs to be confident that he can anticipate my thinking and respond as circumstances and events dictate."

He was still looking straight at Bek. "Quentin's purpose is obvious, as well, although he doesn't realize it yet. Quentin is a Leah, the oldest of his father's sons, and heir to a powerful magic. There is no one else I can recruit for this journey who will have such a magic to lend to our cause. Once, we might have relied upon the use of Elfstones, but those in the possession of the Elves were lost with Kael Elessedil. The Ilse Witch will have allies she can turn to who possess magic of their own. Moreover, we are certain to encounter other forms of magic during our quest. It will be difficult for anyone to stand alone against them all. Quentin must support me."

The Highlander looked as if the Druid had lost his mind. "You can't mean that old sword, the one my father gave me several years back when I crossed into manhood? That old relic is symbolic and nothing more! The Sword of Leah, handed down for generations, carried by my great-great-grandfather Morgan against the Federation when he fought for the liberation of the Dwarves in the wake of the Shadowen defeat—everyone knows the tale, but . . . but . . ."

He seemed to run out of words, shaking his head in disbelief and turning to Bek for support.

But it was Walker who spoke first. "You are familiar with the weapon, Quentin. You've held it in your hands, haven't you? When you took it out of its scabbard to examine it, you must have noticed that it was in perfect condition. The weapon is centuries old. How do you account for that if it is not infused with magic?"

"But it doesn't do anything!" Quentin exclaimed in exasperation.

"Because you tried to summon the magic, and failed?"

The Highlander sighed. "It feels foolish to admit it. But I knew the stories, and I just wanted to see if there was any truth to them. Honestly, I admire the weapon. Its balance and weight are exceptional. And it does look as if it is new." He paused, his broad, open Highlander face suffused with a mix of doubt and cautious expectation. "Is it really magic?"

Walker nodded. "But its magic does not respond to whim; it responds to need. It cannot be called forth simply out of curiosity. There must be a threat to the bearer. The magic originated with Allanon and the shades of the Druids who preceded him in life. No magic of theirs would be wild or arbitrary. The Sword of Leah has value, Highlander, but you will discover that only when you are threatened by the dark things you must help protect against."

Quentin Leah kicked at the earth with the heel of his boot. "If I go with you, I'll get my chance to discover this, won't I?"

The Druid stared at him without answering.

"Thought so." Quentin studied his boot a moment, then glanced at Bek. "A real adventure, cousin. Something more challenging than boar hunting. What do you think?"

For a moment, Bek didn't respond. He didn't know what he thought about any of it. Quentin was more trusting, more willing to accept what he was told, particularly when what it offered was what he was seeking. For several years he had asked for permission to join the Free-born and fight against the Federation, but his father had forbidden it. Quentin's obligations were to his family and his home. As the oldest son, he was expected to help in the raising and training of his younger siblings and of Bek. Quentin wanted to travel the whole of the Four Lands, to see what else was out there. So far, he had not been allowed to go much farther than the borders of the Highlands.

Now, all at once, he was being offered a chance to experience what had been denied him for so long. Bek was excited, too. But he was not so willing as his cousin to jump into the adventure with both feet.

"Bek is probably wondering why I'm asking him to come, as well," Walker said suddenly, his gaze fixed once more on the boy.

Bek nodded. "I guess I am."

"I'll tell you then." The Druid hunched forward once more. "I need you for an entirely different reason than Hunter or Quentin. It has to do with who you are and how you think. You have displayed a healthy dose of skepticism about what you are hearing. That's good. You should. You like to think things through carefully before giving credence to them. You like to measure and balance. For what I require of you, such an attitude is essential. I need a cabin boy on this journey, Bek, someone who can be anywhere and everywhere without questions being asked, someone whose presence is taken for granted, but who hears and sees everything. I need someone to keep watch for me, someone to investigate when it is called for and to report back on things I might have missed. I need an extra pair of hands and eyes. A boy like you has the intelligence and instincts to know when and how to put those hands and eyes to work."

Bek frowned. "You've only just met me; how can you be so sure of all this?"

The Druid pursed his lips reprovingly. "It is my business to know, Bek. Do you think I'm wrong about you?"

"You could be. What if you are?"

The Druid's smile was slow and easy. "Why don't we find out?"

He looked away. "One more thing," he said, speaking to all of them now. "When we begin this voyage, we shall do so with certain expectations regarding the character of those chosen to go. Over time, those expectations will change. Circumstances and events will touch all of us in ways we cannot foresee. Our company will number close to forty. I would like to believe that all would persevere and endure; they will not. Some will prove out, but some will fail us when we have need of them most. It is in the nature of things. The Ilse Witch will continue to try to stop us from leaving and, when that fails, to prevent us from reaching our goal. Moreover, she may not prove to be the most dangerous enemy we encounter. So we must learn to rely on ourselves and on those we discover we can depend upon. It is a formidable responsibility to shoulder, but I have great confidence in all three of you."

He leaned back, his dark face unreadable. "So, then. Are you with me? Will you come?"

Hunter Predd spoke first. "I've been with you from the start, Walker. I guess maybe I'll stick around for the finish. As for how dependable or trustworthy I'll turn out to be, all I can say is that I will do my best. One thing I do know—I can find the Wing Riders you need for this expedition."

Walker nodded. "I can ask no more." He looked at the cousins. "And you?"

Quentin and Bek exchanged a hurried glance. "What do you say, Bek?" Quentin asked. "Let's do it. Let's go."

Bek shook his head. "I don't know. Your father might not want us to—"

"I've spoken to him already," Walker interrupted smoothly. "You have his permission to come if you wish to do so. Both of you. But the choice is yours, and yours alone."

In that instant, Bek Rowe could see the future he had been searching for as clearly as if he had already lived it. It wasn't so much the specific events he would experience or the challenges he would face or the creatures and places he would encounter. These could be imagined, but not yet firmly grasped. It was the changes he would undergo on such a voyage that were discernible and thereby both intimidating and frightening. Many of them would be profound and lasting, affecting his life irrevocably. Bek could feel these changes as if they were layers of skin peeled back one at a time to demonstrate his growth. So much would happen on a journey like this one, and no one who returned—for he was honest enough with himself to accept that some would not—would ever be the same.

"Bek?" Quentin pressed softly.

He had come from nowhere to be where he was, an outsider accepted into a Highland home, a traveler simply by having come from another place and family. Life was a journey of sorts, and he could travel it by staying put or by going out. For Quentin, the choice had always been easy. For Bek, it was less so, but perhaps just as inevitable.

He looked at the Druid called Walker and nodded. "All right. I'll go."

TEN

On the way home the next day, Bek Rowe agonized over his decision. Even though it was made and he was committed, he could not stop second-guessing himself. On the face of things, he had made the right choice. There were lives at stake and responsibilities to be assumed in questing for the mysterious magic, and if the result of his going was to secure for the people of all nations a magic that would further their development and fulfill their needs—a result that Walker had taken great pains to assure him was possible—it was the right thing to do.

But in the back of his mind a whisper of warning nagged at him. The Druid, he felt, had told the truth. But the Druid was also reticent about giving out information, a tradition among the members of his order, and Bek was quite certain he was keeping something to himself. More than one something, in all likelihood. Bek could sense it in his voice and in the way he presented his cause to them. So careful with his words. So deliberate with his phrasing. Walker knew more than he was saying, and Bek worried that some of his misgivings about how a journey of this sort would influence his and Quentin's lives had their source in the Druid's secrets.

But there was a secondary problem with not going. Quentin had made up his mind even before Bek had agreed and would likely have gone without him. His cousin had been looking for an excuse to leave Leah and go elsewhere for a long time.

That his father had apparently agreed to his going on this particular journey—a decision that Bek found remarkable—removed the last obstacle that stood in Quentin's path. Quentin was like a brother. Much of the time, Bek felt protective toward him, even though Quentin was the older of the two and looked at the matter the other way around. Whatever the case, Bek loved and admired his cousin and could not imagine staying behind if Quentin went.

All of which was fine except that it did nothing to alleviate his misgivings. But there was no help for that, so he was forced to put the matter aside as they journeyed home. They walked steadily all day, crossing through the Highlands, navigating the deep woods, scrub wilderness, flowering meadows, streams and small rivers, misty valleys and green hills. They left much more quickly than they had gone in, Quentin setting the pace, anxious to return home so that they could prepare to set out again.

Which was another sticking point with Bek. Walker had asked them to come with him on a journey and then promptly departed for regions unknown. He hadn't waited for them to join him or offered to take them with him. He hadn't even told them when they would see him again.

"I want you to return to Leah on the morrow," he had advised just before they had rolled into their blankets and drifted off to an uneasy sleep. "Speak with your father. Satisfy yourselves that he has given you his permission to leave. Then pack your gear—not forgetting the sword, Quentin—saddle two strong horses, and ride east."

East! East, for cat's sake! Isn't that the wrong direction? Bek had demanded instantly. Didn't the Elves live west? Wasn't that where their journey to follow the map was supposed to initiate?

But the Druid had only smiled and assured him that traveling east was what was needed before going on to Arborlon. They must carry out a small errand for him, an errand he had insufficient time to run. Maybe it would offer Quentin a chance to test the magic of his blade. Maybe Bek would be given an opportunity to test his intuitive abilities. Maybe they would have a chance to meet someone they would come to depend upon in the days ahead.

Well, there wasn't much they could say to all that, so they had agreed to do as he asked. Just as Walker had known they would, Bek felt. He sensed, in fact, that Walker knew exactly how to present a request so that it would always be agreed to. When Walker spoke, Bek could feel himself agreeing almost before the words were out. Something in the Druid's voice was compelling enough to make him want to acquiesce out of hand.

Magic's sway, he supposed. Wasn't that a part of the Druid history? Wasn't that one reason why people were so afraid of them?

"This fellow we're supposed to find," he spoke up suddenly, halfway through the long walk home, glancing over at Quentin.

"Truls Rohk," his cousin said.

Bek shifted the heavy pack on his back. "Truls Rohk. What kind of name is that? Who is he? Doesn't it bother you that we don't know the first thing about him, that Walker didn't even tell us what he looks like?"

"He told us how to find him. He told us exactly where to go and how to get there. He gave us a message to deliver and words to speak. That's all we need to get the job done, isn't it?"

"I don't know. I don't know what we need because I don't know what we're getting ourselves into." Bek shook his head doubtfully. "We jumped awfully quick at the chance to get involved in this business, Quentin. What do we know about Walker or the Druids or this map or any of it? Just enough to get excited about traipsing off to the other side of the world. How smart is that?"

Quentin shrugged. "The way I look at it, we have a wonderful opportunity to travel, to see something of the world, something beyond the borders of Leah. How often is that kind of chance going to come along? And Father agrees that we can go. Talk about miracles!"

Bek huffed. "Talk about blackmail—that's more likely."

"Not Father." Quentin shook his head firmly. "He would die first. You know that."

Bek nodded reluctantly.

"So let's give this a chance before we start passing judgment. Let's see what things look like. If we think we're in over our heads, we can always give it up."

"Not if we're flying somewhere out over the Blue Divide, we can't."

"You worry too much."

"Sure enough. And you worry too little."

Quentin grinned. "True. But I'm happier worrying too little than you are worrying too much."

That was Quentin for you, never spending too much time on what might happen, content to live in the moment. It was hard to argue with someone who was so happy all the time, and that was Quentin right down to the soles of his boots. Give him a sunny day and a chance to walk ten miles and he was all set. Never mind that a thunderstorm was approaching or that Gnome Hunters prowled the region he traveled. Quentin's view was that bad things happened mostly when you thought too much about them.

Bek let the matter drop for the rest of the way back. He wasn't going to change Quentin's mind, and he wasn't sure he even ought to try. His cousin was right—he should give the idea a chance, let things develop a bit, and see where they were going.

The sun had set and the blue-green haze of twilight had begun to shroud the Highlands when the city of Leah at last came in sight. They walked out of the trees and down a long, gently sloped hillside to where Leah sat on a high plain overlooking the lowlands east and south and the Rappahalladran and the Duln Forests west. Leah sprawled outward from its compact center in a series of gradually expanding estates, farms, and cooperatives owned and managed by its citizenry. Leah had been a monarchy in the time of Allanon, and various members of the Leah family had ruled in unbroken succession for nine hundred years. But eventually the monarchy had dissolved and the Highlands had fallen under Federation sway. It was only in the last fifty years that the Federation had withdrawn to the cities below the Prekkendorran Heights, and a council of elders had taken over the process of governing. Coran Leah, as a member of one of the most famous and prestigious Highland families, had gained a seat on the council and recently been elected First Minister. It was a position that he occupied reluctantly, but worked hard at, intent on justifying the trust his people had shown him.

Quentin thought the whole governing business an appropriate one for old men. Leah was a drop in an ocean, to his way of thinking. There was so much more out there, so much else happening, and none of it was affected in even the tiniest way by events in Leah. Entire nations had never even heard of the Highlands. If he wanted to have an impact on the future of the Four Lands, and possibly even on countries that lay beyond, he had to leave home and go out into the world. He had talked about it with Bek until his cousin was ready to scream. Bek didn't think like that. Bek wasn't interested in affecting the rest of the world. Bek was quite content to stay pretty much where he was. He viewed Quentin's relentless search for a way out of Leah as an obsession that was both dangerous and wrongheaded. But, he had to admit, at least Quentin had a plan for his life, which was more than Bek could say for himself.

They passed through farmlands, across horse and cattle fields, and past estate grounds and manor houses until they had reached the outskirts of the city proper. The Leah house occupied the same site on which their palace had been settled when the family ruled the Highlands. The palace had been destroyed during Federation occupation—burned, it was rumored, by Morgan Leah himself in defiance of its occupiers. In any case, Coran's father had replaced it with a two-story traditional home, multiple eaves and dormers, long rooflines and deep alcoves, casement wraps and stone fireplaces. The old trees remained, flower gardens dotted the grounds front and rear, and vine-draped arbors arched above crushed-stone walkways that wound from the front and rear entry doors to the surrounding streets.

Lights already burned in the windows and along the paths. They gave a warm and friendly feel to the big house, and as the cousins walked up to it Bek found himself wondering how long it would be before he would enjoy this feeling again.

They ate dinner that night with the family, with Coran and Liria and the four younger Leahs. The children spent the meal clamoring for details about their adventures, especially the boar hunt. Quentin made it all sound much more exciting than it really was, accommodating his younger brothers and sisters with a wild and lurid tale about how they barely escaped death on the tusks and under the hooves of a dozen rampaging boars. Coran shook his head and Liria smiled, and any discussion of Walker's unexpected appearance and proposed journey was postponed until later.

When dinner was finished and Liria had taken the younger children off to bed, Bek left Quentin to speak alone with his father about the Druid and took a long, hot bath to wash off the dirt from their outing. He gave himself over to the heat and damp, letting go of his concerns long enough to close his eyes and soak away his weariness. On finishing, he went to Quentin's room and found his cousin sitting on the bed holding the old sword and studying it thoughtfully.

Quentin looked up as he entered. "Father says we can go."

Bek nodded. "I never thought he wouldn't. Walker wouldn't be foolish enough to lie to us about something like that." He brushed a lock of damp hair off his forehead. "Did he tell you why he's had this change of heart about our leaving?"

"I asked. He said he owed the Druid a favor for something that happened a long time ago. He wouldn't say what. Actually, he changed the subject on me." Quentin looked thoughtful. "But he didn't seem disturbed about our going or about Walker's appearance. He seemed more . . . oh, sort of determined, I guess. It was hard to read him, Bek. He was very serious about this matter—calm, but intense. He made sure I knew to take the sword."

He looked down at the weapon in his hands. "I've been sitting here looking at it." He smiled. "I keep thinking that if I look hard enough, I'll discover something. Maybe the sword will speak to me, tell me the secret of its magic."

"I think you have to do what Walker said. You have to wait until there's a need for it before you learn how it works." Bek sat down on the bed next to him. "Walker was right. The sword is perfect. Not a mark on it. Hundreds of years old and in mint condition. That's not something that could happen if magic wasn't warding it in some way."

"I suppose not." Quentin turned the blade over and back again, running his fingers along the smooth, flat surface. "I feel a little strange about this. If the blade is magic and I'm to wield it, will I know what to do when it's time?"

Bek chuckled. "When did you ever not know what to do when it was time? You were born ready, Quentin."

"And you were born twice as smart and a lot more intuitive than I was," his cousin replied, and there was no joking or laughter in his response. His steady, open gaze settled on Bek. "I know my strengths and weaknesses. I can be honest about them. I know I rush into things, the way I did the chance to go on this expedition. Sometimes that's okay, and sometimes it isn't. I rely on you to keep me from wandering too far astray."

Bek shrugged. "Always happy to bring you back into line." He grinned.

"You remember that." Quentin looked back down at the sword. "If I don't see what needs doing, if I miss the right and wrong of things, I'm counting on you not to. This sword," he said, hefting it gently, "maybe it is magic and can do wonderful things. Maybe it can save lives. But maybe it's like all magic and can be harmful, as well. Isn't that the nature of magic? That it can work both ways? I don't want to cause harm with it, Bek. I don't want to be too quick to use it."

It was a profound observation for Quentin, and Bek thought his cousin did not give himself nearly enough credit. Nevertheless, he nodded in agreement. "Now go take a bath," he ordered, standing up again and moving toward the door. "I can't be expected to think straight when you smell like this!"

He returned to his room and began putting together clothes for their journey. They would leave early in the morning, getting a quick start on their travels. It would take them a week to track down Truls Rohk and then to reach Arborlon. How much longer would they be gone after that? What would it be like in the lands beyond their own, across the Blue Divide? Would the climate be hot or cold, wet or dry, bitter or mild? He looked around his room helplessly, made aware again of how little he knew about what he had let himself in for. But that kind of thinking wasn't going to help, so he put it aside and went back to work.

He was almost finished when Coran Leah appeared in the doorway, grave and thoughtful. "I wonder if I might talk to you a minute, Bek?"

Without waiting for a response, he stepped into the room and closed the door behind him. For a moment he just stood there, as if undecided about what to do next. Then he walked over to the bench on which Bek was laying out clothing, made a place for himself, and sat down.

Bek stared, still holding a shirt he was folding up to put in his backpack. "What is it? What's the matter?"

Coran Leah shook his gray head. He was still a handsome man, strong and fit at fifty, his blue eyes clear and his smile ready. He was well liked in Leah, well regarded by everyone. He was the kind of man who made it a point to do the small things others would overlook. If there were people in need, Coran Leah was always the first to try to find help for them or, failing that, to help them himself. He had raised his children with kind words and gentle urgings, and Bek didn't think he had ever heard him shout. If he could have chosen a father for himself, Bek wouldn't have looked farther than Coran.

"I have been thinking about this since Walker came to see me yesterday and told me what he wanted. There are some things you don't know, Bek—things no one knows, not even Quentin, only Liria and I. I've been waiting for the right time to tell you, and I guess maybe I've waited as long as I can."

He straightened himself, placing his hands carefully on his knees. "It wasn't your father who brought you here all those years ago. It was Walker. He told me your father had died in an accident, leaving you alone, and he asked me to take you in. The fact is, I wasn't close to Holm Rowe. I hadn't seen him in more than ten years before you came to live with us. I didn't know he had children. I didn't even know he had a wife. I thought it very strange that your father would choose to send you to me, to live with my family, but Walker insisted that this was what he wanted. He convinced me that it was the right thing to do."

He shook his head anew. "He can be very persuasive when he chooses. I asked him how your father had come to know him well enough to put you in his care. He said it wasn't a matter of choice, that he was there when no one else was, and your father had to trust him."

Bek put down the shirt he was holding. "Well, I know how persuasive he can be. I've seen it for myself. How did he talk you into agreeing with him on this present business?"

Coran Leah smiled. "He told me the same thing I assume he told you—that he needed you both, that people's lives depended on it, that the future of the Four Lands required it. He said you were old enough to make the decision for yourselves, but that I must give you the freedom to do so. I didn't like hearing that, but I recognized the truth in what he was

saying. You are old enough, almost grown. Quentin is grown.
I've kept you with me as long as I can." He shrugged. "Maybe
he's right. Maybe people's lives do depend on it. I guess I owe
it to you both to let you find out."

Bek nodded. "We'll be careful," he reassured him. "We'll
look after each other."

"I know you will. I feel better with both of you going
rather than only one. Liria doesn't think you should go at all,
either of you, but that's because she's a mother, and that's how
mothers think."

"Do you think Quentin's sword really does have magic? Do
you think it can do what Walker says?"

Coran sighed. "I don't know. Our family history says so.
Walker seems certain of it."

Bek sat down across from him on the edge of his bed. "I'm
not sure we're doing the right thing by going, and I realize we
don't know everything yet, maybe not even enough to appreciate the risk we're taking. But I promise we won't do anything foolish."

Coran nodded. "Be careful of those kinds of promises,
Bek. Sometimes they're hard to keep." He paused. "There's
one thing more I have to say. It has occurred to me before, but
I've kept it to myself. I thought about it again yesterday, when
Walker reappeared on my doorstep. Here it is. I have only the
Druid's word that Holm Rowe really was your father and that
he sent you here to live with me. I tried to check on this later,
but no one could tell me where or when Holm had died. No
one could tell me anything about him."

Bek stared at him in surprise. "Someone else might be my
real father?"

Coran Leah fixed him with his steady gaze. "You are like
one of my own sons, Bek. I love you as much as I love them. I
have done the very best I could to raise you in the right way.
Both Liria and I have. Now that you are about to leave, I want
no secrets between us."

He stood up. "I'll let you get back to your packing."

He started for the door, then changed his mind and came back across the room. He put his strong arms around Bek and hugged him tightly. "Be careful, son," he whispered.

Then he was gone again, leaving Bek to conclude that there was as much uncertainty about his past as there was about his future.

ELEVEN

It was raining again by the time Hunter Predd and Walker arrived aboard Obsidian at the seaport of March Brume, some distance north of Bracken Clell on the coast of the Blue Divide. They had flown into the rain just before sunset after traveling west all day from the Highlands of Leah, and it felt as if the dark and damp had descended as one. March Brume occupied a stretch of rocky beach along a cove warded by huge cliffs to the north and a broad salt marsh to the south. A stand of deep woods backed away from the village into a shallow valley behind, and it was just to the south of that valley, on a narrow plateau, that the Roc deposited her passengers so that they might take refuge for the night in an old trapper's shack.

March Brume was a predominately Southland community, although a smattering of Elves and Dwarves had settled there, as well. For centuries, the seaport had been famous for the construction of her sailing ships, everything from one-man skiffs to single-masted sloops to three-masted frigates. Craftsmen from all over the Four Lands came to the little village to ply their trades and offer their services. There was never a shortage of need for designers or builders, and there was always a good living to be made. Virtually everyone who lived in the seaport was engaged in the same occupation.

Then, twenty-four years ago, a man named Ezael Sterret, a Rover of notorious reputation, a sometime pirate and brigand with a streak of inventive genius, had designed and built the first airship. It had been unwieldy, ungainly, and unreliable, but it had flown. Other efforts by other builders had followed, each increasingly more successful, and within two decades, travel had been revolutionized and the nature of shipbuilding in March Brume had been changed forever. Sailing ships were still built in the shipyards of the old seaport, but not in the same numbers as before. The majority of ships constructed now were for air travel, and the customers whose pockets were deepest and whose needs were greatest came from the Federation and Free-born army commands.

None of which had anything to do with Walker's primary reason for choosing to come here rather than to one of a dozen other shipbuilding ports along the coast. What brought him to March Brume was the nature of the shipbuilders and designers who occupied the seaport—Rovers, a people universally disliked and distrusted, wanderers for the whole of their history, who even as mostly permanent residents still came and went from the seaport whenever the urge struck. Not only were they the most skilled and reliable of those engaged in shipbuilding and flying, but they accepted work from all quarters and they understood the importance of keeping a bargain and a confidence once engaged.

Walker was about to test the truth of this generally held belief. His instincts and his long association with Rovers persuaded him that it was his best option. His cousin, the Elven Queen Wren Elessedil, had been raised by Rovers as a child and taught the survival skills that had kept her alive when she had journeyed to the doomed island of Morrowindl to recover the lost Elven people. Rovers had aided various members of Walker's family over the years, and he had found them tough, dependable, and resourceful. Like him, they were wanderers. Like him, they were outcasts and loners. Even living in settled communities, as many of them were doing now, they remained mostly isolated from other peoples.

This was fine with Walker. The less open and more secretive his dealings in this matter, the better. He did not think for a moment that he could keep secret for long either his presence or his purpose. The Ilse Witch would be seeking to discover both. Sooner or later, she would succeed.

Hunter Predd managed a fire in the crumbling hearth of the old trapper's cabin, and they slept the night in mostly dry surroundings. At dawn, Walker gave the Wing Rider orders to replace their dwindling provisions and to wait for his return from the village. He might be gone for several days, he cautioned, so the Wing Rider shouldn't be concerned if he did not reappear right away.

The day had cleared somewhat, the rain turned to a cold, damp mist that clung to the forests and cliffs like a shroud, and the skies brightened sufficiently to permit a hazy glimpse of the sun through banks of heavy gray clouds. Walker navigated the woods until he found a trail, then the trail until it led to a road, and followed the road into the village. March Brume was a collection of sodden gray buildings, with the residences set back from the shoreline toward the woods, and the shipyards and docks set closer to the water. The sounds of building rose in a din above the crash of waves, a steady mix of hammers and saws punctuated by the hiss of steam rising from hot iron hauled from the forge and by the shouts and curses of the laborers. The village was crowded and active, residents and visitors alike clogging the streets and alleys, going about their business in the damp and gloom in remarkably cheerful fashion.

Walker, wrapped in his cloak to hide his missing arm, was not remarkable enough to draw attention. People of all sorts came and went in March Brume, and where a Rover population dominated, it was best to mind your own business.

The Druid moved unhurriedly toward the docks through the businesses at the center of town. Federation soldiers dressed in silver and black uniforms lounged about while waiting to take delivery of their orders. There were Free-born soldiers, as well, not so obvious or bold in revealing their presence, but come to March Brume for the same reason. It was odd, the Druid thought, that they would shop at the same store as if it were the most natural thing in the world, when in any other situation they would attack each other on sight.

He found the man he was looking for in a marketplace toward the south end of the village, not far from the beginnings of the docks and building yards. He was a scarecrow dressed in brilliant but tattered scarlet robes. He was so thin that when he braced himself against the occasional gusts of wind that blew in off the water, he seemed to bend like a reed. A wisp of black beard trailed from his pointed chin, and his dark hair hung long and unkempt about his narrow face. A vivid red scar ran from hairline to chin, crossing the bridge of his broken nose like a fresh lash mark. He stood just off the path of the traffic passing the stalls, close by a fountain, head cocked in a peculiarly upward tilted fashion, as if searching for guidance from the clouded skies. One hand held forth a metal cup, and the other gestured toward passersby with a fervor that suggested you ignored him at your peril.

"Come now, don't be shy, don't be hesitant, don't be afraid!" His voice was thin and high pitched, but it caught the attention. "A coin or two buys you peace of mind, pilgrim. A coin or two buys you a glimpse of your future. Be certain of your steps, friend. Take a moment to learn of the fate you might prevent, of the misstep you might take, of the downward path you might unwittingly follow. Come one, come all."

Walker stood across the square from the man and watched silently for a time. Now and then, someone would stop, place a coin in the metal cup, and bend close to hear what the man had to say. The man always did the same thing: he took the giver's hand in his own and held it while he talked, moving his fingers slowly over the other's open palm, nodding all the while.

Once or twice, when the man shifted positions or moved to take a drink from the fountain's waters, the scarlet robes shifted to reveal that he had only one leg and wore a wooden peg for the other.

Walker held his position until the rain quickened sufficiently to drive most of the crowd elsewhere and force the man to back away under the shelter of an awning. Then he crossed the square, approached the man in the scarlet robes as if seeking to share his shelter, and stood quietly at his side.

"Perhaps you could read the future of a man who seeks to take a long and hazardous journey to an unknown land?" he queried, looking out at the rain.

The man's gaze shifted slightly, but stayed directed skyward. "Some men have made journeys enough for five lifetimes already. Perhaps they should stay home and quit tempting fate."

"Perhaps they have no choice."

"Paladins of shades revealed only to them, questers of answers to secrets unknown, ever searching for what will put an end to their uncertainty." The hands gestured helplessly. "You've been away for a long time, pilgrim. Up there, in your high castle, alone with your thoughts and dreams. Do you really seek to make a journey to a faraway land?"

Walker smiled faintly. "You are the forecaster of fates, Cicatrix. Not me."

The scarred face nodded. "A teller of futures this day, a disabled soldier the next, a madman the third. Like yourself, Walker, I am a chameleon."

"We do what we must in this world." The Druid bent closer. "But I didn't seek you out for any of the skills you've listed, formidable though they are. I require instead a small piece of information from that vast storehouse you manage— and I would keep that information from reaching other ears."

Cicatrix reached for the Druid's hand and took it in his own, running his fingers over the palm, keeping his ruined face directed skyward as he did so. "You intend to make a trip to an unknown land, pilgrim?" His voice had dropped to a whisper. "Perhaps you seek transport?"

"Of the sort that flies. Something fast and durable. Not a

warship, but able to be fitted to withstand an attack by one. Not a racer, but able to fly as if born to it. Her builder must have vision, and the ship must have heart."

The thin man laughed softly. "You seek miracles, pilgrim. Do I seem to you the sort that can provide them?"

"In the past, you have."

"The past comes back to haunt me, then. There lies the trouble with having to live up to another's expectations, when those expectations are founded on questionable memories. Well." He kept running his hands over Walker's palm. "Your enemy in this endeavor wouldn't happen to wear silver and black?"

Walker glanced out into the rain. "Mostly, my enemy would have eyes everywhere and kill with her song."

Cicatrix hissed softly. "A witch with a witches' brew, is it? Stay far from her, Walker."

"I'll try. Now listen carefully. I need a ship and a builder, a Captain and a crew. I need them to be strong and brave and willing to ally themselves with the Elves against all enemies." He paused. "March Brume's reputation will be tested in this as it has not been tested before."

"And mine."

"And yours."

"If I disappoint you, I shall not see you again, pilgrim?"

"You will at least wish as much."

Cicatrix chuckled mirthlessly. "Threats? No, not from you, Walker. You never threaten; you only reveal your concerns. A poor cripple like myself is advised to pay close attention, but not to act out of fear." His fingers stopped moving on Walker's hand. "Are the rewards for those who become involved reasonable, given the risks?"

"Well beyond that. The Elves will open wide the doors to their vaults."

"Ah." The other man nodded, head tilted strangely, gaze directed at nothing. He released Walker's hand. "Come to the docks at the end of Verta Road after nightfall. Stand where you can be seen. Mysteries shall unfold and secrets be revealed. Perhaps a journey shall be taken to an unknown land."

Walker produced a pouch filled with gold coins, and Cicatrix pocketed it smoothly. He turned slowly and limped away. "Farewell, pilgrim. Good fortune to you."

Walker spent the remainder of the day walking the docks, studying the ships under construction and the men building them, listening to talk of sailing, and garnering small amounts of information. He ate at a large, dockside tavern, where he was one of many, and pretended disinterest while keeping close watch for the Federation spies he knew to be there. The Ilse Witch would be looking for him, determined to find him. He had no illusions. She was relentless. She would attack him wherever and whenever she could, hoping to finish what she had started in Arborlon. If she could kill or disable him, the quest he sought to mount would fall apart and her own path to the map's treasure would be left unobstructed. She did not have the map, but she probably had the castaway's memories to guide her, and for all he knew, they would prove sufficient.

He pondered at length the implications of an encounter with her, of a confrontation he was almost certain he could not avoid. He mulled the consequences of cruel chance and unkind fate, of opportunities lost and games played, and waited patiently for nightfall.

When it was dark, he made his way through March Brume, his progress hidden by a mist come in off the water with the temperature's drop and the rain's passing. The forges and shipyards had emptied with the end of the workday, and the sound of the surf lapping against the shoreline was clearly audible in the ensuing silence. Vendors had closed their shops, and peddlers had stowed their wares. The taverns, eating establishments, and pleasure houses were packed full and boisterous, but the streets were mostly deserted.

Several times, he stopped in the shadows and waited—listening and watching. He did not pursue a direct route to his destination, but instead worked his way through the village in an oblique fashion, making certain he was not followed. Even so, he was uneasy. He was inconspicuous enough to those who did not know to look for him, but easily recognizable by those who did. The Ilse Witch would have advised her spies of his appearance. He might have been wiser to disguise himself. But that was hindsight talking, and hindsight was of little use now.

At the end of Verta Road, cloaked in the mist and silence, he stood in the faint light of a streetlamp. The docks stretched away oceanside, the stark, spectral forms of partially formed ship hulls and support cradles outlined by the lights of the village. No one moved in the night's gloom. No sounds broke the steady roll and hiss of the surf.

He had been in place for only a few minutes when a man materialized out of the dark and walked toward him. The man was tall and had flaming red hair worn long and tied back with a brightly colored scarf. A Rover, by the look of him, he walked with the slightly rolling gait of a sailor, and his cloak billowed open to reveal a set of flying leathers. The man smiled easily as he came up to Walker, as if they were old friends reuniting after a long separation.

"Are you called Walker?" he asked, coming to a stop before the Druid. His gold earrings glittered faintly in the streetlamp's hazy light.

Walker nodded.

The other bowed slightly. "I'm Redden Alt Mer. Cicatrix tells me you have plans for a journey and need help with the preparations."

Walker frowned. "You don't have the look of a shipbuilder."

Redden Alt Mer grinned broadly. "That's probably because I'm not one. But I know where to find the man you need. I know how to put you aboard the fastest, most agile ship ever built, enlist the best crew who ever sailed the open sky, and then fly you to wherever you want to go—because

I'll be your Captain." He paused, cocking his head. "All for a price, of course."

Walker studied him. The man was cocky and brash, but with a dangerous edge to him, as well. "How do I know you can manage all this, Redden Alt Mer? How do I know you're the man I need?"

The Rover managed a look of complete astonishment. "Cicatrix sent me to you; if you trusted him enough to find me in the first place, that should be enough."

"Cicatrix has been known to make mistakes."

"Only if you cheated him of his fee, and he wants to teach you a lesson. You didn't, did you?" The Rover sighed. "Very well. Here are my credentials, since I see that my name means nothing to you. I was born to ships and have sailed them since I was a boy. I have been a Captain for most of my life. I have sailed the entire Westland coast and explored most of the known islands off the Blue Divide. I have spent the last three years flying airships for the Federation. More to the point, I have never, ever, been knocked out of the skies."

"And should I trust you enough to believe you speak the truth?" Walker moved a step closer. "Even though you place an assailant at my back with a drawn dagger, waiting to strike me down should you feel I do not?"

Alt Mer nodded slowly, the grin still in place. "Very good. I know something of Druids and their powers. You are the last of your kind and not well respected in the Four Lands, so I felt it wise to test you. A real Druid, I am told, would sense an assailant's presence. A real Druid would know if he was threatened." He shrugged. "I was simply being cautious. I meant you no offense."

Walker's dark face did not change expression. "I take none. This is to be a long and dangerous journey, should we agree that you are the right man to make it, Redden Alt Mer. I understand that you don't want to attempt it in the company of a fool or a liar." He paused. "Of course, neither do I."

The Rover laughed softly. "Little Red!" he called.

A tall, auburn-tressed woman emerged from the misty dark behind Walker, eyes sweeping the shadows, suggesting she was even less trusting of him than her companion was. When she nodded to Alt Mer, and he back to her, agreeing between them that all was well, the resemblance was unmistakable.

"My sister, Rue Meridian," Alt Mer said. "She'll be my navigator when we sail. She'll also watch my back, just as she did here."

Rue Meridian extended her hand in greeting, and Walker took it. Her grip was strong and her eyes steady as they met his own. "Welcome to March Brume," she said.

"Let's move out of the light while we conduct our business," Alt Mer suggested cheerfully.

He led his sister and Walker away from the streetlamp's hazy light and into a darkened alleyway that ran between the buildings. On the road behind them, a small boy darted past, chasing after a metal hoop he rolled ahead of him with a stick.

"Now then, to business," Redden Alt Mer said, rubbing his hands with enthusiasm. "Where is this journey to take us?"

Walker shook his head. "I can't tell you that. Not until we're safely away."

The Rover seemed taken aback. "Can't tell me? You want me to sign on for a voyage that has no destination? Do we go west, east, north, south, up or down—?"

"We go where I say."

The big man grunted. "All right. Do we carry cargo?"

"No. We go to retrieve something."

"How many passengers will we carry?

"Three dozen, give or take a few. No more than forty."

The Rover frowned. "For a ship that size, I'll need a crew of at least a dozen, including Little Red and myself."

"I'll allow you ten."

Alt Mer flushed. "You place a good many constraints on us for someone who knows nothing of sailing!"

"How well do you intend to pay?" his sister interjected quickly.

"What would be your normal rate of pay for a long voyage?" Walker queried. Now they were down to the part that mattered most. Rue Meridian glanced at her brother. Alt Mer thought about it, then provided a figure. Walker nodded. "I'll pay that much in advance and double it when we return."

"Triple it," Rue Meridian said at once.

Walker gave her a long, considering look. "What did Cicatrix tell you?"

"That you have rich friends and powerful enemies."

"Which are good reasons to hire us," her brother added.

"Especially if the latter are allied with someone whose magic is as powerful as your own."

"Someone who can kill with little more than the sound of her voice." Redden Alt Mer smiled anew. "Oh, yes. We know something of the creatures that live in the Wilderun. We know something of witches and warlocks."

"Rumor has it," his sister said softly, "that you were standing next to Allardon Elessedil when he was killed."

"Rumor has it that he struck some sort of bargain with you, and that the Elves intend to honor it." Alt Mer cocked one eyebrow quizzically.

Walker glanced out at the darkness of Verta Road, then back at the red-haired siblings again. "You seem to know a great deal."

The Rover Captain shrugged. "It is our business to know, when we are being asked to put our lives at risk."

"Which brings up an interesting point." The Druid gave them both a considering look. "Why do you want to come with me on this voyage? Why choose to involve yourselves in this venture when there are other, less dangerous expeditions?"

Redden Alt Mer laughed. "A good question. A question that requires several answers. Let me see if I can provide them for you. First, there is the money. You offer more than we can make from anyone else. A great deal more. We're

mercenaries, so we pay close attention when the purse offered is substantial. Second, there are the unfortunate circumstances surrounding our recent leave-taking from the
Federation. It wasn't altogether voluntary, and our former
employers could decide to come looking for us to settle ac-
counts. It might be best if we were somewhere else if that
happens. A long voyage out of the Four Lands would provide
them with sufficient time to lose interest.

"And third," he said, smiling like a small boy with a piece
of candy, "there is the challenge of making a voyage to a new
land, of going somewhere no one else has gone before, of
seeing something for the first time, of finding a new world."
He sighed and gestured expansively. "You shouldn't under-
estimate what that means to us. It's difficult to explain to
someone who doesn't fly or sail or explore like we do, like
we've done all our lives. It is who we are and what we do, and
sometimes that counts for more than anything."

"Especially after our experience with the Federation,
where we hired out just for the money," his sister growled
softly. "It's time for something else, something more ful-
filling, even if it is dangerous."

"Don't be so quick to demystify our thinking, Little Red!"
her brother reproved her sharply. He cocked a finger at the
Druid. "Enough about the reasons for our choices. Let me
tell you something about yours, about why you chose to involve yourself with us. I don't mean Little Red and myself,
personally—though we're the ones you want. I mean the
Rovers. You are here, my friend, because you're a Druid and
we're Rovers, and we have much in common. We are outsiders and always have been. We are outcasts of the lands, just
barely tolerated and suspiciously viewed. We are comfortable
with wanderlust and the wider view of the world, and we do
not see things in terms of nationalities and governments. We
are people who value friendship and loyalty, who prize
strength of heart and mind as well as of body, but who value
good judgment even more. You can be the bravest soul who

ever walked the earth and be worthless if you do not know when and where to choose your battles. How am I doing?"

"A little long-winded," Walker offered.

The tall Rover laughed gleefully. "A sense of humor in a Druid! Who would have thought it possible? Well, you catch my drift, so I needn't go on. We are made for each other—and for quests that most would never dream of even considering. You want us, Walker, because we will stand against anything. We will go right into death's maw and give a yank of his tongue. We will do it because that is what life is for, if you are a Rover. Now tell me—am I wrong?"

Walker shook his head, as much in dismay as in agreement.

"He actually believes all this," his sister declared ruefully. "I worry that it might prove contagious and that one day soon we will both become infected and then neither one of us will be able to think straight."

"Now, now, Little Red. You're supposed to stand up for me, not knock me down!" Alt Mer sighed and stared at Walker with his cheerful gaze. "There is also, of course, the inescapable fact that almost no one else of talent and nerve would give you the time of day in this business. Rovers are the only ones bold enough to accept your offer while still respecting your need for secrecy." He grinned. "So, what's it to be?"

Walker pulled his black robes more closely about him, and the mist that had filtered into their dark alleyway stirred in response. "Let's sleep on it. Tomorrow we can have a talk with your shipbuilder and see if he backs you up. I'll want to see his work and judge the man himself before I commit to anything."

"Excellent!" the big Rover exclaimed joyfully. "A fair response!" He paused, a shadow of regret crossing his broad face. "Except for one thing. Sleep is out of the question. If you're interested in our services, we'll have to leave here tonight."

"Leave?" Walker didn't bother to hide his surprise.

"Tonight."

"And go where?"

"Why, wherever I say," the Rover answered, feeding Walker's words back to him. He grinned at his sister. "I'm afraid he thinks me none too bright after all." He turned back to Walker. "If the shipbuilder you wanted could be found in March Brume, you wouldn't need us to locate him for you, would you? Nor would he be of much use if he conducted his business openly."

Walker nodded. "I suppose not."

"A short journey is required to provide you with the reassurances you seek—a journey that would best be begun under cover of darkness."

Walker glanced skyward, as if assessing the weather. He couldn't see moon or stars or fifty feet beyond the fog. "A journey we will make on foot, I hope?"

The big Rover grinned anew. His sister cocked her eyebrow reprovingly.

Walker sighed. "How soon do we leave?"

Redden Alt Mer draped one companionable arm over Rue Meridian's shoulders. "We leave now."

The boy with the iron hoop and stick remained hidden in the deep shadows of the dockyards across the way until the trio emerged from the alleyway and disappeared up the road. Even then, he did not move for a long time. He had been warned about the Druid and his powers, and he did not wish to challenge either. It was enough that he had found him; nothing more was required.

When he was confident he was alone again, he left his hiding place, hoop and stick abandoned, and raced toward the woods backing the village. He was small for his age and wild as an animal, lean and wiry and unkempt, not quite a child of the streets, but close. He had never known his father and had lost his mother when he was only two. His half-blind grandmother had raised him, but had lost all control before he was six. He was bright and enterprising, however, and he had found ways to support them both in a world that otherwise would have swallowed them whole.

In less than an hour, sweaty and dirt-streaked from his run, he reached the abandoned farm just beyond the last residences of March Brume. His labored breathing was the only sound that broke the silence as he entered the ruined barn and moved to the storage bins in back. Within the more secure one on the far right were the cages. He released the lock, slipped inside the bin, lit a candle, and scribbled a carefully worded note.

The lady for whom he gathered information from time to time would pay him well for this bit, he thought excitedly. Enough that he could buy that blade he had admired for so long. Enough that he and his grandmother could eat well for weeks to come.

He fastened the message to the leg of one of the odd, fierce-eyed birds she had given him, walked back outside with the bird tucked carefully under his arm, and sent it winging off into the night.

TWELVE

Redden Alt Mer and Rue Meridian took Walker along the dockside for several hundred yards, then turned onto a narrow pier bracketed by skiffs. Stopping at a weathered craft with a knockdown mast and single sail and a rudder attached to a hand tiller at the stern, they held her steady while the Druid boarded, then quickly cast off. Within seconds, they were out of sight of the dock, the village, and any hint of land. The Rovers placed Walker in the bow with directions to keep an eye open for floating debris, and went about putting up the mast and sail. Walker glanced around uneasily. As far as he could determine, they had no way of judging where they were or where they were going. It did not seem to matter. Once the sail was up and filled with a steady wind off the sea, they sat back, Alt Mer at the stern and his sister amidships, tacking smoothly and steadily into the night.

It was a strange experience, even for the Druid. Now and then a scattering of stars would appear through the clouds, and once or twice the moon broke through, high and to their right. But for that, they sailed in a cauldron of fog and darkness and unchanging sea. At least the water was calm, as black and depthless as ink, rolling and sloshing comfortably below the gunwales. Redden Alt Mer whistled and hummed, and his sister stared off into the night. No bird cries sounded. No lights appeared. Walker found his thoughts drifting to a renewed consideration of the ambiguity and uncertainty of

what he was about. It was more than just the night's business
that troubled him; it was the entire enterprise. It was as vague
and shrouded as the darkness and the fog in which he drifted,
all awash in unanswered questions and vague possibilities.
He knew a few things and could guess at a few more, but
the rest—the greater part of what lay ahead—remained a
mystery.

They sailed for several hours in their cocoon of changeless
sounds and sights, wrapped by the darkness and silence as if
sleepers who drowsed before waking. It came as a surprise
when Rue Meridian lit an oil lamp and hooked it to the front
of the mast. The light blazed bravely in a futile effort to
cut through the darkness, but seemed able to penetrate no
more than a few feet. Redden Alt Mer had taken a seat on the
bench that ran across the skiff's stern, his arm hooked over
the tiller, his feet propped up on the rail. He nodded to his
sister when the light was in place, and she moved forward to
change places with Walker.

Shortly after, a sailing vessel appeared before them, loom-
ing abruptly out of the night, this one much larger and better
manned. Even in the darkness, Walker could estimate a crew
of six or seven, all working the rigging on the twin masts. A
rope was tossed to Rue Meridian, who tied it to the bow of the
skiff. Her brother put out the lamp, hauled down the sail, took
down the mast, and resumed his seat. Their work was done in
moments, and the towrope tightened and jerked as they were
hauled ahead.

"Nothing to do now until we get to where we're going," the
Rover Captain offered, stretching out comfortably on the
bench. In moments, he was asleep.

Rue Meridian sat with Walker amidships. After a few moments, she said, "Nothing ever seems to bother him. I've
seen him sleep while we're flying into battle. It isn't that he's
incautious or unconcerned. Big Red is always ready when
he's needed. It's just that he knows how to let go of everything
all at once and then pick it up again when it's time."

Her eyes swept the dark perfunctorily as she talked. "He'll tell you he's the best because he believes it. He'll tell you he should be your Captain because he's confident he should be. You might think him boastful or brash; you might even think him reckless. He's neither. He's just very good at flying airships." She paused. "No, not just good. He's much better than that. He's great. He's gifted. He is the best I've ever known, the best that anyone's ever seen. The soldiers talked about him on the Prekkendorran like that. Everyone who knows him does. They think he's got luck. And he does, but it's mostly luck he makes by being brave and smart and talented."

She glanced at him. "Do I sound like a younger sister talking about a big brother she idolizes?" She snorted softly. "I am, but I'm not deceived by my feelings for him. I've been his protector and conscience for too long. We were born to the same mother, different fathers. We never knew either father very well, just vague memories. They were sailors, wanderers. Our mother died when we were still very young. I looked after him for much of his life; I was better at it than he was. I know him; I understand him. I know his abilities and shortcomings, strengths and weaknesses. I've seen him succeed and fail. I wouldn't lie about him to anyone, least of all to myself. So when I tell you Big Red is worth two of any other man, you should listen to me. When I tell you he's the best man you'll find for your journey, you ought to pay attention."

"I am," Walker said quietly.

She smiled. "Well, where would you go if you didn't want to? You're my captive audience." She paused, studying him. "You have intelligence, Walker. I can see you thinking all the time. I look inside your eyes and see your mind at work. You listen, you measure, and you judge accordingly. You'll make your own decision about this expedition and us. What I say won't influence you. That's not why I'm telling you how I feel about Big Red. I'm telling you so you will know where I stand."

She paused and waited, and after a moment, he nodded. "That's fair enough."

She sighed and shifted on the seat. "Frankly, I don't care about the money. I have enough of that. What I don't have is peace of mind or a sense of future or something to believe in again. I had those once, when I was younger. Somewhere along the way, I lost them. I'm sick at heart and worn-out. The past three years, fighting on the Prekkendorran, chasing Free-born back and forth across the heights, killing them now and then, burning their airships, spilling fire on their camps—it charred my soul. The whole business was stupid. A war over land, over territorial rights, over national dominion—what does any of it matter? Except for the money, I have nothing to show for that experience."

She fixed him with her green eyes. "I don't sense this about your expedition. I don't feel that a Druid would bother with something so petty. Tell me the truth—is your enterprise going to offer anything more?"

She was so intense as she stared at him that he was momentarily taken aback by her depth of feeling. "I'm not sure," he said after a moment. "There is more to what I'm asking you to do than the money I've offered. There are lives at stake besides our own. There are freedoms to be lost and maybe a world to be changed for better or worse. I can't see far enough into the future to be certain. But I can tell you this much. By going, we might make a difference that will mean something to you later."

She smiled. "We're going to save the world, is that it?"

His face remained expressionless. "We might."

The smile disappeared. "All right, I won't make a joke of it. I won't even suggest you might be overstating what's possible. I'll allow myself to believe a little in what you're promising. It can't hurt. A little belief on both sides might be a good beginning to a partnership, don't you think?"

He nodded, smiling. "I do."

Bird cries heralded the arrival of dawn, and as the early

light broke through the darkness, massive cliffs rose against the skyline, craggy and barren facings lashed by wind and surf. At first it appeared as if there was no way through the formidable barrier. But the ship ahead lit a lantern and hoisted it aloft, and a pair of lamps responding from shoreside indicated the approach. Even then, it was not apparent that an opening existed until they were almost on top of it. The light was thin and faint, the air clogged by mist and spray, and the thunder of waves crashing on the rocks an unmistakable warning to stay clear. But the Captain of the ship ahead proceeded without hesitation, navigating between rocks large enough to sink even his craft, let alone the skiff in which Walker rode.

Redden Alt Mer was awake again, standing at the tiller, steering the skiff with a sure hand in the wake of the two-master. Walker glanced back at him, and was surprised to find his features alive with happiness and expectation. Alt Mer was enjoying this, caught up in the excitement and challenge of sailing, at home in a way most could never be.

Standing next to him, Rue Meridian was smiling, as well.

They passed through the rocks and into a narrow channel, the skiff rising and falling on the roiling sea. Gulls and cormorants circled overhead, their cries echoing eerily off the cliff walls. Ahead lay a broad cove surrounded by forested cliffs with waterfalls that tumbled hundreds of feet out of the misted heights. As they sailed from the turbulence of the channel into the relative calm of the harbor, the sounds of wind and surf faded and the waters smoothed. Behind them, the lamps that had been lit to guide their way in winked out.

Etched out of gloom and mist, the first signs of a settlement appeared. There was no mistaking its nature. A sprawling shipyard fronted the waters of the cove, complete with building cradles and docks, forges, and timber stores. A cluster of ships lay anchored at the north end of the cove, sleek and dark against the silvery waters, and by the glint of radian draws and the odd slant of light sheaths furled and waiting for release, Walker recognized them as airships.

As they neared the shoreline, the towing ship dropped anchor, and a small transport was lowered with a pair of sailors at the oars. It rowed back to the skiff and took Walker and the Rovers aboard. Alt Mer and his sister greeted the sailors familiarly, but did not introduce the Druid. They rowed ashore through hazy light and swooping birds and disembarked at one of the docks. Dockworkers were hauling supplies back and forth along the waterfront, and laborers were just beginning their workday. The sounds of hammers and saws broke the calm, and the settlement seemed to come awake all at once.

"This way," Redden Alt Mer advised, starting off down the dock toward the beach.

They stepped onto dry land and proceeded left through the shipyards, past the forges and cradles, to where a building sat facing the water. A broad covered porch fronted the building, with narrow trestle tables set along its length. Sheaves of paper were spread upon the tables and held in place by bricks. Men worked their way from one set of papers to the next, examining their writings, marking them for adjustments and revisions.

The man who supervised this work looked up at their approach and then came down the steps to meet them. He was a huge, burly fellow with arms and legs like tree trunks, a head of wild black hair, and a ruddy, weathered face partially obscured by a thick beard. He wore the bright sashes and gold earrings favored by Rovers, and his scowl belied the twinkle in his bird-sharp eyes.

"Morning, all," he growled, sounding less than cheerful. His black eyes lit on Walker. "Hope you're a customer who's deaf, dumb, and blind, and comes ready to share a small fortune with those less fortunate than yourself. Because if not, I might as well kill you now and have done with it. Big Red knows the rules."

Walker did not change expression or evidence concern, even when he heard Redden Alt Mer groan. "I've been told that by coming here I have a chance to do business with the best shipbuilder alive. Would that be you?"

"It would." The black eyes shifted to Alt Mer suspiciously, then back to Walker. "You don't look stupid, but then you don't look like a man with a fat purse, either. Who are you?"

"I'm called Walker."

The burly man studied him in silence. "The Druid?"

Walker nodded.

"Well, well, well. This might prove interesting after all. What would bring a Druid out of Paranor these days? Don't think it would be anything small." He stuck out a massive hand. "I'm Spanner Frew."

Walker accepted the hand and shook it. The hand felt as if it had been cast in iron. "Druids go where they are needed," he said.

"That must be extremely difficult when there is only one of you." Spanner Frew chuckled, a deep, booming rasp. "How did you have the misfortune to fall in with these thieves? Not that young Ruo wouldn't turn the head of any man, mine included."

"Cicatrix sent them to me."

"Ah, a brave and unfortunate man," the shipbuilder allowed with a solemn nod, surprising Walker. "Lost everything but his mind in a shipwreck that wasn't his fault but was blamed on him nevertheless. Do you know about it?"

"Only the rumors. I know Cicatrix from other places and times. Enough to trust him."

"Well said. So you've tied in with Big and Little Red and come looking for a shipbuilder. That must mean you have a voyage in mind and need a ship worthy of the effort. Tell me about it."

Walker provided a brief overview of what it was he required and how it would be used. He gave Spanner Frew no more information than he had Redden Alt Mer, but was encouraging where he could be. He had already decided he liked the man. What remained to be determined was his skill as a craftsman.

When Walker was finished, Spanner Frew's scowl deepened and his brow creased. "This would be a long voyage you're planning, one that could take years perhaps?"

Walker nodded.

"You'll need your ship for living quarters, supplies, and cargo when you arrive at your destination. You'll need it for defense against the enemies you might encounter. You'll need it to be weatherworthy, because there's storms on the Blue Divide that can shred a ship of the line in minutes." He was listing Walker's requirements in a matter-of-fact way, no longer asking questions. "You'll need weapons that will serve on both land and air. You'll need replacement parts that can't be found on your travels—radian draws and ambient-light sheaves, parse crystals and the like. A big order. Very big."

He glanced at the workmen behind him, then off at the harbor. "But your resources are plentiful and your purse is deep?"

Walker nodded once more.

Spanner Frew folded his beefy arms. "I have the ship for you. Just completed, a sort of prototype for an entire line. There's nothing else like her flying the Four Lands. She's a warship, but built for long-range travel and extended service. I was going to offer her on the open market, a special item for those fools who keep trying to kill each other above the Prekkendorran. If they liked her well enough, and I think they would, I'd build them a few dozen more and retire a rich man." His scowl became a menacing grin. "But I would rather sell her to you, I think. Care for a look?"

He took them north all the way through the shipyards to where the beach opened on a series of rocky outcroppings and the fleet Walker had seen earlier when entering the harbor lay at rest. There were nearly a dozen ships of various sizes, but only one that caught the Druid's eye. He knew it was the ship Spanner Frew had been talking about even before the other spoke.

"That's her," the burly shipbuilder indicated with a nod and a gesture. "You picked her out right away, didn't you?"

She was built like a catamaran, but much larger. She was low and sleek and wicked looking, her wood and stays and even her light sheaves dark in color, and her twin masts raked ever so slightly, giving her the appearance of being in motion even when she lay at rest. Her decking rested on a pair of pontoons set rather close together, their ends hooking upward into twin horns at either end, their midsections divided into what appeared to be fighting compartments that could hold men and weapons. Her railings slanted away and back from her sides, bow, and stern to allow for storage and protection from weather and attacks. The pilothouse sat amidships between the masts, raised well above the decking and enclosed by shields that gave ample protection to the helmsman. Low, flat living quarters and storage housing sat forward and aft of the masts, broad but curved in the shape of the decking and pontoons to minimize wind resistance. The living and sleeping quarters were set into the decking and extended almost to the waterline, giving an unexpected depth to the space.

Everything was smooth and curved and gleamed like polished metal, even in the faint, misted light of the cove.

"She's beautiful," Walker said, turning to Spanner Frew. "How does she fly?"

"Like she looks. Like a dream. I've had her up myself and tested her. She'll do everything you ask of her and more. She lacks the size and weapons capability of a ship of the line, but she more than makes up for it in speed and agility. Of course," he added, glancing now at Redden Alt Mer, "she needs a proper Captain."

Walker nodded. "I'm looking for one. Do you have any suggestions?"

The shipbuilder broke into a long gale of laughter, practically doubling over from the effort. "Oh, that's very good, very funny! I hope you caught the look on Big Red's face when you said that! Why, he looked as if he'd been jerked by his short hairs! Hah, you do make me laugh, Druid!"

Walker's solemn face was directed back toward the ship. "Well, I'm glad you're amused, but the question is a serious one. The bargain we strike for the purchase of the ship includes the builder's agreement to come with her."

Spanner Frew stopped laughing at once. "What? What did you say?"

"Put yourself in my position," Walker replied mildly, still looking out at the harbor and the ship. "I'm a stranger seeking the help of a people who are notorious for striking bargains that have more than one interpretation. Rovers don't lie in their business dealings, but they do shade the truth and bend the rules when it benefits them. I accept this. I am a part of an order that has been known to do the same. But how do I protect myself in a situation where the advantage is all the other way?"

"You had best place a tight hold on—" the shipbuilder began, but Walker cut him short with a gesture.

"Just listen a moment. Redden Alt Mer tells me he is the best airship Captain alive. Rue Meridian agrees. You tell me you are the best shipbuilder alive and this craft you wish to sell me is the best airship ever built. I will assume all of you agree that I can do no better, so I won't even ask. In fact, I'm inclined to agree, from what I've seen and heard. I believe you. But since I'm going to give you half your money in advance, how do I reassure myself that I haven't made a mistake?"

He turned now and faced them squarely. "I do it by taking you with me. I don't think for a moment you would sail in a ship or with a Captain you don't trust. If you go, it means you have faith in both and I know I haven't been misled."

"But I can't go!" Spanner Frew shouted in fury.

Walker paused. "Why not?"

"Because . . . because I'm a builder, not a sailor!"

"Agreed. That's mostly why I want you with me. Those repairs you spoke of earlier, the ones that would be required after an encounter with enemies or storms. I would feel better if you were supervising them."

The shipbuilder gestured expansively at the shore behind them. "I can't leave all these projects half completed! They need my skills here! There are others just as competent who can go in my place!"

"Leave them," Walker said calmly. "If they are as competent as you, let them complete your work here." He stepped forward, closing the distance between them until they were almost touching. Spanner Frew, his face flushed and scowling, held his ground. "I haven't told this to many, but I will tell it to you. What we go to do is more important than anything you will ever do here. What is required of those who do go is a courage and strength of will and heart that few possess. I think you are one. Don't disappoint me. Don't refuse me out of hand. Give some thought to what I'm saying before you make up your mind."

There was a momentary silence. Then Redden Alt Mer cleared his throat. "That sounds fair, Spanner."

The shipbuilder wheeled on him. "I don't care a whit what you think is fair or not, Big Red! This has nothing to do with you!"

"It has everything to do with him," Rue Meridian cut in sharply. She gave him a slow, mocking smile. "What's the matter, Black Beard? Have you grown old and timid?"

For just a moment, Walker thought the burly shipbuilder was going to explode. He stood there shaking with fury and frustration, his big hands knotted. "I wouldn't let anyone else alive speak to me like that!" he hissed at her.

A knife appeared in her hand as if by magic. She flipped it in the air above her, caught it, and made it vanish in the blink of an eye. "You used to be a pretty fair pirate, Spanner Frew," she prodded. "Wouldn't you like the chance to be one again? How long since you've sailed the Blue Divide?"

"How long since you've ridden the back of the wind to a new land?" her brother added. "It would make you young again, Spanner. The Druid's right. Come with us."

Rue Meridian looked at Walker. "You'll pay him, of course. The same as you'll pay Big Red and me."

She made it a statement of fact for him to affirm, and he did so with a nod. Spanner Frew looked from face to face in disbelief. "You're committed to this, aren't you?" he demanded of Walker.

The Druid nodded.

"Shades!" the shipbuilder breathed softly. Then abruptly he shrugged. "Well, let it lay for now. Let's sit for breakfast and see how we feel when we have full stomachs. I could eat a horse, saddle and all. Hah!" he roared, pounding his midsection. "Come along, you bunch of thieves! Trying to drag an honest man off on a voyage to nowhere! Trying to make a poor shipbuilder think he might have something to offer a clutch of madmen and madder women! Spare me, I hope you've not picked my purse, as well!"

He wheeled back in the direction of the settlement, shouting out epithets and protests as he went, leaving them to follow after.

They ate breakfast in a communal dining hall assembled beneath a huge tent, the cooking fires and pots all set toward the back of the enclosure where they could vent, the tables and benches toward the front. Everything had a makeshift, knockdown look to it, and when Walker asked Spanner Frew how long the settlement had been there, the shipbuilder advised him that they moved at least every other year to protect themselves. They were Rovers in the old tradition, and the nature of their lives and business dealings involved a certain amount of risk and required at least a modicum of secrecy. They valued anonymity and mobility, even when they weren't directly threatened by those who found them a nuisance or considered them enemies, and it made them feel more secure to shift periodically from one location to another. It wasn't difficult, the big man explained. There were dozens of coves like this one located up and down the coast, and only the equally reclusive and discreet Wing Riders knew them as well.

As they dined, Spanner Frew explained that those who worked and lived here frequently brought their families, and that the settlement provided housing and food for all. The younger members of the family were trained in the shipbuilding crafts or pressed into service in related pursuits. All contributed to the welfare of the community, and all were sworn to secrecy concerning the settlement's location and work. These were open secrets in the larger Rover community, but Rovers never revealed such things to outsiders unless first ascertaining that they were trustworthy. So it was that Walker would not have found Spanner Frew if Cicatrix had not first assured Redden Alt Mer of the Druid's character.

"Otherwise, you would have been approached in March Brume and a business deal struck there," the shipbuilder grunted around a mouthful of hash, "which, come to think of it, might have been just as well for me!"

Nevertheless, by the time breakfast was finished, Spanner Frew was talking as if he might be reconsidering his insistence on not going with Walker. He began cataloguing the supplies and equipment that would be required, advising as to where they might best be stored, mulling over the nature of the crew to be assembled, and weighing the role he might play as helmsman, a position he had mastered years earlier in his time at sea. He reassured Walker that Redden Alt Mer was the best airship Captain he knew and was the right choice for the journey. He said little about Rue Meridian, beyond commenting now and then on her enchanting looks and sharp tongue, but it was clear he believed brother and sister a formidable team. Walker said little, letting the garrulous shipbuilder carry the conversation, marking the looks that passed between the three, and taking mental notes on the way they interacted with one another.

"One thing I want understood from the beginning," Redden Alt Mer said at one point, addressing the Druid directly. "If we agree to accept you as expedition leader, you must agree in turn that as Captain I command aboard ship. All decisions regarding the operation of the vessel and the safety of the crew and passengers while in flight will be mine."

Neither Rue Meridian nor Spanner Frew showed any inclination to disagree. After a moment's consideration, Walker nodded, as well.

"In all things," he corrected gently, "save matters of destination and rate of progress. In those, you must give way to me. Where we go and how fast we get there is my province alone."

"Save where you endanger us, perhaps unknowingly," the other declared with a smile, unwilling to back down completely. "Then, you must heed my advice."

"Then," Walker replied, "we will talk."

They rowed out to the ship afterwards, and Spanner Frew walked them from bow to stern, explaining how she was constructed and what she could do. Walker studied closely the ship's configuration, from fighting ports to pilothouse, noting everything, asking questions when it was necessary, growing steadily more confident of the ship's ability to do what was needed. But already he was reassessing the amount of space he had determined would be available for use, realizing that more would be needed for weapons and supplies than he had anticipated. Consequently, he would have to scale down the number of expedition members. The crew was already pared down to a bare minimum, even with the addition of Spanner Frew. That meant he would have to reduce his complement of fighting men. The Elves would not like that, but there was no help for it. Forty men were too many. At best, they could take thirty-five, and even that would be crowding the living space.

He discussed this at length with the Rovers, trying to find a way to make better use of the available space. Redden Alt Mer said the crew could sleep above decks in hammocks strung between masts and railings, and Spanner Frew suggested they could reduce their supplies and equipment if they were willing to chance that foraging in the course of their travels would produce what was needed in the way of replacements. It was a balancing act, an educated guessing game at determining what would suffice, but Walker was somewhat reassured by the fact that they would have the aid of Wing Riders for foraging purposes and so could afford to take chances they might otherwise never have considered.

By the close of the day, they had settled on what was needed in the way of onboard adjustments and compiled a list of supplies and equipment to be secured. A crew of Redden Alt Mer's choosing would be found in the surrounding seaports and could be readily assembled. Ship, Captain, and crew, Spanner Frew included, could be in Arborlon within a week.

Walker was satisfied. Everything was proceeding as he had hoped. After a good night's sleep, he would depart for March Brume.

But he was to get little rest that night.

The attack on the settlement came just before sunset. A sentry perched high on a cliff overlooking the cove blew a ram's horn in warning, three sharp blasts that shattered the twilight calm and sent everyone scurrying. By the time the dark hulls of the airships hove into view through the gap in the cove entry, sailing out of the glare of the setting sun, the Rover women and children and old people were already fleeing into the forests and mountains and the Rover men were preparing to defend them.

But the attacking ships outnumbered those of the Rovers by more than two to one, and they were already airborne and readied for their strike. They streamed through the harbor entrance in a dark line, flying less than a hundred feet above the water, railings and fighting ports bristling with men and weapons. Fire from casks of pitch and catapults rained down on the exposed vessels and their crews. Spears and arrows filled the air. Half of the Rover ships burned and sank before their sails could even be hoisted. Dozens of men died in the ensuing conflagrations and many more died in the small boats attempting to reach them.

Solely by chance, Walker and his three Rover companions were spared the fate of so many. Just before the attack arrived, they had been testing the responsiveness of their ship. As a result, they were still aboard when the warning was given, light sheaths yet unfurled, radian draws in place, and the anchor barely down. The Rovers acted instantly, leaping to tighten the stays and reset the draws, cutting the anchor with a sword stroke, and casting off. In seconds, they were airborne, lifting toward their attackers like a swift, black bird. Even with only three hands to sail her, she responded with a quickness and agility that left the enemy ships looking as if they were standing still.

A safety line secured about his waist, Walker crouched just in front of the pilothouse and behind the forward mast and watched the land and water spin away in a dizzying rush. With Spanner Frew and Rue Meridian manning the starboard and port draws respectively, Redden Alt Mer wheeled their sleek craft recklessly through the dark line of attackers, nearly colliding with those nearest. The hulls of ships loomed on either side, sliding past like night phantoms, great massive ghosts at hunt. Some passed so close that Walker could identify the Federation uniforms worn by the soldiers who knelt in the fighting ports firing their arrows and launching their spears.

"Hold tight!" Alt Mer shouted down to him from atop his precarious station, hauling back on the steering levers to gain more height and speed.

Missiles flew everywhere, dark projectiles against the twin glows of the sunset and the fires in the harbor. Walker flattened himself against the rough wall of the pilothouse, protecting his back. He did not want to use magic. If he did, he would reveal his presence, and he thought it best not to do so. To his right, crouched deep in one of the fighting ports, so close to the nearest ship that he could have reached out and touched it, Spanner Frew was cursing loudly under a hail of bow fire. Across from him, Rue Meridian was dashing recklessly from draw to draw, miraculously avoiding the barrage of arrows that sailed all around her, dark face grim and determined as she set the lines.

Their wild, hair-raising escape was punctuated by the underside of their ship raking across the mastheads of the last attacker as they finally gained the safety of the open skies. All about them, the remaining Rover airships were fleeing into the darkness, skimming across the cliff tops, and disappearing down the coast. Below, their attackers were descending on the settlement buildings, setting fire to everything, and driving the last of the residents into the surrounding forests. Masts jutting sharply against the flaming debris, dark hulls glided everywhere.

As their vessel steadied and their passage smoothed, Rue Meridian appeared at Walker's side. "Those were Federation ships!" she snapped angrily. Her face was streaked with soot and sweat. "They must be madder at us than I thought! All those people driven out or killed, their ships and homes burned, just to make a point?"

Walker shook his head. "I don't think it was you they were after." He caught her startled gaze and held it. "Nor do I think it was the Federation who was behind this witch hunt."

She hesitated a moment, then let her breath out in a long, slow hiss of understanding.

Behind them, hidden by the cliffs they were fleeing and reduced to a reddish-yellow glow against the darkness of night, Rover buildings burned unhindered to the ground and gutted airships sank into the deep.

THIRTEEN

Provisioned and readied, Bek Rowe and Quentin Leah departed at daybreak and rode east through the Highlands. The day was cool and clear, with the smell of new grass and flowers heavy on the scented air and the sun warm on their faces. Clouds were massing west, however, and there was a clear possibility of rain by nightfall. Under the best of conditions it would take them several days just to navigate as far as the Eastland and the beginning of their search for the mysterious Truls Rohk. In the old days, before invasion and occupation by the Federation army, they could never have gone this way. Directly in their path lay the Lowlands of Clete, a vast, dismal bog choked with deadwood and scrub, shrouded in mist and devoid of life. Beyond that were the Black Oaks, an immense forest that had claimed more victims than either of the young men cared to count, most to mishap and starvation, but some, in earlier times, to the huge wolves that were once its fiercest denizens. All this was daunting enough, but even after navigating bog and woods, a traveler wasn't safe. Just east of the Black Oaks was the Mist Marsh, a treacherous swamp in which, it was rumored, creatures of enormous power and formidable magic prowled. Below the marsh, and running south for a hundred miles, were the Battlemound Lowlands, another rugged, difficult stretch of country populated by Sirens, deadly plants that could lure and hypnotize by mimicking voices and shapes, seize with tentacle-like roots, paralyze with flesh-numbing needles, and devour their victims at leisure.

None of this was anything the cousins wanted to encounter, but all were difficult to avoid in making passage below the Rainbow Lake. Any route that would take them above the Rainbow Lake would cost them an additional three days at least and involved dangers of their own. Traveling farther south required a detour of better than a hundred miles and would put them almost to the Prekkendorran, a place no one in his right mind wanted to be.

But the Federation had realized this, as well, during the time of its occupation of Leah and so had built roads through Clete and the Black Oaks to facilitate the movement of men and supplies. Many of these roads had fallen into disrepair and could no longer be used by wagons, but all were passable by men on horseback. Quentin, because he was the older of the two, had explored more thoroughly the lands they intended to pass through, and was confident they could find their way to the Anar without difficulty.

True to his prediction, they made good progress that first day. By midday, they had ridden out of the Highlands and into the dismal morass of Clete. Sun and sky disappeared and the cousins were buried beneath a dismal gray shroud of mist and gloom. But the road remained visible, and they pressed on. Their pace slowed as the terrain grew more treacherous, scrub and tree limbs closing in so that they were forced to duck and weave as they went, guiding their horses around encroaching pools of quicksand and bramble patches, picking their way resolutely through the haze. Shadows moved all about them, some cast by movements of light, others by things that had somehow managed to survive in this blasted land. They heard sounds, but the sounds were not identifiable. Their conversation died away and time slowed. Their concentration narrowed to keeping safely on the road.

But by the approach of nightfall, they had navigated the lowlands without incident and moved into the forbidding darkness of the Black Oaks. The road here was less uneven and better traveled, the way open and clear as they rode into a steadily lengthening maze of shadows. With twilight's fall, they stopped within a clearing and made camp for the night. A fire was built, a meal prepared and eaten, and bedding laid out. The cousins joked and laughed and told stories for a time, then rolled into their blankets and fell asleep.

Sleep lasted until just after midnight, when it began to rain so hard that the clearing was flooded in a matter of minutes. Bek and Quentin snatched up their gear and retreated to the shelter of a large conifer, covering themselves with their travel cloaks as they sat beneath a canopy of feathery branches and watched the rain sweep through unabated.

By morning they were stiff and sore and not very well rested, but they resumed their travels without complaint. In other circumstances, they would have come better equipped, but neither had wanted the burden of pack animals and supplies, and so they were traveling light. A few nights of damp and cold were tolerable in the course of a week's passage if it meant shaving a few days off their traveling time. They ate a cold breakfast, then rode all morning through the Black Oaks, and by afternoon the rain had abated and they had reached the Battlemound. Here they turned south, unwilling to chance crossing through any part of the Mist Marsh, content to detour below the swamp and come out to the east, where they would turn north again and ride until they reached the Silver River.

By sunset, they had succeeded in accomplishing their goal, avoiding Sirens and other pitfalls, keeping to the roadway until it meandered off south, then sticking to the open ground of the lowlands as the terrain changed back to forests and low hills and they could see the glittering ribbon of the river ahead. Finding shelter in a grove of cottonwood and beech, they made camp on its banks, the ground sufficiently dry that they could lay out their bedding and build a fire. They watered and fed the horses and rubbed them down. Then they made dinner for themselves and, after eating it, sat facing out toward the river and the night, sipping cups of ale as they talked.

"I wish we knew more about Truls Rohk," Bek ventured after the conversation had been going on for a time. "Why do you think Walker told us so little about him?"

Quentin contemplated the star-filled sky thoughtfully. "Well, he told us where to go to find him. He said all we had to do was ask and he would be there. Seems like enough to me."

"It might be enough for you, but not for me. It doesn't tell us anything about why we're looking for him. How come he's so important?" Bek was not about to be appeased. "If we're to persuade him to come with us to Arborlon, shouldn't we know why he's needed? What if he doesn't want to come? What are we supposed to do then?"

Quentin grinned cheerfully. "Pack up and go on. It isn't our problem if he chooses to stay behind." He grimaced. "See, there you go again, Bek, worrying when there isn't any reason for it."

"So you're fond of telling me. So I'll tell you something else that's worrying me. I don't trust Walker."

They stared at each other in the darkness without speaking, the fire beginning to burn down, the sounds of the night lifting out of the sudden silence. "What do you mean?" Quentin asked slowly. "You think he's lying to us?"

"No." Bek shook his head emphatically. "If I thought that, I wouldn't be here. No, I don't think he's that sort. But I do think he knows something he's not telling us. Maybe a lot of somethings. Think about it, Quentin. How did he know about you and the Sword of Leah? He knew you had it before he even talked to us. How did he find out? Has he been keeping an eye on you all these years, waiting for a chance to summon you on a quest? How did he manage to convince your father to let us go with him, when your father wouldn't even consider your request to fight for the Free-born?"

He stopped abruptly. He wanted to tell Quentin what Coran had said about his parentage. He wanted to ask Quentin why he thought Coran hadn't said a word about it until the Druid appeared. He wanted to ask his cousin if he had any idea how the Druid had ended up ferrying him to the Leah doorstep in the first place, not a task a Druid would normally undertake.

But he was not prepared to talk about any of this just yet; he was still mulling it over, trying to decide how he felt about it before sharing what he knew.

"I think you're right," Quentin said suddenly, surprising him. "I think the Druid's keeping secrets from us, not the least of which is where we're going and why. But I've listened to you expound on Druids and their history often enough to know that this is normal behavior for them. They know things we don't, and they keep the information mostly to themselves. Why should that trouble you? Why not just let things unfold in the way they're intended rather than worry about it? Look at me. I'm carrying a sword that's supposed to be magic. I'm supposed to trust blindly in a weapon that's never shown a moment's inclination to be more than what it seems."

"That's different," Bek insisted.

"No, it isn't." Quentin laughed and rocked back onto his elbows, stretching out his long legs. "It's all the same thing. You can live your life worrying about what you don't know, or you can accept your limitations and make the best of it. Secrets don't harm you, Bek. It's fussing about them that does you in."

Bek gave him a disbelieving look. "That's entirely wrong. Secrets can do a great deal of harm."

"All right, let me approach it another way." Quentin drained off his ale and sat forward again. "How much can you accomplish worrying about secrets that may not exist? Especially when you have no idea what they are?"

"I know. I know." Bek sighed. "But at least I'm prepared for the fact that some nasty surprises might lie ahead. At least I'm ready for what I think is going to happen down the road.

And by keeping an eye on Walker, I won't be caught off guard by his shadings of the truth and purposeful omissions."

"Great. You're prepared and you won't be fooled. Me, too, believe it or not—even if I don't worry about it as much as you." Quentin looked off into the darkness, where a shooting star streaked across the firmament and disappeared. "But you can't prepare against everything, Bek, and you can't save yourself from being fooled now and then. The fact is, no matter what you do, no matter how hard you try, sometimes your efforts fall short."

Bek looked at him and said nothing. True enough, he was thinking, but he didn't care for the implications.

He slept undisturbed by rain and cold that night, the skies clear and the air warm, and he did not dream or toss. Even so, he woke in the deep sleep hours of early morning, bathed in starlight and infused by a feeling of uneasiness. The fire had burned itself out and lay cold and gray. Beside him, Quentin was snoring, wrapped in his blankets. Bek did not know how long he had been asleep, but the moon was down and the forest about him was silent and black.

He rose without thinking, looking around cautiously as he did so, trying to pinpoint the source of his discomfort. There seemed to be no reason for it. He pulled on his great cloak, wrapping himself tightly against a sudden chill, and walked down to the banks of the Silver River. The river was swollen with spring rains and snowmelt off the Runne Mountains, but its progress this night was sluggish and steady and its surface clear of debris. As he stood there, a night bird swooped down and glided into the trees, a silent, purposeful shadow. He started at the unexpected movement, then quieted once more. Carefully, he studied the glittering surface of the waters, searching for what troubled him, then shifted his attention to the far bank and the shadowed trees. Still nothing. He took a deep breath and exhaled. Perhaps he had been mistaken.

He was turning back toward Quentin when he saw the

light. It was just a glimmer of brightness at first, as if a spark had been struck somewhere back in the trees across the river. He stared at it in surprise as it appeared, faded, reappeared, faded anew, then steadied and came on. It bobbed slightly with its approach to the river, then glided out of the trees, suspended on air and floating free as it crossed the water and came to a halt just yards away from him.

It flashed sharply in his eyes, and he blinked in response. When his vision cleared, a young girl stood before him, the light balanced in her hand. She was somehow familiar to him, although he could not say why. She was beautiful, with long dark hair and startling blue eyes, and there was an innocence to her face that made his heart ache. The light she held emanated from one end of a polished metal cylinder and cast a long, narrow beam on the ground between them.

"Well met, Bek Rowe," she said softly. "Do you know me?"

He stared, unable to answer. She had appeared out of nowhere, perhaps come from across the river on the air itself, and he believed her to be a creature of magic.

"You have chosen to undertake a long and difficult journey, Bek," she whispered in her childlike voice. "You go to a place where few others have gone and from which only one has returned. But the greater journey will not carry you over land and sea, but inside your heart. The unknown you fear and the secrets you suspect will reveal themselves. All will be as it must. Accept this, for that is the nature of things."

"Who are you?" he whispered.

"This and that. What you see before you and many things you do not. I am a chameleon of time and age, my true form so old I have forgotten it. For you, I am two things. The child you see and think you might perhaps know, and this."

Abruptly, the child before him transformed into something so hideous he would have screamed if his voice had not frozen in his throat. The thing was huge and twisted and ugly, all wrapped in scarred and ravaged skin, hair burnt to a black stubble about its head and face, eyes maddened and red, mouth twisted in a leer that suggested horrors too terrible to contemplate. It loomed over him, tall even when bent, its clawed and crooked hands gesturing hypnotically.

"Thiss am I, too, Bek. Thiss creature of the pitss. Would you ssee me thiss way or the other? Hsss. Which do you prefer?"

"Change back," Bek managed to whisper, his voice harsh, his throat gone dry and raw and tight with fear.

"Sso, foundling of ill fortune. What are you willing to do to make it happen? Hsss. How much of yoursself are you prepared to ssacrifisse to make it sso?"

The thing almost touched him, claws brushing against the front of his tunic. He would have run if he could, would have called out to Quentin, sleeping not fifty feet away. But he could do nothing, only stand in place and stare fixedly at the apparition before him.

"Yourss iss the power to change me from one to the other," the creature hissed. "Do not forget thiss. Do not forget. Hsss."

Once more the creature transformed in the blink of an eye, and Bek found himself looking into the kind, pale eyes of an old, weathered man.

"Do not be afraid, Bek Rowe," the old man said softly, his voice warm and reassuring. "Nothing comes to harm you this night. I am here to protect you. Do you know me now?"

Surprisingly, he did. "You are the King of the Silver River."

The old man nodded approvingly. A legend in the Four Lands, a myth whose reality only a few had ever encountered, the King of the Silver River was a spirit creature, a magical being who had survived from times long before even the Great Wars had destroyed the world. He was as old as the Word, it was said, a creature who had been born into and survived the passing of Faerie. He lived within and gave protection to the Silver River country. Now and then, a traveler would encounter him, and sometimes when it was needed, he would give them aid.

"Heed me, Bek," the old man said softly. "What I have shown you is the past and the present. What remains to be determined is the future. That future belongs to you. You are both more and less than you believe, an enigma whose secret will affect the lives of many. Do not shy from discovering what you must, what you feel compelled to know. Do not be deterred in your search. Go where your heart tells you. Trust in what it reveals."

Bek nodded, not certain he understood, but unwilling to admit as much.

"Past, present, and future, the symbiosis of our lives," the old man continued quietly, gently. "Our birth, our life, our death, all tied into a single package that we spend our time on this earth unwrapping. Sometimes we see clearly what it is we are looking at. Sometimes we do not. Sometimes things happen to distract or deceive us, and we must look more carefully at what it is we hold."

He reached into his robes then and produced a chain from which hung a strange, silver-colored stone. He held up the stone for Bek to see. "This is a phoenix stone. When you are most lost, it will help you find your way. Not just from what you cannot see with your eyes, but from what you cannot find with your heart, as well. It will show you the way back from dark places into which you have strayed and the way forward through dark places into which you must go. When you have need of it, remove it from the chain and cast it to the ground, breaking it apart. Remember. In your body, heart, and mind—all will be revealed with this."

He passed the stone and its chain to Bek, who took it carefully. The depths of the phoenix stone seemed liquid, swirling as if a dark pool into which he might fall. He touched the surface gingerly, testing it. The movement stopped and the surface turned opaque.

"You may use it only once," the old man advised. "Keep it concealed from others. It is an indiscriminate magic. It will serve the bearer, even if stolen. Keep it safe."

Bek slipped the chain about his neck and tucked the stone into his clothing. "I will," he promised.

His mind was racing, trying to find words for the dozens of questions that suddenly filled it. But he could not seem to think straight, his concentration riveted on the old man and the light. The King of the Silver River watched him with his kind, appraising eyes, but did not offer to help.

"Who am I?" Bek blurted out in desperation.

He spoke without thinking, the words surfacing in a rush of need and urgency. It was this question that troubled him most, he realized at once, this question that demanded an answer above all others, because it had become for him in the last few days the great mystery of his life.

The old man gestured vaguely with one frail hand. "You are who you have always been, Bek. But your past is lost to you, and you must recover it. On this journey, that will happen. Seek it, and it will find you. Embrace it, and it will set you free."

Bek was not certain he had heard the old man right. What had he just said? Seek it, and it will find you—not, you will find it? What did that mean?

But the King of the Silver River was speaking again, cutting short Bek's thoughts. "Sleep, now. Take what I have given you and rest. No more can be accomplished this night, and you will need your strength for what lies ahead."

He gestured again, and Bek felt a great weariness descend. "Remember my words when you wake," the old man cautioned as he began to move away, the light wavering, back and forth, back and forth. "Remember."

The night was suddenly as warm and comforting in its darkness and silence as his bedroom at home. There was so much more that Bek wanted to ask, so much he would have known. But he was lying on the ground, his eyes heavy and his thinking clouded. "Wait," he managed to whisper.

But the King of the Silver River was fading away into the night, and Bek Rowe drifted off to sleep.

FOURTEEN

When Bek woke the next morning, he was back where he had started the night before, rolled into his blankets next to the defunct fire. It took him several minutes to shake off his confusion and decide that what he remembered about the King of the Silver River was real. It felt as if he had dreamed it, the events hazy and disjointed in his mind. But when he checked inside his tunic, there were the chain and phoenix stone, tucked safely away, just where he had put them before falling asleep.

He sleepwalked through breakfast and cleanup, thinking he should say something about the encounter to Quentin, but unable to bring himself to do so. It was a pattern he was developing with the events surrounding this journey, and it worried him. Normally, he shared everything with his cousin. They were close and trusted each other. But now he had kept from Quentin both his conversation with Coran and his midnight encounter with the being that claimed to be the King of the Silver River. Not to mention, he amended quickly, his possession of the phoenix stone. He wasn't entirely sure why he was doing this, but it had something to do with wanting to come to terms with the information himself before he shared it with anyone else.

He supposed that he was being overly cautious and perhaps even selfish, but the greater truth was that he was feeling confused and somewhat unnerved by all of this happening at once. It was difficult enough coming to grips with the idea of making a journey that would take him halfway around the world. This was Quentin's dream, not his. It was Quentin, with his sword of magic and his great courage, of whom the Druid Walker had need, and not Bek. Bek had agreed to go out of loyalty to his cousin and a rather fatalistic acceptance of the fact that if he stayed behind, he would be second-guessing himself forever. It was only in these recent developments with Coran and the King of the Silver River that he began to wonder if perhaps he had his own place on the expedition, a place he had never even imagined might exist.

So he kept what he knew to himself as they ate their food and packed their gear and set out once more, into a day that was bright and sunny. Loose and easy as always, Quentin joked and laughed and told stories as they rode, leaving Bek to play the role of the audience and to simmer in his own uncertainty. They rode upstream along the banks of the Silver River through a morning filled with spring smells and birdsong, through a backdrop of mingled green hues splashed with clusters of colorful wildflowers and the glint of sunlight off the river. They sighted fishermen seated on the banks of the river and anchored in skiffs just offshore in quiet coves, and they passed travelers on the road, mostly tradesmen and peddlers on their way between villages. The warm day seemed to infect everyone with a spirit of good humor, inviting smiles and waves and cheerful greetings from all.

By midday, the cousins had forded the Silver River just west of where it disappeared into the deep forests of the Anar and were traveling north along the treeline. It was a short journey from there to the Dwarf village of Depo Bent, a trading outpost nestled in the shadow of the Wolfsktaag, and the sun was still high when they arrived. Depo Bent was little more than a cluster of homes, warehouses, and shops sprung up around a clearing in the woods that opened up at the end of the sole road leading in or out from the plains. It was there that Bek and Quentin were to ask for Truls Rohk, although they had no idea of whom they were supposed to make inquiry.

They began their undertaking by leaving their horses at a stable where the owner promised a rubdown and feeding and watering. Bluff and to the point, in the way of Dwarves, he agreed for a small extra charge to store their gear. Freed of horses and equipment, the cousins walked to a tavern and enjoyed a hearty lunch of stew, bread, and ale. The tavern was visited mostly by the Dwarves of the village, but no one paid them any attention. Quentin was wearing the Sword of Leah strapped across his back in the fashion of Highlanders, and both wore Highlander clothing, but if the residents found it curious that the cousins were so far from home, they kept it to themselves.

"Truls Rohk must be a Dwarf," Quentin ventured as they ate. "No one else would be living here. Maybe he's a trapper of some sort."

Bek nodded agreeably, but he couldn't quite fathom why Walker would want a trapper on their journey.

After lunch, they began asking where they could find the man they were looking for and promptly discovered that no one knew. They started with the tavern's barkeep and owner and worked their way up and down the street from shop to warehouse, and everyone looked at them blankly. No one knew a man named Truls Rohk. No one had ever heard the name.

"Guess maybe he doesn't live here after all," Quentin conceded after more than twenty unsuccessful inquiries.

"Guess maybe he's not going to be as easy to find as Walker led us to believe," Bek grumbled.

Nevertheless, they pressed on, continuing their search, moving from one building to the next, the afternoon slipping slowly away from them. Eventually they had worked their way back around to the stables where they had left their horses and supplies. The stableman was nowhere in sight, but a solid-looking Dwarf dressed in woodsman's garb was sitting on a bench out front, whittling on a piece of wood. As the cousins approached, he glanced up, then set aside his knife and carving and rose.

"Quentin Leah?" he asked in a way that suggested he already knew the answer. Quentin nodded, and the Dwarf stuck out his gnarled hand. "I'm Panax. I'm your guide."

"Our guide?" Quentin repeated, extending his own hand in response. He winced at the other's grip. "You're taking us to Truls Rohk?"

The Dwarf nodded. "After a fashion."

"How did you know we were coming?" Bek asked in surprise.

"You must be Bek Rowe." Panax extended his hand a second time, and Bek shook it firmly. "Our mutual friend sent word. Now and then I do favors for him. There's a few of us he trusts enough to ask when he needs one." He glanced around idly. "Let's move somewhere less public while we talk this over."

They followed him down the road to a patch of shade where a clutch of weathered benches was grouped around an old well that hadn't seen much use lately. Panax gestured them to one bench while he took a second across from them. It was quiet and cool beneath the trees, and the traffic on the road and in the village suddenly seemed far away.

"Have you eaten?" he asked. He was a rough-featured, bearded man, no longer young. Deep lines furrowed his forehead, and his skin was browned and weathered from sun and wind. Whatever he did, he did it outdoors and had been at it for quite a while. "You look a little footsore," he observed.

"That's probably because we've tramped all over this village searching for Truls Rohk," Bek said sourly.

The Dwarf nodded. "I doubt that anyone in Depo Bent even knows who he is. If they do, they don't know him by his name." His brown eyes had a distant look, as if they were seeing beyond what was immediately visible.

Bek glared openly. "You could have saved us a lot of trouble by finding us sooner."

"I haven't been here all that long myself." Panax seemed unruffled. "I don't live in the village, I live in the mountains. When I got word you were coming, I came down to find you." He shrugged. "I knew you'd be back for your horses sooner or later, so I decided to wait for you at the stables."

Bek would have said more on the matter, but Quentin cut him short. "How much do you know about what's going on, Panax? Do you know what we're doing here?"

Panax snorted. "Walker is a Druid. A Druid doesn't feel it necessary to tell anyone more than what he feels they absolutely have to know."

Quentin smiled, unperturbed. "Do you think Truls Rohk knows more than you do?"

"Less." Panax shook his head, amused. "You don't know anything about him, do you?"

"Just that we're supposed to deliver a message from Walker," Bek said rather more sharply than he intended. He took a steadying breath. "I have to tell you that I don't like all this secrecy. How is anyone supposed to make a decision about anything if there's no information to be considered?"

The Dwarf laughed, a deep, booming sound. "You mean, how is Truls supposed to give you an answer to whatever question you're bringing from Walker? Hah! Highlander, that's not what you're doing here! Oh, I know you're carrying a message from the Druid. Let me guess. He wants you to tell Truls something about what he's up to now and see if Truls wants to be a part of it. Is that about right?"

He looked so smug that Bek wanted to tell him it wasn't, but Quentin was already nodding agreeably. "You have to understand something," Panax continued. "Truls doesn't care what Walker is up to. If he feels like going with him, which he usually does, he will. It doesn't take you two coming all the way here to determine that. No, Walker sent you here for something else."

Bek exchanged a quick glance with Quentin. To test the power of the Sword of Leah, Bek was thinking. To put them in a situation that would measure their determination and toughness. Suddenly, Bek was very worried. What sort of challenge were they being asked to measure up to?

"Maybe we should go talk with Truls Rohk right now," he suggested quickly, wanting to get on with things.

But the Dwarf shook his head. "We can't do that. First off, he won't be out until after dark. He doesn't do anything in the daylight. So we have to wait until nightfall. Second, it isn't a matter of going to him to have our talk. He has to come to us. We could hunt for him until next summer and never catch even a glimpse." He gave Bek a wink. "He's up in those mountains behind us, running with things you and I don't want anything to do with, believe me."

Bek shivered at the implication. He had heard stories of the things that lived in the Wolfsktaag, creatures out of myth and legend, nightmares come to life. They couldn't hurt you if you were careful, but a single misstep could lead to disaster.

"Tell us something about Truls Rohk," Quentin asked quietly.

Panax regarded him solemnly for about two heartbeats and then smiled almost gently. "I think I'd better wait and let you see for yourselves."

He changed the subject then, asking them for news about the Southland and the war between the Federation and the Free-born, listening intently to their answers and comments as he resumed work on the carving he had been shaping while awaiting their return to the stables. Bek was fascinated by the Dwarf's ability to divide his attention so completely between the tasks. His eyes were focused on the speakers, but his hands continued to whittle at the piece of wood with his knife. His blocky, solid body settled into a comfortable position and never shifted, still save for the careful, precise movement of his hands and the occasional nod of his bearded head.

He might have been there or gone somewhere else entirely inside his head; it was impossible to tell.

After a time, he placed the carving on the bench next to him, a finished piece, a bird in flight, perfectly realized. Without so much as a glance at it, he reached into his tunic, produced a second piece of wood, and went back to work. When Bek managed to work up sufficient courage to ask him what he did for a living, he deflected the question with a shrug.

"Oh, a little of this and a little of that." His bluff face was wreathed momentarily in an enigmatic smile. "I do some guiding for those who need help getting through the mountains."

Who, Bek wondered, would need help getting through the Wolfsktaag? Not the people who lived in this part of the world, the Dwarves and Gnomes who knew enough to avoid passing that way. Not the hunters and trappers who made their living off the forests of the Anar, who would choose better and safer working grounds. Not anyone who led a normal life, because there was no reason for those people to be here in the first place.

He must guide people like us, he concluded, who needed to go into the mountains to find someone like Truls Rohk. But how many like us can there be?

As if reading his thoughts, the Dwarf glanced at him and said, "Not many people, even Dwarves, know their way through these mountains—not well enough to know all the pitfalls and how to avoid them. I know because Truls Rohk taught me. He saved my life, and while I was healing from my wounds, he instructed me. Perhaps he thought he owed it to me to help me find a way to stay alive when I left him."

He stood up, stretched, and picked up his carvings. He handed the bird to Bek. "It's yours. Good luck against the things that frighten you now and again. Like a good carving, such things can be better understood when we give them shape and form. Whatever undertaking Walker has in store for you, you'll need all the protection you can get."

He started away without waiting for their response. "Time to be going. My place, first, then up into the mountains. We should be there by midnight and back again by sunrise. Take what you need for the hike in and leave the rest here. It'll be safe."

Bek tucked the carving into his tunic, and the cousins followed after obediently.

They walked out of Depo Bent and up into the shallow foothills fronting the peaks of the Wolfsktaag, the shadows lengthening before them as the sun settled into the west and twilight descended. The air cooled and the light failed, and a crescent moon appeared overhead to the north. They proceeded at a steady pace, climbing gradually out of the flats into more rugged country. Within a short while, the village had disappeared into the trees, and the trail had faded. Panax led the way, head up and eyes alert, giving no indication of having to think about where he was going, saying nothing to either of them. Bek and Quentin kept silent in turn, studying the forest around them, listening to the sounds of the approaching night begin to filter out of the twilight's hush—the cries of night birds, the buzz of insects, and the occasional huff or snort of something bigger. Nothing threatened, but the Wolfsktaag loomed ahead like a black wall, craggy and forbidding, its reputation a haunt at play in their minds.

It was fully dark by the time they reached Panax's cabin, a small, neat shelter built of logs and set back in a clearing near the crest of the foothills, well out of sight. A stream ran nearby, one they could hear but not see, and the trees formed a sheltering wall against the weather. Panax left them standing outside while he went into his home, then reappeared almost immediately carrying a sling looped through his belt and a long-handled double-edged battle-ax laid comfortably over one shoulder.

"Stay close to me and do whatever I tell you," he advised as he came up to them. "If we're attacked, use your weapons to defend yourselves, but don't go looking for trouble and don't become separated from me. Understood?"

They nodded uneasily. Attacked by what? Bek wanted to ask.

They left the cabin and the clearing behind, hiked through the trees to the lower slopes of the mountains, and began to climb. The way was unmarked, but Panax seemed to know it well. He took them in switchback fashion through clumps of boulders, stands of old growth, and shadowy ravines and defiles, steadily ascending the Wolfsktaag's rugged slopes. The night sky was clear and bright with moon and stars, and there was sufficient light to navigate by. They climbed for several hours, growing more alert as the trees began to thin, the rocks to broaden, and the silence to deepen. It grew colder, as well, the mountain air thin and sharp even on this windless night, and they could watch their breath cloud before them. Shadows passed overhead in smooth, silent flight, night hunters at work, secretive and swift.

Bek found himself thinking of his own life, a past wrapped in vague possibility and shrouded in concealments. Who was he, that a Druid had brought him to Coran Leah's doorstep all those years ago? Not just the orphaned scion of a relative with a family no one had ever heard anything about. Not just a homeless child. Who was he, that the King of the Silver River would appear so unexpectedly to give him a phoenix stone and a warning of dark and hidden meanings?

He found himself remembering all the times he had asked about his parents and had his questions deflected by Coran or Liria. Their actions had never seemed all that important before. It was bothersome sometimes not to be given the answers he sought, to be put off in his inquiries. But his life had been good with Quentin's family, and his curiosity had never been compelling enough to persuade him to insist on a better response. Now he wondered if he had been too accepting.

Or was he making something out of nothing, his parentage no more than what it had always seemed—an accident of birth of no consequence at all, incidental to his upbringing at the capable hands of his stepparents? Was he looking for secrets that didn't exist, simply because Walker had appeared in Leah so unexpectedly?

The night deepened and swelled with cold and silence, and their efforts to climb higher slowed. Then a gap opened in a cliff face, and they were passing through a deep defile into a valley beyond. There the forest was thick and sheltering, and what lived within could only be imagined. Panax continued on, his thoughts his own. The defile opened into a draw that angled down onto the valley floor. Beyond, the peaks of the Wolfsktaag rose in stark relief against the moonlit sky, sentries standing watch, each a little more misted and a little less clear than the one before.

Within the valley's center, Panax called an unexpected halt in a small clearing hemmed in by towering elm. "We will need to wait here."

Bek glanced around at the encroaching shadows. "How long?"

"Until Truls notices we've come." He laid down his ax and moved toward the shadows. "Help me build a fire."

They gathered deadwood and used tinder and flint to strike a spark and coax a flame to life. The fire built swiftly and threw light across the open space of the clearing, but could not penetrate the wall of shadows beyond. If anything, it seemed to emphasize how isolated the travelers were. The burning wood crackled and popped as it was consumed, but the surrounding night remained silent and enigmatic. The Dwarf and the Highland cousins sat in silence on the ground, backed up against each other so that they could share the warmth and watch the shadows. Now and again, one of them would add fuel to the blaze from the small pile of wood collected earlier, keeping the clearing lit and the signal steady.

"He might not be in the valley tonight," Panax said at one point, shifting against Bek so that the youth was bent forward under the weight of his stocky frame. "He might not return until morning."

"Does he live here?" Quentin asked.

"As much as he lives anywhere. He doesn't have a cabin or a camp. He doesn't keep possessions or even stash his food for when he might have need of it." The Dwarf paused, reflecting. "He isn't anything at all like you and me."

He let the matter drop, and neither Quentin nor Bek chose to pursue it. Whatever the cousins were going to learn would have to await the other's appearance. Bek, for one, was growing less and less certain that this was an event he should anticipate. Perhaps they would all be better off if the night passed, morning arrived, and nothing happened. Perhaps they would be better off if they let the matter drop here and now.

"I was just twenty when I met him," Panax said suddenly, his gruff voice quiet and low. "Hard to remember what that was like now, but I was young and full of myself and just learning that I wanted to be a guide and spend my time away from the settlements. I'd been alone for a while. I'd left home young and stayed gone, not missing it much, not thinking I should have reconsidered. I was always apart from everyone else, even my brothers, and it was probably a relief to everyone when I wasn't there anymore."

He glanced over his shoulder at Bek. "I was a little like you, cautious and doubtful, not about to be tricked or misled, knowing enough to take care of myself, but not much yet about the world. I'd heard the stories about the Wolfsktaag and decided to go there to see for myself. I thought that lying as it did across the backbone of the Eastland it would have to be crossed frequently enough that a guide could earn a living. So I tied in with some men who did this, but who didn't know as much as they pretended. I made a few crossings with them and lived to tell about it. After a year or two, I struck out on my own. Thought I'd be better off alone.

"Then one day I got myself so lost I couldn't find my way out. I was exploring, trying to teach myself how the passes connected, how the crossings could best be made. I knew something of the things that lived in the Wolfsktaag, having learned of them from the older guides, having seen most of them for myself. Some, you never saw, of course—unless you were unlucky. Most could be avoided or driven off, at least the ones made of flesh and blood. The ones that were spirit or wraith you had to stay clear of or hide from, and you could learn to do that. But this time I forgot to pay attention. I got lost and desperate, and I made a mistake."

He sighed and shook his head. "It hurts to admit it, even now. I backtracked into a stretch of land I knew I shouldn't go into, thinking I could do so just long enough to get clear of the mess I was in. I fell and twisted my ankle badly enough that I could barely walk. It was almost nightfall, and when it got dark enough, a werebeast came for me."

The fire snapped loudly, and Bek jumped in spite of himself. Werebeasts. They were something of a legend in the Southland, one half believed in by most, but seen only by a few. Part animal, part spirit, difficult even to recognize, let alone defend against, they fed off your fear and took shape from your imagination and almost nothing could stand against them, not even the great moor cats. The possibility that they might encounter one here was not comforting. "I thought they only lived in the deep Anar, farther east and north."

Panax nodded. "Once, maybe. Times change. Anyway, the werebeast attacked, and I did battle with it for most of the night. I fought so long and so hard I don't think I even knew what I was doing in the end. It changed shape on me repeatedly, and it tore me up pretty good. But I held my ground, backed up against a tree, too stubborn to know that I couldn't possibly win that sort of contest, growing weaker and more tired with every rush."

He stopped talking and stared off into the dark. The cousins waited, thinking him lost in thought, perhaps remembering. Then abruptly he came to his feet, battle-ax gripped in both hands.

"Something's moving out there—" he started to say.

A fleet, dark shape hurtled out of the night, followed by a second and then a third. It seemed as if the shadows themselves had come alive, taking form and gathering substance. Panax was knocked to the ground, grunting with the force of the blow he was struck. Quentin and Bek rolled aside, the shadows hurtling past them, dark shapes with just a flash of teeth and claws and deep-throated growls.

Ur'wolves! Bek snatched his long knife from its loop at his belt, wishing that he had something more substantial with which to defend himself. An ur'wolf pack was even capable of bringing down a full-grown Koden.

Panax had recovered and was wielding the two-edged ax, shifting his weight left and then right as the shadows flitted all around him at the edges of the light, looking for an opening. Every so often, one would launch itself at him, and he would meet the attack with a sweep of his curved blade and find nothing but air. Bek shouted at Quentin, who had tumbled away from the fire and was struggling to climb back to his feet. Finally Panax moved to aid him, but the moment he shifted his gaze to the Highlander, an ur'wolf slammed into him, knocking him flat and sending the battle-ax spinning away.

For an instant, Bek thought they were lost. The ur'wolves were coming out of the darkness in a rush, so many the Dwarf and the Highlanders could not have stopped them even had they been ready to do so. As it was, Panax and Quentin were both down, and Bek was trying to defend them with nothing more than his long knife.

"Quentin!" Bek screamed in desperation, and was knocked flying by a sleek form that materialized out of nowhere to catch him from behind.

Then the Highlander was beside him, the Sword of Leah unsheathed and gripped in both hands. Quentin's face was bloodless and raw with fear, but his eyes were determined. As the ur'wolves came at them, he swept the ancient weapon

in a wide arc and cried out *"Leah! Leah!"* in challenge.
Abruptly, his sword flared white-hot, threads of fire racing up
and down its polished length. Quentin gasped in surprise and
staggered back, almost falling over Bek. The ur'wolves scattered, twisting away frantically and disappearing back into
the dark. Quentin, shocked by what had happened, but exhilarated, as well, impulsively gave chase.

"Leah! Leah!" he called out.

Back came the ur'wolves, attacking anew, sheering off
at the last moment as the sword's fire lanced out at them.
Panax was back on his feet, astonishment mirrored in his
eyes as he retrieved his battle-ax and moved to stand next to
the Highlander.

Magic! Bek thought as he rushed to join them. There was
magic in the Sword of Leah after all! Walker had been right!

But their problems weren't over. The ur'wolves were not
breaking off their attack, just working around the edges of
the defense that had been raised against them, waiting for a
chance to break through. They were too wily to be caught off
guard and too determined to give up. Even the sword's magic
could do little more than keep them at bay.

"Panax, there are too many!" Bek shouted above the din of
the ur'wolves' howls and snarls. He snatched up the cold end
of a burning brand to thrust into the jaws of their attackers.

Half-blinded by ash and sweat, the three put their backs to
the fire and faced out into the darkness. The ur'wolves flitted
through the shadows, their liquid forms all but invisible.
Eyes glimmered and disappeared, pinpricks of brightness
that taunted and teased. Unable to determine where the next
attack would come from, Bek swept the air before him with
the long knife. He wondered suddenly if he should use the
magic of the phoenix stone. But he couldn't see how it would
help them.

"They'll rush us soon!" Panax shouted. His voice was
raspy and filled with grit. "Shades! So many of them! Where
have they all come from?"

"Bek, do you see, do you see?" Quentin was laughing almost hysterically. "The sword is magic after all, Bek! It really is!"

Bek found his cousin's enthusiasm entirely unwarranted and would have told him so if he could have spared the strength. But it was taking everything he had to stay focused on the movements of their attackers. He had no energy to waste on Quentin.

"Leah! Leah!" his cousin howled, darting out from their little circle, faking a strike at the shadows, then quickly retreating. "Panax!" he cried. "What are we supposed to do?"

Then something even darker and quicker than the ur'wolves crossed in front of them, trailing shards of cold wind in its wake. The three defenders shrank from it instinctively. The night hissed as if steam had been released from a fissure, and the ur'wolves began to howl wildly and to snap at nothing. Bek couldn't see them in the darkness, but he could hear the sounds they were making, sounds of madness and fear and loathing. A moment later, they were in full flight, gone back into the forest as it swallowed whole.

Bek Rowe held his breath in the ensuing silence, crouching so far down he was almost kneeling, his long knife extended blindly toward the trees. Beside him, Quentin was as still as carved stone.

Suddenly the darkness shifted anew, and a huge, tattered form that was not quite human, but not quite anything else, rose against the flicker of the firelight. It came together in a slow gathering of shadows, taking shape but not assuming identity, never quite becoming anything recognizable, formed of dreams and nightmares in equal parts.

"What is it?" Quentin Leah whispered.

"Truls Rohk," Panax breathed softly, and his words were as chill and brittle as ice in deep winter.

FIFTEEN

Hunkered down in the sprawling, treacherous tangle of the Wilderun, Grimpen Ward was ablaze with light and suffused with sound. Patrons of the ale houses and pleasure dens overflowed into the dirt streets, celebrating nothing, as lost to themselves as to those who had once known them. Grimpen Ward was the last rung on the ladder down, a melting pot for those who had no other place to go. Inquiries of strangers were as apt to get your purse stolen or your throat cut as your questions answered, fights broke out spontaneously and for no particular reason, and the only rule of behavior that mattered was to keep your nose out of what didn't concern you.

Even Hunter Predd, a veteran of countless reckonings and narrow escapes, was wary of those who lived in Grimpen Ward.

Once, Grimpen Ward had been a sleepy village catering to trappers and hunters seeking game within the vast and little explored expanse of the Wilderun. Too remote and isolated to attract any other form of commerce, it had subsisted as an outpost for many years. But there was little money to be made in hunting game and much to be made in gambling, and slowly the nature of the village began to change. The Elves shunned it, but Southlanders and Rovers found that its location suited their needs perfectly. Men and women seeking escape from their past, from pursuers who would not let them be, and from failed dreams and constant disappointment;

men and women who could not live under the constraints of
rules that governed elsewhere and who needed the freedom
that came with knowing that being quickest and strongest
was all that mattered; and men and women who had lost
everything and were hoping to find a way to begin anew
without having to be anything but clever and immoral; eventually all such found their way to Grimpen Ward. Some
stayed only a short time and moved on. Some stayed longer. If
they failed to stay alive, they stayed forever.

In daylight, it was a squalid, sleepy village of clapboard
buildings and sheds, of rutted dirt roads and shadowed alley-
ways, and of a populace that remained inside and slept,
waiting for nightfall. The forests of the Wilderun closed it
about, ancient trees and choking scrub, and it was always on
the verge of being swallowed completely. Nothing of what it
was seemed permanent, as if everything had been thrown together on a whim, perhaps within a few desperate days, and
might be torn down again by the end of the week. Its populace
cared nothing for the town, only for what the town had to
offer. There was a sullen, angry cast to Grimpen Ward that
suggested a caged and malnourished animal waiting for a
chance to break free.

Hunter Predd walked its streets cautiously, staying back
from the light, keeping clear of the knots of people crowded
about the doorways and porches of the public houses. Because he was a Wing Rider, he preferred open spaces.
Because he was a sensible man who had been to Grimpen
Ward and places like it before, he knew what to expect.

He slowed and then stopped at the entrance of an alley
where three men were beating another with clubs, already
pulling at his clothes, searching for his purse. The man was
pleading with them not to kill him. There was blood on his
face and hands. One of his attackers looked over at Hunter
Predd, feral eyes bright and hard, assessing his potential as
an adversary. The Wing Rider did as he had been instructed.

He held the other's gaze for a moment to demonstrate he was not afraid, then turned aside and walked on.

Grimpen Ward was not a place for the faint of heart or those seeking to redress the wrongs of the world. Neither could survive in the claustrophobic atmosphere of this breeding ground of cruelty and rage. Here, everyone was either prey to or hunter of someone else, and there was no middle ground. Hunter Predd felt the pall of hopelessness and despondency that shrouded the village, and he was sickened by it.

He moved out of the central section of the village, away from the brighter lights and louder noises, and entered a cluster of hovels and shacks occupied by those who had fallen into a twilight existence of drug-induced escape. The beings who lived here never emerged from their private, self-indulgent worlds, from the places they had created for themselves. He could smell the chemicals burning on the air as he passed through. He could smell the sweat and excrement. Everything they needed to escape life was free, once they forfeited everything they had.

He turned up a pathway that disappeared back into the trees, glanced about cautiously to be certain he had not been followed, and proceeded into the shadows. The trail wound back a short distance to a cabin set within a small grove of ash and cherry. The cabin was neat and well tended with flower boxes hung from the windows and a garden out back. It was quiet, an oasis of calm amid the tumult. A light burned in the front window. The Wing Rider walked to the door, stood quietly for a moment listening, and then knocked.

The woman who opened the door was heavy and flat-faced, her hair cropped short and graying, her body shapeless. She was of indeterminate age, as if she had passed out of childhood sometime back and would not change her look again until she was very old. She regarded Hunter Predd without interest, as if he were just another of the lost souls she encountered every day.

"I've got no more rooms to let. Try somewhere else."

He shook his head. "I'm not looking for a room. I'm looking for a woman called the Addershag."

She snorted. "You've come too late for that. She's been dead these past five years. News travels slowly where you come from, I guess."

"You know this to be so? Is she really dead?"

"As dead as yesterday. I buried her out back, six feet down, standing upright so she could greet those who tried to dig her up." She smirked. "Want to give it a try?"

He ignored the challenge. "You were her apprentice?"

The woman laughed, her face twisting. "Not hardly. I was her servant woman and the caretaker of her house. I hadn't the stomach for what she did. But I served her well and she rewarded me in kind. You knew her, did you?"

"Only by reputation. A powerful seer. A worker of magic. Few would dare to challenge her. None, I think, even now that she is dead and buried."

"Only fools and desperate men." The woman glanced out at the village lights and shook her head. "They come here still, now and then. I've buried a few, when they didn't listen to me about letting her be. But I haven't her power or abilities. I just do what I was brought here to do, looking after things, taking care. The house and what's in it are mine now. But I keep them for her."

She stared at him, waiting.

"Who reads the future of those in Grimpen Ward now that she is gone?" he asked.

"Pretenders and charlatans. No-talent thieves who would steal you blind and send you to your death pretending it was something else entirely. They moved in the moment she was gone, laying claim to what she was, to what she could do." The woman spit into the earth. "They'll all be found out and burned alive for it."

Hunter Predd hesitated. He would have to be careful here. This woman was protective of her legacy and not inclined to help. But he needed what she could give him.

"No one could replace the Addershag," he agreed soberly. "Unless she chose someone herself. Did she ever train an apprentice?"

For a long moment, the woman just looked at him, suspicion mirrored in her sharp eyes. She brushed roughly at her ragged hair. "Who are you?"

"An emissary," he said truthfully. "But the man who sent me knew your mistress well and shared her passion for magic and secrets. He, too, has lived a long time."

Her features scrunched up like crumpled paper, and she folded her heavy arms before her defensively. "Is he here?"

"Close by. He prefers not to be seen."

She nodded. "I know of whom you speak. But name him anyway if you wish me to believe you are his man."

The Wing Rider nodded. "He is called Walker."

"Hah!" Her eyes were bright with glee. "Even the vaunted Druid needed her help from time to time! That was how powerful she was, how well regarded!" There was triumph and satisfaction in her voice. "She might have been one of his order, had she wanted it. But she was never inclined to be anything other than a seer."

"Is there, then," he pressed gently, "another he might turn to, now that she is gone?"

The silence pressed in about them as she stood studying him anew, thinking the matter over. She knew something, but was not inclined to share it. He waited patiently on her.

"One," the woman said finally, but spoke the word as if it left a bitter taste in her mouth. "One only. But she was not suitable. She was flawed in character and made waste of her talent. My mistress gave her every chance to be strong, and each time the girl failed. Finally, she left."

"A girl," Hunter Predd repeated carefully.

"Very young when she was here. Still a child. But old even then. Like she was already grown inside her child's body. Intense and secretive, which was to her credit, but passionate, as well, which was not. Very powerful in her talent. She could see the future clearly, could mark its progress and read its signs." The woman spat once more, her voice suddenly weary. "So gifted. More than just a seer. That was her undoing."

The Wing Rider was confused. "What do you mean?"

The woman glared and shook her head. "There's no reason for me to talk about it. If you're so curious to know, ask her yourself. Ryer Ord Star is her name. She lives nearby. I can give you the directions. Do you want them or not?"

Hunter Predd took the directions she had offered and thanked her for her help. In return she gave him a look that suggested both pity and disdain. He had barely turned away before she had closed the cottage door behind her.

It felt empty and silent in the woods where Walker waited outside Grimpen Ward for Hunter Predd's return. Nothing moved in the darkness. No sound came from the gloom. He waited patiently, but reluctantly, uncomfortable with leaving the search for the Addershag to the Wing Rider. It wasn't that he thought Hunter Predd lacking in ability; in fact, he thought the Wing Rider better able than most. But he would have preferred to handle the matter himself. Contacting her was his idea. Seeking her out was something he knew how to do. But it was clear after the attack on Spanner Frew's safehold that the Ilse Witch was determined to disrupt his efforts to retrace the route on the castaway's map. It might have appeared it was the Federation who attacked the Rover settlement, but the Druid was convinced it was the Ilse Witch. Her spies must have caught sight of him in March Brume, and she had tracked him north to Spanner Frew. He had been lucky to elude her on the coast—luckier still to escape with his new airship intact. His Rover allies—Redden Alt Mer, Rue Meridian, and Spanner Frew—had flown him back to March Brume under cover of darkness and early morning mist, dropped him close to where he had left Hunter Predd, and then taken the airship in search of a crew. Once that crew was assembled, they would fly north to Arborlon, present themselves to the Elves and their new ruler, and await the Druid's arrival.

All of which would take time, but Walker needed that time to accomplish two things. First, he must wait for Quentin Leah and Bek Rowe to find Truls Rohk, then reach Arborlon. Second, he must confer with a seer.

Why a seer? Hunter Predd had asked as they flew aboard Obsidian across the peaks of the Irrybis toward Grimpen Ward. What need did they have of a seer when Walker had already determined the purpose of the map? But their journey, Walker explained, was not so easily fathomed. Think of the Blue Divide as a depthless void and its islands as stepping-stones. The stability of those stones and the dark secrets of the waters all around were unknown. The Addershag might help them better understand their dangers. She could see some of what would threaten, what would lie in wait, what would steal away their lives if they weren't prepared.

A seer could always provide insights, and no seer could provide more than the Addershag. Her abilities were renowned, and while she was dangerously unpredictable, she had never been antagonistic toward him. Once, long ago, she had helped his cousin, the Elf Queen Wren Elessedil, in her search for the missing Elven nation. It was the beginning of a connection he had carefully preserved. The Addershag had accommodated him now and again over the years, always with a grudging nod of admiration for the magic he could wield, always with a veiled hint of warning that her own was a match. She had been alive almost as long as he had, without the benefit of the Druid Sleep. He had no idea how she had managed this. She was both burdened and conflicted by her talent, and her life was a closely guarded secret.

Walker was not certain that Hunter Predd could succeed in persuading her to speak to him. She might well refuse. But it made sense to try. If he were to accomplish anything, he would have to do so both swiftly and surreptitiously.

Still, he chafed at the waiting and the uncertainty, and wished he could involve himself openly. Time was precious and success uncertain. The Addershag's aid was vital. She would never agree to go with him, but she could open his eyes to the things he must know if he were to go himself. She would do so reluctantly and with carefully crafted words and confusing images, but even that would help.

A soft rustle broke his concentration, and he looked up as Hunter Predd materialized out of the night. The Wing Rider was alone.

"Did you find her?" the Druid asked at once.

Hunter Predd shook his head. "She's been dead five years. The woman who looked after her told me so."

Walker took a long, slow breath and exhaled. Disappointment welled up inside. A lie? No, a lie of that sort wouldn't stand up for long. He should have known of the seer's death, but he had shut himself away in Paranor for the better part of twenty years and much of what had happened in the world had passed him by completely.

The Wing Rider seated himself on a stump and drank from his water skin. "There is another possibility. Before she died, the seer took an apprentice."

"An apprentice?" Walker frowned.

"A girl called Ryer Ord Star. Very talented, according to the woman I spoke with. But she had some sort of falling out with the Addershag. The woman hinted that it had something to do with a flaw in the girl's character, but wouldn't say more. She said I should ask her myself if I wanted to know. She lives not far from here."

Walker thought it through quickly, weighing the possible risks and gains. Ryer Ord Star? He had never heard of her. Nor had he heard of the Addershag taking an apprentice. But then he hadn't heard of the seer's death either. What he knew or didn't know of the larger world the past few years was not the most accurate measure of its truths. Better to find things out for himself before deciding what was or wasn't so.

"Show me where she is," he said.

Hunter Predd led him along a series of trails that circumvented the center of Grimpen Ward and avoided contact with its denizens. Darkness hid their passage, and the forests were a vast, impenetrable maze into which only they appeared to have ventured. Distant and removed, the sounds of the village rose up in tiny bursts within the cloaking silence, and slivers of light appeared and faded like predators' eyes. But both Wing Rider and Druid knew how to walk undetected, and so their passing went unnoticed.

As he slipped through the dark tangle of the trees, Walker's thoughts crowded in on him. His opportunities, he sensed, were slipping away. Too many he had depended on were dead—first Allardon Elessedil, then the castaway, and now the Addershag. Each represented information and assistance that would be difficult, if not impossible, to replace. The loss of the Addershag troubled him most. Could he manage without a seer's visions in this endeavor? Allanon had done so, years earlier. But Walker was not chiseled from the same rock as his predecessor and made no claims to being his equal. He did what he could with what he had, mostly because he understood the need for doing so and not because he coveted the role into which he had been cast. Druids had traditionally desired their positions in the order. The mold had been broken with him.

He did not like thinking about who he was and how he had gotten to be that way. He did not like remembering the road he had been forced to travel to become what he had never intended to be. It was a bitter memory he carried and a difficult burden he bore. He had become a Druid because of Allanon's machinations and Cogline's urgings and in spite of his own considerable misgivings because, in the end, the need for his doing so was overwhelming. He had never thought to have anything to do with the Druids, never thought to be part of what they represented. He had grown up with a determination to stay apart from the legacy that had claimed so many of his family—the legacy of the Shannara. He had vowed to take his life in another direction.

But this is old news, he admonished himself even as he remembered the early fire of his doomed commitment to change what was fated. He supposed what pained him most, what weighed so heavily on his conscience, was not the breaking of the vow itself, which he could justify in light of the need it served, but the distance he had strayed from his appointed path in taking up his role. He had sworn he would not be a Druid like those others, like Allanon and Bremen before him. He would not cloak himself in subterfuge and secrecy. He would not manipulate others to achieve the ends he wished. He would not deceive and misdirect and conceal. He would be open and forthright and honest in his dealings. He would reveal what he knew and be truthful always.

He marveled at how naive he had been. How foolish. How terribly, fatally unrealistic.

Because life's dictates did not allow for quick and easy distinctions between right and wrong or good and bad. Choices were made between shades of gray, and there was healing and harm to be weighed on both sides of each. As a result, his life had irrevocably followed the path of his predecessors, and in time he had taken on the very characteristics he had despised in them. He had assumed their mantles more completely than he had ever intended. Without ever wishing it to be so, he had become like them.

Because he could see the need for doing so.

Because he was then required to conduct himself accordingly.

Because, always and forever, the greater good must be considered in determining his course of action.

Tell that to Bek Rowe when this is over, he thought darkly. Tell it to that boy.

They emerged suddenly from the forest into a clearing

in which a solitary cottage sat dark and silent. Far removed from everything, the cottage was poorly tended, its windows broken, its roof sagging, its yard choked with weeds, and its gardens bare. It looked as if no one had lived in it for some time, as if it had been abandoned and let run to ruin.

Then Walker saw the girl. She sat in the deep shadows of the porch stoop, perfectly still, at one with the darkness. When his eyes settled on her, she rose at once and stood watching his approach with Hunter Predd. Revealed more clearly by the light of moon and stars, she became older, less a girl, more a young woman. She wore her silver hair long and loose, and it fell about her pale, thin face in thick waves. She was rail thin, so insubstantial it seemed as if a strong wind might blow her away completely. She wore a plain wool dress cinched at her tiny waist by a strip of braided cloth. Sandals that were dusty and worn were strapped to her feet, and an odd collar of metal and leather was clasped about her neck.

He came up to her and stopped, Hunter Predd at his side. She never took her eyes from his, never even glanced at the Wing Rider.

"Are you the one they call Walker?" she asked in a soft, high voice.

Walker nodded. "I am called that."

"I am Ryer Ord Star. I have been waiting for you."

Walker studied her curiously. "How did you know I was coming?"

"I saw you in a dream. We were flying far out over the Blue Divide in an airship. There were dark clouds all about, and thunder rolled across the skies. But within the dark clouds there was something darker still, and I was warning you to beware of it." She paused. "When I had that dream, I knew you would be coming here and that when you did, I would be going with you."

Walker hesitated. "I never intended to ask you to come with me, only to ask—"

"But I must come with you!" she insisted quickly, her hands making sudden, anxious gestures to emphasize her need. "There have been other dreams of you as well, more as time has passed. I am meant to go with you across the Blue Divide. It is my destiny to do so!"

She spoke with such conviction that Walker was momentarily taken aback. He glanced at Hunter Predd. Even the Wing Rider's rugged face reflected surprise.

"See?" she inquired, gesturing down at a canvas bag that sat at her feet. "I am packed and ready to leave with you. I dreamed of you again last night, of your coming here. The dream was so strong it even told me when you would arrive. Such dreams do not come often, even to seers. They almost never come in such numbers. When they do, they must not be ignored. We are bound, you and I—our destinies intertwined in a way we cannot sever. What happens to one, happens to both."

She regarded him solemnly, her thin, pale face questioning, as if she could not understand his inability to accept her words. Walker, for his part, was confounded by her determination.

"You apprenticed with the Addershag?" he inquired, turning the conversation another way. "Why did you leave?"

The thin hands gestured anew. "She was suspicious of what I was. She was distrustful of how I employed my gifts. I am a seer, but I am an empath, too. Both talents are strong within me, and I find the need to use them too compelling to ignore. On occasion, I used the one to alter the other, and the Addershag would scream at me. 'Never do anything to change what is to be!' she would shrill. But if I can take away another's pain through divining the future, where is the harm? I saw nothing wrong in doing so. Such pain can be better borne by me than by most."

Walker stared. "You read the future, determine that something bad will happen, then use your empathic skill to lessen the hurt that will result?" Walker tried to envision it and failed. "How often can you do this?"

"Only now and then. I can only do a little. Sometimes, the use of my gifts is reversed. Sometimes I come to those already in pain, see the future that pain will create, and act to change it. It is an imperfect skill, and I do not use it carelessly. But the Addershag distrusted my empathic side altogether, believing it affected my seer's eyes. Perhaps she was right. The two are equal parts of me, and I cannot separate them out. Does this bother you?"

Walker didn't know. What bothered him most was his own confusion over what to do with the girl. She seemed convinced she was going with him, while he was still struggling with whether he should consult with her at all.

"You are unsure of me," she said. He nodded, seeing no reason to dissemble. "You have no reason to fear that I cannot do what is needed. You are a Druid, and a Druid's instincts never lie. Trust what yours tell you about me."

She took a step forward. "An empath can give you peace you can find in no other way. Give me your hand."

He did so without thinking, and she took it in her own. Her hands were soft and warm, and they barely enclosed his. She ran her fingers slowly over his palm and closed her eyes. "You are in such pain, Walker," she said. A tingling began that turned slowly to sleepy calm, then to a sudden, soaring euphoria. "You feel yourself beset on all sides, your chances slipping away from you, your burden almost too much to bear. You hate yourself for what you are because you believe it is wrong for you to be so. You conceal truths that will affect the lives of those who—"

He jerked his hand free and stepped back, shocked at how easily she had penetrated his heart. Her eyes opened and lit on him anew. "I could free you of so much of your pain if you would let me," she whispered.

"No," he replied. He felt himself naked and revealed in a way he didn't care for. "The pain is a reminder of who I am."

At his side, Hunter Predd stirred uneasily, a witness to words he shouldn't hear. But Walker could do nothing about it now.

"Listen to me," Ryer Ord Star intoned softly. "Listen to what I have seen in my dreams. You will make your voyage across the Blue Divide in search of something precious—more to you than to any who go with you. Those who accompany you will be both brave and strong of heart, but only some will return. One will save your life. One will try to take it. One will love you unconditionally. One will hate you with unmatched passion. One will lead you astray. One will bring you back again. I have seen all this in my dreams, and I am meant to see more. I am meant to be your eyes, Walker. We are bound as one. Take me with you. You must."

Her small voice was filled with such passion that it left the Druid transfixed. He thought momentarily of the Addershag, of how black and twisted she had always seemed, her words sharp edged and threatening, her voice come out of a dark pit into which no one should venture. How different, then, was Ryer Ord Star? He could see how difficult it must have been for the girl to train at the feet of someone so different from herself. She must have struggled in her training and would have lasted as long as she did because of her passion for her gift. He could see that in her. Trust your instincts, she had urged him. He always did. But his instincts here were mixed and his conclusions uncertain.

"Take me with you," she repeated, and her words were a whisper of need.

He did not look at Hunter Predd. He knew what he would find in the Wing Rider's eyes. He did not even look into his own heart, because he could already feel what was lurking there. He read, instead, her face, to be certain he had missed nothing, and he gave counsel to his mission and his need. A seer was required for the dark places into which he must venture. Ryer Ord Star had the gift, and there was no time to seek it in another. That she was not the Addershag was troubling.

That she was not only willing, but eager to go with him, was a gift he could not afford to spurn.

"Pick up your bag, Ryer Ord Star," he said softly. "We fly tonight to Arborlon."

SIXTEEN

Bek Rowe froze as the huge apparition swung away from the fleeing wolves to face them. Quentin took an involuntary step back, his earlier euphoria over the rediscovered magic of the Sword of Leah forgotten. Neither dared even to breathe as the thing before them rippled like windblown cedar limbs, a kind of shimmering movement that suggested an image cast on a rain-drenched window or a ghost imagined in a sudden change of light.

Then the tattered cloak that wrapped Truls Rohk's broad, rangy form billowed once and settled about his shoulders, the edges trailing stray threads and ragged strips of cloth. Hands and feet moved like clubs within the circle of darkness he cast, but no face could be seen within the shadows of his cowl. If not for his vaguely human form, Truls Rohk could as easily have been a beast of the sort that prowled those mountains.

"Panax," he hissed. "Why are you here?"

He spoke the Dwarf's name with recognition, but without warmth or pleasure. His voice bore the sharp whine of metal scraping metal, and ended with the sound of steam released under pressure. Bek had forgotten the Dwarf. Battle-ax lowered to his side, Panax stood straight and unbowed in the presence of the dark creature that confronted them. But there was a tenseness in his rough features and wariness in his eyes.

"Walker has sent you a message," he said to the apparition.

Truls Rohk made no move to come forward. "Walker," he repeated.

"These are Highlanders," Panax continued. "The tall one is Quentin Leah. The younger is his cousin, Bek Rowe. They were entrusted to carry the message to you."

"Speak it," Truls Rohk said to the cousins.

Bek looked at Quentin, who nodded. Bek cleared his throat. "We've been asked to tell you that Walker is preparing to undertake a journey by airship across the Blue Divide. He goes in search of a safehold in an unknown land. The safehold contains a treasure of great value. He says to tell you that others search for it, as well, one of them a warlock called the Morgawr and one a sorceress called the Ilse Witch."

"Hssshh! Dark souls!" Truls Rohk spat sharply, the sound so venomous it stopped Bek right in the middle of his speech. "What else, boy?"

Bek swallowed thickly. "He says to tell you that his enemies have already killed the Elf King, Allardon Elessedil, and a castaway who carried back a map of the safehold. He says to tell you he needs you to come with him to help in the search and to protect against those who would prevent it."

There was a long silence, then a cough that might have been a laugh or something less pleasant. "Lies. Even with only one arm, Walker can protect himself. What does he really need?"

Bek stared at the other in confusion and fear, then glanced at both Quentin and Panax, found no help, and shook his head. "I don't know. That was all he told us. That was the whole message, just as he gave it to us. He wants you to—"

"He wants more than he says!" The raspy voice grated and hissed. "You, Highlander." He gestured vaguely within his cloak toward Quentin. "What magic do you wield?"

Quentin did not hesitate. "An old magic, just this night recovered. This sword belongs to my family. It was given its magic, I'm told, in the time of Allanon."

"You wield it poorly." The words were cutting and dismissive. "You, boy." Truls Rohk spoke once more to Bek. "Have you magic as well?"

Bek shook his head. "No, none."

He was aware that Truls Rohk was studying him carefully, and in the stillness that followed, it seemed as if something reached out and touched him, brushing against his forehead with feathery lightness. It was there and gone so quickly that he might only have imagined it.

Truls Rohk moved a step to his right, and the movement revealed a flash of arm and leg of huge proportions, all muscle and thick hair, bare to the mountain night. Bek had a strong sense that the other was stooped within his cloak, affecting a kind of guarded crouch, a readiness that never left him. As big as Truls Rohk already seemed, Bek believed he would be much bigger still if he was to stand upright. Nothing got that big that wasn't a Rock Troll, but Truls Rohk lacked a Rock Troll's thick hide and cumbersome, deliberate movements. He was too quick and fluid for that, and his skin was human.

"The Druid sent you to be tested," he growled softly. "Tested against your own fears and superstitions. Your magic and your grit are untried weapons." He gave a low chuckle that died away into the familiar hiss. "Panax, are you party to this game?"

The Dwarf grunted irritably. "I play no games with anyone. I was asked to see these Highlanders into the Wolfsktaag and out again. You seem to know more about this than I do."

"Games within games," the shadowy form murmured, stalking a few steps to the right, then turning back again. This time Bek caught a glimpse of a face within the hood, just a momentary illumination by the edges of the firelight. The face was crisscrossed with deep, scarlet welts, and the flesh looked as if it had been melted like iron in a furnace. "Druid games," Truls Rohk went on, disappearing again into shadow. "I do not like them, Panax. But Walker is always interesting to watch." He paused. "Maybe these two, as well, hmmm?"

Panax seemed confused and said nothing. Truls Rohk

pointed at Quentin. "Those wolves would have had you if not for me. Better practice your sword's magic if you expect to stay alive for very long."

Bek felt the other's eyes shift and settle on him. "And you, boy, had better not trust anyone. Not until you learn to see things better than you do now."

Bek was conscious that both Quentin and Panax were looking at him, as well. He wanted to ask Truls Rohk what he was talking about but cowed by the giant's size and dark mystery, he was afraid to question him.

Truls Rohk spat and wheeled away. "Where do you go to meet Walker?" he called over his shoulder.

"Arborlon," Bek answered at once.

"Then I'll see you there." His words were soft and whispery. "Now get out of these mountains, quickly!"

There was a rush of wind, cold and sharp, and a whisper of movement in the night. Bek and Quentin shrank involuntarily from both, shielding their eyes. Behind them, the fire flickered and went out.

When they looked back toward the silent darkness, Truls Rohk was gone.

Far south, below the Highlands of Leah, the Prekkendorran Heights, and the older, more industrialized cities, Wayford and Sterne, in the Federation capital city of Arishaig, Minister of Defense Sen Dunsidan was awakened by a touch on his shoulder.

His eyes blinked open and he stared through the gloom toward the ceiling without seeing anything, uncertain what had disturbed him. He was lying on his back, his big frame sprawled on the oversize bed, the sleeping room cool and silent.

"Wake up, Minister," the Ilse Witch whispered.

His eyes settled on her slender, cloaked form as she bent over him. "Dark Lady of my dreams," he greeted with a sleepy smile.

"Don't say anything more, Minister," she advised, stepping back from him. "Rise and come with me."

She watched him do as he was told, his strong face calm and settled, as if it were not at all unexpected that she should appear to him like this. He was a powerful man, and the effective exercise of his power relied in part on never seeming surprised or afraid. He had been Minister of Defense of the Federation for better than fifteen years, and he had achieved his longevity in that position in part by burying a lot of men who misjudged him. He seemed mild and even detached at times, just an observer on the edges of the action, just a man eager to make things right for everyone. In truth, he had the instincts and morals of a snake. In a world of predators and prey, he preferred to take his chances as the former. But he understood clearly and unequivocally that his survival depended on keeping his preference secret and his ambitions concealed. When he felt threatened, as perhaps he did now, he always smiled. But the smile, of course, hid the teeth behind.

The Ilse Witch led him wordlessly from his sleeping chamber down the hall to his study. His study was his place of business, and he would understand from her taking him there that there was business to be done. He was a man of huge appetites, and he was accustomed to satisfying them when he chose. She did not want him mistaking her purpose in coming to his bedchamber for something other than what it was. She had seen the way he looked at her, and she did not care for what she saw in his eyes. If he were to attempt to put his hands on her, she would have to kill him. She did not mind doing so, but it would accomplish nothing. The best way to prevent that from happening was to make it clear from the outset that their relationship was not about to change.

Sen Dunsidan was both her spy and her ally, a man well placed in the Federation hierarchy to do favors for her in exchange for favors she might do for him. As Minister of Defense, he understood the uses of power in government, but he was mindful, too, of the need for cautious selection. He was clever, patient, and thorough, and his work ethic was legendary. Once he set his mind to something, he did not give up. But it was his ambition that attracted the Ilse Witch. Sen Dunsidan was not satisfied with being Minister of Defense. He would not be satisfied if he were to become Minister of War or Minister of State or even if he were chosen Prime Minister. He might not be satisfied with being King, a position that didn't even exist in the current structure of the Federation government, but it was closer to the mark. What he desired was absolute power—over everything and everyone. She had learned early on in their relationship that if she could show him ways of achieving this, he would willingly do whatever she asked.

They reached his study and entered. The room was wood paneled and austere, an intimidating lair. Disdaining the brighter light that the torches set in wall brackets would have afforded, the minister moved to light a series of candles on a broad-topped desk. Tall and athletic, his silvery hair worn long and flowing freely, he moved from place to place unhurriedly. He was an attractive man with a magnetic personality until you got to know him, and then he was just someone else to be watched carefully. The Ilse Witch had encountered more than her share of these. Sometimes it seemed the world was full of them.

"Now, then," he said, seating himself comfortably on one end of a long couch, taking time to adjust his dressing gown.

She stayed somewhat removed from him, still wrapped in her hooded cloak, her face hidden in shadows. He had seen what she looked like on several occasions, mostly because it was necessary to let him do so, but she had been careful never to encourage his obvious interest in her. She did not treat him as she did her spies, because he considered himself an equal and his pride and ambition would not allow for anything less. She could reduce him to servitude easily enough, but then his usefulness would be ended. She must let him remain strong or he could not survive in the arena of Federation politics.

"Did those airships I sent you not do what was needed?" He pressed, his brow furrowing slightly.

"They did what they could," she said in a neutral tone of voice. She chose her words carefully. "But my adversary is clever and strong. He is not easily surprised, and he was not surprised there. He escaped."

"Unfortunate."

"A momentary setback. I will find him again, and when I do, I will destroy him. In the meantime, I require your help."

"In finding him or destroying him?"

"Neither. In pursuing him. He has the use of an airship, with a Captain and a crew. I will need the same if I am to catch up to him."

Sen Dunsidan studied her thoughtfully. Already he was working it through, she could tell. He had determined quickly that there was more to this than she was telling him. If she was chasing someone, there had to be a reason. He knew her well enough to know she would not waste time hunting someone down simply to kill him. Something else was involved, something of importance to her. He was trying to figure out what might be in it for him.

She decided not to play games. "Let me tell you a little about my interest in this matter," she offered. "It goes well beyond my determination to see my adversary destroyed. We compete for the same prize, Minister. It is a prize of great and rare value. It would benefit both of us, you and I, if I were to gain possession of it first. My request to you for aid in this endeavor presupposes that whatever success I enjoy, I intend to share with you."

The big man nodded. "As you have always so graciously done, Dark Lady." He smiled. "What sort of prize is it you seek?"

She hesitated deliberately, as if debating whether to tell him. He must be made to think it was a difficult decision, the result of which would favor him. "A form of magic," she confided finally. "A very special magic. If I was to gain possession of this magic, I would become much more powerful than I am. And if I was to share possession with you, you would become strongest among those who seek power within the Federation government." She paused. "Would you like that?"

"Oh, I don't know," he said, laughing softly. "Such power might be too much for a simple man like me." He paused. "Do I have your assurance that I will share in the use of this magic on your return?"

"My complete and unequivocal assurance, Minister."

He bowed slightly in acknowledgment. "I could ask for nothing more." She had convinced him a long time ago that she would keep her word once she gave it. She also knew that his confidence was buttressed by his belief that even if she broke it, her betrayal would not cost him much.

"Where do you go to seek this magic?" he asked.

She gave him a long, careful look. "Across the Blue Divide, to a new land, an old city, a strange place. Only a few others have gone there. None have returned."

She did not mention the castaway or the Elves. There was no reason for him to know of them. She gave him just enough to keep him interested.

"None have returned," he repeated slowly. "Not very reassuring. Will you succeed where everyone else has failed?"

"What do you think, Minister?"

He laughed softly. "I think you are young for such machinations and intrigue. Do you never think of taking time for more casual pleasures? Do you never wish that you could put aside your obligations, just for a few days, and do something you never imagined?"

She sighed wearily. He was being obtuse. He was refusing to accept that his advances were not welcome. She must put a stop to it now before it got out of hand. "If I were to consider such a thing," she purred, "do you know a place to which I might escape?"

His gaze on her was steady and watchful. "I do."

"And would you be my guide and companion?"

He straightened expectantly. "I would be honored."

"No, Minister, you would simply be dead, probably before the first day was out." She paused to let him absorb the impact of her words. "Put aside your dreams of what you think I might be. Do not let them enter your mind or be persuaded to speak of them again. Ever. I am nothing of what you imagine and less of what you would hope. I am blacker than your worst deeds could ever be. Don't presume to know me. Keep far away from me, and maybe you'll stay alive."

His face had stilled, and there was uncertainty in his eyes. She let him wrestle with it a moment, then whispered words of calming in the silence, and laughed like a girl, soft and low. "Come now, Minister. Harsh words are unnecessary. We are old friends. We are allies. What of my request? Will you aid me?"

"Of course," he answered swiftly. A political animal first and always, Sen Dunsidan could recognize reality quicker than most. He did not want to anger or alienate her or sever their mutually advantageous connection. He would attempt to move past his clumsy attempt at an assignation as if it had never happened. She, of course, would let him. "A ship, a Captain, and crew," he assured her, grateful for a chance to accommodate, to be back in her good graces. He brushed at his silver hair and smiled. "All at your disposal, Dark Lady, for as long as you need them."

"Your best of each, Minister," she warned. "No weak links. This voyage will not be easy."

He rose, walked to the study window, and looked out over the city. His home sat in a cluster of Federation government buildings, some residences, some offices, all warded by a walled park into which no one was admitted without invitation. The Ilse Witch smiled. Except for her, of course. She could go anywhere she wished.

"I'll give you *Black Moclips*," Sen Dunsidan announced

suddenly. "She is the best of our warships, a Rover-built ship of the line, a proven vessel. Her history is remarkable. She has fought in over two hundred engagements and never been defeated or even disabled. Just now, she has a new Captain and crew, and they are eager to prove themselves. Veterans all, don't misunderstand me, but new to this ship. They were brought aboard when her Rover crew deserted."

She studied him. "They are seasoned and reliable? They are tested in battle?"

"Two full years on the Prekkendorran, all of them. They are a strong and dependable unit, well led and thoroughly trained."

And a full complement of Federation soldiers, she was about to say when the Morgawr's rough-edged voice stopped her. *No soldiers,* he hissed, so that only she could hear. It was an unmistakable reminder of his earlier warning, when she had insisted she must have soldiers to combat the Elven forces. *A ship, a Captain, and a crew—nothing more. Do not question me.* She froze under the lash of his voice, projected from the shadows behind Sen Dunsidan, where he waited in hiding.

"Lady?" the Minister of Defense asked solicitously, sensing the hesitation in her.

"Supplies for a long voyage," she said, forging ahead as if nothing had intruded on her thinking, looking directly toward the Morgawr, unwilling to concede him anything. She resented his insistence on trying to control matters when he himself had no intention of being involved in the expedition. He saw himself as her mentor, and he was, but she was his equal now and no longer in his thrall. She had always possessed magic, even before he came to her and helped her to rebuild her shattered life. She had never been helpless or unaware, and he seemed too quick to forget how strong she was.

"The ship will be delivered to you fully outfitted and ready to sail." Sen Dunsidan reclaimed her attention. "I'll have her ready in a week."

"Four days," the Ilse Witch said softly, holding his gaze firmly with her own. "I'll come for her myself. Have her Captain and crew under orders to obey me in everything. Everything, Minister. There are to be no questions, no arguments, and no hesitations. All decisions are to be mine."

The Federation Minister nodded without enthusiasm. "The Captain and crew will be advised, Dark Lady."

"Go back to bed," she ordered, and turned away, dismissing him.

Standing with her gaze directed out the windows and into the night, she waited until he was gone, then wheeled back to face the Morgawr, who had emerged from hiding, tall and dark and spectral. He had come with her to the city, but kept hidden while she did the talking. He told her that it was best if Sen Dunsidan believed she was the one he must listen to, the one in control. As in fact I am, she had wanted to reply, but instead held her tongue.

"You did well," he said, sliding into the faint light.

"I don't appreciate your interference with my efforts!" she snapped, unappeased. "Or your reminders of what you think I should or shouldn't do! I am the one who risks life and limb to gain possession of the magic!"

"I only seek to supply help where help is needed," he replied calmly.

"Then do so!" she snapped. Her patience was exhausted. "We need soldiers! We need hardened warriors! Where are they to come from, if not from the Federation?"

He dismissed her anger and displeasure with a wave of his gloved hand. "From me," he replied casually. "I have already arranged for it. Three dozen Mwellrets, commanded by Cree Bega. They will be your warriors, your fighters. You will have nothing to fear with them beside you."

Mwellrets. She cringed at the idea. He knew she hated rets. As fighters, they were savage and relentless, but they were deceivers, as well. She did not trust them. She could not see inside their minds. They resisted her magic and employed subterfuges and artifices of their own. It was why the Morgawr liked them, why he was using them. They would be effective fighters in her behalf, but they would act as her keepers, as well. Giving her Mwellrets was a means of keeping her in line.

She could refuse his offer, she knew. But to do so would demonstrate weakness. Besides, the warlock would simply insist that she do as he asked, having already made up his mind that the rets were necessary—

She caught herself in midthought, realizing suddenly what sending the rets really meant. It wasn't just that the Morgawr no longer trusted her or that he was no longer certain she would do as he ordered.

He was afraid of her.

She smiled, as if deciding she was pleased with his suggestion, careful to keep her true feelings veiled. "You are right, of course," she agreed. "What better fighters could we find? Who would dare to challenge a ret?"

Only me, she thought darkly. *But by the time you discover that, Morgawr, it will already be too late for you.*

SEVENTEEN

Four days after departing the Wolfsktaag Mountains, Bek Rowe, his cousin Quentin Leah, and the Dwarf Panax arrived at the Valley of Rhenn.

Bek had heard stories of the valley his entire life, and as the trio rode their horses slowly out of the plains and down its broad, grassy corridor, he found himself remembering them anew. There, more than a thousand years ago, the Elves and their King, Jerle Shannara, stood against the hordes of the Warlock Lord in three days of ferocious fighting that culminated in the renegade Druid's defeat. There, more than five hundred years ago, the Legion Free Corps rode to the aid of the Elven people when they were beset by the demon hordes freed from the Forbidding. There, less than 150 years ago, the Elf Queen Wren Elessedil commanded the Free born allies in their defense against the Federation armies of Rimmer Dall, breaking the back of the Federation occupation and destroying the cult of the Shadowen.

Bek glanced upward at the steepening valley slopes and sharp ridgelines. So many critical battles had been fought and pivotal confrontations had taken place within only a few miles of that gateway to the Elven homeland. But as he looked at it, quiet and serene and bathed in sunshine, there was nothing to indicate that anything of importance had ever happened there.

Once, Bek heard a man remark to Coran that this ground was sacred, that the blood of those who had given up their lives to preserve freedom in the Four Lands had made it so. It was a fine and noble thought, Coran Leah replied, but it would mean more if the sacrifice of those countless dead had bought the survivors something more permanent.

The boy thought about that as he rode through the midday silence. The valley narrowed to a defile at its western end, a natural fortress of cliff walls and twisting passes through which all traffic gained entry into the Westland forests leading to Arborlon. It had served as a first line of defense for the Elves each time their homeland was invaded. Bek had never been here, but he knew its history. Remembering his father's words, he was surprised at how different it felt being here rather than picturing it in his mind. All the events and the tumult faded in the vast quiet, the open spaces, the scent of wildflowers, the soft cool breeze, and the warm sun, masked as if they had never taken place. The past was only an imagining here. He could barely put a face to it, barely envision how it must have been. He wondered if the Elves ever thought of it as he did now, if it was ever for them a reminder of how transitory victories in battle so often were.

He wondered if the journey he was making now would feel any different to him when it was finished. He wondered if he would accomplish anything lasting.

His travel west had been uneventful. All four days had passed without incident. The Highland cousins and the Dwarf had come down out of the Wolfsktaag after their encounter with Truls Rohk, spent what remained of the night and the early morning hours sleeping at Panax's cabin, then packed their gear, collected their horses, and set out for Arborlon at midday. They traveled light, choosing to forgo pack animals and supplies, foraging on the way. There were countless settlements scattered across the Borderlands, and they had little difficulty obtaining what they needed. Their passage west was straightforward and unobstructed. They crossed the Rabb Plains above the Silver River, followed the north shore of the Rainbow Lake below the Runne, bypassed Varfleet and Tyrsis through Callahorn's hill country to the flats above the Tirfing, then angled north along the Mermidon River toward the Valley of Rhenn. They traveled steadily, but without haste, the days clear and sunny and pleasant, the nights cool and still.

Not once did they catch sight of or hear from Truls Rohk. Panax said they wouldn't, and he turned out to be right.

Their encounter with the shadowy, formidable Truls had left both Bek and Quentin shaken, and it wasn't until the next day, when they were well away from Depo Bent and the Wolfsktaag, that they had felt comfortable enough to pursue the subject. By then, Panax was ready to tell them the rest of what he knew.

"Of course, he's a man, just like you or me," he replied to Bek's inevitable question regarding what sort of creature Truls Rohk really was. "Well, not just like you or me, I guess, or anyone else I've ever come across. But he's a man, not some beast or wraith. He was a Southlander once, before he went into the mountains to live. He came out of the border country below Varfleet, somewhere in the Runne. His people were trappers, poor migrants who lived close to the bone. He told me this once, long time ago. Never spoke of it again, though. Especially not the part about the fire."

They were somewhere out on the Rabb by then, chasing the sun west, the daylight beginning to fade to twilight. Neither cousin spoke as the Dwarf paused in his narration to gather his thoughts.

"When he was about twelve, I guess, there was a fire. The boy was sleeping with the men in a makeshift shelter of dried skins and it caught fire. The others got out, but the boy ran the wrong way and got tangled up in the tent folds and couldn't get free. The fire burned him so badly he was unrecognizable afterwards. They thought he was going to die; I think they thought it would be better if he did. But they did what they could for him, and it turned out to be just enough. He says he was a big lad in any case, very strong even then, and some part of him fought back against the pain and misery and kept him alive.

"So he lived, but he was disfigured so badly even his family couldn't stand to look at him. I can't imagine what that must have been like. He says he couldn't look at himself. He kept away from everyone after that, trapping and hunting in the woods, avoiding other people, other places. When he was old enough to manage it, he set out on his own, intending to live apart from everyone. He was bitter and ashamed, and he says that what he really wanted was to die. He went east into the Wolfsktaag, having heard the stories of what lived there, thinking no other man would try living in such a place, so he could at least be alone for whatever time he had left.

"But something happened to him in those mountains—he won't say what, won't talk about it. It changed his way of thinking. He decided he wanted to live. He decided he wanted to be healed. He went to the Stors for medicines and balms, for whatever treatments they could offer, then began some sort of self-healing ritual. He won't talk about that, either. I don't know whether it worked or not. He says it did, but he still hides himself in that cloak and hood. I've never seen him clearly. Not his face, not any part of his body. I don't think anyone has."

"But there's something else about him," Bek interjected quickly. "You say he's human, that he's a man underneath, a man like you and me, but he doesn't seem so. He doesn't seem like any man I've ever come across."

"No," Panax agreed, "he doesn't. And for good reason. I say he's a man like you and me mostly so you don't think he was born anything else. But he's become something more, and it's difficult to say just what that something is. A little of it, I know, I understand. He's found a way of assimilating with the things that live in the Wolfsktaag, a way of becoming like they are. He's able to shape-shift; I know that for a fact. He can takc on the look and feel of animals and spirit creatures; he can become like they are—or, when he chooses, like the things that frighten them. That's what he did back there with those ur'wolves. That's why they ran from him. He's like some force of nature you don't want to cross; he's able to become anything he needs to become to kill you. He's big and strong and quick and fast to begin with; the shape-shifting only enhances that. He's feral and he's instinctive; he knows how to fit in where you and I would only know enough to want to run. He's at home in those mountains. He's at home in places other men never will be. That's why the Druid wants him along. Truls Rohk will get past obstacles no one else would dare even to challenge. He'll solve problems that would leave others scratching their heads."

"How did Walker meet him?" Quentin asked.

"Heard about him, I believe, rumors mostly, then tracked him down. He's the only man I know who could do that." Panax smiled. "I'm not sure he really did track Truls, only that he got close enough to attract his attention. There might not be anyone alive who can track Truls Rohk. But Walker found him somehow and talked him into coming with him on a journey. I'm not sure where they went that first time, but they formed some kind of a bond. Afterwards, Truls was more than willing to go with the Druid."

He shook his head. "Still, you never know. No one really has his ear. He likes me, trusts me, as much as he likes or trusts anyone, but he doesn't let me get too close."

"He's scary," Bek offered quietly. "It's more than how he hides himself or appears like a ghost out of nowhere or shape-shifts. It's more than knowing what's happened to him, too. It's how he looks right through you and makes you feel like he sees things you don't."

"He was right about me and the sword," Quentin agreed. "I didn't know what I was doing. I was just fighting to keep the magic under control, to keep those wolves at bay. If he hadn't come along, they probably would have had us."

Truls Rohk had seen or recognized something about Bek, as well, but had chosen to keep it to himself. Bek wasn't able to stop thinking about it. Trust no one, the shape-shifter had said, until you learn to see things better. It was an admonition that revealed Truls Rohk had gained an insight into him that he himself had not yet experienced. All the way down from the Wolfsktaag and on the journey across the Borderlands to Arborlon, he found himself remembering how it had been to have the shape-shifter looking at him, studying him, penetrating beyond what he could see. It was an old Druid trait, Bek knew. Allanon had been famous for the way his eyes looked right through you. There was something of that in Walker, as well. Truls Rohk was not a Druid, but when he looked at you, you felt as if you were being flayed alive.

The discussion of the shape-shifter pretty much died away after the first night, since Panax seemed to have exhausted his store of knowledge and Quentin and Bek chose to keep their thoughts to themselves. Conversation turned to other matters, particularly the journey ahead, of which the Dwarf was now part but knew little. He had been drafted into the cause because Walker had insisted he join them if Truls Rohk agreed to come. So Bek and Quentin filled Panax in on what little they knew, and the three spent much of their time tossing back and forth their ideas about exactly where they might be going and what they might be looking for.

The Dwarf was blunt in his assessment. "There is no treasure big or rich enough to interest a Druid. A Druid cares only for magic. Walker seeks a talisman or spell or some such. He goes in search of something so powerful that to let it fall into the hands of the Ilse Witch or anyone else would be suicide."

It was a compelling and believable assessment, but no one could think of anything that dangerous. There had been magic in the world since the new races had been born out of the Great Wars, reinvented by the need to survive. Much of it had been potent, and all of it had either been tamed or banished by the Druids. That there might be a new magic, undiscovered all these years and now released solely by chance, felt wrong. Magic didn't exist in a vacuum. It wouldn't just appear. Someone had conjured it, perfected it, and set it loose.

"Which is why Walker is taking people like you, Highlander, with your magic sword, and Truls Rohk," Panax insisted bluntly. "Magic to counter magic, linked to men who can wield it successfully."

This did nothing to explain why Bek was going, or Panax either, for that matter, but at least Panax was a seasoned hunter and skilled tracker; Bek was untrained at anything. Now and again, his hand would stray to the smooth hard surface of the phoenix stone, and he would remember his encounter with the King of the Silver River. Now and again, he would remember that perhaps he was not his father's son. Each time, of course, he would question everything he thought he knew and understood. Each time, he would feel Truls Rohk's eyes looking at him in the Eastland night.

Elven Hunters met them at the far end of the valley and escorted them back through the woods to Arborlon. An escort was unusual for visitors, but it was clear from the moment they gave their names to the watch that they were expected. The road to the city was broad and open, and the ride through the afternoon hours was pleasant. It was still light when they arrived at the city, coming out of the shadow of the trees onto a stretch of old growth that thinned and opened through a sprawl of buildings onto a wide bluff. Arborlon was much bigger and busier than Leah, with shops and residences spreading away for as far as the eye could see, traffic on the roads thick and steady, and people from all the races visible at every turn. Arborlon was a crossroads for commerce, a trading center for virtually every form of goods. Absent were the great forges and factories of the deep Southland and of the Rock Trolls north, but their products were in evidence everywhere, brought west for warehousing and shipping to the Elven people living farther in. Caravans of goods passed them going in and coming out, bound for or sent from those less accessible regions—the Sarandanon west, the Wilderun south, and the Troll nations north.

Quentin glanced about with a broad smile. "This is what we came for, Bek. Isn't it all grand and wonderful—just what you imagined?"

Bek kept his thoughts to himself, not trusting them to words. Mostly he wondered how a people who had just lost a King to assassination could carry on with so little evidence of remorse—though he had to admit he couldn't think of how they should otherwise behave. Life went on, no matter the magnitude of the events that influenced it. He shouldn't expect more.

They passed through the city proper and turned south into a series of parks and gardens to reach what were clearly the Elessedil palace grounds. It was late by then, the light failing quickly, the torches on street poles and building entries lit against the encroaching gloom. The crowds of people they had passed earlier had been left behind. Home Guard materialized out of the shadows, the King's own protectors and the heart of the Elven army, stoic, silent, and sharp-eyed. They took the travelers' horses away, and the Dwarf and cousins were led down a pathway bordered by white oak and tall grasses to an open-air pavilion somewhere back from the palace buildings and overlooking the bluffs east. High-backed benches were clustered about the pavilion, and pitchers of ale and cold water sat on trays beside metal tankards and glasses.

The Home Guard who had escorted them from the road gestured toward the benches and refreshments and left.

Alone, the pavilion empty except for them, the surrounding grounds deserted, they stood waiting. After a few minutes, Panax moved to one of the benches, took out his carving knife and a piece of wood, and began to whittle. Quentin looked at Bek, shrugged, and walked over to help himself to a tankard of ale.

Bek stayed where he was, glancing about warily. He was

thinking of how the Ilse Witch had orchestrated the death of an Elven King not far from that spot. It did not give him a good feeling to think that killing someone in the heart of the Elven capital city was so easy, since all of them were now eligible targets.

"What are you doing?" Quentin asked, sauntering over to join him, tankard of ale in hand. He wore the Sword of Leah strapped across his back as if it was something he had been doing all his life instead of for less than a week.

"Nothing," Bek replied. Already Quentin was evidencing the sort of changes that would affect them both in the end, growing beyond himself, shaking loose from his life. It was what his cousin had come to do, but Bek was still struggling with the idea. "I was just wondering if Walker is here yet."

"Well, you look as if you expect Truls Rohk to appear again, maybe come right out of the earth."

"Don't be too quick to discount the possibility," Panax muttered from the bench.

Quentin was looking around, as well, after that, but it was Bek who spied the two figures coming up the walk from the palace. At first neither cousin could make out the faces in the gloom, catching only momentary glimpses as they passed through each halo of torchlight on their approach. It wasn't until they had reached the pavilion and come out of the shadows completely that Bek and Quentin recognized the short, wiry figure in the lead.

"Hunter Predd," Quentin said, walking forward to offer his hand.

"Well met, Highlander," the other replied, a faint smile creasing his weathered features. He seemed genuinely pleased to see Quentin. "Made the journey out of Leah safely, I see."

"Never a moment's concern."

"That old sword strapped to your back reveal any secrets on the way?"

Quentin flushed. "One or two. You don't forget a thing, do you?"

Bek shook the Wing Rider's hand, as well, feeling a little of his earlier uneasiness fade with the other's appearance. "Is Walker here?" he asked.

Hunter Predd nodded. "He's here. Everyone's here that's going. You're the last to arrive."

Panax rose from his bench and wandered over, and they introduced him to the Wing Rider. Then Hunter Predd turned to his companion, a tall, powerfully built Elf of indeterminate age, with close-cropped gray hair and pale blue eyes. "This is Ard Patrinell," the Wing Rider said. "Walker wanted you to meet him. He's been placed in command of the Elven Hunters who will go with us."

They clasped hands with the Elf, who nodded without speaking. Bek thought that if ever anyone looked the part of a warrior, it was this man. Scars crisscrossed his blunt features and muscular body, thin white lines and rough pink welts against his sun-browned skin, a testament to battles fought and survived. Power radiated from even his smallest movements. His grip when shaking hands was deliberately soft, but Bek could feel the iron behind it. Even the way he carried himself suggested someone who was always ready, always just a fraction of a second away from swift reaction.

"You're a Captain of the Home Guard," Panax declared, pointing to the scarlet patch on the Elf's dress jacket.

Ard Patrinell shook his head. "I was. I'm not anymore."

"They don't keep you on as Captain of the Home Guard if the King is assassinated on your watch," Hunter Predd observed bluntly.

Panax nodded matter-of-factly. "Someone has to bear the blame for a King's death, even when there's no blame to be found. Keeps everyone thinking something useful's been done." He spat into the dark. "So, Ard Patrinell, you look a seasoned sort. Have you fought on the Prekkendorran?"

Again, the Elf shook his head. "I fought in the Federation Wars, but not there. I was at Klcpach and Barrengrote fifteen years ago, when I was still an Elven Hunter, not yet a Home

Guard." If Patrinell was irritated by the Dwarf's questions, he didn't show it.

For his part, Bek was wondering how a failed Captain of the Home Guard could end up being given responsibility for the security and safety of Walker's expedition. Was his removal only ceremonial, made necessary because of the King's death? Or was something else at work?

There was an enormous calm in Ard Patrinell's face, as if nothing could shake his confidence or disrupt his thinking. He had the look of someone who had seen and weathered a great deal and understood that loss of control was a soldier's worst enemy. If he had failed the King, he did not carry the burden of that failure openly. Bek judged him a man who understood better than most the value of patience and endurance.

"What remains to be done before we leave?" Quentin asked suddenly, changing the subject.

"Impatient to be off, Highlander?" Hunter Predd chided. "It won't be long now. We've got an airship and a Captain and crew to speed us on our way. We're gathering supplies and equipment. Loading is already under way. Our Captain of the Home Guard has selected a dozen Elven Hunters to accompany us."

"We're ready then," Quentin declared eagerly, his grin broadening with expectation.

"Not quite." The Wing Rider seemed reluctant to continue, but unable to think of a way not to. He glanced out at the encroaching night, as if his explanation might be found somewhere in the gloom. "There's still a few adjustments to be made to the terms of our going, a couple of small controversies to be resolved."

Panax frowned. "What might these small controversies be, Hunter Predd?"

The Wing Rider shrugged rather too casually, Bek thought. "For one thing, Walker feels we have too many members assigned to the expedition. Space and supplies won't support them all. He wants to reduce by as many as four or five the number that will go."

"Our new King, on the other hand," Ard Patrinell added softly, "wants to add one more."

"What you are asking is not only unreasonable, it is impossible," Walker repeated patiently, stymied by Kylen Elessedil's intransigence on the matter, but fully aware of its source. "Thirty is all we can carry. The size of the ship will allow for no more. As it is, I have to find a way to cut the number who expect to go."

"Cut that number to twenty-nine, then add one back in," the Elven King replied with a shrug. "The problem is solved."

They stood in what had been Allardon Elessedil's private study, the one in which he had perused the castaway's map for the first time, but more to the point the one in which he had conducted business with those with whom he did not want to be seen on matters he did not wish to discuss openly. When the Elven King desired a public audience or a demonstration of authority, he held court in the throne room or the chambers of the Elven High Council. Allardon Elessedil had been a believer in protocol and ceremony, and he had employed each in careful and judicious measure. His son, it appeared, was inclined to do the same. Walker rated courtesy and deference, but only in private and only to the extent to which the old King had obligated his son before dying.

Kylen Elessedil understood what must be done regarding the matter of Kael Elessedil and the Elves who had disappeared with him. There was to be a search, and the Druid was to command it. The Elves were to assign funds for the purchase of a ship and crew, secure supplies and equipment for the journey, and provide a command of Elven Hunters to ensure the ship's safety. It was the command of a dying King, and his son was not about to challenge it as his first official act of office.

This did not mean, however, that he viewed the idea of a

search for ships and men gone thirty years as a sane one, the appearance of the castaway, the Elessedil bracelet, and the map notwithstanding. Kylen was not his father. He was a very different sort. Allardon Elessedil had been tentative, careful, and unambitious in his life's goals. His son was reckless and determined to leave his mark. The past meant little to Kylen Elessedil. It was the present and, to an even greater extent, the future that mattered to him. He was an impassioned youth who believed without reservation that the Federation must be destroyed and the Free-born made victorious. Nothing less would guarantee Elven security. He had spent the last six months fighting aboard airships over the Prekkendorran and had returned only because his father was dead and he was next in line for the throne. He did not particularly want to be King, except to the extent that it furthered his efforts to crush the Federation. Imbued with the fever of his commitment to a victory over his enemies, he wanted only to remain on the front in command of his men. In short, he would have preferred it if his father had stayed alive.

As it was, eager to return to the battle, he was chafing already at the delay his coronation had occasioned. But he would not go, Walker knew, until this matter of the search for Kael Elessedil was resolved and, even more important, until he was certain the Elven High Council was settled on the terms of his succession. This last, Walker was beginning to understand, was at the source of his insistence on adding his younger brother's name to the ship's roster.

Kylen Elessedil stopped pacing and faced the Druid squarely. "Ahren is almost a man, nearly fully grown. He has been trained by the man I personally selected to command your Elven Hunters on this expedition. My father arranged for my brother's training five years ago. Perhaps he foresaw the need for it better than you or I."

"Perhaps he believed it should continue until Ahren is older, as well," Walker offered mildly, holding the other's gaze. "Your brother is too young and too unseasoned for a journey like this. He lacks the experience needed to justify including him. Better men will be asked to remain behind as it is."

The Elven King dismissed the argument with a grunt. "That's a judgment you cannot make. Is Ahren less a man than this cabin boy you insist on including? Bek Rowe? What does he have to offer? Is he to be left behind?"

Walker held his temper. "Your father left it to me to make the decision about who would go and who would stay. I have chosen carefully, and there are good reasons for my choices. What is at issue is not why I should take Bek Rowe, but why I should take Ahren Elessedil."

The Elf King took a moment to walk over to a window and look out into the night. "I don't have to support you in this matter at all, Druid. I don't have to honor my father's wishes if I deem them wrongheaded or if I decide circumstances have changed. You are pressing your luck with me."

He turned back to Walker, waiting.

"There is a great deal at stake in this matter," Walker replied softly. "Enough at stake that I will find a way to make this voyage, with your blessing and assistance or without. I would remind you that your father died for this."

"My father died *because* of this!"

"Your father believed me when I told him that what the Elven people stood to gain from completing this voyage successfully was of enormous importance."

"Yet you refuse to tell me what that something is!"

"Because I am not yet certain myself." Walker walked over to the King's desk and rested the tips of his fingers on its polished surface. "It is a magic that may yield us many things, but I will have to discover what form that magic will take. But think, Elven King! If it is important enough for the Ilse Witch to kill your father and your uncle as well, important enough for her to try to kill me and to stall this expedition at all costs, isn't it important enough for you?"

The young King folded his arms defensively. "Perhaps your concerns in this matter are overstated. Perhaps they are not as important as you would have me believe. I do not see the future of the Westland Elves tied to a magic that may not even exist, may not be able to be traced if it does, and may not even be useful if found. I see it tied to a war being waged with the Federation. The enemy I can see is a more recognizable threat than the one I can imagine."

Walker shook his head. "Why are we arguing? We have covered this ground before, and there is nothing to be gained by covering it again. I am committed to this journey. You have determined that your father's wishes should be followed regarding any support from the Elves. What we are arguing about is the inclusion on this expedition of a youth who is untested and inexperienced. Shall I tell you why I think you want me to take him?"

Kylen Elessedil hesitated, but Walker began speaking anyway.

"He is your younger brother and next in line for the throne. You are not close. You are the children of different mothers. If you were to be killed in the fighting on the Prekkendorran, he would be named Regent, if not King. You wish to secure the throne for your children instead. But your oldest boy is only ten. Your brother, if available, would be named his protector. That worries you. To protect your son and heir to the throne, you would send your brother with me, on a journey that will consume months and perhaps years. That removes your brother as a possible successor, either as King or Regent. It removes him as a threat."

He spoke calmly, without malice or accusation. When he was finished, Kylen Elessedil stared at him for a long time, as if weighing carefully his response.

"You are awfully bold to speak those words to me," he said finally.

Walker nodded. "I am only telling you this so that I may

better understand your thinking on the matter. If Ahren Elessedil is to go with me, I would like to know why."

The young King smiled. "My father never liked you. He respected you, but he never liked you. Were you this bold with him?"

"More so, I would guess."

"But it never helped you, did it? He never agreed to support you in your bid for an independent Druid Council, convened anew at Paranor. I know. He told me."

Walker waited.

"You risk all that now by challenging me. Part of your bargain with my father was his agreement to support a new Council of Druids on your successful return. You've worked twenty-five years for that end. Would you give it all up now?"

Still Walker waited, silent within his black robes.

Kylen Elessedil stared at him a moment more, then judging that nothing further was to be gained, said, "Ahren will accompany you as my personal representative. I cannot go, so he will go in my place. This is an Elven expedition, and its goals and concerns are peculiarly Elven in nature. Kael Elessedil's disappearance must be explained. The Elfstones, if they can be found, must be returned. Any magic that exists must be claimed. These are Elven matters. Whatever happens, there must be an Elessedil in attendance. That is why my brother is going, and that is the end of the matter."

It was a firm decision, one rendered and dismissed for good. Walker could see that nothing was to be gained by arguing further. Whatever his convictions and concerns on the subject of Ahren Elessedil, Walker knew when it was time to back off. "So be it," he acknowledged, and turned the discussion to other matters.

It was after midnight when Quentin shook Bek awake from the sleep that had claimed him an hour before. With no further word from Walker on the fate of the expedition and its members, they had retired from the palace gardens and been shown to their sleeping quarters by another of the silent Home Guard. Panax was snoring in another room. Ard Patrinell and Hunter Predd had disappeared.

"Bek, wake up!" Quentin urged, pulling on his shoulder.

Bek, still catching up on sleep lost during their journey west out of the Wolfsktaag, dragged himself out of his cottony slumber and opened his eyes. "What's the matter?"

"Hunter Predd just returned from the palace, where he's spoken with Walker." Quentin's eyes were bright and his voice excited. "I heard him come in and went to see what he'd learned. He said to tell you good-bye for now. He's been sent to the coast to recruit two more Wing Riders from the Hove. The decision's been made. We leave in two days!"

"Two days," Bek repeated, not yet fully awake.

"Yes, cousin, but you didn't hear me clearly. I said *we* are going, you and I!" Quentin laughed gleefully. "Walker kept us both! He's leaving behind three of the Home Guard and taking only a single Healer. I don't know, maybe there was someone else left off the list, as well. But he kept us! That's what matters! We're going, Bek!"

Afterwards, Quentin fell into bed and off to sleep so quickly that Bek, now awake, was unable to measure the time lapse between the two. It seemed somehow inevitable that he should be going. Even when Hunter Predd had warned that there were too many chosen for the voyage and some would be left behind, it had never occurred to him that he would be one of them. It was logical that he would be, of course. He was the youngest and the least skilled. On the face of things, he was the most expendable. But something in the Druid's insistence that he come, coupled with his encounters with the King of the Silver River and Truls Rohk, had convinced him that his selection was no afterthought and was tied inextricably to secrets of the past and to resolution of events yet to be determined. Bek was there because it was necessary for him to be so, and his life was about to change forever.

It was what Quentin had wanted for them both. But Bek Rowe was inclined to wonder if one day soon they would have cause to remember the danger of getting what you wish for.

EIGHTEEN

Bek Rowe woke the following morning to sunshine and blue skies and no sign of Quentin Leah. He took a moment to orient himself, decided he was still in Arborlon, and jumped out of bed to dress. When he checked the adjoining bedrooms, he found that Panax was missing as well. A quick glance out the window revealed the sun at midmorning height, a clear indicator of how late he had slept. There was grain cereal, cheese, and milk on the table in the anteroom, and he wolfed them down hungrily before charging out the door in search of his friends.

He was running so fast and so hard he ran right into the black-cloaked figure coming in.

"Walker!" he gasped in shock and embarrassment, and jumped back quickly.

"Good morning, Bek Rowe," the Druid said formally. A faint smile played at the corners of his mouth. "Did you sleep well?"

"Too well," Bek answered, chagrined. "I'm sorry. I didn't mean to be such a layabout—"

"Please, young traveler, don't be so anxious to apologize." Walker was chuckling softly now. He put his big hand on Bek's shoulder. "You haven't missed anything. Nor have you neglected any obligations. You were right to sleep. That was a long journey up to Depo Bent and then west to here. I would rather have you rested when we set out from here."

Bek sighed. "I guess I just assumed that since Quentin and Panax are already up and gone I was lagging in some way."

Walker shook his head. "I passed the Highlander on my way here. He had just gotten up. Panax rose a little earlier, but he doesn't sleep much. Don't think on it again. Did you eat?"

Bek nodded.

"Then you're ready to go out to the airfield and have a look around. Come with me."

They left the sleeping quarters and walked through the palace grounds, moving away from the city and out toward the south end of the Carolan. They passed any number of Elven Hunters and Home Guard on the way, but few regular citizens. No one paid them any attention. It was quieter where they walked than in the main sections of the city, less traveled by those who lived and worked there. On the backside of the Gardens of Life, they passed a pair of Black Watch guarding one of the entrances. The pair stood as if frozen, towering over everyone in their sleek black uniforms and tall hats, everything smooth and clean and trimmed in red. Within the gardens, birds darted and sang, and butterflies flitted from bush to bush, as bright as the flowers they touched upon, but the Black Watch might have been carved from stone.

Somewhere deep in the center of those gardens was the legendary Ellcrys. Even Bek, who had traveled so little, knew her story. The Ellcrys was a tree imbued with magic that formed a Forbidding to shut away the demons banished by the Word from the Faerie world centuries ago at the beginning of life. She had begun her life as an Elf, a member of an order called Chosen, and had transformed into the tree as a result of exposure to the Bloodfire. So long as she remained strong and healthy in her changed state, her magic would keep the Forbidding in place. When she began to fail, as she one day must, another would take her place. The need for replacement did not happen often; the Ellcrys on average lived for a thousand years. But the order of the Chosen was kept filled and ready even so. Once, not so long ago, almost all had been slaughtered by demons that had escaped a weakened Forbidding. Only one had survived, a young Elessedil girl named Amberle, and she had sacrificed herself to become the present Ellcrys.

Bek thought of how Coran had told him that story when he was still very little. Coran had told him any number of Elven stories, and it had always seemed to Bek that the history of the Elves must be more colorful and interesting than those of the other races, even without knowing what they were. Seeing the Gardens of Life now and having passed through the Valley of Rhenn earlier, a visitor at last to the city of Arborlon, he could believe it was so. Everything had a feeling of magic and enchantment, and all that history imparted to him by Coran felt newly alive and real.

It made him think that coming on the journey was not such a bad idea after all, though he would never admit it to Quentin.

"Did Truls Rohk arrive?" he asked Walker suddenly.

Walker did not look at him. "Did you ask him to come?"

Bek nodded. "Yes."

"Did he say he would?"

"Yes."

"Then he's here."

Walker seemed perfectly willing to accept the shapeshifter's presence on faith, so Bek let the matter drop. It wasn't his concern in any case. Another encounter with Truls Rohk could wait. Walker had already moved on, talking about their plans for departure on the following morning, the airship fitted and supplied, its crew and passengers assembled, and everything in readiness for their journey. He was confident and relaxed as he detailed their preparations, but when Bek glanced over, he caught a distant look in the other's dark eyes that suggested his thoughts were somewhere else.

Away from the buildings of the city, the Gardens of Life, and the Carolan, they passed down a well-traveled road through woods that opened onto a bluff farther south. Bek could hear the activity before he could see it, and when they emerged from the trees, an airfield and a dozen Elven airships were visible. Bek had never seen airships up close, only flying over the highlands now and then, but there was no mistaking them for anything other than what they were. They hung motionless above the earth as if cradled by the air on which they floated, tethered like captured birds to anchoring pins. From the ground they looked much bigger, particularly from where Bek stood looking up at them. Broad stretches of decking, single and multilevel, were fastened to pontoons fitted out and armored as fighting stations. On some of the airships, cabins and steering lofts were affixed aft; on others, they were settled amidships. Various forms of housing could be found both atop and beneath the decking. Single, double, and triple masts speared the clear blue sky.

"There's our vessel, Bek," Walker announced softly, his voice gone distant and soft.

Even without being told, Bek knew which of the airships the Druid was talking about. The ship in question was so different from the others that his eyes were drawn to it immediately. Its profile was low and sleek, and while it did not appear less formidable as a fighting vessel, it had a look of quickness and maneuverability that the others lacked. Its twin masts were raked and its cabins were recessed deep into the decking both fore and aft, adding to the long, smooth look. Its elevated pilot box sat amidships between the masts. Several sets of fighting ports were built into the pontoons, which curved upward at both ends like horns and were fashioned as battering rams. Other sets of fighting ports were integrated into the deck railings, which were slanted inward to provide maximum protection against attack. The airship had a dark and wicked look to it, even at rest, and a shiver went down Bek's spine as he imagined it in motion.

Men were swarming all over its decking, some working on sails and lines, some carrying aboard supplies and equipment. On this morning, it was the center of activity, with preparations for its voyage long since under way.

"If you wait here, I'll send someone over to put you to work," Walker said. Without waiting for a response, he moved away.

Bek stood looking at the shadowy form of the airship, trying without success to imagine what it would feel like to fly in her, to have this strange vessel as his home. He knew a journey of the sort they were planning would take weeks and probably months. All that time, they would live and travel aboard this ship. Thirty men and women, confined in a small, constantly moving wood-and-iron shell, adrift in the world. It was a sobering image.

"She's a striking lady, isn't she," a voice broke into his thoughts.

He glanced over as the speaker came up to him, a tall man with long red hair and clear green eyes and dressed in a wild combination of black leather and bright scarves. "She is," Bek agreed.

"You'd be Bek Rowe?" the man inquired with a grin, his manner open and friendly and immediately disarming. Bek nodded. "I'm this lady's Captain. Redden Alt Mer." He stuck out his hand in greeting, and Bek took it. "You're to be my cabin boy, Bek. You can call me Captain or sir. Or you can call me Big Red, like nearly everyone else does. Have you sailed before?"

Bek shook his head. "Not really. On the Rainbow Lake once or twice and on rivers and streams in the Highlands."

The tall man laughed. "Goodness, they've given me a cabin boy with no sea legs at all! No experience on open water or free air either, Bek? What am I to do with you?"

Bek grimaced. "Hope for the best?"

"No, no, no, we can't be relying on hope to see you through." He grinned anew. "Are you a quick study?"

"I think so."

"Good, that will help our cause. This morning is all I've

got to teach you what I know before we set out, so we must make the most of it. You know about airships, do you?"

"A little." Bek was feeling foolish and slow, but the tall man was not unkind or intimidating.

"You'll know everything by the time I'm done." He paused. "A few words of advice to begin with, Bek. I'm a Rover, so you know two things right off. One, I've forgotten more about airships than other men have learned, and with the crew of Rovers I've chosen to serve under me, I can see us through anything. So don't ever question or doubt me. Second, don't ever say anything bad about Rovers—not even if you think I can't hear you."

He waited for Bek to answer, so Bek said, "No, sir."

"Good. Now here's the really important thing to remember." The cheerful face took on a serious, almost contemplative cast. "The Druid's in charge of this expedition, so I am obliged to respect his wishes and obey his orders save where the safety of the ship and crew are concerned. He's ordered me to take you on as cabin boy. That's fine. But you and I need to understand each other. The Druid intends you to serve as his eyes and ears aboard ship. He wants you to watch everyone and everything, me included. That's fine, too. I expect you can do this and do it well. But I don't want you thinking I don't know why you're really here. Fair enough?"

Bek flushed. "I'm not a spy."

"Did I say you were? Did I suggest that you were anything of the sort?" The Rover shook his head reprovingly. "Smart lads keep their eyes and ears open in any case. I don't begrudge any man that advantage. My purpose in bringing this up is to make sure you understand that as clever as the Druid thinks he is, he's no more clever than I am. I wouldn't want you to make a foolish assumption about your Captain."

Bek nodded. "Me either."

"Good lad!" Redden Alt Mer seemed genuinely pleased. "Now let's put all that behind us and begin our lessons. Come with me."

He took Bek over to the airship and had him climb the rope ladder to the decking. There, standing amidships with the boy, he began a step-by-step explanation of the ship's operation. The sails were called light sheaths. Their function was to gather light, either direct or ambient, from the skies for conversion to energy. Light could be drawn from any source, day or night. Direct light was best, but frequently it was not to be found, so the availability and usefulness of ambient light was the key to an airship's survival. Light energy gathered by the sheaths was relayed by lines called radian draws. The draws took the heat down to the decking and into containers called parse tubes, which housed diapson crystals. The crystals, when properly prepared by craftsmen, received and converted the light energy to the energy that propelled and steered the airship. Hooding and unhooding the crystals determined the amount of thrust and direction the airship took.

Redden Alt Mer had Bek repeat all this back when he was finished, word for word. Intrigued by the process and interested to learn everything about how it worked, the boy did so faultlessly. The Rover was pleased. Understanding the principles of airship flight was crucial to learning how to operate her. But it took years to learn how to fly an airship properly, as the Federation pilots had not yet discovered. The nuances of hooding and unhooding the crystals, of riding and sideslipping wind currents, and of avoiding downdrafts and lightfalls that could change the momentum and responsiveness of an airship in an instant were not easily mastered. Rovers were the best pilots, he offered without a trace of boasting. Rovers were born to the free life, and they adapted and understood flight better than other men.

Or women, a tall, red-haired woman who might have been his twin offered pointedly, coming up beside them. Redden Alt Mer only barely managed to salvage his gaffe by introducing his sister, Rue Meridian, as the best airship pilot he had ever known and a better fighter than any man he had flown with. Rue Meridian, with her striking looks and flaming hair, her confident, no-nonsense attitude, and her smiling eyes and ready laugh, made Bek feel shy and awkward. But she made him feel good, too. She did not challenge him as her brother had done or question his presence in any way. She simply told him she was glad to have him aboard. Still, there was an iron core to her that Bek did not misjudge, a kind of redoubt beneath the cheerful facade that he suspected he did not want to come up against.

She chatted with them for a few minutes more, then left to oversee the loading of the vessel. Her departure left a void in Bek that was tangible and startling.

With Redden Alt Mer leading, they continued to walk the airship end to end, the Rover explaining what everything was as they went. Each time he finished an explanation, he made Bek repeat it back to him. Each time, he seemed satisfied with the answer he received. He explained the pilot box and the connectors that ran to the parse tubes, hoods, rudders, and main draws. For the most part, the crew raised and lowered the sheaths and set the draws, but in an emergency, everything could be controlled from the pilot box. There were anchors and stays for landing. There were weapons of all sorts, some handheld, some attached to the decking of the ship. The Rover took Bek into the sleeping quarters and supply bins. He took the boy all the way up the pegged climbing steps of the masts to see how the sheaths were attached to the draws, then down to the parse tubes to see how the draws were attached to the diapson crystals. He was quick with his explanations, but thorough. He seemed intent on the boy's learning, and Bek was eager to comply.

There was only one component of the airship that the Rover avoided assiduously, a large rectangular box set upright against the foremast in front of the pilot box. It was covered with black canvas and lashed to the mast and decking with a strange type of metal-sheathed cable. They walked right by it repeatedly, and after they had done so for about the third or fourth time, Bek could contain himself no longer.

"Captain, what's under the canvas?" he asked, pointing at the box.

The Rover scratched his head. "I don't know. It belongs to the Druid. He had it brought aboard in the dead of night without my knowing two days ago, and when I found it there, he told me it was necessary that we take it with us, but he couldn't tell me what it was."

Bek stared at it. "Has anyone tried to get a look under the canvas?"

The Rover laughed. "A lad after my own heart! Shades, Bek Rowe, but you are a wonder! Of course, we tried! Several of us!" He paused dramatically. "Want to know what happened?"

Bek nodded.

"Try looking for yourself and see."

Bek hesitated, no longer so eager.

"Go on," the other urged, gesturing, "it won't hurt you."

So Bek reached for the canvas, and when his hand got to within a foot of it, lines of thin green fire began to dance all over the cables that lashed the box in place, jumping from cable to cable, a nest of writhing snakes. Bek jerked his hand back quickly.

Redden Alt Mer chuckled. "That was our decision, as well. A Druid's magic is nothing to trifle with."

His instruction of Bek continued as if nothing had happened. After Bek had been aboard for a time and his initial excitement had died down, he became aware of a movement to the airship that had not been apparent before, a gentle swaying, a tugging against the anchoring lines. There was no apparent wind, the day calm and still, and there was no movement from the other ships that might account for the motion. When Bek finally asked about it, Redden Alt Mer told him it was the natural response of the ship to the absorption of light into their sheaths. The converted energy kept her aloft, and it was only the anchor cables that kept her from floating away completely, because her natural inclination was to take flight. The Rover admitted that he had been flying for so long that he didn't notice the motion himself anymore.

Bek thought it gave the airship the feel of being alive, of having an existence independent of the men and women who rode her. It was a strange sensation, but the longer he stayed aboard, the more he felt it. The ship moved like a great cat stirring out of sleep, lazy and unhurried, coming slowly awake. The motion radiated through the decking and into his body, so that he soon became a part of it, and it had something of the feel of floating in water that was still and untroubled.

Redden Alt Mer finished with him at midday and sent him off to help inventory supplies and equipment with a bluff, burly fellow Rover called Furl Hawken. The Rover everyone called Hawk barely gave him a second glance, but was friendly enough and pleased at his quickness in picking up the instructions he was given. Once or twice, Rue Meridian came by, and every time Bek was mesmerized.

"She affects everyone that way," Furl Hawken observed with a grin, catching the look on his face. "Little Red will break your heart just by looking at you. Too bad it's wasted effort."

Bek wanted to ask what he meant but was too embarrassed to pursue the matter, so he let it drop.

By the end of the day, Bek had learned most of what there was to know about the operation of their airship, the components that drove her, and the nature of the supplies and equipment she would be carrying. He had met most of the crew as well, including the ship's builder, a truly frightening Rover named Spanner Frew, who yelled and cursed at everyone in general and looked ready to knock down anyone who dared question him. He acknowledged Bek with a grunt and afterwards ignored him completely. Bek was just as happy.

He was on his way back across the airfield with the sun at his back when Quentin caught up with him.

"Did you go aboard the ship?" he asked eagerly, falling into step with his cousin. He was sweating through his rumpled, stained clothes. His long hair was matted, and the skin of his hands and forearms was cut and bruised.

"I've hardly been *off* the ship," Bek said. He gave the other a smirk. "What have you been doing, wrestling bears?"

Quentin laughed. "No, Walker ordered me to train with the Elven Hunters. Ard Patrinell worked with me all day. He knocked me down so many times and skinned me up so many different ways that all I can think about is how little I know." He reached back for his sword. "This thing's not all it's cracked up to be, Bek."

Bek grinned mischievously. "Well, it's probably only as good as its bearer, Quentin. Anyway, count your blessings. I spent all day learning how much I don't know about airships and flying. I'd be willing to bet that there's a lot more I don't know about flying than you don't know about fighting."

Quentin laughed and shoved him playfully, and they joked and teased each other all the way back to the palace compound as the last of the sunlight disappeared below the horizon and the twilight began to shadow the land. With the setting of the sun, a stillness enveloped the city as her people drifted homeward and the bustle and clamor of traffic faded away. In the woods through which the cousins passed close by the palace grounds and parks, the only sounds were of voices, indistinct and distant, carried in the silence from other places.

They were approaching the pathway that led to their sleeping quarters when Bek said quietly, "Quentin? What do you think we're really doing here?"

They stopped, and his cousin looked at him in confusion. "What do you mean?"

Bek put his hands on his hips and sighed. "Think about it. Why are we here? Why us, with all these others that Walker's chosen?"

"Because Walker thinks we—"

"I know what Walker told us." Bek cut him short impatiently. "He told us he wanted two young, clever fellows to share his thoughts. He told us he wanted you for your magic sword and me for my keen eyes and ears or some such thing. I know what he said, and I've been trying to make myself believe it since we set out. But I don't. I don't believe it at all."

Quentin nodded matter-of-factly, unperturbed. Sometimes Bek just wanted to throttle him. "Are you listening to me?" he snapped.

His cousin nodded. "Sure. You don't believe Walker. Why not?"

"Because, Quentin, it just doesn't feel right." Bek emphasized his words with chopping gestures. "Everyone selected for this expedition has years of experience exploring and fighting. They've been all over the Four Lands, and they know how to deal with all sorts of trouble. What do we know? Nothing. Why take two inexperienced nobodies like us?"

"He's taking Ahren Elessedil," Quentin offered. "And what about the seer? Ryer Ord Star? She doesn't look very strong."

Bek nodded impatiently. "I'm not talking about strength alone. I'm talking about skill and experience and talent. I'm talking about purpose! What's ours? We've just spent the entire day training, for goodness' sake! Did you see anyone else training for this trip? Are you really the only one Walker could turn to who could back him up with magic? In all the Four Lands, the only one? Given what happened in the Wolfsktaag, how much use do you think you would be to him at this point? Be honest!"

Quentin was quiet a moment. "Not much," he admitted grudgingly, and for the first time a hint of doubt crept into his voice.

"What about me?" Bek pursued his argument with a vengeance. "Am I the only clever pair of eyes and ears he can call on? Am I really that useful to him that he would drop several Elven Hunters with years of experience and training behind them and a skilled Healer, as well? Are you and I all that wondrous that he just can't afford to leave us behind, even though we know he's pressed for space?"

They stared at each other in the growing dark without speaking, eyes locked. Somewhere in the compound ahead, a door slammed and a voice called out a name.

Quentin shook his head. "What are you saying, Bek?" he asked softly. "That we shouldn't go? That we should give this whole business up?"

Oddly enough, that wasn't his intent. It might have been a logical suggestion, given his arguments and conclusions. It might have been what another man would have done under the circumstances, but Bek Rowe had decided he would make the voyage. He was committed. He was as determined to go as Quentin was. Maybe it had something to do with the secrets he had discovered since Walker had appeared to them in the Highlands—of his father's identity and his own origins, of the King of the Silver River and the phoenix stone, of Truls Rohk and his cryptic warning not to trust anyone. Maybe it was just that he was too stubborn to quit when so many would know and judge him accordingly. Maybe it was his belief that he was meant to make the journey, whatever his fears or doubts, because going would determine in some important and immutable way the course of his life.

A small voice of reason still whispered that he should tell Quentin, *Yes, we should give this business up and go home.* He squelched that voice with barely a second's thought.

"What I'm saying," he replied instead, "is that we should be careful about what we accept at face value. Druids keep secrets and play games with ordinary men like you and me. That's their history and tradition. They manipulate and deceive. They are tricksters, Quentin. I don't know about Walker. I don't know much of anything about what he really intends for us. I just think we ought to be very careful. I think we . . ."

He ran out of words and stood there, looking at his cousin helplessly.

"You think we ought to look out for each other," Quentin finished, nodding slowly. "We always have, haven't we?"

Bek sighed. "But maybe we need to do more of it here. And when something doesn't sit right, like this business, I think we have to tell each other so. If we don't, Quentin, who will?"

"Maybe no one."

"Maybe not."

Quentin studied him in silence once more, then smiled suddenly. "You know what, Bek? If you hadn't agreed to come on this journey, I wouldn't have come either."

Bek stared at him in surprise. "Really?"

Quentin nodded. "Because of what you've just said. There isn't anyone else I would trust to watch my back or tell me the truth about things. Only you. You think I look at you like a bothersome younger brother that I let tag along because I have to. I don't. I want you with me. I'm bigger and stronger, sure. And I'm better at some things than you. But you have a gift for figuring things out that I don't. You get at the truth in a way I can't. You see things I don't even notice."

He paused. "What I'm trying to say is that I think of us as equals as well as brothers. I pay pretty close attention to how you feel about things, whether you realize it or not. That's the way it's always been. That's the way it will be here. I won't accept anything I'm told without talking it over with you. You don't have to ask me to do that. I'd do it anyway."

Bek felt awkward and foolish. "I guess I just needed to say what I was thinking out loud."

Quentin grinned. "Well, who knows? Maybe I needed to hear you say it, too. Now it's done. Let's go eat."

They went inside then, and for the rest of the night until he fell asleep Bek found himself thinking how close he was to Quentin—as a brother, a friend, and a confidant—closer than he was to anyone in the world. They had shared everything growing up, and he could not imagine it being any other way. He made a promise to himself then, the sort of promise he hadn't made since he was a small boy filled with the sort of resolve that age tempered and time wore down. He did not know where they were going or what they would encounter in the days ahead, Quentin and he, but whatever happened he would find a way to keep his brother safe.

NINETEEN

Dawn broke in a bright golden blaze at the line between sky and earth on the eastern horizon, and the airfield south of Arborlon began to fill with Elves come to watch the launch of the expedition. Thousands approached, crowding down the roads and walks, slipping along the narrow forest trails and pathways, filling the spaces at the edges of the field until their eager, excited faces ringed the bluff. Organized by unit and company, a sizable contingent from the Elven army was already in place, drawn up in formation at both ends of the field, Elven Hunters in their soft green and taupe dress uniforms, Home Guard in emerald trimmed with crimson, and Black Watch standing tall and dark and forbidding like winter trees. Overhead, Elven airships that had already lifted off circled like silent phantoms, sailing on the back of a slow, soft morning wind.

At the center of the airfield, solitary and proud, the sleek, dark airship that was the object of everyone's attention hung just off the ground in the new light, her sails unfurled and her lines taut, straining to be free.

Quentin on one side and Panax on the other, Bek Rowe stood watching from the bow. All about the railings fore and aft were gathered the Rovers who would crew the ship, the Elven Hunters who would defend her, and the few other members of the expedition chosen by Walker. The Druid stood with Redden Alt Mer in the pilot box, talking quietly, sharp eyes shifting left and right as he spoke, hands folded into his black robes.

Ahren Elessedil stood alone amidships by the foremast, isolated from everyone. He was a small, slight Elf with boyish features and a quiet manner. Whereas his brother Kylen was fair and blond in the traditional manner of the Elessedils, Ahren was dusky of skin and brown of hair, closer in appearance to the great Queen Wren. He had come aboard with the other Elves, but quickly separated from them and had remained apart since. He seemed lost and uncertain of himself as he stood looking out at the crowds. Bek felt sorry for him. He was in a difficult position. Officially, he was a representative of the Elessedil family and the crown, but everyone knew that Walker had been forced to include him because Kylen had insisted on it. Rumor had it that Kylen wanted him out of the way.

That accounted for everyone but Truls Rohk. Of the shapeshifter, there was still no sign.

A blare of trumpets drew Bek's eyes to where the crowd was parting to make way for the Elven King and his retinue. A long line of Home Guard marched through the gap, flanking standard bearers who bore the flags of all the Elven Kings and Queens dead and gone, personal icons sewn on brightly colored fields swirling in the breeze. When they had passed onto the airfield, the Elessedil family banner hove into view, a crimson image of the Ellcrys emblazoned on a field of green. Kylen Elessedil followed on horseback, raised high enough above the heads of the crowd so that all could see him. His wife and children rode on horses behind him followed on foot by the more distant members of his family and his personal retinue. The long column marched out of the trees and onto the airfield and took up a position directly in front of the airship's curved bow.

The trumpets sounded once more and went still. The crowd quieted, and Kylen Elessedil lifted his arms in greeting.

"Citizens of Arborlon! Friends of the Elven!" His booming

voice carried easily from one end of the field to the other. "We are gathered to witness and to celebrate an epochal event. A band of men and women of great courage will go forth this day on our behalf and on behalf of all free and right-thinking men and women everywhere. They sail the winds of the world in search of truths that have eluded us for thirty years. On their journey, they will attempt to discover the fate of my father's brother's expedition, lost those thirty years ago, of those ships and men, and of the Elfstones they carried, which are our heritage. On their journey, they will seek out treasures and magics that are rightfully ours and that can be put to the uses for which they were intended by the men and women for whom they were meant—Elves, one and all!"

A cheer rose from the crowd, swelling quickly to a roar. Bek glanced about at the faces of those gathered close, but found no expression on any save Quentin's, where a kind of vague amusement flickered like candlelight in the wind and was gone.

"My brother Ahren leads this expedition on behalf of my family and our people," Kylen continued as the cheering died away. "He is to be commended and respected for his bravery and his sense of duty. With him go some of the bravest of our Elven Hunters; our good friend from the Druids of Paranor, Walker; a complement of skilled and capable Rovers to captain and crew the ship; and a select band of others drawn from the Four Lands who will lend their talents and courage to this most important effort. Acknowledge them all, my friends! Praise them well!"

Again, the roar went up, the banners waved, and the air was filled with sound and color, and Bek, in spite of his cynicism, found himself infused with unmistakable pride.

Kylen Elessedil held up his hands. "We have lost a good and well-loved King in these past weeks. Treachery and cowardice have taken my father, Allardon Elessedil, from us. It was his dying wish that this expedition set forth, and I would be a poor son and subject indeed if I failed to honor his wishes. These men and women"—he gestured behind him toward the ship—"feel as I do. Everything possible has been done to assure their success and speedy return. We send them off with our good wishes, and we will not cease to think of them until they are safely home again."

Clever, Bek thought, to lay everything off on the old King, dead and gone. Kylen had learned something of politics already. If the expedition failed, he had made certain the blame would not be laid at his feet. If it succeeded, he would be quick to share in the rewards and claim the credit.

Bek shook his head at Quentin, who just shrugged and grinned ruefully.

The crowd was cheering anew, and while the people did so, a member of the Elven High Council carried to the King a long, slender green bottle. The King accepted it, wheeled his stallion about, and walked him to just below the bow of the airship. Hands raised anew, he turned once more to the crowd.

"Therefore, as King of the Land Elves and Sovereign Lord of the Westland, I wish this brave company success and good sailing, and I give to their ship the cherished name of one of our own, revered and loved over the years. I give to this ship the name *Jerle Shannara*!"

He turned back to the airship, standing tall in the stirrups of his saddle, and swung the bottle against the metal-sheathed horns of the bow rams. The green glass shattered in a spray of bright liquid, and the air was filled with silver and gold crystals, then with rainbow colors erupting in showers that geysered fifty feet skyward and coated in a fine crystalline mist all those who stood with the King and those aboard ship. Bek, who had shielded himself automatically, brushed at his tunic sleeves and watched the mist come away in a soft, warm powder that fizzled on his hands like steam, then faded on the air.

The crowd cheered and shouted anew, "Long live the *Jerle Shannara*" and "Long live Kylen Elessedil." The cheering went on and on, rising across the open bluff and sailing off into the distant forests beyond, echoes on the wind. Trumpets blew and drums boomed, and the banners of the dead Elven Kings waved and whipped at the end of their lofted standards. The ropes that bound the *Jerle Shannara* were released, and the sleek black airship rose swiftly, wheeled away from the sun toward the still-dark west, and began to pick up speed. The bluff below and those assembled on it fell away, turning small and faint in the light morning haze. The cheers died and the shouts faded, and Arborlon and her people were left behind.

That first day passed quickly for Bek, though not as quickly as he would have liked. It started out well enough, with Redden Alt Mer bringing the boy into the pilot box to stand next to him while he conducted a series of flight tests on the *Jerle Shannara*, taking her through various maneuvers intended to check her responses and timing. The Rover even let the boy steer the great ship at one point, talking him through the basics of handling the rudder and line controls. Bek repeated once more what he had learned the previous day about the components of the airship and their functions.

All this helped take his mind off the motion of the ship as it rocked and swayed on the back of the wind, but it wasn't enough to save him. In the end, his stomach lurched and knotted with deliberate and recognizable intent. Redden Alt Mer saw the look on his face and pointed him toward the bucket that sat at the foot of the box.

"Let her go, lad," he advised with an understanding smile. "It happens to the best of us."

Bek doubted that, but there was nothing he could do to save himself. He spent the next few hours wishing he were dead and imagining that if the weather was even the least bit severe, he would be. He noted between heaves that the frail young seer, Ryer Ord Star, looked equally distressed where she sat alone at the aft railing with her own bucket in hand,

and that even the stalwart Panax had gone green around the gills.

No one else seemed to be affected, not even Quentin, who was engaged in combat practice with the Elven Hunters in a wide space on the foredeck, working his way through a series of blows and parries, advances and retreats, urged on by the immutable Ard Patrinell. Most of the others aboard, he was told later by Big Red, had sailed airships before and so were accustomed to their motion. Bek would never have believed that so little movement could make anyone feel so sick, but, his safety line securely in place, he forced himself to stay upright and interested in what was happening about him, and by midafternoon he was no longer struggling.

Walker came by once or twice to inquire after him. The Druid's dark face and somber demeanor never changed when he did so, and nothing in his words suggested reproval or disappointment. He simply asked both the boy and the ship's Captain how the former's training was coming and seemed satisfied with their answers. He was there and gone so quickly that Bek wasn't entirely sure Walker had noticed how ill "the boy" was—although it seemed impossible to imagine he hadn't.

In any case, Bek got through the experience and was grateful when later in the day the Elven Healer Joad Rish gave him a root to chew that would aid in staving off further attacks. He tried a little, found it bitter and dry, but quickly decided that any price was worth keeping his stomach settled.

It was nearing sunset, his flying lessons complete for the day and his equilibrium restored, when Ahren Elessedil approached Bek. He was standing at the portside railing looking out at the sweep of the countryside below, the land a vast, sprawling checkerboard of green and brown, the sun sliding westward into the horizon, when the young Elf came up to stand beside him.

"Are you feeling better now?" Ahren asked solicitously.

Bek nodded. "Although I thought I was going to turn myself inside out for a while there."

The other smiled. "You did well for your first time. Better than me. I was sent up when I was twelve to learn about airships. On my father's orders. He believed his children should be schooled often and early in the world's mechanics. I was not a very strong boy, and the flying didn't agree with me at all. I was up for two weeks and sick every day. The Captain of the ship never said a word, but I was humiliated. I just never got the hang of any of it."

"I was surprised at how quickly I got sick."

"I think it builds up inside you, so that by the time you realize how badly you feel, it seems like it's happening all at once." The Elf paused and turned toward him. "I'm Ahren Elessedil."

Bek shook the other's hand. "Bek Rowe."

"The Druid brought you with him, didn't he? You and the Highlander? That says you are someone special. Can you work magic?"

There it was again. Bek smiled ruefully. "Quentin has a sword that can work magic, although he doesn't know how to use it very well yet. I can't do anything." He thought about the phoenix stone, but kept the thought to himself. "Can you?"

Ahren Elessedil shook his head. "Everyone knows why I'm here. My brother doesn't want me anywhere near Arborlon. He's worried that if something happens to him, I'll be placed on the throne ahead of his own children because they're too young to rule. It's an odd concern, don't you think? If you're dead, what does any of it matter?" He seemed sad and distant as he spoke. "My father would probably agree with me. He didn't think all that much about succession and order of rule, and I guess I don't either. Kylen does. He's been training for it all his life, so it matters to him. We don't like each other very much. I suppose it's better that I'm out here, on this airship, on this expedition, than back in Arborlon. At least we're out of each other's hair."

Bek nodded and said nothing.

"Did you know that my father and Walker didn't like each other?" Ahren asked, looking at him sharply. Bek shook his head no. "They had a terrible fight some years ago about establishing a Druid Council at Paranor. Walker wanted Father's help, and Father wouldn't give it. They didn't speak for years and years. It's odd that they agreed on this expedition when they couldn't agree on anything else, don't you think?"

Bek furrowed his brow.

"But maybe they found more in the way of common ground on the issue of this expedition than they did on the issue of a Druid Council." Ahren didn't wait for his reply. "There's some sort of Elven magic involved, and both would have wanted possession of that. I think the truth of the matter is that they needed each other. There is this map that only Walker can read, and there is the cost of the airship and crew that only Father could manage. And he would have agreed to provide the Elven Hunters to keep us all safe. If anyone can manage to do so. My uncle carried Elfstones, and that wasn't enough to save him."

He was being so forthright about matters that Bek was encouraged to ask a question he otherwise would not have asked. "And Patrinell was removed as Captain of the Home Guard when your father was killed. If he's out of favor with your brother and the High Council, why has he been sent to command the Elven Hunters on this expedition?"

Ahren grinned. "You don't understand how these things work, Bek. It is because he is out of favor that he's been sent with us. Kylen wants him out of Arborlon almost as much as he wants me out. Ard is my friend and protector. He trained me personally at my father's express command. Everything I know about fighting and battle tactics, I learned from him. Kylen doesn't trust him. My father's death gave my brother the perfect excuse to strip Ard of his command, and this expedition offered him a way to remove both Ard and me from the city."

He gave Bek a cool look of appraisal. "You seem pretty smart, Bek. So let me tell you something. My brother doesn't think we're coming back—any of us. Maybe, deep down inside where he hides his darkest secrets, he even hopes it. He's supporting this expedition because he can't think of a way out of it. He's doing this because Father decreed it as he lay dying, and a newly crowned King can't afford to ignore that sort of deathbed admonition. Besides, in a single stroke of good fortune he manages to get rid of me, Ard Patrinell, and the Druid, none of whom he has any particular use or liking for. If we don't come back, that solves his problem for good, doesn't it?"

Bek nodded. "I suppose so." He paused, thinking about the implications of it all. "It doesn't make me feel very good about being part of the expedition, however."

Ahren Elessedil cocked his head reflectively. "It's not supposed to. On the other hand, maybe we'll fool him. Maybe we'll survive."

That night, when dinner was complete, the airship coasting on ambient starlight, and crew and passengers alike beginning to settle into their quarters for sleep, Walker called together a small number of the ship's company for a meeting. Bek and Quentin were among those summoned, which surprised both, since neither considered himself a part of the vessel's leadership. By then Bek had shared with his cousin his conversation with Ahren Elessedil, and the two of them had debated at length how many others aboard ship understood as the young Elf did how expendable they were considered by the Elven King who had dispatched them. Certainly Walker appreciated the situation. Ard Patrinell probably understood it as well. That was about it. Everyone else would be operating under the assumption that Kylen Elessedil and the Elven High Council fully supported the expedition and anticipated its safe and successful return.

Except perhaps the Rovers, Bek added, almost as an afterthought. Big Red and his sister seemed pretty quick, and it was common knowledge in the Four Lands that Rovers had ears everywhere.

Bek was of the opinion that he should tell all of this to Walker in any case, since the Druid wanted to know everything the boy saw or heard while aboard ship, but there had been no opportunity as yet to talk with him. Now they were gathered in Redden Alt Mer's quarters below the aft decking for the meeting Walker had called, and Bek put the matter aside. In addition to the Druid and the Highland cousins, others present included Big Red and his sister, Ahren Elessedil and Ard Patrinell, and the frail-looking seer, Ryer Ord Star. As the others crowded close to Walker, who stood at a table with a hand-drawn chart spread out before him, the seer alone hung back in the shadows. Childlike and shy, her strange eyes luminescent and her skin as pale as parchment, she watched them as if she were a wild thing ready to bolt.

"Tomorrow midday we will reach the coast of the Blue Divide," Walker began, looking at each of them in turn. "Once there, we meet up with Hunter Predd and two other Wing Riders who will accompany us on our voyage, serving as scouts and foragers. Our journey from there will take us west and north, where we will seek out three islands. Each requires a stop and a search for a talisman that we must claim in order to succeed in our quest. The islands are familiar to no one aboard, myself included. They lie beyond the regions explored either by airships or Rocs. They are named on the map we follow, but they are not well described."

"Nor are we certain of the distances to each," Redden Alt Mer added, drawing all eyes momentarily to him. "Headings are clearly marked, but distances are vague. Our progress may depend greatly on the weather we encounter."

"Our Captain believes from the information I've been able to extract from the original map that the first island requires about a week's travel," Walker continued. He pointed at the map. "This copy is an approximation of the one we follow and will be left out for anyone who wishes to view it during the course of our travels. I've made it larger so that it will be easier to see. The islands we seek lie here, here, and here." He pointed to each. "Flay Creech is the first, Shatterstone the second, and Mephitic the third. They will have been chosen deliberately by whoever concealed the talismans we seek. Each talisman will be protected. Each island will be warded. Going ashore will be a dangerous business, and we will limit each search party to the smallest number possible."

"What sort of talismans do we search for?" Ard Patrinell asked quietly, leaning forward for a better look at the map.

"Keys," Walker said. "Of their size and shape, I can't be sure. I think from the writing on the map they are all the same, but possibly they are not."

"What do they do?" Ahren Elessedil asked boldly, his young face wearing its most determined look.

Walker smiled faintly. "What you might expect, Elven Prince. They open a door. When we have the keys in our possession, we will sail until we reach Ice Henge." He pointed to a symbol drawn on the map. "Once there, we search for the safehold of Castledown. The keys will gain us entrance when we have found it."

There was momentary silence as they studied the map in earnest. In the shadows, Ryer Ord Star's eyes were locked on Walker's dark face, an intense and feverish gaze, and it seemed to Bek, glancing over at her, as if she fed herself in some way by what she found there.

"How will you get ashore on these islands?" Rue Meridian asked, breaking the silence. "Will you use the ship or the Rocs?"

"The Rocs, when and where I can, because they are more mobile," the Druid answered.

She shook her head slowly. "Reconsider your decision. If we use the ship, we can lower you by winch basket or ladder from the air. If you rely on the Rocs, they will have to land. When they are grounded, they are vulnerable."

"Your point is well taken," Walker said. He glanced around. "Does anyone else wish to speak?"

To Bek's surprise, Quentin responded. "Does the Ilse Witch know all this, too?"

Walker paused to study the Highlander carefully, then nodded. "Most of it."

"So we are engaged in a race of sorts?"

Walker seemed to consider his answer before giving it. "The Ilse Witch does not have a copy of the map. Nor has she had the opportunity to study its markings as I have. She has probably gleaned her information from the mind of the castaway who carried the map. Of our general purpose and route, she will have full knowledge, I think. But of the particulars, there is some doubt. The castaway's mind was nearly gone, and I have reason to think he did not know all of what the map revealed."

"But knowing what she does she will have left by now on an airship of her own," Ard Patrinell interrupted. "She will be looking for us, either following behind or lying in wait ahead."

He made it a statement of fact, and Walker did not contradict him. Instead, he looked around once more. "I think we all appreciate the dangers we face. It is important that we do. We must be ready to defend ourselves. That we will be required to do so, probably more than once, is almost certain. Whether or not we are successful depends on our preparation. Be alert, then. Wherever you are, look about you and keep careful watch. Surprise will undo us quicker than anything."

He made a small gesture of dismissal. "I think we've talked enough about it for tonight. Go to your berths and sleep. We will meet again tomorrow night and each night hereafter to discuss our plans."

Leaving Redden Alt Mer to his cabin, they filed silently out, dispersing in the corridors belowdecks. As Bek followed Quentin, Walker stopped him with a light touch and took him aside. Quentin glanced back, then continued on without comment.

"Walk with me," the Druid said to Bek, taking him down the corridor that led to the supply room. From there, they climbed topside and stood together at the portside railing, alone beneath a canopy of black sky and endless stars. A west wind brushed at their faces with a cool touch, and Bek thought he could smell the sea.

"Tell me what Ahren Elessedil had to say to you today," Walker instructed softly, looking out into the night.

Bek did so, surprised the Druid had even noticed his conversation with the Elf. When he was finished, Walker did not speak again right away, continuing to stare off into the darkness, lost in thought. Bek waited, thinking that nothing he had repeated would be news to the Druid.

"Ahren Elessedil is made of tougher material than his brother knows," was all the other said of the matter, when he finally spoke. Then his eyes shifted to find Bek's. "Will you be his friend on this voyage?"

Bek considered the question, then nodded. "I will."

Walker nodded, seemingly satisfied. "Keep your eyes and ears open, Bek. You will come to know things that I will not, and it will be important that you remember to tell me of them. It might not happen for a time, but eventually it will. One of those things might save my life."

Bek blinked in surprise.

"Our young seer has already forecast that at some point I will be betrayed. She doesn't know when or by whom. But she has seen that someone will try to kill me and someone else will try to lead me astray. Maybe they are the same person. Maybe it will be purposeful or maybe an accident. I have no way of knowing."

Bek shook his head. "No one I've met aboard this ship seems disposed to wish you harm, Walker."

The Druid nodded. "It may not be anyone aboard ship. It may be the enemy who tracks us, or it may be someone we will meet along the way. My point is that four eyes and ears are better than two. You still suspect you have no real function on this journey, Bek. I can see it in your eyes and hear it in your voice. But your importance to me—to all of us—is greater than you think. Believe in that. One day, when the time is right, I will explain it fully to you. For now, keep faith in my word and watch my back."

He glided silently into the darkness, leaving Bek staring after him in confusion. The boy wanted to believe what the Druid had told him, but that he might have any real importance on their journey was inconceivable. He considered the matter in silence, unable to come to terms with the idea. He would watch Walker's back because he believed it was right to do so. How successful he would be was another matter, one he did not care to look at too closely.

Then, suddenly, he was aware of being watched. The feeling came over him swiftly and unexpectedly, attacking, not stealing. The force of it stunned him. He scanned quickly across the empty decking from bow to stern, where at each end an Elven Hunter as still and dark as fixed shadow kept watch. Amidships, the burly figure of Furl Hawken steered the airship from the pilot box. None of them looked at him, and there was no one else to be seen.

Still, Bek could feel hidden eyes settled on him, their weight palpable.

Then, as suddenly as the feeling had swept over him, it disappeared. All about, the star-filled night was wrapped in deepest silence. He stood at the railing a few moments longer, regaining his equilibrium and screwing his courage back into place, then hurried quickly below.

TWENTY

Early the following afternoon, the *Jerle Shannara* arrived on the coast and swung out over the vast expanse of the Blue Divide into the unknown. Within moments Hunter Predd and two other Wing Riders soared skyward from the cliffs below the Irrybis to meet them. Hunter Predd glided close to the airship to offer greetings, then angled away to take up a flanking position. For the remainder of that day and for most of the days that followed, the Wing Riders flew in formation off the bow and stern of the ship, two forward and one aft, a silent and reassuring presence.

When Bek asked Walker at one point what happened to them at night, the Druid told him it varied. Sometimes they flew right on through until daybreak, matching the slower pace that the airship set in darkness. Rocs were enormously strong and resilient, and they could fly without stopping for up to three days. Most of the time, however, the Wing Riders would take their Rocs ahead to an island or atoll and land long enough to feed, water, and rest the birds and their riders before continuing on. They worked mostly in shifts, with one Wing Rider always warding the ship, even at night, as a protective measure. With the Rocs on watch, nothing could approach without being detected.

They traveled without incident for ten days, the time sliding away for Bek Rowe in a slow, unchanging daily routine. Each morning he would rise and eat his breakfast with the Rovers, then follow Redden Alt Mer as he completed a thorough inspection of the airship and its crew. After that, he would stand with the Rover Captain in the pilot box, sometimes just the two of them, sometimes with another Rover at the controls, and Bek would first recite what he knew about a particular function of the ship's operating system and then be instructed in some further area or nuance. Later, he would operate the controls and rudders, drawing down power from the light sheaths or unhooding the crystals or tightening the radian draws.

Sometimes, when Big Red was busy elsewhere, Bek would be placed in the care of Little Red or Furl Hawken or even the burly Spanner Frew. The shipbuilder mostly yelled at him, driving him from pillar to post with his sharp tongue and acid criticism, forcing him to think harder and act faster than normal. It helped steady him, in an odd sort of way. After an hour or two of surviving Spanner Frew, he felt he was ready for anything.

Between sessions with the Rovers, he would perform a cabin boy's chores, which included running messages from Captain to crew and back again, cleaning the Captain's and his sister's quarters, inventorying supplies every third day, and helping serve the meals and clear the dishes. Most of it wasn't very pleasant or exciting, but it did put him in close proximity to almost everyone several times a day and gave him a chance to listen in on conversations and observe behavior. Nothing of what he saw seemed of much use, but he did as Walker had asked and kept his eyes and ears open.

He saw little of Quentin during the day, for the Highlander was constantly training with the Elven Hunters and learning combat skills and technique from Ard Patrinell. He saw more of Ahren Elessedil, who never trained with the others and was often at loose ends. Bek took it upon himself to include the young Elf in most of what he did, teaching him what little he knew of airships and how they flew and sharing confidences and stories. He did not tell Ahren any more than he told Quentin, but he told him almost as much. As they spent more

time together, he began to see what Walker had meant about
Kylen Elessedil misjudging his brother. Ahren was young,
but he had grown up in a family and political situation that
did not foster or tolerate naïveté or weakness. Ahren was
strong in ways that weren't immediately apparent, and Bek
gained a new measure of respect for him almost daily.

Now and again he visited with Panax and even Hunter
Predd, when the Wing Rider came aboard to speak with
Walker or Redden Alt Mer. Bek knew most of the Rovers by
name, and they had accepted him into their group in a loose
and easy sort of way that offered companionship if not necessarily trust. The Elves had little to do with him, mostly because they were always somewhere else. He did speak with
the Healer, Joad Rish, a tall, stooped man with a kind face and
reassuring manner. The Healer, like Bek, was not certain of
his usefulness and felt more than a little out of place. But he
was a good conversationalist, and he liked talking with
the boy about cures and healings that transcended the standard
forms of care and were the peculiar province of Elven Healers.

Bek even talked once or twice with the wistful seer, Ryer
Ord Star, but she was so reclusive and shy that she avoided
everyone except Walker, whom she followed everywhere. As
if in thrall to the Druid, she was his shadow on the airship,
trailing after him like a small child, hanging on his every
word and watching his every move. Her fixation was a steady
topic of conversation for everyone, but never within Walker's
hearing. No one cared to broach the strangeness of the young
woman's attachment directly to the Druid when it was apparent it did not matter to him.

Of Truls Rohk, there was still no sign. Panax insisted he
was aboard, but Bek never saw any evidence of it.

Then, ten days out of land's view, they came in sight of
the island of Flay Creech. It was nearing midday, the sky
clouded and gray, the weather beginning to turn raw for the
first time since they had set out. Thunderheads were massed
to the west, approaching at a slow, steady roll across the back

of a still-calm wind, and the burn of the sun through gaps in the thinner clouds east was giving way before cooler air. Below them, the sea rose and fell in gentle waves, a silver-tipped azure carpet where it broke against the shores of the island ahead, but beyond, out on the horizon, it was dark and threatening.

Flay Creech was not a welcoming sight. The island was gray and barren, a collection of mostly smooth mounds irrigated by an irregular patchwork of deep gullies that deposited seawater in shallow ponds all across its surface. Save for clusters of scrub trees and heavy weed patches, nothing grew. The island was small, barely a half mile across, and marked by a rocky outcropping just off the coast to the south that bore a distinct resemblance to a lizard's head with its mouth agape and its crest lifted in warning. On the map that Walker had drawn for the ship's company, the lizard's head was the landmark that identified the island.

Redden Alt Mer took the *Jerle Shannara* slowly around the island, keeping several hundred feet above its surface, while the ship's company gathered at the railings to survey the forbidding terrain. Bek looked downward with the others, but saw nothing of interest. There was no sign of life and no movement of any kind. The island appeared deserted.

When they had completed several passes, Walker signaled to Hunter Predd, who with his complement of Wing Riders had been gliding silently overhead. The grizzled rider swung close aboard Obsidian and shook his head. They had seen nothing either. But they would not descend to the island for a closer look, Bek knew, because they were under orders from the Druid not to land on any of the three islands where the talismans were hidden until a party from the airship had gone down first. The Rocs and their riders were too valuable to risk; if lost, they could not be replaced.

Walker called Redden Alt Mer and Ard Patrinell to his side, and Bek and Quentin eased nearer to listen to what was being said.

"What do you see?" the Druid was asking the Rover Captain as they drew close enough to hear.

"The same as you. Nothing. But there's something not right about the look of the island. What made those gullies that crisscross everything?"

However unhappy Redden Alt Mer was, Ard Patrinell was even more so. "I don't like what I'm seeing at all. The terrain of this island doesn't fit with anything I've ever come across. It's the shape of it. False, somehow. Unnatural."

Walker nodded. Bek could tell that he was troubled, too. There was something odd about the formation of the gullies and the smoothness of the island.

The Druid walked over to where Ryer Ord Star stood watching and bent down to speak softly with her. The seer listened carefully, then pressed her thin, small hands against her breast, closed her eyes and went completely still. Bek watched with the others, wondering what was happening. Then her eyes opened, and she began to speak to the Druid in rapid, breathless sentences. When she was finished, he held her gaze for a moment, squeezed her hand, and turned away.

He came back to where Ard Patrinell and Redden Alt Mer stood waiting. "I'm going down for a closer look," he said quietly. "Lower me in the basket and stand ready to bring me up again when I signal. Don't come down for me with either the ship or the Rocs if anything goes wrong."

"I don't think you should go alone," Ard Patrinell said at once.

Walker smiled. "All right. I'll take one man with me."

Leaving them, he walked over to Quentin Leah. "Highlander, I need a swift, sure blade to protect me. Are you interested in the job?"

Quentin nodded instantly, a grin breaking out on his sunbrowned face. He hitched up the Sword of Leah, where it was strapped across his back, and gave Bek a wink before hastening to follow the Druid, who was already walking over to stand with Furl Hawken while he readied the winch basket for lowering.

Ahren Elessedil appeared at Bek's elbow and put a hand on his shoulder. Panax came up beside him, as well. "What's going on?" the Dwarf rumbled.

Bek was too stunned to answer, still trying to come to grips with the idea of his untested cousin being selected to go with the Druid rather than the Elf Captain or one of his Hunters. Walker was already in the basket, his dark robes drawn close, and Quentin quickly climbed in after him. Redden Alt Mer was at the airship's controls, swinging her around and then descending to within twenty feet of a flat place at the island's eastern tip. Bek wanted to shout something encouraging to his cousin, to warn him to be careful and to come back safe. But he couldn't manage to get the words out. Instead, he just stood there staring as the Rover crew winched the basket and its occupants aloft, then pushed them out over the railing and into space.

With the remainder of the ship's company looking on, the crew slowly lowered the basket and the two men who rode within it toward Flay Creech.

Walker's mind was working swiftly as the basket began its descent to the island, the words of the seer repeating over and over in his mind with harsh urgency.

"Three dark holes in place and time do I see, Walker. Three, that would swallow you up. They lie in deep blue waters that spread away forever beneath skies and wind. One is blind and cannot see, but will find you anyway. One has mouths that would swallow you whole. One is everything and nothing and will steal your soul. All guard keys that look to be other than what they are and are nothing of what they seem. I see this in a haze of shadow that tracks you everywhere and seeks to place itself about you like a shroud."

These were the words she had spoken to him last night when she had come to him unexpectedly after midnight, waking from a dream that had shown her something new of their quest. Wide-eyed and frightened, her childlike face twisted with fear for him, she had shaken him from his sleep to share her strange vision. It had come unbidden, as they almost always did, buried in a mix of other dreams and no dreams, the only part of her mind's sight that had reason for being, clear and certain to her, a glimpse of a future that would unfailingly come to pass.

He steadied her, held her because she was shaking and not yet even fully awake. She was tied to him, he knew, in a way neither of them yet understood. She had accompanied him on the voyage because she believed it was her destiny, but her bonds to him were as much emotional as psychic. She had found in him a kindred soul, another part of her being, and she had given herself into his care completely. He did not approve and would have it otherwise, but he had not found a way as yet to set her free.

Her eyes glistened with tears and her hands clasped his arm as she told him of the dream and struggled with what it meant. She saw no more than what she was given to see, had no insights to aid him, and therefore felt inadequate and useless. But he told her that her vision was clear to him and would help to keep him safe, and he held her for a time until she quieted and went back to sleep.

But his words to her were false, for he did not understand her vision beyond what was immediately apparent. The black holes were the islands they sought. On each, something dark and dangerous awaited. The keys he would find did not look like the keys with which he was familiar. The haze of shadow that followed after and sought to wrap about him was the Ilse Witch.

Of the eyes and mouths and spirits, he had no opinion. Had she seen them in order of appearance? Were they manifestations of real dangers or metaphors for something else? He had gone to her again, just before making this descent, asking her to repeat what she had seen, everything. He had hoped she might reveal something new, something she had forgotten in the rush of last night's telling. But her description of

the dream remained unchanged. Nor had there been a new vision from which to draw. So he could not know what waited
on the island, and he must look for any of the three dangers
she had foreseen until one revealed itself.

Taking the Highlander with him was a risk. But Quentin
Leah possessed the only other true magic of those accompa-
nying him, save Truls Rohk, and he must have someone at his
back while he sought out the first of the three keys. Quentin
was young and inexperienced, but the Sword of Leah was a
powerful weapon, and Quentin had trained for almost two
weeks now with Ard Patrinell, whom Walker believed to be the
finest swordsman he had ever seen. No mention had been made
of Patrinell's great skill by the other Elves, but Walker had
watched him spar for days now with the Highlander and could
tell it was there. Quentin was a quick study, and already he was
showing signs that one day he might be a match for the Elf. It
was enough to persuade the Druid to take a chance on him.

It could be argued that Truls Rohk was a more logical
choice for this than Quentin, but it would have meant waiting
until nightfall. Walker did not like the look of the storm approaching, and he felt it better in any case to keep the shape-
shifter's presence a secret for a little longer.

The basket bumped against the surface of the island, and
the Druid and the Highlander scrambled out. The latter had
his sword held ready, gripped in both hands, blade upward.
"Stay close to me, Quentin," Walker ordered. "Do not stray.
Watch my back and your own, as well."

They hastened across the flats in a low crouch, eyes watchful. The surface was rocky and slick with dampness and
moss. Up close, the deep furrows were even more mysterious, worn into the rock like open irrigation runnels, not
straight and even, but twisty and irregular, some of them as
deep as four feet, their strange network laid all across the island. Walker cast about for bolt-holes in the rock in which
something might burrow and hide, but there was nothing to
be seen, only the exposed rock and the shallow ponds.

They continued on, Walker searching now for a trace of the key, a hint of its presence in the solid rock and shifting seawaters that lay all about. Where would such a key be hidden? If it was infused with magic, he should detect its presence quickly. If not, their search would take longer—time, perhaps, they did not have.

He glanced about warily. The island lay still and unmoving save for the soft wave of sea grasses buffeted by the approaching storm winds.

Suddenly Walker sensed something unfamiliar, not the magic he had anticipated, but an object that nevertheless had a living presence—though not one he could identify. It was over to his left, within a jumble of broken rock that formed a pocket on the high ground close to the southern tip of the island. The Druid swung toward it at once, working his way along the lip of one of the odd gullies, staying where he could see what lay about him. Pressed close to the dark-robed leader, Quentin Leah followed, his sword gleaming in the sunlight.

Then the sun slipped behind a bank of heavy clouds, and the island of Flay Creech was cloaked in shadow.

In the next instant, the sea came alive in a frenzy of movement.

Aboard ship, Bek Rowe gasped sharply as the waters surrounding Flay Creech began to boil and surge with terrible ferocity. The bright azure color darkened, the crystalline stillness churned, and dozens of squirming dark bodies surged from the ocean's depth in a twisting mass. Giant eels, some more than thirty feet long, their huge bodies sleek and speckled and their mouths agape to reveal hundreds of razorsharp teeth, squirmed out of the water and onto the island. They came from everywhere, sliding smoothly into the deep channels that fit their bodies perfectly, that Bek could see now had been formed by their countless comings and goings over the years. In a rush they slithered from the ocean onto the land, then along the gullies from shallow pond to shallow pond, closing on the two men who were racing for a cluster of broken rocks to make a stand against them.

"Shades!" Bek heard Panax hiss as he watched the eels advance in a thrashing, frenzied mass.

The eels were so maddened they were colliding with each other as they twisted and squirmed down the gullies toward their prey. Some ascended the high ground long enough to gain a momentary advantage over their brethren before dropping back into the grooved channels they favored. Some, perhaps enraged at being crowded, perhaps simply ravenous with hunger, snapped and tore at others. It gave the impression that the entire island was being overrun at once, all slithery bodies and movement. Bek had never heard of such huge eels or imagined that so many could be in any one place. What could possibly sustain such a massive number on this barren atoll? Even the occasional presence of other creatures could not be enough to keep them all alive.

Walker was digging frantically in the rocks, his back to the approaching monsters. Quentin faced them alone, standing close to the Druid, elevated on an abutment so that he could bring his sword to bear without hindrance. He shifted from right to left and back again on his chosen defensive ground, watching the mass of sea hunters come at him, readying himself.

Oh, but there were so many! Bek thought in horror.

The first eel reached Quentin and launched itself like a striking snake, snapping its body from the depression. The Highlander brought the Sword of Leah around in a short whipping motion, the magic flaring to life along the length of the heavy blade, and the eel was severed just behind its gaping maw and fell back again, thrashing in pain and confusion. Other eels fed upon it instantly, tearing it to shreds. A second eel struck at Quentin, but he brought his sword to bear again, swift and steady, and that one fell away, too. On the backswing, he dispatched a third that had come up behind him, flinging it away.

Walker straightened from his crouched position within the rocks long enough to summon the Druid fire. It lanced from his fingers in an explosion of blue flame, burning into the advancing eels and forcing them back down into the gullies. Then he was bending down again, searching anew.

Back came the eels in only moments, breaking past the already diminishing ring of fire, mouths gaping hungrily.

There's too many! Bek thought again, hands gripping the railing of the airship helplessly as a fresh wave of attackers closed on Quentin and the Druid.

"Captain!" Ard Patrinell shouted at Redden Alt Mer in desperation.

The flame-haired Rover swung into the pilot box in response. "Safety lines!" he roared. "We're going after them!"

Bek had barely managed to secure himself when the *Jerle Shannara* went into a steep, swift dive toward the island.

Quentin Leah struck down his nearest attacker and swung instantly about to face the next. He had driven back the first assault, but the second seemed even more frenzied and determined. The Highlander's strokes were steady and smooth, and he wheeled skillfully to keep his back from being exposed for more than a few seconds at a time, just as Patrinell had taught him in their exercises. The Highlander was strong and quick, and he did not panic in the face of the overwhelming odds he faced. He had hunted the Highlands since he was old enough to run, and he had faced great odds and terrible dangers before. But he understood that here, in this place, time was running out. The giant eels were vulnerable to the magic of his weapon but undeterred by the deaths of their fellows. They would keep coming, he knew, until they had what they wanted. There were so many that eventually they would succeed. Already his arms were growing tired and his movements jerky. Use of the sword's magic was draining him of his energy and breaking down his will. He could feel it happening and could do nothing to stop it. Wounds had been opened on both arms and one leg where the razor-sharp teeth of his attackers had slashed him, and his face was bathed in sweat and salt spray from the sea.

Walker gave a grunt and uncoiled from his search in the rocks, swinging up to stand beside him. "I have it!" he shouted, jamming something into his robes. "Run now! This way!"

They leapt out from the rocks and raced toward an open flat that lay less than a hundred feet away, scrambling through the shallow, slippery ponds. The eels thrashed after them, their huge bodies twisting and squirming along the deep channels. Overhead, the *Jerle Shannara* was dropping swiftly, sails full and radian draws taut, her sleek dark form plummeting out of the gray sky. The eels were closing on Quentin and Walker, who turned to stand one final time, the Druid with his fire exploding from his extended arm, the Highlander with his sword's magic flashing.

Then the shadow of the airship fell over them and a trailing rope ladder swung past, their lifeline to safety. They reached for it instinctively, grasped it, and were whisked off the ground and into the air as eel jaws snapped only inches away.

Seconds later, they were clear of the island once more and climbing the ladder to safety.

Bek was among those who helped pull the Druid and the Highlander back aboard the airship as it lifted high above Flay Creech and its twisting mass of frustrated, maddened eels. When he had his cousin standing before him, torn and bloodied, but smiling, as well, Bek tried to say something to him about agreeing to take risks and scaring him half to death, then gave it up and threw his arms about the other in a warm, grateful hug.

"Ouch, you're hurting me!" Quentin yelped. When Bek hurriedly backed off, his cousin's smile broadened. "Happy to see me safe, Bek? Never a moment's doubt, was there? You could tell. We had a clear path all the way."

Walker was at his elbow, fumbling in his robes for what he had recovered, and the rest of the ship's company crowded close. What he produced was a flat metal rectangle with symmetrical ridges that connected in a geometrical pattern to a small raised square that vibrated softly. A red light embedded in the square blinked on and off. Everyone stared at it in wonder. Bek had never seen anything like it before.

"What is it?" Panax asked finally.

"A key," Walker answered. "But not a key of the sort we know. This key belongs to the technology of the Old World, from before the Great Wars, from the old civilization of Man. It is a form of machine and has a life of its own."

He let them study it a moment longer, then slipped it back into his robes. "It has secrets to tell us if we can unlock them," he said quietly, then clasped Quentin's shoulder in thanks, and walked away.

The remainder of the company dispersed to their stations and work, the adventure of Flay Creech behind them. Joad Rish was already stripping off the Highlander's tunic to clean his wounds. Quentin accepted congratulations from a few of the ship's company who lingered, then sat heavily on a barrel top and winced as the Healer began to work on him in earnest. Bek stayed close, silent company, and alone saw the hint of raw fear that flashed in his cousin's green eyes as he looked down at his torn body and realized momentarily how close he had come to dying.

But then he was looking up again, himself once more, smiling rakishly as he held up a single finger.

One down, Quentin was saying.

Bek smiled back. One down, he was thinking in response, but two still to go.

TWENTY-ONE

It took two more months of travel to reach the island of Shatterstone. Bek had thought they would arrive more quickly since it had taken them only ten days to gain Flay Creech. But Walker's rough-drawn map showed the distance to be considerably greater, and it was.

Nevertheless, the days between passed swiftly, eaten up by routine tasks and small crises. Bek continued to learn about airships—how they were constructed, why they flew, and what was needed to maintain them. He was given a chance to try his hand at almost everything, from polishing the diapson crystals to threading the radian draws. He was allowed to go topside to see how the draws were attached to the light sheaths so as to draw down their power. He was given time at the ship's rudders and controls and a chance at plotting courses. By the end of the two months, Redden Alt Mer thought him competent enough to leave him alone in the pilot box for several hours at a stretch, allowing him to become accustomed to the feel of the airship and the ways she responded to his touch.

For the most part, the weather continued to favor them. There were storms, but they did not cause the ship damage or ship's company to fear. A few were severe enough that ship and passengers sought shelter in an island's protective cove or windward bluffs. Once or twice they were badly lashed by heavy winds and rain while still aloft, but the *Jerle Shannara* was well made and able to endure.

Certainly it helped having the ship's builder aboard. If something malfunctioned or failed, Spanner Frew found the problem and fixed it almost instantly. He was ferociously loyal to and protective of his vessel, a mother hen with teeth, and he was quick to reprimand or even assault anyone who mistreated her. Once Bek watched him cuff one of the Rover crew so hard he knocked the man down, all because the crewman had removed a diapson crystal improperly.

The only one who seemed able to stand up to him was Rue Meridian, who was intimidated by no one. Of all aboard ship, save Walker, she was the coolest and calmest presence. Bek remained in awe of Little Red, and when he had the chance to do so, he watched her with an ache he could not quite manage to hide. If she noticed, she kept it to herself. She was kind to him and always helpful. She would tease him now and then, and she made him laugh with her surreptitious winks and clever asides. She was the airship's navigator, but Bek soon discovered that she was much more. It was apparent from the beginning that she knew as much as her brother about flying airships and was his most valued adviser. She was also extremely dangerous. She carried knives everywhere she went, and she knew how to use them. Once, he watched her compete against the other Rovers in a throwing contest, and she bested them easily. Neither her brother nor Furl Hawken would throw against her, which told Bek something. He thought she might not be as skilled at the use of weapons as Ard Patrinell, but he would not have wanted to put it to a test.

Much of his time was spent with Ahren Elessedil. Together, they would walk the ship from end to end, discussing everything that interested them. Well, not quite everything. A few things, he did not share with anyone. He still hid, even from the Elf, the presence of the phoenix stone. He still told no one of his meeting with the King of the Silver River. But it was growing harder and harder to keep these secrets from Ahren. With time's passage, he was becoming as close to the young Elf as to Quentin, and sometimes he thought that

Ahren would have been his best friend if Quentin hadn't claimed the position first.

"Tell me what you want to do with your life, Bek," the Elf said one evening as they stood at the railing before sleep. "If you could do anything at all, what would it be?"

Bek answered without thinking. "I would find out the truth about myself."

There it was, right out in the open without his meaning for it to happen. He would have swallowed the words if there had been a way, but it was too late.

"What do you mean?" Ahren looked sharply at him.

Bek hesitated, seeking a way to recover. "I mean, I was brought to Coran and Liria when I was a baby, given to them when my parents died. I don't know anything about my real parents. I don't have any family history of my own."

"You must have asked Quentin's father and mother. Didn't they tell you anything?"

"I asked them only a little. Growing up, I felt it didn't matter. My life was with them and with Quentin. They were my family and that was my history. But now I want to know more. Maybe I'm just beginning to realize that it's important to me, but now that I find it so, I want to know the truth." He shrugged. "Silly to wonder about it, out here in the middle of nowhere."

Ahren smiled. "Out in the middle of nowhere is exactly the right place to wonder who you are."

Every day at high noon, usually while Bek was eating lunch with the Rovers or steering the airship from the pilot box or perhaps languishing in the narrow shade of the foremast with Panax, Ahren Elessedil stood out in the midday sun with Ard Patrinell and for the better part of two hours honed his skills with Elven weapons. Sometimes it was with swords and knives. Sometimes it was with bow and arrow, axes, or slings. At times the two simply sat and talked, and Bek would watch as hand gestures and sketches were exchanged. The former Captain of the Home Guard worked his young charge hard. It was the hottest time of the day and the training rendered was the most exhaustive. It was the only time Bek ever saw the two together, and finally he asked Ahren about it.

"He was your teacher once," Bek pointed out. "He was your friend. Why don't you spend any time with him aside from when you train?"

Ahren sighed. "It isn't my idea. It's his. He was dismissed from his position because my father's life was his responsibility. The Elven Hunters he commands accept his leadership because the King, my brother, ordered it and because they value his experience and skill. But they do not accept his friendship with me. That ended with my father's death. He may continue to train me, because my father ordered it. Anything more would be unacceptable."

"But we are in the middle of the ocean." Bek was perplexed. "What difference does any of that make here?"

Ahren shrugged. "Ard must know that his men will do what he orders of them without question or hesitation. He must have their respect. What if they believe he curries favor with me in an effort to get back what he has lost, perhaps with my help? What if they believe he serves more than one master? That is why he trains me at midday, in the heat. That is why he trains me harder than he does them. That is why he ignores me otherwise. He shows me no favoritism. He gives them no reason to doubt him. Do you see?"

Bek didn't see, not entirely, but he told Ahren he did anyway.

"Besides," Ahren added, "I'm the second son of a dead King, and second sons of dead Kings have to learn how to be tough and independent enough to survive on their own."

Panax, gruff and irascible as always, told Ahren that if Elves spent less time worrying about stepping on each other's toes and more time trusting their instincts, they would better off. It used to be like that, he declared bluntly. Things had changed since this current crop of Elessedils had taken office. How he arrived at this conclusion, living in the backwoods

beyond Depo Bent, was beyond Bek. But for all that he lived
an isolated and solitary existence, the Dwarf seemed to have
his finger firmly on the pulse of what was happening in the
Four Lands.

"You take this ridiculous war between the Free-born and
the Federation," he muttered at one point, while they sat
watching Patrinell and Ahren duel with staves. "What is
the point? They've been fighting over the same piece of
ground for fifty years and over control of the Borderlands for
more than five hundred. Back and forth it goes; nothing ever
changes, nothing ever gets resolved. Wouldn't you think after
all this time, someone would have found a way to get them all
to sit down and work it out? How complicated can it be? On
the surface, it's an issue of sovereignty and territorial influence, but at heart it's about trade and economics. Find a way
to stop them from posturing about whose birthright it is to
govern and get them to talk about trade alliances and dividing
the wealth those alliances would generate, and the war will be
over in two days."

"But the Federation is determined to rule the Borderlands," Bek pointed out. "They want the Borderlands to be
part of their Southland empire. What about that?"

The Dwarf spat. "The Borderlands will never be part of
any one land because it's been part of all four lands for as
long as anyone can remember. The average Southlander
doesn't give a rat's behind if the people in the Borderlands are
a part of the Federation. What the average Southlander cares
about is whether those ash bows that are so good for hunting and those silk scarves the women love and those great
cheeses and ales that come out of Varfleet and those healing
plants grown on the Streleheim can find their way south to
them! The only ones who care about annexing the Borderlands are the members of the Coalition Council. Send them to
the Prekkendorran for a week, and then see how they feel
about things!"

There were small adventures to be enjoyed during those

eight-odd weeks of travel between islands, as well. One day, a huge pod of whales came into view below the airship, traveling west in pursuit of the setting sun. They breached and sounded with spouts of water and slaps of tails and fins, great sea vessels riding the waves with joy and abandon, complete within themselves. The Highlander and the Elf peered down at them, tracking their progress, reminded of the smallness of their own world, envious of the freedom these giants enjoyed. On another day, hundreds of dolphins appeared, leaping and diving in rhythmic cadence, small glimmers of brightness in the deep blue sea. There were migrating schools of billfish at times, some with sails, some brightly colored, all sleek and swift. There were giant squids with thirty-foot tentacles, as well, who swam like feathered arrows, and dangerous-looking predators with fins that cut the water like knives.

Now and again something aboard ship would break down, and what was required to complete repairs could not be found. Sometimes supplies ran low. In both instances, the Wing Riders were pressed into service. While the third rider remained with the airship, the other two would explore the surrounding islands to forage for what was needed. Twice, Bek was allowed to accompany them, both times when they went in search of fresh water, fruit, and vegetables to supplement the ship's dietary staples. Once he rode with Hunter Predd aboard his Roc, Obsidian, and once with a rider named Gill aboard Tashin. Each time, the experience was exhilarating. There was a freedom to flying the Rocs that was absent even on an airship. The great birds were much quicker and smoother, their responses swifter, and the feeling of riding something alive and warm far different from riding something built of wood and metal.

The Wing Riders were a fiercely independent bunch and kept apart from everyone. When Bek screwed up his courage to ask the taciturn Hunter Predd about it, the Wing Rider explained patiently that life as a Wing Rider necessitated believing you were different. It had to do with the time you

spent flying and the freedom you embraced when you gave up
the safeties and securities others relied upon living on the
ground. Wing Riders needed to view themselves as independent in order to function. They needed to be unfettered and
unencumbered by connections of any kind, save to their Rocs
and to their own people.

Bek wasn't sure that much of it wasn't just a superior attitude fostered by the freedom that flying the Rocs engendered
in Wing Riders. But he liked Hunter Predd and Gill, and he
didn't see that there was anything to be gained by questioning
their thinking. If he were a Wing Rider, he told himself, he
would probably think the same way.

When Bek told Ahren of his conversation with Hunter
Predd, the Elf Prince laughed. "Everyone aboard this ship
thinks their way of life is best, but most keep their opin-
ions to themselves. The reason the Wing Riders are so free
with theirs is that they can always jump on their Rocs and fly
off if they don't like what they hear back!"

But there were few conflicts in the weeks that passed after
their departure from Flay Creech, and eventually everyone
settled into a comfortable routine and developed a compla-
cency with life aboard ship. It wasn't until one of the Wing
Riders finally sighted the island of Shatterstone that everything began to change.

It was the Wing Rider, Gill, patrolling in the late afternoon
on Tashin, who sighted Shatterstone first. The expedition had
been looking for it for several days, alerted by Redden Alt
Mer, who had taken the appropriate readings and made the
necessary calculations. An earlier sighting of a group of three
small islands laid out in a line corresponded to landmarks
drawn on the map and confirmed that the island they sought
was close.

Walker was standing with the Rover Captain in the pilot
box behind Furl Hawken, who was in command of the helm
that afternoon, discussing whether they needed to correct

their course at sunrise on the following day, when Gill
appeared with the news. All activity stopped as the ship's
company hurried to the rails, and Big Red swung the *Jerle
Shannara* hard to the left to follow the Wing Rider's lead.

Finally, the Druid thought as they sailed toward the setting
sun. The prolonged inactivity, the seductive comfort of routine, and the lack of progress bothered him. The men and
women of the expedition needed to stay sharp, to remain
wary. They were losing focus. The only solution was to get on
with things.

But when the island came into view, he felt his expectations fade. Whereas Flay Creech had been small and compact, Shatterstone was sprawling and massive. It rose out of
the Blue Divide in a jumble of towering peaks that disappeared into clouds and mist and fell away at every turn into
canyons thousands of feet deep. The coastline was rugged
and forbidding, almost entirely devoid of beaches and shal-
lows, with sheer rock walls rising straight out of the ocean.
The entire island was rain-soaked and lush, heavily overgrown by trees and grasses, tangled in vines and scrub, and
laced with the silver threads of waterfalls that tumbled out of
the mist into the emerald green landscape below. Only at its
peaks and on its windswept cliff edges was it bare and open.
Birds wheeled from their aeries and plummeted in white
flashes to the sea, hunting food. Below the cliff walls, the surf
crashed against the rocks in long, rolling waves and turned to
milky foam.

Walker had the *Jerle Shannara* circle the island twice
while he noted landmarks and tried to get a feel for the terrain. A thorough search of Shatterstone by ordinary methods
would take weeks, maybe even months. Even then, they might
not discover the key if it was buried deep enough in those
canyons. He found himself wondering which of the three horrors of Ryer Ord Star's vision guarded this key. The eels
would have been the mouths that could swallow you whole.
That left something that was blind but could find you anyway

or something that was everything and nothing and would steal your soul. He had hoped the seer would dream again before they reached Shatterstone, but she had not. All they had to work with was what she had given them before.

He watched the rugged sweep of the island pass away below, thinking that whatever he decided, it would have to wait for morning. Nightfall was close upon them, and he had no intention of landing a search party in the dark.

But he might consider sending down Truls Rohk, he thought suddenly. The shape-shifter preferred the dark anyway, and his instincts for the presence of magic were nearly as keen as the Druid's.

The Wing Riders landed on an open bluff high above the pounding surf on the island's west coast and, leaving their Rocs tethered, began a short exploration of the area. They found nothing that threatened and determined that it was safe enough for them to remain there for the night. No attempt would be made to journey inland until morning. Redden Alt Mer anchored the airship some distance away on an adjoining bluff, fixing the anchor lines in place and letting the ship ride about twenty feet off the ground. Again, no one would leave the ship until morning, and a close watch would be kept until then. Darkness was already beginning to settle in, but it appeared that the coastal skies would remain clear. With the illumination provided by a half-moon and stars, it would be easy to see anything that tried to approach.

After dinner was consumed, Walker called his small group of advisers together in Redden Alt Mer's cabin and told them his plan for the coming day. Though he didn't say so, he had abandoned for the moment the idea of using Truls Rohk. Instead, he would fly with one of the Wing Riders over the peaks and into the canyons in an attempt to locate the hidden key using his Druidic instincts. Because the key had such a distinctive presence and would likely be the only thing like it on the island, he had a good chance of determining its location. If it were in a place he could reach without endangering

the Wing Rider and his Roc, he would retrieve it himself. But
the canyons were narrow and not easily navigated by the
great birds with their broad wingspans, so retrieval might
have to be undertaken by the ship's company.

Everyone agreed that the Druid's plan seemed sensible,
and the matter was left at that.

The following morning, the dawn a bright golden flare on
the eastern horizon, Walker set off with Hunter Predd and
Obsidian to conduct a methodical sweep of the island's west
coast. They searched all day, dipping into every canyon and
defile, soaring over every bluff and peak, crisscrossing the island from the coastal waters inland so that nothing was
missed. The day was sunny and bright, the weather fair, the
winds light, and their search progressed without difficulty.

By sunset, Walker had found exactly nothing.

He set out again the next day with Po Kelles, seated behind
the whip-thin Wing Rider on his gray-and-black-dappled
Roc, Niciannon. They rode the back of a strong wind south
along the most forbidding stretch of the island's shoreline,
and it was here just after midday that Walker detected the
presence of the key. It was buried deep in a coastal valley that
opened off a split between a pair of towering cliffs and ran inland into heavy jungle for better than five miles. The valley
was unnavigable from the air, and after ascertaining the ap-
proximate location of the key, Walker had Po Kelles fly them
back to the airship. Postponing any further effort for the day,
he asked Redden Alt Mer to move the *Jerle Shannara* to a
bluff just above the valley he intended to explore at dawn, and
they settled in for the night.

He waited until everyone but the watch was asleep and
then summoned Truls Rohk. He had neither seen nor spoken
with the shape-shifter since he had come aboard, although he
had detected the other's presence and knew him to be close.
Walker stood at the back of the ship, just down from the aft
rise where the Elven Hunter on sentry duty peered out at the
jungled island darkness, and sent out a silent call to Rohk. He

was still looking for the shape-shifter when he realized Rohk was already there, crouching next to him in the shadows, virtually invisible to anyone who might be looking.

"What is it, Druid?" Rohk hissed, as if the summoning were an irritation.

"I want you to explore the valley below before it gets light," Walker answered, unruffled. "A quick search, no more. There is a key, and the key feels like this."

He produced the one he carried and let the other touch it, hold it, feel its energy.

Truls Rohk grunted and handed it back. "Shall I bring it to you?"

"Do not go near it." Walker found the other's eyes and held them. "It isn't that you couldn't, but the danger might be greater than either of us suspects. What I need to know is where it is. I'll go after it myself in the morning."

The shape-shifter laughed softly. "I would never deny you a chance to risk your life over mine, Walker. You think so much less of the risk than I do."

Without a word, he vaulted over the side of the ship and was gone.

Walker waited for him until nearly dawn, dozing at the railing, his back to the island, his thoughts gone deep inside. No one disturbed him; no one tried to approach. The night was calm and warm; the winds of the day died away into soft breezes that carried the smells of the ocean to higher ground. Inland, the darkness enfolded and blanketed everything in black silence.

He might have dreamed, but if he had, his memory of it was lost when Truls Rohk's touch brought him awake.

"Sweet dreams of an island paradise, Walker?" the other asked softly. "Of sand beaches and pretty birds? Of fruit and flowers and warm winds?"

Walker shook his head, coming fully awake.

"That's just as well, because there are none of these in the valley you seek to explore." The dark form shifted against the railing, liquid black. "The key you seek lies three miles inland, close to the valley floor, in a cavern of some size. The jungle hides it well, but you will find it. How it is concealed within the cave, I could not say. I did not enter because I could tell that something keeps watch."

Walker stared at him. "Something alive?"

"Something dark and vast, something without form. I felt no eyes on me, Walker. I felt only a presence, a stirring in the air, invisible and pervasive and evil."

No eyes. Was it something blind, perhaps? Walker mulled the shape-shifter's words over in his mind, wondering.

"That presence was with me all the way up the valley, but it did not bother with me until I got close to the cavern." Truls Rohk seemed to reflect. "It was in the earth itself, Druid. It was in the valley's soil, in its plants and trees." He paused. "If it decides to come after you, I don't think you can run from it. I'm not certain you can even get out of its way."

Then he was gone, disappeared as suddenly as he had come, and Walker was left standing at the railing alone.

Dawn broke brilliant and warm across a still, flat sea. The winds had died completely, and the sky was a cloudless silver blue. Everywhere, the horizon was a depthless void where air and water joined. Seabirds wheeled and shrieked, then dived past the cliffs and down to the ocean's surface. Thick patches of mist clung to the island's peaks and nestled in her valleys, hiding her secrets, obscuring her in gloom.

Walker chose Ard Patrinell and three of his Elven Hunters to go with him. Experience and quickness would count for more than power in the confines of the valley jungle, and the Druid wanted veterans to face whatever kept watch there. Redden Alt Mer would take them into the valley aboard the *Jerle Shannara* for as far as the airship could go in the narrow confines. Then the Druid and the Elven Hunters would descend in the winch basket to the valley floor and walk the rest of the way in. With luck, they would not have to walk far.

Once Walker had retrieved the key, the five would make their way back to the basket and be pulled up again.

As the ship's company assembled, Walker saw edginess in the eyes of the veterans and uncertainty in the eyes of the rest. Ryer Ord Star seemed particularly distressed, her thin face white with fear. Perhaps all were remembering the cels of Flay Creech, the devouring mouths and rending teeth, though none would say so. There, the Druid had retrieved the hidden key and everyone had escaped harm. Perhaps they were wondering if their good fortune would carry over here.

With safety lines secured, Redden Alt Mer sailed the *Jerle Shannara* slowly from the bluff down the cliff wall and into the haze of the valley. Dawn's light faded behind them as the airship slid silently between the massive peaks and disappeared into the gloom. Visibility diminished to less than two dozen yards. Alt Mer occupied the helm, taking his vessel ahead cautiously, his speed reduced to dead slow. Rue Meridian stood at the curve of the forward rams, peering ahead into the fog, calling out sightings and navigational corrections to her brother. Everyone else crouched at the railings in silence, watching and listening. The mist clung to them in a fine damp sheen, gathering in droplets on their skin and clothing, causing them to blink and lick their lips. Except for the mist, which moved like an ancient behemoth, lumbering and slow, everything about them was still.

As the minutes passed and the gloom persisted, Walker began to worry about visibility on the valley floor. If they could see no more than this from the air, how could they find their way once they were off the ship? His Druidic instincts would give them some help, but no amount of magic could replace the loss of sight. They would be virtually blind.

He caught himself. There it was again, that word. Blind. He was reminded of Ryer Ord Star's vision and the thing that waited on one of these islands, a thing that was blind but could find you anyway. He pricked his senses for what Truls

Rohk had felt the night before, coming here alone. But from the air, he could sense nothing.

Ahead, the mist cleared slightly, and the cliff walls reappeared, closing in on them sharply. Redden Alt Mer brought the airship to a complete stop, waiting for Little Red to call back to him. She hung from the bow on her safety line, peering into the gloom, then motioned him ahead cautiously. Tree branches reached out of the haze, spectral fingers that seemed to clutch for the airship. Vines hung from the trees and the cliff face in a ropy tangle.

Then the mist disappeared altogether, and the *Jerle Shannara* eased into a canyon that was unexpectedly open and clear. The sky reappeared overhead, blue and welcoming, and the valley floor opened in a sea of green dappled with striations of damp color. Redden Alt Mer took the airship lower, down to within a few feet of the treetops, then slid her cautiously ahead once more. Walker searched the far end of the pocket, finding the cliff walls narrowed down so completely that the tree limbs almost touched. They had come as far as they could by air. From here, they must walk.

When they arrived at the canyon's far end, Redden Alt Mer brought the *Jerle Shannara* right down to where the treetops scraped the hull. Walker and the four Elven Hunters released their safety lines and climbed into the winch basket. A dozen hands swung them out over the ship's railing, and they were lowered slowly into the trees.

Once grounded and out of the basket, Walker signaled back to Rue Meridian, who was still hanging off the bow, that they were safely down. Then he stood motionless in the silence to get his bearings and search for hidden danger. Nothing. Though he probed their surroundings carefully, he could find no threatening presence.

Yet something was clearly out of place.

Then he realized what it was. The jungle was a thick, impenetrable wall of emptiness and silence. No birds, Walker thought. No animals. Nothing. Not even the smallest chirp of an insect. Except for what was rooted in the earth, nothing lived here.

Walker could see a gap in the cliffs ahead, and he nodded to Ard Patrinell to proceed. The Elven leader did not reply, but turned to his Hunters and used hand signals to communicate his orders. A burly Elf named Kian was given the lead. Walker followed just behind, then Patrinell with lean Brae and tall Dace trailing. They moved from the canyon into the narrow gap, casting about warily as they proceeded, mindful of the danger they could expect to find waiting. Walker continued to probe the jungle gloom with tendrils of magic that brushed softly like feathers and then withdrew. The gap tightened about them, narrowing to a corridor less than fifty feet wide where trees and vines clogged everything. There was passage to be found, but it was circuitous and required them to push their way through the vegetation that grew everywhere. All about, the jungle was silent.

They moved ahead steadily, still without encountering any sign of life. Their narrow corridor broadened into another canyon, and the sky reappeared in a blue slash overhead. Sunlight dappled the trees and illuminated the dampness. They crossed to yet another defile and passed down its narrow corridor into a third canyon, this one larger still.

Suddenly, Walker was rocked by something that seized him as a giant hand would a tiny bug. It came out of the earth in a rush, sweeping over him so fast that he did not have time to react and was left momentarily stunned. Perhaps it had been there all along and had masked its presence; perhaps it had only just now found him. Pervasive and powerful, it had no identifiable form, no substantive being. It was everywhere at once, all around him, and though invisible to his eye, it was unmistakably real. He went limp in its grasp, offering no resistance, letting it think him helpless. The Elven Hunters stared at him in confusion, not realizing what was happening. He did not acknowledge them, gave no indication that he even knew they were there. He disappeared inside himself, down where nothing could touch him. There, closed away, he waited.

A few moments later, the presence withdrew, sliding back into the earth, satisfied perhaps that it was not threatened.

Walker shook off the lingering effects of its touch and took a deep, steadying breath. The attack had shaken him badly. Whatever lived in this valley possessed power that dwarfed his own. It was old, he could tell, perhaps as old as the Faerie world. He signaled to the Elves that he was all right, then glanced around quickly. He did not want to stay where he was. A rise of barren, empty rock formed a smooth hump at the center of the canyon, a sun-drenched haven within the jungle gloom. Perhaps from there he could see better where to go next.

Beckoning to the Elven Hunters, he moved out of the undergrowth and gloom and climbed onto the stone rise. The last traces of the hateful presence faded as he did. Odd, he thought, and moved to the center of the rise. From this new elevation, he surveyed the canyon. There was not much to see. At its far end, the canyon broadened and rose in a long, winding slope that disappeared into mist and shadow. The Druid could not determine what lay beyond. He glanced around at the portion of the canyon in which he stood and saw nothing helpful.

Yet something tugged at him. Something close. He closed his eyes, cleared his mind, and began to probe gently outward with his senses. He found what he was looking for almost at once, and his eyes snapped open to confirm his vision.

He could just make out a darkening through the green of the jungle wall in a cliffside a hundred yards or so away. It was the cavern Truls Rohk had found the night before.

He stood looking at the darkness and did not move. The second key was in there, waiting. But the thing that guarded it was waiting, as well. He considered for a moment how best to approach the cavern. No solution presented itself. He turned to the Elven Hunters and gestured for them to remain where they were. Then he walked down off the jumble of rock toward the cave.

He felt the presence return almost instantly, but he had already turned his thoughts inward. He was nothing, an object without purpose, random and devoid of thought. He walled himself away before the sentry that guarded the key could read his intentions or discover his purpose and walked straight into the cavern.

Within, he stopped to collect his thoughts. He could no longer feel the presence shadowing him. It had left him at the entrance of the cave as it had left him at the foot of the rise. Rock did not offer it passage, he decided. Only the soil from which it drew its power. Could he use that to protect himself in some way?

He put the thought aside, and looked around carefully. The cavern opened into a series of chambers, which were dimly lit by splits in the rock that admitted small streamers of light from above the jungle canopy. Walker began to hunt for the key and found it almost immediately. It was sitting out in the open on a small rock shelf, unguarded and unwatched. Walker studied it for a moment before picking it up, then studied it some more. Its configuration was similar to the one he already had, with a flat power source and a blinking red light, but the ridged metal lines on this one formed different patterns.

Walker glanced about the cavern warily, searching for the key's sentry, for some hint of an alarm, for anything dangerous or threatening, and found nothing.

He walked to the cave entrance once more and stood looking out at the clearing. Ard Patrinell and his Elven Hunters were clustered on the rocky mound, looking back at him. In the surrounding jungle, nothing moved. Walker stayed where he was. Something would try to stop him. Something had to. Whatever warded the key would not simply let him walk away. It was waiting for him, he sensed. Out there, in the trees. There, in the soil from which it drew its strength.

He was still debating what to do next when the earth before him erupted in an explosion of green.

Aboard the *Jerle Shannara*, which hovered in a cloud of mist two clearings away, Bek Rowe was watching Rue Meridian tie off a fresh radian draw close by the horns of the bow when Walker's voice cried out sharply in the silence of his mind.

Bek! We're under attack! Two canyons farther in! Have Alt Mer bring the airship! Drop the basket and pull us out! Quick, now!

Startled by the unexpected assault, the boy jumped at the sound of the Druid's voice. Then he was racing for the pilot box. It never occurred to him to question whether he was being misled. It never occurred to him that the voice might not be real. The urgency it conveyed catapulted him across the decking in a rush, crying out to Big Red as if stung.

In moments, the airship was sailing skyward through the rugged peaks, lifting over the defiles it could not navigate to reach the beleaguered men.

Walker stared from the cavern entrance at the Elven Hunters marooned on the rocky rise. The entire floor of the canyon had risen up in a tangle of writhing vines and limbs, all of them grasping for anything that came within reach. They had gotten the Elven Hunter Brae before he could even defend himself, dragged him from the rise, and pulled him apart as he screamed for help. The other three had backed to the center of their island, swords drawn, and were striking frantically at the tentacles that snatched for them.

The Druid shoved the second key deep inside his robes and called up the Druid fire against the wall that had formed before him. Blue flames lanced into the tangle and burned everything they touched, momentarily clearing a path. Walker continued his assault, burning through the twisting mass of foliage toward the rise, seeking to reach his companions. But the jungle refused to give way, thrusting back at him from both sides, driving him back. An enormous, implacable weight settled on him, driving him to his knees. He backed from the entrance, recoiling from the assault, and the weight lessened. The key's guardian could not reach him while he remained protected by the cave's stone. But it would keep him there forever.

He realized then what had happened, both here and at Flay Creech. The guardians of the keys had been set at watch against any foreign presence and all threatened thefts of the keys. They were not thinking entities and did not rely on reason; they acted out of pure instinct. Eels and jungle both had been conditioned to serve a single purpose. How that had been managed and by whom, Walker had no idea. But their power was enormous, and while probably confined to a small area, it was more than sufficient to subdue anyone who came within reach.

The jungle reached for him through the cavern entrance, and he responded with the Druid fire, charring vines and limbs, filling the air with clouds of smoke and ash. If Redden Alt Mer didn't reach them soon, they were finished. The Elves could not hope to withstand a prolonged assault on the rise. And even a Druid's magic had its limits.

A hint of desperation driving at him, he thrust his way forward, determined anew to break free. He beat back the jungle wall in an effort to reach the light beyond. As he did so, he caught a glimpse of the *Jerle Shannara* passing overhead and heard the shouts of her company. The Elves trapped on the rise glanced skyward, as well, momentarily distracted, and tall Dace paid the price. Knocked sprawling by a whiplash assault of grasses, his legs became tangled in their implacable weave. Kicking wildly, he fought in vain to break free. Patrinell and Kian reached for him instantly, but he had already been pulled from the rise to his death.

Then a torrent of liquid fire rained down about the rocky isle, encircling the trapped Elven Hunters. Poured from barrels stored aboard ship, it showered onto the vines and grasses and exploded into flame. Down came the winch basket in the fire's wake, jerking up short just above Ard Patrinell and Kian. Breaking off their struggle with the jungle, they scrambled over the basket's side and were pulled to safety.

The jungle turned now on Walker, vines and tall grasses, supple limbs and trunks, twisting and writhing in fury. Walker stood in the cavern opening and burned them with the Druid fire to prevent them from dragging him down. A few moments more and he would be free.

But the guardian of the key was determined to have him. A bramble limb snaked out of the shadows to one side, lashing at the Druid's face. Two-inch needles bit into his flesh, raking his arm and side. Walker felt their poison enter him instantly, a cold fire. He ripped the bramble away, threw it on the ground, and turned it to ash.

Then the winch basket dropped in front of him, and he dragged himself over its side. Vines clutched frantically at him as he rose. With the last of his strength, Walker burned them away, fired them one by one, fighting to stay conscious. The basket lurched free and began to rise swiftly. The airship rose, as well, lifting away into the blue. Anxious faces peered down at him from the railing, blurred and fading quickly. He fought to keep them in focus and failed. Collapsing to the floor of the basket, he lost consciousness.

Below, the floor of the valley writhed in a fiery mass of shriveled limbs and then disappeared in black clouds of roiling smoke.

TWENTY-TWO

For six days and nights, Walker lay near death. A swift and deadly agent, the poison from the brambles had penetrated deep into his body. By the time he was brought back aboard the *Jerle Shannara*, he was already beginning to fail. The Elven Healer Joad Rish recognized his symptoms immediately and roused him long enough to swallow an antidote, then spent the next few anxious minutes applying baen-leaf compresses to his injuries to draw out the poison.

Although the Healer's efforts slowed the poison and blunted its killing effects, they could not counteract it completely. At Redden Alt Mer's insistence, Walker was carried below and placed in the Rover Captain's cabin, and there Joad Rish wrapped the stricken Druid in blankets to keep him warm, gave him liquids to prevent dehydration, changed his dressings regularly, and sat back to wait. Walker's own body was doing more than the Healer could to keep him alive. It waged a silent struggle that was apparent to him but that he could do little more to aid.

Bek Rowe was there for most of it. Since his summoning by Walker during the jungle attack, he felt tied to the Druid in a new and unexpected way. There was considerable wonder and confusion among the members of the ship's company at the fact that he alone had heard Walker's summons. No one had made much of it as yet, but Bek could tell what they were thinking. If the Druid could have summoned anyone, he would have summoned Redden Alt Mer, who piloted the airship and could respond more directly than Bek Rowe. But Big Red had heard nothing. Nor had Quentin or Panax or even Ryer Ord Star. Perhaps not even Truls Rohk had heard. Only Bek. How could that be? Why would Bek be able to receive a summons of that sort when no one else could? How had Walker known that Bek could hear and so chosen to call to him?

The questions plagued him, and there would be no answers unless the Druid recovered from his wounds. But it was not for that reason that Bek chose to keep watch over the Druid. It was because he was afraid that Walker, locked inside his body while unconscious and stricken, in need of help that he could communicate in no other way, would call to him again. Perhaps distance wasn't a problem for the Druid when he was well, but what if it was while he was sick? If Bek were not close and listening, a cry for help might go unheard. Bek did not want that on his conscience. If there was a way to save the Druid's life, he had to be there to provide it.

So he sat with Walker in Redden Alt Mer's cabin and watched in silence while Joad Rish worked. He slept now and then, but only in short naps and never deeply. Ahren Elessedil brought him his meals, and Quentin and Panax came to visit. No effort was made to remove him from the cabin. If anything, the ship's company seemed to feel he belonged at the Druid's side.

To no one's surprise, he did not keep his vigil over Walker alone. Sitting with him the whole of the time was the young seer, Ryer Ord Star. As she had since their departure from Arborlon, she stayed as close to the Druid as his shadow. She studied him intently during his struggle, her head bent in concentration. She watched while Joad Rish worked, asking occasionally what he was doing, nodding at his responses, giving silent approval and support to his efforts. Now and then she spoke to Bek, a word or two here and there, never more, always with her eyes directed toward the Druid. Bek studied her surreptitiously, trying to read her thoughts, to see inside her mind deep enough to discover if she had caught a glimpse of Walker's fate. But the seer revealed nothing, her thin, youthful face a mask against whatever secrets she kept.

Once, when Joad Rish had left them alone and they sat together on a wooden bench at the Druid's side in candlelit gloom, Bek asked her if she thought Walker would live.

"His will is very strong," she replied softly. "But his need for me is greater."

He had no idea what she was talking about and could not think of a way to ask. He was silent long enough that Joad Rish returned, and the matter was dropped. But he could not shake the feeling that the young woman was telling him that in some inextricable way Walker's life was linked to hers.

As he discovered two nights later, he was right. Joad Rish had announced earlier in the day that he had done everything he could think to do for the Druid and that further healing was up to the Druid himself. He had not abandoned hope or given up on his treatment, but he was seeing no change in Walker and was clearly worried. Bek could tell that the Druid had reached a critical juncture in his battle. He was no longer sleeping quietly, but thrashing and twisting in his unconsciousness, delirious and sweating. His great strength of will seemed to have hit a wall, and the poison was pushing back against it relentlessly. Bek had an uneasy feeling that Walker was losing ground.

Ryer Ord Star must have decided the same. She rose suddenly as the midnight hour approached and announced to Joad Rish that he must step back from Walker and give her a chance to help him. The Healer hesitated, then decided for whatever reason to comply. Perhaps he knew of her reputation as an empath and hoped she could do something to relieve his patient's distress. Perhaps he felt there was nothing more he could do, so why not let someone else try? He moved to the bench beside Bek, and together they watched the young seer approach.

She bent to the Druid soundlessly. Like the shadow she so often seemed, she hovered over him, her hands placed carefully on the sides of his face, her slender form draped across his own. She spoke softly and gently, the words lost to Bek and Joad Rish, murmurings that faded into the sounds of the airship as it sailed on the back of the night wind. She continued for a long time, linking herself to Walker, Bek decided, by the sound of her voice and her touch. She wanted him to feel her presence. She wanted him to know she was there.

Then she laid her cheek against his forehead, keeping her hands on his face, and went silent. She closed her eyes and breathed deeply and steadily. Walker began to convulse, arching off the bed in violent spasms, gasping and moaning. She held on to him as he thrashed, and her own body jerked in response to his. Sweat appeared on her thin face, and her pale brow furrowed in anguish. Joad Rish started to go to them, then sat back again. Neither he nor Bek looked at each other, their eyes riveted on the drama taking place.

The strange dance between Druid and seer went on for a long time, a give and take of sudden motion and harsh response. She's taking the poison with its sickness and pain into herself, Bek realized at one point, watching her body knot and her face twist. She's absorbing what's killing him into herself. But won't it then kill her? How much stronger can she be than the Druid, this tiny frail creature? He felt helpless and frustrated watching her work. But he could do nothing.

Then she collapsed to the floor so suddenly that both Bek and the Healer sprang to their feet to go to her. She was unconscious. They laid her on some spare bedding on the cabin floor and covered her with blankets. She was sleeping deeply, locked within herself, carrying Walker's poison inside, carrying his sickness and pain; Walker was sleeping peacefully, the thrashing stopped, the delirium faded. Joad Rish examined them both, feeling for heartbeat and pulse, for temperature and breathing. He looked at Bek when he was finished and shook his head uncertainly. He couldn't tell if she'd been successful or not. They were alive, but it was impossible for him to judge as yet if they would stay that way.

He returned to the bench, and the waiting began anew.

At dawn, the *Jerle Shannara* encountered the worst storm of the voyage. Redden Alt Mer had felt it coming all night as it was signaled by sudden drops of temperature and changes in the wind. When dawn broke iron gray and bloodred, he ordered the sails reefed and all but the main draws shortened. Lightning flashed in long, jagged streaks across the northwest skies, and thunderheads rolled out of the horizon in massive dark banks. Placing the dependable Furl Hawken at the helm, Big Red moved down to the main deck to direct his Rover crew. Everything not already secured was lashed down. Everyone who was not a part of the crew was sent belowdecks and told to stay there. Rue Meridian was dispatched to her brother's cabin to make certain that Walker was tied to his bed and to warn Bek, Ryer Ord Star, and Joad Rish that rough weather lay ahead.

By the time this was done and Little Red was back, the wind was howling across the decking and through the masts and spars as if a living thing. Rain washed down out of the clouds, and darkness descended on the airship in a smothering wave. Redden Alt Mer took the helm back from Furl Hawken, but ordered him to stand by. Spanner Frew was already stationed aft where he could see everything forward of his position. Little Red moved to the bow. All of the crew had secured safety lines and were crouched in the shelter of the railings and masts in anticipation of what was to come.

What came was ferocious. The storm swallowed them in a single gulp of black fury that shut out every other sight and sound, drenched them in rain, and lashed at them with winds so fierce it seemed the ship must surely come apart. Searching for a place to ride out of the storm, Big Red took the *Jerle Shannara* down to a little over a hundred feet above the ocean surface. He would not take the ship all the way down, because the ocean was more dangerous than the wind. What he could see of the Blue Divide, as intermittent flashes of lightning illuminated it, convinced him he had made the right choice. The surface of the ocean was a boiling cauldron of swirling foam and wicked dark troughs with waves cresting thirty and forty feet. In the air, they were buffeted hard, but they would not sink.

Even so, the Rover Captain began to fear they might break apart. Spars and lines were crashing to the decking, flying off into the windswept void. The airship was sleek and smooth and could sideslip the worst of the wind's gusts, but, it was taking a beating. It tossed and dipped wildly. It slewed left and right with sudden lurches that caused stomachs to drop and jaws to clench. Redden Alt Mer stood tall in the pilot box, trying to keep his ship level and directed, but even that soon became hopeless. He could not tell in what direction they traveled, what speed they held, or where within the storm they lay. All he could manage was to keep them turned into the wind and upright above the sea.

The struggle went on all morning. Several times Big Red gave up the wheel to Furl Hawken and sank down in the shelter of the pilot box for a few moments of rest. His hearing was lost temporarily to the howl of the wind, and the skin of his face and hands felt raw. His body ached, and there was a thrumming in his arms and legs from fighting to hold the wheel steady. But each time he rested, he worried that he was taking too long. A few minutes were all he would spare himself. Responsibility for the ship and crew belonged to him, and he would not yield that responsibility to anyone else. Furl Hawken was as able as they came, but the safety of the ship and her company belonged to the Captain. He might have shared his duty with Little Red, but he had no idea where she was. He hadn't seen her in hours. He could no longer see the ship's bow or stern or anyone on them.

Eventually the storm passed, leaving all aboard ship sodden and battered and grateful to be alive. It was the worst storm

Redden Alt Mer could remember. He thought they were lucky to have had a vessel as well built as the *Jerle Shannara* to weather it, and one of the first things he did after a hurried best-guess correction of their heading was to relinquish the helm to Furl Hawken so he could tell Spanner Frew as much. A quick check of the ship's company revealed that everyone was still with them, although a few members had sustained minor injuries. Little Red appeared out of the shelter of the forward rams to advise him they had lost several spars and a couple of radian draws, but sustained no major damage. The most immediate problem they faced was that a forward hatch had fallen in on the water casks and all of their fresh water was lost. Foraging for more would be necessary.

It was at that point that Alt Mer remembered the Wing Riders and their Rocs, who had ridden out the storm on their own. He searched the skies in vain. All three had disappeared.

Well, there was nothing he could do about it. Half a day's light remained to them, and he intended to take advantage of it. They were still following Walker's map, sailing on toward the last of the three islands. Even though the Druid was lost to them for now, continuing on made better sense than turning back or standing still. If the Druid died, a different decision might be necessary, but he would make it only then.

"Bring everyone topside and put them to work cleaning up," he told his sister. "And check on the Druid."

She left at once, but it was Bek Rowe who appeared with the news he sought. "He's sleeping better now, and Joad Rish thinks he will recover." Bek looked exhausted, but pleased. "I don't need to be down there anymore. I can help with what's needed up here."

Alt Mer smiled and clapped the boy on the back. "You are a game lad, Bek. I'm lucky to have you for my good right hand. All right, then. You go where you want for now. Lend a hand where it's needed."

The boy went at once to join Rue Meridian, who was clearing away one of the broken spars. Big Red watched him

for a moment, then moved back into the pilot box with Furl
Hawken and watched Bek some more.

"That boy's in love with her, Hawk," he declared with a
wistful sigh.

Furl Hawken nodded. "Aren't they all. Much good that it
will do him or any of them."

Redden Alt Mer pursed his lips thoughtfully. "Maybe Bek
Rowe will surprise us."

His friend grunted. "Maybe cows will fly."

They turned their attention to determining the ship's position, taking compass and sextant readings, and beginning a
search for landmarks. For now, they could do little but wait.
The stars would give them a better reading come nightfall.
Tomorrow would see a return of good weather and clear
sailing. Maybe the Wing Riders would reappear from wherever they had gone. Maybe Walker would be back on his feet.

Redden Alt Mer glanced over at his sister and Bek Rowe
once more and smiled. Maybe cows would fly.

It was almost twenty-four hours later when the Wing
Riders soared into view out of the eastern horizon, winging
for the airship across clear skies and over placid waters.
Hunter Predd rode the lead bird. He was steady and calm as
he swung close enough to shout across at Redden Alt Mer.

"Well met, Captain! Are you all right?"

"We survived, Wing Rider! What kept you?"

Hunter Predd grimaced. Rover humor. "We saw the storm
coming and found an island on which to wait it out! You don't
want to be caught aloft on a Roc in a storm like that! You've
been blown well off course, you know!"

Alt Mer nodded. "We're working our way back! What we
need now is fresh water! Can you find us some?"

The Wing Rider waved. "We'll take a look! Don't wander
off while we're gone!"

With Gill and Po Kelles in tow, he swung Obsidian south
and west and began tracking the path of the sun in search of

an island. The Wing Riders had weathered the storm on an island some miles east, in a cove sheltered by hills and trees. They had lost all contact with the airship and its company, but there was no help for that. Flying their Rocs in winds that heavy would have killed them all. Experience had taught them to take whatever shelter they could find when a bad storm appeared. They had remained on the island through the night and set off again at dawn. Rocs were intelligent birds possessed of extraordinary eyesight, and their tracking instincts were almost infallible. Using a method they had employed countless times before, the Wing Riders had flown a spiral search pattern that eventually brought them back on course with the *Jerle Shannara*.

Hunter Predd sighed. Storms and other navigational challenges did not concern him all that much. Losing Walker was a different matter. He assumed that Walker was still alive from the simple fact that Redden Alt Mer hadn't said otherwise. Perhaps the Druid had even improved. But having him incapacitated even temporarily pointed up dramatically the weak link in the chain that anchored this entire expedition—only Walker understood what it was that they were trying to accomplish. Granted, a handful of others knew about the keys and the islands and the nature of their destination. Granted, as well, the seer had her visions and whatever information they supplied. Perhaps there were even a few additional things known to one or two others that were crucial to the success of the voyage.

But Walker was the glue that held them all together and the only one who understood completely the larger picture. He had told Hunter Predd that he needed the Wing Rider's experience and insight to help him succeed on this expedition. He had intimated that the Wing Rider was to keep a sharp eye out. But half the time Hunter felt as if he were groping in the dark. He was never entirely sure what he was watching out for, save in the very narrow context of momentary circumstance. It was bad enough to operate in this fashion with

Walker safe and sound. But if the Druid was incapacitated, how were the rest of them supposed to function reliably knowing as little as they did? It would be guesswork at best.

He made up his mind that he could not allow this situation to continue. Foraging and scouting in unknown territory, miles from any mainland, were sufficiently dangerous. But doing so without a clear idea of their purpose was intolerable. Certainly others aboard ship must feel the same. What about Bek Rowe and Quentin Leah? They had been taken into the Druid's confidence, as well. They had been given the same charge he had. He had barely spoken to either since they had set out, but surely they must be having the same misgivings he was.

Still, Hunter Predd was reluctant to force the issue. He was a trained Rider of the Wing Hove, and he understood the importance of obeying orders without questioning them. Leaders did not always impart everything they knew to those they led. Certainly he did not do so with Gill and Po. They were expected to accept the assignments they were given and to do as they were told.

He shook his head. If there was no order, you ran the risk of anarchy. But if there was too much, you ran the risk of revolt. It was a fine line to walk.

He was still pondering this dilemma, trying to reason it through, when he sighted the island.

There were storm clouds lingering ahead, and at first he thought the island was a part of them. But as he drew nearer, he saw that what he had mistaken for dark clouds were rugged cliffs of the sort they had encountered on Shatterstone, their craggy faces exposed and windswept. The island's foliage grew thick and lush inland on the lee side. The Wing Rider squinted against the glare of waterfalls cascading out of the rocks in long silver streams and sunlight where it reflected off the brilliant green of the trees. There would be fresh water available here, he thought.

Then something strange caught his eye. Hundreds of dark spots dotted the cliffs, making it look as if deep pockmarks had formed in the crevices and ridges after long years of severe weathering.

"What is that?" Hunter Predd muttered to himself.

He swung Obsidian about, motioning for Gill to move off to his left and Po Kelles to flank him on the right. On a long, sweeping glide, they approached the island and its cliffs, peering through the brightness of the afternoon sun.

Hunter Predd blinked. Had one of the dark spots moved? He glanced over at Po. The young Wing Rider nodded in response. He had seen it, too. Hunter Predd motioned for him to fall back.

He was trying to signal Gill, whose concentration had been distracted by a passing pod of whales, when several of the dark spots lifted away from the cliffs entirely.

Beneath him, Obsidian tensed and then screamed in alarm. Wings were unfolding from the black dots, giving them size and shape. Hunter Predd went cold. The Roc had recognized the danger before he had. Shrikes! War Shrikes! The fiercest and most savage of the breed. This island, which the Rocs and Wing Riders had stumbled upon unwittingly, must be their nesting ground. The War Shrikes would not ignore a trespass on their home ground, regardless of the reason for it. Rocs were their natural enemies, and the Shrikes would attack.

Hunter Predd wheeled Obsidian around hurriedly, watching Po Kelles and Niciannon follow his lead. To his astonishment, Gill continued to advance. Either he hadn't seen the Shrikes or hadn't recognized what they were. It was useless to yell warnings from that distance, so he used the signal whistle. Startled, Gill glanced over his shoulder and saw his companions pointing. Then he caught sight of the Shrikes. Frantically, he reined in Tashin. But the Roc panicked, and instead of wheeling back, he went into a steep dive, spiraling toward the ocean, pulling up and leveling out only at the last possible moment.

Then he was streaking after Obsidian and Niciannon, but he was still far behind and the Shrikes were closing. War

Shrikes were swift and powerful short-range fliers. A Roc's best hope was to gain height and distance. Hunter Predd realized that Tashin had failed to do either and would not escape.

He brought Obsidian back around swiftly and flew at the Shrikes in challenge, trying to distract them. Po Kelles and Niciannon were beside him almost instantly. Both Rocs screamed in fury at the approaching Shrikes, their hatred of their enemies as great as that of their enemies for them. Secured to their riding harnesses by safety lines and gripping their mounts with knees and boots, both Wing Riders brought out their long bows and the arrows that were dipped in an extract from fire nettles and nightshade. Close enough now to find their targets, they began to fire on the Shrikes.

Some of their missiles struck home. Some of the Shrikes even broke off the attack and wheeled back toward the island. But the bulk, more than twenty, descended on Gill and Tashin like a black cloud and caught them just off the surface of the water. Gill was torn from his Roc's back on the first pass. Sharp talons and hooked beaks scattered parts of him everywhere in a red spray. Tashin lasted only seconds longer. Shuddering from the blows he received, he righted himself momentarily, then disappeared under a swarm of black bodies. Forced down into the ocean, he was quickly ripped to shreds.

Hunter Predd stared down at the carnage in helpless rage and frustration. It had happened so fast. One minute there, the next gone. Alive, and then a memory, a senseless loss of life that shouldn't have happened. But what could have been done to avoid it? What could he have done?

He wheeled Obsidian about. Po Kelles and Niciannon followed. Swiftly they gained height and then distance, and in a matter of moments, they were safely away. Their pursuers did not give chase; they were otherwise occupied, wheeling above the broad patch of rolling ocean streaked with feathers and blood. The Wing Riders flew on and did not look back.

TWENTY-THREE

After having their number reduced by three in a matter of a few days, the men and women of the *Jerle Shannara* continued their voyage for another six weeks without incident. Even so, tempers flared more easily than before. Perhaps it was the strain of prolonged confinement or the increased uncertainty of their fate or just the change in climate as the ship turned north, the air grew cold and sharp, and storms became more frequent, but everyone was on edge.

The change in Walker was pronounced. Recovered from his ordeal on Shatterstone, he had nevertheless grown increasingly aloof and less approachable. He seemed as sure of himself as ever and as fixed of purpose, but he distanced himself in ways that left no doubt that he preferred his own company to that of others. He consulted regularly on the ship's progress with Redden Alt Mer and spoke in a civil way to everyone he came upon, but he seemed to do so from a long way off. He canceled the nightly meetings in the Rover Captain's quarters, announcing that they were no longer necessary. Ryer Ord Star still followed him around like a lost puppy, but he seemed unaware of her. Even Bek Rowe found him difficult to talk to, enough so that the boy put off asking why he, in particular, had been mind-summoned on Shatterstone.

Nor was Walker the only member of the company affected. Ard Patrinell still worked his Elven Hunters daily, as well as

Quentin Leah and Ahren Elessedil, but he was virtually invisible the rest of the time. Spanner Frew was a thunderhead waiting to burst. One time he engaged in a shouting match with Big Red that brought everyone on deck to stare at them. Rue Meridian grew tight-lipped and somber toward everyone except her brother and Bek. She clearly liked being with Bek, and spent much of her time exchanging stories with him. No one understood her attraction for the boy, but Bek basked in it. Panax shook his head at everything and spent all of his time whittling. Truls Rohk was a ghost.

Once, Hunter Predd came aboard for a hard-edged, whispered confrontation with Walker that seemed to satisfy neither and left the Wing Rider angry when it was finished.

They had been gone for almost four months, and the voyage was beginning to wear on them. Days would pass with no land sighted, and sometimes those days would stretch into weeks. The number of islands they passed diminished, and it became necessary to ration their stores and water more strictly. Fresh fruit was seldom available, and rainwater was caught in tarps stretched over the decking to supplement what was foraged. Routines grew boring and change more difficult to invent. The course of their lives settled into a numbing sameness that left everyone disgruntled.

There was no help for it, Rue Meridian explained to Bek one day as they sat talking. Life aboard ship did that to you, and long voyages were the worst. Some of it had to do with the fact that explorers and adventurers detested confinement. Even the members of the Rover crew liked to move around more than was permitted here. None of them had ever sailed on a voyage of such length, and they were discovering feelings and reactions they hadn't even known were there. It would all change when they reached their destination, but until then they simply had to live with their discomfort.

"There's a lot of luck involved in being a sailor, Bek," she told him. "Flying airships is tricky business, even with a Captain as experienced as Big Red. His crews like him more for his luck than his skill. Rovers are a superstitious bunch, and they're constantly looking for favorable signs. They don't feel good about new experiences and unknown places if they come at the price of their shipmates' lives. They're drawn to the unknown, but they take comfort in what's familiar and reassuring. Sort of a contradiction, isn't it?"

"I thought Rovers might be more adaptable," he replied.

She shrugged. "Rovers are a paradox. They like movement and new places. They don't like the unknown. They don't trust magic. They believe in fate and omens. My mother read bones to determine her children's future. My father read the stars. It doesn't always make sense, but what does? Is it better to be a Dwarf or a Rover? Is it better to have your life fixed and settled or to have it change with every shift in the wind? It depends on your point of view, doesn't it? The demands of this particular voyage are a new experience for everyone, and each of us has to find a way to deal with them."

Bek didn't mind doing that. He was by nature an accepting sort, and he had learned a long time ago to live with whatever conditions and circumstances he was provided. Maybe this came from being an orphan delivered into the hands of a stranger's family and being brought up with someone else's history. Maybe it came from an approach to life that questioned everything as a matter of course, so that the uncertainties of their expedition didn't wear at him so cruelly. After all, he hadn't gone into this with the same high spirits as many of the others, and his emotional equilibrium was more easily balanced.

To a measurable extent, he found he was a calming influence on the other members of the company. When they were around him, they seemed more at ease and less irritable. He didn't know why that was, but he was pleased to be able to offer something of tangible value and did his best to soothe ruffled feathers when he encountered them. Quentin was of some use in this regard, as well. Nothing ever seemed to change Bek's cousin. He continued as eager and bright-eyed and hopeful as ever, the only member of the company who genuinely enjoyed each day and looked forward to the next. It was the nature of his personality, of course, but it provided a needed measure of inspiration to those who possessed a less generous attitude.

Shortly after their encounter with the Shrikes, the airship assumed a more northerly heading in accordance with the dictates of the map. As the days passed, the weather turned colder. Autumn had arrived at home, and a fresh chill was apparent in the sea air as well. The sky took on an iron-gray cast much of the time, and on the colder mornings a thin layer of ice formed on the railings of the ship. Furl Hawken broke out heavy coats, gloves, and boots for the company, and warming fires were lit on deck at night for the watch. The days grew shorter and the nights longer, and the sun rose farther south in the eastern sky with each new dawn.

Snow flurries appeared for the first time only two nights before the *Jerle Shannara* arrived at the island of Mephitic.

Walker stood at the bow of the airship to study the island during their approach. The Wing Riders had discovered it several hours earlier while making their customary sweep forward and to either side of the ship's line of flight. Redden Alt Mer had adjusted their course at once on being informed, and now Mephitic lay directly ahead, a green jewel shining brightly in the midday sun.

This island was different from the other two, as Walker had known it would be. Mephitic was low and broad, comprising rolling hills, thickly wooded forests, and wide smooth grasslands. It lacked the high cliffs of Shatterstone and the barren rocky shoals of Flay Creech. It was much larger than either, big enough that in the haze of the midday autumn light, Walker could not see its far end. It did not appear forbidding. It had the look of the Westland where it bordered the Plains of Streleheim north and abutted the Myrian south. As the airship descended toward its shores and began a slow circle about its coastline, he could see small deer grazing peacefully and flocks of birds in flight. Nothing seemed out of place or dangerous. Nothing threatened.

Walker found what he was looking for on their first pass. A massive castle sat on a low bluff facing west, backed up against a deep forest and fronted by a broad plain. The castle was old and crumbling, its portcullis collapsed, its windows and doors dark empty holes, and its battlements and courtyards deserted. It had been a mighty fortress in another age and time, and its walls and outbuildings sprawled across the grasslands for perhaps a mile in all directions. The castle proper was as large as Paranor and every bit as formidable.

Unlike the other two islands, where only the name had been given, Mephitic had been carefully drawn on the castaway's map. The fortress, in particular, had been noted. The third and final key, the map indicated, was hidden somewhere inside.

Walker folded himself into his black robes and stared at the castle. He was aware of the growing dissatisfaction of the ship's company. He understood that some of it was due entirely to him. He had indeed distanced himself from them in a very deliberate fashion, but not without consideration for the consequences and not for the reasons they thought. Their disgruntlement and unrest were side effects he could not avoid. He knew things they did not, and one of them had prompted him to keep everyone at arm's length since his recovery.

That would change once he had possession of the third key and could instill in the ship's company a reasonable expectation of reaching the safehold the keys would unlock.

Not that anything was as simple as it appeared on the surface, or even that anything was *what* it appeared.

He felt a bitter satisfaction in knowing the truth, but it did nothing to make him feel better. Hunter Predd had a right to be angry with him for keeping secrets. They all had a right to be angry, more so than they realized. It reminded him anew of his own bitter feelings toward the Druids in times past. He knew the nature of their order. They were wielders of power and keepers of secrets. They manipulated and deceived. They specialized in creating events and directing lives for the greater good of the Four Lands. He had wanted no part of them then and wanted little now. Although he had become one of them, a part of their order and their history, he had promised himself that things would be different with him. He had sworn that in carrying out the admittedly necessary task of implementing order and wielding magic in a way that would unite the Races, he would not resort to their tactics.

He was finding out anew how hard that vow was to keep. He was discovering firsthand the depth of his own commitment to their cause and to his duty.

He ordered Redden Alt Mer to take the *Jerle Shannara* down to the plain in front of the castle and to anchor her several hundred yards away and in the open so that all approaches could be watched. He called the ship's company together and told them he would take a scouting party into the castle now, before dark, for a look around. Perhaps they would find the key at once, as they had on the other two islands. Perhaps they would even manage to secure it quickly and escape. But he did not want to run the risks of Shatterstone, so he would proceed cautiously. If he sensed any form of danger, they would turn back at once and begin again tomorrow. If it took them longer to achieve their objective because of his caution, so be it.

He chose Panax, Ard Patrinell, and six Elven Hunters to go with him. He considered Quentin Leah, then shook his head. He did not even glance at Bek.

The scouting party descended from the airship by rope ladder and set off across the flats for the castle. Wading through waist-high grasses, they reached the castle's west entry, a drawbridge that was lowered and rotting and a portcullis that was raised and rusted in place. They stopped long enough for the Druid to read the shadows that lay pooled at every silent opening, dark hollows within the walls of stone and mortar, then crossed the drawbridge warily and entered the main courtyard. Dozens of doors opened through walls and dozens of stairs led into towers. Walker scanned them all for whatever might threaten and found nothing. There was no sign of life and no indication of danger.

But he could sense the presence of the key, faint and distant, somewhere deep inside the keep. What sort of guardian kept watch over it? *One is everything and nothing and will steal your soul.* The words of the seer echoed in the silence of his mind, enigmatic and troubling.

Walker stood in the courtyard for a long time making sure of what his senses told him, then started ahead once more.

They combed the ruins from tower to cellar, dungeon to spire, hall to courtyard, and parapet to battlement, crisscrossing its maze swiftly, but thoroughly. Nothing interfered with their efforts, and no dangers presented themselves. Twice, Walker thought they were close to the key, able to sense its presence more strongly, to feel its peculiar mix of metal and energy reaching out to him. But each time he believed himself close, it eluded him. The second time, he divided the Elven Hunters into pairs and sent two with Ard Patrinell, two with Panax, and two with himself in an effort to surround it. But no one found anything.

Their search was frustrating in other ways, as well. The fortress was a puzzling warren of chambers, courtyards, and halls, and all sense of direction disappeared once they were inside. The searchers constantly found themselves going around in circles and ending up back where they started. Worse, led astray by a deceived sense of direction, they were as likely to find themselves outside the walls at the end of a corridor's turn or stairwell's twist as they were inside. It was irksome and somewhat troubling to the Druid, but he could find no reason for it beyond the construction of the keep. Probably it had been designed to confuse enemies. Whatever the case, all efforts at completing a successful search were thwarted as they found themselves starting over time and again.

Finally, they gave it up. The afternoon sun had drifted west to the horizon, and Walker did not want to get caught inside the castle after dark. The keep might be less friendly then, and he didn't want to find that out the hard way. Even though they hadn't discovered it, he knew the key was close at hand. It was only a matter of time before their search was concluded.

He returned to the ship and called his first meeting of the company's inner circle in almost two months to give his report and express his confidence. Redden Alt Mer, Rue Meridian, Ard Patrinell, Ahren Elessedil, Ryer Ord Star, Quentin Leah, and Bek Rowe were all there, and all were heartened by what they heard. Tomorrow they would resume their search for the final key, he concluded, and this time their efforts would prove successful.

At dawn, Walker took everyone with him but the Rovers, Ryer Ord Star, Truls Rohk, and Bek. He could see the disappointment and hurt in Bek's eyes, but there was no help for it. Again they searched diligently, taking all day to do so, and again they found nothing. Walker sensed the presence of the key just as he had the day before, unmistakable and clear. But he could not find it. Without results, he combed the castle for magic that might conceal it. He kept a wary eye out for whatever guarded it—for he knew something must be doing so— but could identify nothing.

For three more days, Walker searched. He took the same members of the ship's company with him each time, splitting them up into different groups, hoping that some new combination would see what the others had missed. From dawn until dusk, they crisscrossed the ruins. Again and again, they found themselves traveling in circles. Over and over, they found themselves starting their search inside and ending up outside. Nothing new was uncovered. No one caught even a glimpse of the key.

On the fifth night, weary and discouraged, he was forced

to admit to himself, if to no one else, that he was getting nowhere. He had reached a point where he felt failure's grip tightening on his hopes. His patience was exhausted and his confidence was beginning to erode. Something about this business was wearing at him in a very unpleasant and subtle way.

While the other members of the company drifted off to sleep, he stood at the bow of the ship for a long time trying to decide what he should do. He was missing something. The key was there; he could feel it. Why was it so difficult for him to pinpoint its location? Why was it so hard to discover how it had been concealed? If no magic was protecting it and no guardian was evident, how could it continue to elude him?

Another approach was needed. Something new must be tried. Perhaps someone should go into the castle at night. Perhaps the darkness would change the way things looked.

It was time to call on Truls Rohk.

Far astern of the *Jerle Shannara*, south and east of the island and well out of sight below the horizon, *Black Moclips* hung silently above the water, anchored in place for the night. Mwellret sentries prowled across her sleek, armored decking, their spidery forms hooded and cloaked as they drifted through the shadows. The Federation crew was belowdecks in the sleeping quarters, all save for the helmsman, a whip-thin veteran corded with muscle and wrapped in his disdain and repulsion for the lizardlike creatures his ship was forced to carry.

The Ilse Witch shared his feelings. The Mwellrets were loathsome and dangerous, but there was nothing she could do about them. The presence of the Morgawr's minions was the price she had been forced to pay in order to pursue her search for the map's promised magic. Had she been free to do so, she would have turned them all to chum and fed them to the big fish.

Not that she was much better regarded than they were by

Commander Aden Kett and his crew. The Federation soldiers disliked her almost as much; she was a shadowy presence who stayed aloof from them, who gave them no reasons for what she did, and who had on the very first day made a small example of one of their number who had disobeyed her. That she was apparently human was her only saving grace. That she commanded power beyond their understanding and had little regard for them beyond what they could do for her made her someone they went out of their way to avoid.

Which was as it should be, of course. Which was as it had always been.

Wrapped in her gray robes, she stood before the foremast and looked off into the night. She had been shadowing the *Jerle Shannara* and her company ever since the departure from Arborlon. *Black Moclips* was a formidable and efficient craft, and her Federation crew was as well trained and experienced as Sen Dunsidan had promised. Both had done what was needed to track the Elven airship. Not that there was ever any real danger they might lose contact with her. The Ilse Witch had seen to that.

But what was happening here? What was keeping the other ship at anchor for so long? For six days and nights she had waited for the Druid to secure the final key. Why had he failed to do so? Apparently the puzzle offered by this island was proving more difficult to solve than that of the previous two. Was this where Walker would fail? Was this as far as he would get without her help?

She sniffed in disdain at the thought. No, not him. Even crippled, he would not be so easily defeated. She might hate and despise him, but she knew him to be formidable and clever. He would solve the puzzle and continue on to the safehold they both journeyed to find. It would be settled between them there, and a lifetime of anger and hatred would be put to rest at last. It would happen as she had foreseen. He would not disappoint her.

Yet her uncertainty persisted, nagging and insidious. Perhaps she gave him too much credit. Did he realize yet the ways in which he was being manipulated in his quest? Had he reasoned out, as she had, the hidden purpose of the castaway and the map?

Her brow furrowed. She must assume so. She could not afford to assume otherwise. But it would be interesting to know. Her spy could tell her, perhaps. But the risk of compromise was too great to attempt any contact.

She walked forward to the ship's bow and stood looking off into the dark for a time, then produced a small milky glass sphere from within her robes and held it up to the light. Softly, she sang to the sphere, and the milkiness faded and turned clear and captured within it an image of the *Jerle Shannara*, anchored above the grasslands running west from the ruined castle. She studied it carefully, searching for the Druid, but he was nowhere to be found. Elven Hunters kept watch fore and aft, and a burly Rover lounged at the helm. At the center of the ship, the strange case the Druid had brought aboard remained covered and warded by magic-enhanced chains.

What was hidden in it and behind those chains? What, that he must guard it so carefully?

"Elvess do not ssusspect our pressensse, Misstress," a voice hissed at her elbow. "Killss them all while they ssleepss, perhapss?"

White-hot rage surged through her at the interruption. "If you come into my presence again without permission, Cree Bega, I will forget who sent you and why you are here and separate you from your skin."

The Mwellret bowed in obsequious acknowledgment of his trespass. "Apologiess, Misstress. But we wasste our time and opportunitiess. Let uss kill them and be done with it!"

She hated Cree Bega. The Mwellret leader knew she would not harm him; the Morgawr had given him a personal guarantee of protection against her. She had been forced to swear to it in his presence. The memory made her want to retch. He was not afraid of her in any case. Although not completely immune, Mwellrets were resistant to the controlling powers of her magic, and Cree Bega more so than most. The combination of all this added to his insufferable arrogance toward and open disdain for her and made their alliance all but intolerable.

But she was the Ilse Witch, and she showed him nothing of her irritation. No one could penetrate her defenses unless she allowed it.

"They do our work for us, ret. We will let them continue until they are finished. Then you can kill as many as you like. Save one."

"Knowss your claim upon the Druid, misstress," he purred. "Givess the resst to me and mine. We will be ssatissfied. Little peopless, Elvess, belongss to uss."

She passed her hand across the sphere. The image of the *Jerle Shannara* disappeared and the sphere went white again. She tucked it back inside her robes, all without glancing once at the creature hovering next to her. "Nothing belongs to you that I do not choose to give you. Remember that. Now get out of my sight."

"Yess, Misstress," he replied tonelessly, without a scintilla of respect or fear, and slid away into the shadows like oil over black metal.

She did not look to see that he had gone. She did not trouble herself. She was thinking that it did not matter what she had promised the Morgawr. When this matter was finished, so were these treacherous toads. All of them, her promise to the Morgawr notwithstanding. And Cree Bega would be the first.

The night was silent and windless, and she cradled the *Jerle Shannara* like a slumbering child rocked gently in her arms. Bek Rowe sat up suddenly, staring into the darkness of his sleeping room, listening to the snores and breathing of Quentin and Panax and the others. Someone had called his name, whispered it in his mind, in a voice he did not recognize, in words that were lost instantly on waking. Had he imagined it?

He rose, pulled on his boots and cloak, and climbed topside to the decking. He stood without moving at the top of the stairs and looked about as if he might find the answer in the darkness. He had heard his name clearly. Someone had spoken it. He brushed back his curly hair and rubbed the sleep from his eyes. The moon and stars were brilliant white beacons in a velvet black sky. The lines and features of the airship and the island were distinct and clear. Everything was still, as if frozen in ice.

He walked to the forward mast, just ahead of the mysterious object Walker kept so carefully warded. He stared about once more, searching now as much inside himself as without for what had drawn him here.

"Looking for something, boy?" a familiar voice hissed softly at his elbow.

Truls Rohk. He jumped in spite of himself. The shape-shifter crouched somewhere in the shadows of the casing, so close Bek imagined he could reach out and touch him. "Was it you who called me?" he breathed.

"It is a good night for discovering truths," the other whispered in that rough, not-quite-human voice. "Care to try?"

"What are you talking about?" Bek struggled to keep his voice steady and calm.

"Hum for me. Just a little, soft as a kitten's purr. Hum as if you were trying to move me back with just your voice. Do you understand?"

Bek nodded, wondering what in the world Truls Rohk was trying to prove. Hum? Move him back with his voice?

"Do it then. Don't question me. Think about what you want to do and then do it. Concentrate."

Bek did as he was asked. He imagined the shape-shifter standing beside him, visualized him there in the darkness, and hummed as if the sound, the vibration alone, might move him away. The sound was barely audible, unremarkable, and so far as Bek could determine, pointless.

"No!" the other spat angrily. "Try harder! Give it teeth, boy!"

Bek tried again, jaw clenched, angry now himself at being chided. His humming buzzed and vibrated up from his throat and through his mouth and nose with fresh purpose. The force of his effort caused the air before his eyes to shimmer as if turned to liquid.

"Yes," Truls Rohk murmured in response, satisfaction reflected in his voice. "I thought so."

Bek went silent again, staring into the shadows, into the night. "You thought so? What did you think?" The humming had revealed nothing to him. What had it revealed to Truls Rohk?

A part of the blackness surrounding the casing detached itself and took shape, rising up against the light of moon and stars. An only vaguely human form, big and terrifying. Not to step away from it took everything Bek had.

"I know you, boy," the other whispered.

Bek stared. "How could you?"

The other laughed softly. "I know you better than you know yourself. The truth of you is a secret. It is not for me to reveal it to you. The Druid must be the one to do that. But I can show you something of what it looks like. Are you interested?"

For an instant, Bek considered turning around and walking away. There was something dark in the other's meaning, something that would change the boy once it was revealed. He understood that instinctively.

"We are alike, you and I," the shape-shifter said. "We are nothing of what we seem or others think they know. We are joined in ways that would surprise and astonish. Perhaps our fates are linked in some way. What becomes of one depends on what becomes of the other."

Bek could not imagine it. He could barely follow what the

shape shifter was saying, let alone fathom what it meant. He made no reply.

"Lies conceal us as masks do thieves, boy. I, because I choose it to be so—you, because you are deceived. We are wraiths living in the shadows, and the truths of identities are carefully guarded secrets. But yours is the darker by far. Yours is the one that has its source in a Druid's games-playing and a magic's dark promise. Mine is simply the result of a twist of fate and a parent's foolish choice." He paused. "Come with me, and I'll tell you of it."

Bek shook his head. "I can't leave—"

"Can't you?" the other shot, cutting him short. "Down to the island and into the castle? Come with me, and we'll bring the third key back to the Druid before he wakes. It's lying there, waiting for us. You and I, we can do what the Druid cannot. We can find it and bring it back."

Bek took a deep breath. "You know where the key is?"

The other shifted slightly, a flowing of darkness against the moonlight. "What matters is that I know how to find it. The Druid asked me earlier this night to seek it out, and so I did. But now I have decided to go back on my own and get it. Want to come along with me?"

The boy was speechless. What was going on here?

"This should be easy for you. I know your heart. You've been allowed to do nothing. You've been kept aboard for no reason you can determine. You've been lied to and put off as if you didn't count. Aren't you weary of it?"

Just two days earlier, Bek had mustered the courage to ask Walker about his use of the mind-summons on Shatterstone. The Druid had told him it was only a coincidence that he had settled his thoughts on Bek, that he had been thinking of the boy just before the attack and had flashed on him instinctively. It was such an obvious lie that Bek had simply walked away in disgust. Truls Rohk seemed to be speaking directly to this incident.

"This is your chance," the shape-shifter pressed. "Come with me. We can do what Walker cannot. Are you afraid?"

Bek nodded. "Yes."

Truls Rohk laughed, deep and low. "You shouldn't be. Not of anything. But I'll protect you. Come with me. Take back something of who you are from the Druid. Give him pause. Make him reconsider how he thinks of you. Find out something about yourself, about who you are. Don't you want that?"

To be honest, Bek wasn't sure. All of a sudden he wasn't sure of anything. The shape-shifter frightened him for more reasons than he cared to consider, but chief among them was his dark intimation that Bek was nothing of who and what he assumed himself to be. Revelations of that sort usually damaged as much as they healed. Bek wasn't sure he wanted them revealed by this man, in this way.

"I'll keep my promise to you, boy," Truls Rohk whispered. "I'll tell you my truth. Not what you've heard from Panax. Not what you've imagined. The truth, as it really is."

"Panax said you were burned in a fire—"

"Panax doesn't know. No one does, save the Druid, who knows it all."

Bek stared. "Why would you choose to tell me?"

"Because we are alike, as I've said already. We are alike, and perhaps by knowing me you will come to know yourself, as well. Perhaps. I see myself in you, a long time ago. I see how I was, and I ache with that memory. By telling you my story, I can dispel a little of that ache."

And give it to me, Bek thought. But he was curious about the shape-shifter. Curious and intrigued. He glanced off into the night, toward the castle bathed in moonlight. Truls Rohk was right about the key, as well. Bek wanted to do something more than serve as a cabin boy. He resented being kept aboard ship all the time. He wanted to feel a part of the expedition, to do something other than study airships and flying.

He wanted to contribute something important. Finding the third key would accomplish that.

But he remembered the eels of Flay Creech and the jungle of Shatterstone, and he wondered how he could even think of going down to Mephitic and whatever waited there. Truls Rohk seemed confident, but the shape-shifter's reasons for taking him were questionable. Still, others had gone and returned safely. Was he to hide aboard this ship from everything they encountered? He had known when he agreed to come that there would be risks. He could not avoid them all.

But should he embrace them so willingly?

"Come with me, boy," Truls Rohk urged again. "The night passes swiftly, and we must act while it is still dark. The key waits. I'll keep you safe. You'll do the same for me. We'll reveal hidden truths about ourselves on the way. Come!"

For an instant longer, Bek hesitated. Then he exhaled sharply. "All right," he agreed.

Truls Rohk's laugh was wicked and low. Seconds later they slipped over the side of the airship and disappeared into the night.

TWENTY-FOUR

Truls Rohk was born out of fierce passion, misguided choice, and a chance encounter that should never have happened.

His father was a Borderman, a child of frontier parents and grandparents, woodsmen and scouts who lived the whole of their lives in the wilderness of the Runne Mountains. By the time the Borderman was fifteen, he was already gone from his family and living on his own. He was a legend by the time he was twenty, a scout who had traveled the length and breadth of the Wolfsktaag, guiding caravans of immigrants across the mountains, leading hunting parties in and out again, and exploring regions that only a few had ventured into. He was a big man, strong of mind and body, powerfully built and agile, skilled and experienced in a way few others were. He knew of the things that lived within the Wolfsktaag. He was not afraid of them, but he was mindful of what they could do.

He met Truls Rohk's mother in his thirty-third year. He had been guiding and scouting and exploring for half his life, and he was more at home in the wilderness than he was in the camps of civilization. More and more, he had distanced himself from the settlements and their people. Increasingly, he had sought peace and solace in isolation. The world he favored was not always safe, but it was familiar and comforting. Dangers were plentiful and often unforgiving, but he understood and accepted them. He thought them fair trade for the beauty and purity of the country.

He had always been lucky, had never made a serious mistake or taken an unnecessary risk. He had shaped and honed his luck into a mantle of confidence that helped to keep him safe. He learned to think defensively, but positively, as well. He never thought anything would hurt him if he made the right choices. He suffered injuries and sickness, but they were never severe enough to prevent a full and complete recovery.

On the day he met Truls Rohk's mother, however, his luck ran out. He was caught in a storm and seeking shelter when a tree on a slope above him was struck by lightning. It shattered with a huge explosion and tumbled down, along with half the hillside. The Borderman who had escaped so often was a step slow this time. A massive limb pinned his legs. Boulders and debris pummeled him senseless. In seconds, he was completely buried under a mound of rocks and earth, unconscious before he understood fully what had happened.

When he woke, the storm had passed and night had fallen. He was surprised to find that he could move again. He lay in a clearing, away from the slide and the limb, his body aching and his face bloodied, but alive. When he propped himself up on one elbow, he was aware of someone looking at him. The watcher's eyes glimmered in the darkness, well back in the shadows, bright and feral. A wolf, he thought. He did not reach for his weapons. He did not panic. He stared back at the watcher, waiting to see what it would do. When it did nothing, he sat up, thinking it would slink away with his movement. It did not.

The Borderman understood. The watcher had been the one who pulled him free of the limb, of the rocks and earth, of his tomb. The watcher had saved his life.

The staring contest continued for a long time with neither watcher nor Borderman advancing or retreating. Finally the Borderman spoke, calling to the watcher, thanking it for helping him. The watcher stayed where it was. The Border-man spoke for a long time, keeping his voice low and calm in the way he had learned was effective, growing more and more convinced that the watcher was not human. It was, he believed, a spirit creature. It was a child of the Wolfsktaag.

It was nearing dawn when the watcher finally came close enough to be seen clearly. It was a woman, but it was not human. She slid from the shadows as if formed of colored water, changing her look as she came, a beast one moment, a human the next, a cross of each soon after. She seemed to be trying to take form, uncertain of what to be. In all of her variations, she was beautiful and compelling. She knelt by the Borderman and stroked his forehead and face with soft, strange fingers. She whispered words that the Bor-derman could not identify, but in a tone of voice that was unmistakable—sweet, silky, and thick with lust.

She was a shape-shifter, he realized, a creature of the Old World, a thing of magic and strange powers. Something of who and what he was, or perhaps something of her own na-ture, had drawn her to him. She stared at him with such un-bridled passion that he was caught up in her fire. She wanted him in a primal, urgent way, and he found his response to her need equally compelling.

They mated there in the clearing, quick and hard, a coupling more terrible for its frenzy than for its forbidden character. A human and a spirit creature—no good can come of that, the old ones would say.

She carried him to her lair, and for three days they mated without stopping, resting only when it was required, submerged in their passion when it was not. The Borderman forgot his wounds and his misgivings and any sense of reason. He put aside everything for this wondrous creature and what she was giving him. He lost himself in his uncontrollable need.

When it was finished, she was gone. He woke on the fourth day to silence and emptiness. He lay alone, abandoned. He rose, weak and unsteady, but alive in ways he had never thought to be. Her smell and taste lingered in the air around him, on his skin, in his throat. Her presence, the feel of her, was burned into his memory. He wept uncontrollably. He would never be the same without her. She had marked him forever.

For months afterwards, he hunted for her. He combed the Wolfsktaag from end to end, forsaking everything else. He ate, drank, slept, and hunted. He did so ceaselessly. The weather and the seasons changed, then changed back again. A year passed. Two. He never saw her. He never found a trace of where she had gone.

Then one day, a little more than two years later, when he was reduced to searching because he did not know what else to do, when he no longer held out any hope, she came to him again. It was late in the year, and the leaves were changed and beginning to fall in careless pools of bright red and orange and yellow on the forest floor. He was walking toward a spring from which he could drink before continuing on. He did not know where he was or where he was going. He was moving because moving was all that was left to him.

And all at once she was there, standing in front of him, at the pool's edge.

She was not alone. A boy stood beside her, part human, part beast, instantly recognizable from his features. He was the child of the Borderman. Already grown to become nearly as large as his mother, he was too big for a normal boy of two. Sharp-eyed and quick, he stared at his father cautiously. There was recognition and understanding in his eyes. There was acceptance. His mother had told him the truth about his father.

The Borderman came forward and stood awkwardly before them, not knowing what to do. The woman spoke to him in low, compelling tones. Her words, the Borderman found, were clear. She had mated with him when the urge was irresistible and her attraction to him inexplicably strong. They were mismatched and unsuited. But he should know they had a son. He should know and then forget them both.

It was a pivotal moment. The Borderman had searched for her while she had all but forgotten him. She neither needed nor wanted him. She had her own life, a spirit's life, and he could never be part of it. She did not understand that she had destroyed him and he could never forget her, could never go back to being what he had been. He was hers as surely as the boy was his. It did not matter what world he had come from or what life he had led. He was hers, and he would not be sent away.

He begged her to stay. He got down on his knees, this strong and driven man, this man who had endured and survived so much, and he pleaded with her. He wept uncontrollably. It was useless. Worse, it was pointless. She did not understand his behavior. She had no frame of reference for doing so. Spirits did not weep or beg. They acted instinctively and out of need. For her, the choice was clear. She was a creature of the forests and the spirit world. He was not. She could not stay with him.

When finally she turned to leave, her recognition of him already beginning to fade, his desperation turned to rage. Without thinking, his life ruined, his torment too much to bear, he leapt upon her and drove his hunting knife through her back and into her heart. She was dead before he bore her to the earth.

He sprang up instantly then and ripped his knife free to kill the boy as well, but the boy was gone.

The Borderman ran after him, his mind collapsed and turned inward so that nothing else existed. In one hand he carried the hunting knife, wet with the shape-shifter's blood, waving it at the shadows about him, at the fate that had undone him. In the shadowy concealment of the trees, in the silence of the forest, he sought the boy. His madness was thorough and complete. Bloodlust ruled his life.

He ran until he collapsed in exhaustion, and then he slept.

But before he could wake to resume his search, the boy found him, pried the knife from his sleeping hand, and with a sure and practiced touch, cut his throat.

Truls Rohk's low, guttural voice went silent. Crouched and hidden from view, he continued to slide through the tall grass ahead of Bek. Bek waited for him to continue his tale, but he did not. Sweat coated the boy's sun-browned face, a damp sheen prompted as much by his horror as by his exertion. To have watched your father kill your mother and then to have killed your father was an experience too horrifying to contemplate. What must it have felt like to have witnessed and endured such madness at two years of age? Even if you were a spirit creature, a shape-shifter, and not entirely human, what must it have been like? Worse than he could imagine, Bek decided, because Truls Rohk was half human and cloaked in human sensibilities.

"Stay low," the shape-shifter growled in warning.

He stopped and turned back to Bek. His face was hidden in the folds of his hood and his body concealed by his cloak, but Bek could feel the heat of him emanate from beneath his coverings.

"I buried them where they will never be found. I felt nothing at first, not until later, when I had time to think on it." Truls Rohk's voice seemed distant and reflective. "It was not so terrible until I realized I had lost the only two people who were like me—not because we were the same physically, but because we were bonded by blood. These were my parents. No one else would ever care for me as they could. Even my father might have loved me, given time and sanity. If he had not gone mad, perhaps. Now I was alone, not all of one species or the other, human or spirit. I was some of each, and that meant I belonged with neither."

He laughed softly, bitterly. "I never tried living with humans. I knew what their response to me would be. They spied me in the mountains a couple of times and sought to hunt me as they would an animal. I tried living with shape-shifters, for there are bands of them concealed deep in the Wolfsktaag, and I could find their hiding places. But they smelled the part of me that was human, and they knew what I was. My mother had crossed a forbidden line, they said. She had committed an unpardonable act. She had died for her foolishness. It would be best if I died, too. I could never be one of them. I must live out my life alone."

He looked at Bek. "Do you understand yet why we are alike?"

Bek shook his head. He had no idea at all. He was not sure he cared to speculate.

"You will," the other whispered.

He turned away and began moving ahead again through the tall grass, closing swiftly now on the castle entry, another of night's shadows. Bek followed, not knowing what else to do, still waiting to hear why they were alike, still wondering what was going to happen to him. He had come this far on faith and because of his need to be more than a spectator on this voyage. Had he made a mistake?

The castle rose before them, a maze of crumbling stone walls and black holes where doors and windows had fallen away. The moon had dropped toward the horizon, and the shadows cast by towers and battlements fell across the earth like long, black garments. No sound came from within the ruins. Nothing moved in the dark.

Truls Rohk stopped and faced him once more. "The Druid looked for the key's guardian within the castle walls. He did not think to consider the guardian might be the castle itself—his first mistake. He looked for the key's guardian to defend the key by attacking and destroying those who invaded. He did not think to consider the guardian might rely instead on deception—his second mistake. He sought his answers with reason and magic, with a certainty that one or the other must give him the answers he needed. He did not think to consider that his adversary relied on neither—his last mistake."

Smoothly, he retreated through the grasses to hover close. Bek flinched at the other's approach, uncomfortable with looking at the black hole of Truls Rohk's hood and the eyes that haunted there. "The guardian of the third key is a spirit, and it dwells within these castle walls. It has no presence but for the castle itself and wards its treasures equally. The key is but one of its possessions; it has no special value to the spirit. Whoever put it there knew that. The castle wards everything equally, hiding all, revealing nothing, an immutable sentry. It deceives, boy. Like me. Like you."

"How do we penetrate that deception?" Bek asked, glancing up sharply now, eager to know.

The strange eyes glimmered. "We try seeing with different eyes."

They moved forward to the very edge of the grasses, no more than a few yards from the drawbridge and the castle entry. They had stayed low during their approach, hidden by the grasses, concealed by tall stalks, not because the guardian could see them if they stood, for it had no eyes, but because it could sense their presence once they were exposed.

"Time to use other means to conceal ourselves," Truls Rohk advised, hunching down within his robes. "Easy enough for me. I am a shape-shifter and can become anything. Harder for you, boy. But you have the tools. Hum for me again. This time, use your voice as if you were hiding still within the grasses, as if they were all around you. Here, slip this over your head."

He handed Bek a cloak, torn and frayed and dirtied. Bek slipped into it obediently. It smelled of the grasses the shape-shifter wished him to blend into. He took a moment to adjust the garment, then looked at the other questioningly.

Truls Rohk nodded. "Go on. Do as I told you. Hum for me. Use the sound to change the air about you. Stir it like water at the end of a stick. Push what you can away from you. Bury what you can't deep inside. Make yourself a part of the cloak."

Bek did, losing himself in the smells and feel of the cloak, in his vision of the plains, burrowing deep into loam and roots, into a place where only insects and animals ventured. He hummed softly, steadily for a time, then stopped and looked at the shape-shifter again.

"You see a little of it now, don't you?" the other whispered. "A little of how you are? But only a little. Not yet all. Come."

He took Bek out from their concealment into the open, his form changing visibly in front of the boy, turning liquid, losing shape against the night. Bek hummed softly, wrapping himself in the feel and smell of his cloak, masking himself, hiding who and what he was deep within. They entered the castle without difficulty, moving from the darkness of the outer courtyards and into the gloom of the inner halls. They penetrated deep within the ruins, advancing steadily, as if they were no more than a breeze carried off the grasslands. Walls appeared before them, looking solid and impenetrable, but Truls Rohk passed right through them with an astonished Bek following in his wake. Stairs appeared where none had been moments earlier, and they climbed or descended accordingly. Doors materialized and closed behind them. Sometimes the air itself changed from light to dark, from pitch to clear liquid, altering the nature of the path ahead. Gradually, Bek came to see that the entire castle was nothing of what it seemed, but was instead a vast labyrinth of mirages and illusions integrated into the stone and designed to deceive—to provide doorways and paths that led nowhere, to offer obstacles where none existed, to obscure and confuse.

If it wasn't magic, Bek wondered, what was it? Or was it simply that the magic was so vast and so thoroughly infused that it could not be separated from everything else?

They reached a stone wall thick with dust and spider-webbing, a barrier of heavy stone blocks pitted with weather and age. Truls Rohk stopped and gestured for Bek to stay back. He faced the wall and swept the air before him with his arm. The air shimmered and changed, and the shape-shifter turned all but invisible, a hint of a shadow, a stirring of dust in a soft rustle of wind. Then he was gone, melting into the stone, disappearing as if he had never been there at all. Bek searched for him in vain. There was nothing to see.

But an instant later, he was back, materializing out of nowhere, rising up out of the gloom, his cloaked and hooded form as liquid as the shadows he emulated. He paused just long enough to hold out his hand, open his fingers, and reveal the third key.

It was a mistake. In that instant, caught up in the excitement of their success, Bek stopped humming.

At once, his disguise fell away and the feel of the castle changed. The change was palpable, a heavy rush of wind, a flurry of dust and debris, an agonizing sigh that spilled down the stone hallways and across the courtyards, a shudder that emanated from deep within the earth. Bek tried to recover, to conceal himself anew, but it was too late. Something fierce and primal howled down the corridors and rushed across the stones like an uncaged beast. Bek felt his heart freeze and his chest tighten. He stood where he was, trying to muster a defense he didn't have.

Truls Rohk saved him. The shape-shifter snatched him off his feet as if he were a child, tucked him under an arm that felt as if it were banded in iron, and began to run. Back down the halls and passageways and across the courtyards he raced. Leaping over crumbled stone and along worn trenches, he bore the boy away from the enraged spirit. But it was all around, infused in the castle stone, and it came at them from everywhere. Hidden doors dropped into place before them with deafening thuds. Iron gates clanged shut. Spikes rose out of the earth to spear at them. Trapdoors dropped away beneath their feet. Truls Rohk catapulted and twisted his way past every hazard, sometimes using the walls and even the ceilings to find handholds and footholds. Nothing slowed him. He ran as if on fire.

Bek used his voice in an effort to help, humming anew, not

knowing what he did, but needing at least to try. He hummed to make them as swift and elusive as birds, to give them the liquidity of water, to lend them the ethereal qualities of air. He threw up anything and everything he could think of, constantly changing tactics, trying to throw off the thing that pursued them. He melted into the creature that bore him away, disappearing into the smell of earth and grasses, into the feel of iron muscles, into the feral instincts and quick reflexes. He lost himself completely in a being he did not begin to understand. He lost all sense of who he was. He stripped himself of identity and fragmented into the night.

Then suddenly he lay stretched upon the earth, buried in the tall grasses, and he realized they were back outside again. Truls Rohk crouched next to him, head lowered, shoulders heaving, and the sound of his breathing was like an animal's growl. Then he began to laugh, low and guttural at first, then broader and wilder. Bek laughed with him, oddly euphoric, strangely exhilarated, the death that had sought them outrun and outsmarted.

"Oh, you're nothing of what you seem, are you, boy?" the shape-shifter gasped out between laughs. "Nothing of what you were told all these years! Did you know you had a voice that could do this?" He gestured back toward the castle.

"What was it I did?" Bek pressed, convulsed by laughter, as well.

"Magic!"

Bek went still then, his laughter fading to silence. He lay in the tall grasses and stared at the stars, listening to the echoes of the word in his mind. *Magic! Magic! Magic!* No, he thought. That wasn't right. He didn't know any magic. Never had. Oh, yes, he had the phoenix stone, the talisman he wore about his neck, given to him by the King of the Silver River, and perhaps that was what—

"You saved us, boy," Truls Rohk said.

Bek looked over quickly. "*You* saved us."

The dark form shifted and slid nearer. "I took us clear of

the spirit's reach, but you were the one who kept it at bay. It would have had us otherwise. It dwells all through those ruins. It masks the truth of what it is and how it looks. It protects itself with deception. But you were its equal this night. Don't you see? Yours was the greater deception, all movement and sound and color . . . ah, sweet!"

He leaned close, invisible within his cloak and hood. "Listen to me. You saved us this night, but I saved you once before. I carried you from the ruins of your home and the dark fate of your family. That makes us even!"

Bek stared. "What are you talking about?"

"We are the same, boy," Truls Rohk said again. "We were born of the ashes of our parents, of the heritage of our blood, of a history and fate that was never ours to change. We are kindred in ways you can only guess at. The truth is elusive. Some of it you discovered for yourself this night. The rest you must claim from the man who holds it hostage."

He reached out and pressed the third key into Bek's hand, closing the boy's fingers over it. "Take this to the Druid. He should be grateful he did not have to retrieve it himself—grateful enough to give up the truth he wrongfully imprisons. Trust begets trust, boy. Ward yourself carefully until that trust is shared. Keep secret what you have learned this night. Pay heed to what I say."

Then he vanished, sliding away so swiftly and suddenly that he was gone almost before the boy realized he was going. Bek stared into the quivering grasses through which Truls Rohk had vanished, speechless, aghast. Moments later, he watched a shadow lift off the plains and slide upward along one of the airship's anchor lines before disappearing over the side.

The *Jerle Shannara* hung etched against the departing night by the first pale glimmerings of dawn as Bek waited for a glimpse of something more. When nothing came, he rose wearily and began his walk back.

TWENTY-FIVE

"You disobeyed me, Bek," the Druid said quietly, his voice so chilly the boy could feel the ice in it. "You were told not to leave the ship at night, and you did so anyway."

They were alone in Redden Alt Mer's cabin, where as many as nine of the company had gathered comfortably on more than one occasion during their voyage, but where on this morning it felt as if the Druid was taking up all the space and Bek was in danger of being crushed.

"The order I gave extended to everyone, yourself included. It was very clear. No one was to leave the ship without my permission. And particularly not to go into the castle."

Bek stood frozen in front of the Druid, his hand outstretched, the third key held forth. Of all the possible reactions he had anticipated, this was not among them. He had expected to be chastised for his impetuous behavior, certainly. He had expected to be lectured on the importance of following orders. But all of his imagined scenarios ended with Walker expressing his gratitude to the boy for having gained possession of the key. There would be no need for another day of scavenging through the ruins and risking the safety of the ship's company. There would be no more delays. With the third key in hand, they could proceed to their final destination and the treasure that waited there.

Bek saw no hint of gratitude in the Druid's eyes as he stood before him now.

It had not occurred to him until he was back aboard ship

that his plan to hand the key over to Walker in front of the other members of the ship's company so that he could bask in the glow of their praise and be recognized at last as an equal would not work. If he gave the key to Walker in public, he would have to explain how he obtained it. That meant telling everyone about Truls Rohk, which Walker would certainly not appreciate, or about his own magic, which the shape-shifter had warned him not to do. He would have to present the key to the Druid in private and be satisfied with knowing that at least the ship's leader appreciated his value to the expedition.

But it didn't look just now as if appreciation was high on Walker's list of responses. He hadn't even bothered to ask how Bek had obtained the key. The moment he saw it, held out to him just as it was now, he had gone black with anger.

He took the key from Bek's hand, his dark eyes heavy on the boy, hard and piercing. Overhead, the members of the ship's company were preparing for another day's search, not yet advised that it would not be necessary to go ashore again. The sound of their movements across the decking rumbled through the cabin's silence, another world away from what was happening here.

"I'm sorry," Bek managed finally, his arm dropping back to his side. "I didn't think that—"

"Truls Rohk put you up to this, didn't he?" Walker interrupted, new fury clouding his angry features. Bek nodded. "Tell me about it, then. Tell me everything that happened."

To his own astonishment, Bek did not do so. He told Walker almost everything. He told him how the shape-shifter had come to him and urged him to go with him into the castle ruins and bring out the key. He told him how Truls Rohk insisted they were alike and repeated the other's strange story of his birth and parentage. He related their approach and entry into the castle, their discovery of the key, and their escape. But he left out everything about the magic the shape-shifter claimed Bek possessed. He made no mention of the way in which his voice seemed to generate this magic. He kept his discovery to himself, deciding almost without meaning to that this was not the time to broach the subject.

Walker seemed satisfied with his explanation, and some of the fire went out of his eyes and the ice out of his voice when he spoke again. "Truls Rohk knows better than to involve you in this. He knows better than to risk your life needlessly. He is impetuous and unpredictable, so his actions should not surprise me. But you have to use better judgment in these situations, Bek. You can't let yourself be led around by the nose. What if something had happened to you?"

"What if it had?"

The words were out of his mouth before he could stop them. He hadn't intended to speak them, hadn't planned to challenge the Druid in any way this morning, given his unexpected reaction to Bek's recovery of the key. But the boy felt cheated of all recognition for his accomplishment and was angry now himself. After all, it wasn't Truls Rohk who was leading him around by the nose so much as Walker.

"If I hadn't come back," he pressed, "what difference would it make?"

The Druid stared, a look of surprise in his dark eyes.

"Tell me the truth, Walker. I'm not here just because you needed another pair of eyes and ears. I'm not along just because I'm Quentin's cousin." He had gone too far to turn back, so he plowed ahead. "In fact, I'm not really his cousin at all, am I? Coran told me before I left that Holm Rowe didn't bring me to him. You did. You told Coran his cousin gave me to you, but Truls Rohk said he pulled me from the ruins of my home and saved me from the dark fate of my family. His words. Who's telling the truth about me, Walker?"

There was a long pause. "Everyone," the Druid said finally. "To the extent they are able to do so."

"But I'm not a Leah or a Rowe either, am I?"

The Druid shook his head. "No."

"Then who am I?"

Walker shook his head anew. "I'm not ready to tell you that. You must wait a while, Bek."

Bek kept his temper and frustration in check, knowing that if he gave vent to what he was feeling, the conversation would be over and his chance at discovering anything lost. Patience and perseverance would gain him more.

"It wasn't by chance or coincidence that you contacted me on Shatterstone when the jungle had you trapped, was it?" he asked, taking a different approach. "You knew you could reach me with a mind-summons."

"I knew," the Druid acknowledged.

"How?"

Again, the Druid shook his head no.

"All right." Bek forced himself to remain calm. "Let me tell you something I've been keeping from you. Something happened on the journey from Leah to Arborlon that I haven't told anyone, not even Quentin. On our first night out, while we were camped along the Silver River, I had a nighttime visitor."

Quickly, he related the events that surrounded the appearance of the King of the Silver River. He told him how the spirit creature had appeared as a young girl who looked vaguely familiar, then transformed into a reptilian monster, then into an old man. He repeated what he could remember of their conversation and ended by telling Walker of the phoenix stone. The Druid did not change expression even once during the tale, but his dark eyes revealed the mix of emotions he was feeling.

Bek finished and stood shifting his feet nervously in the silence that followed, half anticipating another attack on his lack of judgment. But Walker just stared at him, as if trying to figure him out, as if seeing him in an entirely new light.

"Was it really the King of the Silver River?" the boy asked finally.

The Druid nodded.

"Why did he come to me? What was his reason?"

Walker looked away for a moment, as if seeking his answers in the walls of the vessel. "The images of the young girl and the monster are meant to inform you, to help you make certain decisions. The phoenix stone is to protect you if those decisions prove dangerous."

Now it was Bek's turn to stare. "What sort of decisions?"

The Druid shook his head.

"That's all you're going to tell me?"

The Druid nodded.

"Are you mad at me for this, too?" Bek demanded in exasperation. "For not telling you sooner?"

"It might have been a good idea if you had."

Bek threw up his hands. "I might have done so, Walker, if I hadn't begun to wonder what I was really doing on this expedition! But once I knew you weren't telling me everything, I didn't feel it was necessary for me to tell you everything either!" He was shouting, but he couldn't help himself. "I'm only telling you now because I don't want to go another day without knowing the truth! I'm not asking that much!"

The Druid's smile was ironic and chiding. "You are asking much more than you realize."

The boy set his jaw. "Maybe so. But I'm asking anyway. I want to know the truth!"

The Druid was implacable. "It isn't time yet. You will have to be patient."

Bek felt himself flush dark crimson, his face turning hot and angry. All of his resolve to control himself vanished in a heartbeat. "That's easy for someone to say who has all the answers. You wouldn't like it so much if you were on the other end of this business. I can't make you tell me what you know. But I can quit being your eyes and ears until you do! If you don't trust me enough to share what you know, then I don't see why I should do anything more to help you!"

Walker nodded, calm and unmoved. "That's your choice, Bek. I will miss your help."

Bek stared at him a moment longer, trying to think of what else to say, then gave it up and stalked from the room, slamming the cabin door behind him. There were tears in his eyes as he stomped back up on deck with the others.

Walker stayed where he was for a few moments, thinking through what had happened, trying to decide if he had made the right choice in not revealing what he knew. Eventually, he must. Everything depended on it. But if he told Bek too soon, if the boy was given too much time to dwell on it, he might be paralyzed by fear or doubt when it came time to act. It was better to keep the burden of it from him for as long as possible, even if it meant incurring his anger. It was better to leave him in ignorance awhile longer.

Yet he longed to reveal to Bek Rowe what he had known from the time of the boy's birth and carried hidden inside all these years. He yearned to share what he had so carefully nurtured and protected so that it might find a purpose beyond his own selfish needs.

He looked down at the key in his hand, at the connecting ridges of metal and the flashing red light embedded in the power source. He had all of them now, all three keys, and there was nothing to stop him from gaining entrance to Castledown.

Nothing.

The word echoed in his mind, a bitter and terrifying lie. Of all the lies he fostered by concealing truths he alone understood, this was the most insidious. He closed his eyes. What could he possibly do to keep it from destroying them all?

He walked from the cabin up to the main decking and called everyone together. When they had gathered around him, he held up the third key and announced that with the invaluable aid of Bek Rowe he had recovered it during the night and brought it aboard. It was time to cast off and continue their journey to Ice Henge and the treasure.

Cheers rose from the company, and Bek was hoisted aloft

on Furl Hawken's burly shoulders and paraded around like a hero. The Elven Hunters saluted him with their swords, and Panax clapped him on the back so hard Bek was almost dislodged from his uncertain perch. Finally, Rue Meridian grabbed him by his shoulders and kissed him hard on the mouth. The boy grinned and waved in response, clearly pleased with the unexpected attention. Even so, he avoided looking at Walker.

Fair enough, the Druid thought. It's them who will need you most and whose trust and respect you must earn.

Placing the third key inside his robes with the other two, he turned away.

The weather continued cold and brisk for almost a week as they traveled on toward Ice Henge, sailing crosswise against a north wind with the light sheaves reefed close and their course set to account for the push south and west. Coats and gloves cut the chill of the wind, but everyone felt it gnawing at their bones and thickening their blood, making them sluggish and ill-tempered. They ate and drank sparingly, conserving their supplies. No one knew how far this last leg of the trip would be, but the map indicated it was some distance and therefore would require a considerable amount of time.

After Mephitic, there were no further islands to be found, and the Rocs were forced to roost on makeshift wooden platforms that were constructed from spare lumber. The platforms were lashed to the *Jerle Shannara*'s pontoons by day and dropped into the sea and towed by night. Their progress slowed measurably as a result.

Bek continued his studies with Redden Alt Mer, feeling very much at home at the helm of the airship by now, able to navigate and steer without asking for help, comfortable that he knew what to do in most situations. When Quentin was training with the Elven Hunters, Bek spent his free time with Ahren Elessedil trading stories and life philosophies. All of them had changed in noticeable ways since they had set out, but no one more than Ahren Elessedil. It seemed to Bek that Ahren had grown physically, his body much tougher and stronger from his training, his fighting abilities now almost the equal of any man aboard. He had always seemed a quick learner, but Ard Patrinell had accomplished wonders with him nevertheless. He was still a boy like Bek, but newly confident in himself and less an outsider.

The same could not be said for Bek. Following his confrontation with Walker, he had retreated further inside himself, putting up walls and locking down hatches, persuaded that for the time being, the less accessible he was, the better. It was a decision fueled by his determination not to do anything to put himself back within Walker's sphere of influence. He avoided the Druid very deliberately and kept to those few with whom he shared an established companionship— Quentin, Ahren, Panax, and Big and Little Red. He was friendly and outgoing still, but in a measured way, burdened with the secrets he was carrying and by the questions that haunted him. He thought on more than one occasion to share those secrets with someone, either Quentin or Ahren, but he could not make himself do so. What would it accomplish, after all? It would merely shift his burden to someone else without lightening his own load. No one could help him with what he needed to discover except the Druid. He knew he would simply have to wait Walker out, and it might take a very long time.

At the end of that first week out from Mephitic, the weather changed with the arrival of a warm front blown up from the south. The wind shifted, a wall of thick clouds rolled in, and the temperature rose. The clear, cold air disappeared before a wall of heavy mist and soft, damp wind, and all the colors of the world faded to gray. On the day of the front's arrival, there were still sufficient gaps in the clouds to read the stars at night and set a course. By the second day, there were only glimpses of sky to be found. By the third day, the airship was enveloped completely. The sun was reduced to a bright spot in the sky overhead, then to a barely discernible hazy ball, and then to a faint wash that was everywhere and nowhere at once.

By the fourth day, only a brightening or darkening of the light measured the difference between day and night, and visibility was reduced to less than a dozen yards. Big Red had tried sailing out of this soup without success, and the Wing Riders had been forced to descend to the makeshift rafts to wait out the front's passing. The *Jerle Shannara* was enveloped in swirling mist and impenetrable gloom.

Finally, Redden Alt Mer ordered the sails taken in completely and shut down the airship's power. Unable to see anything, he was afraid that they might sail right into a cliff wall without realizing it was there. Better to wait this weather out, he declared, than to court disaster. Everyone accepted the news stoically and went about their business. There was no help for it, after all. It was unnerving, being unable to see anything—no sky, no sea, no colors of any sort. Not even the cries of seabirds or the splash of fish penetrated the blanket of gloom that enfolded them. It was as if they had been consigned to in-limbo existence. It was as if they were alone in the world. Men gathered at the railing and stared out at the gloom in silent groups, searching for something recognizable. Even the Rovers seemed disconcerted by the immensity of the fog. Off the coast of the Blue Divide and the Wing Hove, fog lasted only a day or two before the winds moved it along. Here, it seemed as if it might last forever.

The fourth day dragged into the fifth and sixth with no change. It had been almost a week since they had seen anything but the airship and each other. The silence was becoming unnerving. Efforts at livening things up with music and song seemed only to exacerbate the problem. As soon as the playing and singing stopped, the silence returned, thick and immutable. The Rover crew had nothing to do while the ship was at rest. Even the training sessions for the Elven Hunters had been shortened as everyone began to spend more and more time staring off into the void.

It was on the sixth night, while Bek and Quentin stood at the aft railing talking about the mist that periodically enveloped the Highlands of Leah, that the boy heard something unfamiliar break the silence. He stopped talking at once, motioning Quentin to be quiet. Together, they listened. The sound came again, a kind of creaking that reminded Bek of the ship's rigging working against spars and cleats. But it did not come from the *Jerle Shannara*. It came from somewhere behind her, off in the mist. Baffled, the cousins stared at each other, then off into the gloom once more. Again they heard the noise, and now Bek turned to see if anyone else was aware of it. Spanner Frew was in the pilot box, his dark, burly form clearly visible as he stood looking over his shoulder at them. Redden Alt Mer had come on deck, as well, and was standing just below the shipwright, confusion mirrored on his strong face. A handful of others stood clustered about the railings on either side.

A long silence descended as everyone waited for some further sound to reach their ears.

Bek bent close to Quentin. "What do you think—?"

He gasped sharply and choked on the rest of what he was going to say. A huge black shape hove into view out of the mist, a massive shadow that materialized all at once and filled the whole of the horizon. It was right on top of them, so close that there was barely time to react. Bek stumbled back, dragging at Quentin's arm as the black shape towered out of the gloom. Shouts of warning went up, and the shrill of a Roc rose above them. The cousins went backwards off the low rise of the aft deck and landed in a jarring heap below as the black shape struck the *Jerle Shannara* in a crash of metal and splintering of wood. The airship lurched and shuddered in response, and the air was filled with cries and curses.

Everything spiraled into instant chaos. Bek rolled to his feet to find the phantom shape locked against the *Jerle Shannara*'s aft battering rams and realized to his shock that he was looking at another airship. The impact of the collision had sent both ships spiraling in a slow, clockwise motion that made it difficult for Bek to keep his feet. One of the Rocs soared past him, lifting out of the gloom, a silent phantom that appeared and was gone again almost immediately.

Then something cloaked and hooded rose off the aft decking and lurched toward him. Bek stared at it in surprise, mesmerized by its unexpected appearance. He did not even have the presence of mind to reach for his weapons as it approached. He just stood there. The shape took form, and the dark opening of the hood lifted into the gray misted light to reveal a reptilian face dominated by lidless eyes and a twisted mouth. Clawed hands lifted toward him, gesturing.

"Little peopless," the creature whispered.

Bek froze, terrified.

"Sstay sstill now," it urged softly, hypnotically, and reached for him.

"No!" he cried out frantically.

He did so without thinking, solely in response to the danger. But he used his voice as he had that night on Mephitic when he had gone into the castle ruins with Truls Rohk, infusing it with the magic he had discovered there. He felt the force of his words strike at the creature, causing it to flinch with the impact.

Then Quentin was yanking him away and leaping into the creature's path. The Sword of Leah cut through the darkness in a single, glittering stroke, severing the creature's head from its body. The creature collapsed without a sound, and its blood sprayed everywhere.

Other creatures of the same look appeared at the railing of the phantom airship, crowding through the gloom and night to look down at them, the glint of their weapons visible. Shouts rose from the Rovers and Elves, and they surged out of the darkness behind the cousins, their own weapons drawn. A hail of missiles showered down off the other ship, and a few sent members of the *Jerle Shannara* to the deck, writhing in pain. Quentin pulled Bek behind a stack of boxes below the rise of the aft deck, yelling at him to stay down and cover himself up.

A moment later both airships lurched anew, and in a grinding of metal and a crunching of wood, unlocked and separated. Slowly, ponderously, the leviathans drifted apart, their occupants still gathered at the railings to stare silently across the void at each other, faceless shadows in the mist.

"Stations!" Redden Alt Mer roared from the pilot box.

Hands working furiously on the controls, he dropped the mainsail to gather what ambient light he could, unhooded the diapson crystals to give the airship power, and swung her about to face the gloom into which the other ship had disappeared. His Rover crew scattered across the decking to lock down the radian draws, and the Elven Hunters, weapons at the ready, dropped quickly into the fighting ports. Everyone was moving at once as Bek climbed back to his feet.

"What happened?" Bek tried to ask Quentin, but his cousin was gone as well.

With a quick glance at the fallen monster in front of him, Bek raced over to join Big Red. The Rover Captain was still shouting out instructions, windburned face grim with determination as he searched the gloom. Bek looked with him. For just an instant, the other ship reappeared, huge and spectral in the night, three masts cutting through the mist, pontoons and decking slicing across the haze. Then it was gone again.

"That's *Black Moclips*!" Bek heard Redden Alt Mer gasp in disbelief.

They searched for the other airship a while longer, but it was nowhere to be found. Walker appeared and ordered Alt Mer to have his men stand down. "Just as well," Big Red muttered, half to himself, still shaken by what he had seen. "Fighting an air battle in this mess is a fool's errand."

The Elven Hunters had gathered about the fallen attacker to examine him, and Bek heard the word *Mwellret* whispered. He didn't know what a Mwellret was, but he knew the thing that lay dead on the deck looked an awful lot like the monster the King of the Silver River had transformed into at their meeting months earlier.

Joad Rish was on deck looking after the wounded. He advised Walker that no one was badly injured. The Druid asked Big Red for a damage report and suggested the watch be increased from two men to four. Bek was standing close to him while an accounting was made, but they didn't speak. It wasn't until everyone had moved away and Redden Alt Mer had given back the helm to Spanner Frew, that Walker bent down to the boy on passing and whispered that Truls Rohk was missing.

TWENTY-SIX

Aboard *Black Moclips*, the chaos was more pronounced, and a deadly confrontation was about to take place.

The Ilse Witch was sleeping when the collision between the airships occurred, and the force of it threw her from her berth onto the floor. She came to her feet swiftly, threw on her gray robes, and hastened from her locked cabin onto the main deck. By then Federation soldiers and Mwellrets were running everywhere, shouting and cursing in the gloom and mist. She strode to where most had gathered and saw the distinctive raked masts of the *Jerle Shannara*. One of the Mwellrets lay dead on the other ship's decking, the first barrage of spears and arrows had been launched, and a full-scale battle was only moments away.

Of Cree Bega and Federation Commander Aden Kett, she saw no sign.

In a cold fury, she strode to the pilot box and swung up beside the helmsman. The man was staring down at the milling ship's company with a look of mingled disbelief and incredulity, his hands frozen on the controls.

"Back her off at once, helmsman!" she ordered.

His eyes filled with fear as he saw who it was, but his hands remained motionless on the levers.

"Back away now!" she snapped, her words lashing at him with such force that his knees buckled.

He reacted instantly this time, drawing down power from the light sheaths and unhooding the diapson crystals. *Black*

Moclips lurched backwards, unhooked from the other ship with a grinding crunch, and slid soundlessly into the gloom. The helmsman glanced over at her without speaking, waiting for further instructions.

"What happened?" she demanded, all fire and sharp edges within her hooded concealment, wrapped in the power of her voice.

"Mistress?" he replied in confusion.

"How did we manage to collide with that other ship? How could that have happened?"

"I don't know, Mistress," the man stammered. "I was just following orders—"

"Whose orders? I gave no orders to proceed! My orders were to stand down!" She was beside herself with rage.

The helmsman made a vague gesture toward the front of the airship. "Commander Kett said the ret ordered him . . ."

She was down out of the pilot box, and striding forward without waiting to hear the rest. Concealed once more by the mist, *Black Moclips* was an island, solitary and adrift. Her Federation crew was already at work on the damage to the bow rams and decking. At the forward railing, a handful of Mwellrets was clustered about Cree Bega, who had finally surfaced. She went up to him without slowing and stopped less than a yard away.

"Who countermanded my orders?" she demanded.

Cree Bega regarded her with a sleepy look, his lidless eyes fixing on her. She could tell what he was thinking. This girl, this child, speaks to me as if she were my better. But she is nothing to me. She is a human, and all humans are inferior. Who is she, to speak to me in this way?

"Misstress," he greeted with a small, perfunctory bow.

"Who countermanded my orders to stand down?" she asked again.

"It wass my misstake, Misstress," he acknowledged without a hint of remorse in his sibilant voice. "There sseemed no reasson not to prosseed, not to sstay closse to the little peopless. I wass worried they might get too far away from uss."

She gave him a long, careful appraisal before she spoke again. She knew where this was heading, but she could not afford to back down. "Who is in command of this expedition, Cree Bega?"

"You, Misstress," he answered coldly.

"Then why would you take it upon yourself to give orders without consulting me first? Why would you assume you had authority to rescind an order I had already given? Do you think, perhaps, you are better able than me to make the decisions that are needed on this voyage?"

He turned slowly to face her, and she could see that he was considering the advisability of a confrontation. Five of his fellows stood directly behind him, and she was alone. Separately, none of them was her equal. Together, they might be. He hated her and wanted her dead. He undoubtedly felt he could accomplish what was needed without her. If she were to disappear on this voyage, the Morgawr would never know what had happened to her.

But that knife cut both ways, of course.

"Sshe sspeakss to uss like children!" the Mwellret to Cree Bega's right snarled, hunching down like a snake.

The Ilse Witch did not hesitate. She stepped to one side, just out of reach of the others, and used her magic on the speaker. Her voice lashed at him with a sound that was bone-chilling and ferocious. Every ounce of power she could muster, she brought to bear. The force of her attack lifted the shocked Mwellret off its feet, twisted it into a shattered and broken mess, so ravaged it was virtually unidentifiable, and dropped the remains over the side. It took only seconds. The Mwellret was gone almost before his fellows understood what had happened.

She faced the remaining Mwellrets calmly. She had needed to make an example of someone to keep the others under control. Better an unknown than Cree Bega, whose leadership was established and effective. Better to keep the enemy she knew than to install one she did not. Changes in command necessitated adjustments that could give rise to new problems. This was enough for now. She looked into his eyes and found what she was looking for. His hatred of her was still apparent, but there was a hint of fear and doubt present, as well. He was no longer seeing her as a slender, vulnerable girl. More to the point, he was no longer measuring her for a coffin.

"Misstress," he hissed, bowing in submission.

"Do not challenge me again, Cree Bega," she warned. "Do not presume to question or alter my orders in any way. Obey me, ret, or I'll find someone who will."

She held his gaze a moment longer, then wheeled away. She did not look back at him, did not act as if she feared him. Let him think she saw herself as invulnerable and he might come to believe she was. Let him see she gave no thought to her safety because there was no need and he would think twice before confronting her again.

As she moved back toward her cabin, her senses searching carefully for any further signs of trouble, she caught a hint of something that was out of place. She stopped at once, motionless within her gray robes. By now, she knew everything that belonged on *Black Moclips*, every member of her company, every stash of supplies and weapons, every timber and metal plate that held her together. She had infused herself with the feel of the airship, so that she was at one with it and always in control, and she could sense if anything changed. She sensed it now, a subtle alteration, so small she'd almost missed it. Carefully, she began to probe for something more. There had been movement and presence, a suggestion of a living creature that didn't belong.

She was still searching when Aden Kett appeared in front of her. "Mistress, we are fully operational and ready to sail on your orders. For now, we are standing down to wait out the fog. Is there anything else?"

His face was pale and drawn; he had witnessed the death of the Mwellret. But he was a ship's Captain and committed enough to being one that he would carry out his duties regardless of his personal feelings. She was angry at the interruption, but knew enough to keep it to herself.

"Thank you, Commander," she acknowledged, and he bowed and moved away.

The distraction had cost her the fragile connection she had made with the unfamiliar presence. She glanced around casually, using the time to probe anew. There was nothing there now. Perhaps a passing seabird had caused her to sense a change. Maybe there was a residual Elven presence from their contact with the *Jerle Shannara*.

She grimaced at the thought of the collision. An entire ocean of air to navigate, and they had somehow managed to find their enemy. It was ironic and maddening. Still, it changed nothing. Walker would already know that she tracked him. Their encounter tonight, while unfortunate, gave away nothing of importance. He would try harder to escape her now that he realized she was close, but he would not be able to do so. Wherever he went, she would be waiting. She had made certain of that.

She took a moment longer to survey the shadows that wrapped the airship, still searching for what had eluded her, then turned away without another glance and disappeared back into her cabin to sleep.

Bek stared after the departing figure of Walker. Truls Rohk was missing, the Druid had said, a whispered utterance in the boy's ear, and then he had walked away. Bek took another moment to let the information sink in, and then did what anyone else would have done. He went after him.

He had reason to believe, thinking it through later, that this was what Walker had intended, that it was a way to break the silence between them. If so, it worked. He caught up with the

Druid as the latter slowed by the bow railing, and without even thinking about it began speaking to him.

"Where is he?" Bek demanded.

Walker shook his head. "I expect he's on the other ship."

With the Ilse Witch, Bek thought, but couldn't bring himself to say so. "Why would he do that?"

"It's difficult to say. With Truls, most things are done instinctively. Perhaps he wanted to see what he could find out over there. Perhaps he has a plan he hasn't shared with us."

"But if the Ilse Witch finds him . . ."

Walker shook his head. "There's nothing we can do about it, Bek. He made the choice to go." He paused. "I saw what you did to that Mwellret before Quentin stepped in. With your voice. Were you aware of what you were doing?"

The boy hesitated, then nodded. "Yes."

"How long have you known you had use of this magic?"

"Not long. Since Mephitic."

Walker frowned. "Truls Rohk, again. He showed you it was there, didn't he? Why didn't you tell me?"

Bek stared at him defiantly, refusing to answer. The Druid nodded slowly. "That's right. I wasn't confiding much in you at the time either, was I?" He studied the boy carefully. "Maybe it's time to change all that."

Bek felt a twinge of expectation. "Are you going to tell me who I am?"

Walker looked off into the mist-shrouded night, and there was a sense of time and place slipping away in his dark eyes. "Yes," he said.

Bek waited for him to say something more, but Walker remained silent, lost in thought, gone somewhere else, perhaps into his memories. Behind them, the Rover crew worked to repair the damage to the aft part of the vessel, where the horns of the battering rams had absorbed most of the shock of their collision with the other airship, but portions of the deck and railing had buckled from the impact. The crew labored alone in the near dark. Almost everyone else, save the watch, had gone back to bed. Even Quentin had disappeared.

In the pilot box, Spanner Frew's fierce dark face stared out over the controls as if daring something else to go wrong.

"I would have told you most of what I know sooner if I hadn't thought it better to wait," Walker said quietly. "I haven't been any happier keeping it from you than you've been not knowing what it was. I wanted to be closer to our final destination, to Ice Henge and Castledown, before speaking with you. Even after the events on Mephitic and the suspicions aroused by Truls Rohk, I believed it was best.

"But now you know you have command of a magic, and it is dangerous for you not to know its source and uses. This magic is of a very powerful nature, Bek. You've only scratched the surface of its potential, and I don't want to risk the possibility that you might choose to use it again before you are prepared to deal with it. If you understand how it works and what it can do, you can control it. Otherwise, you are in grave danger. This means I have to tell you what I know about your origins so you can arm yourself. It isn't going to be easy to hear this. Worse, it isn't going to be easy to live with it afterwards."

Bek stood beside him quietly, listening to him speak. Outwardly, the boy was calm, but inside he was tight and edgy. He was aware of the Druid looking at him, waiting for his response, for permission to continue. Bek met his gaze squarely and nodded that he was ready.

"You are not a Leah or a Rowe or even a member of their families," Walker said. "Your name is Ohmsford."

It took a moment for the boy to recognize the name, to re-member its origins. All the stories he had heard about the Leahs and the Druids came back to him. There had been Ohmsfords in those stories, as well, as recently as 130 years ago when Quentin's great-great-grandfather, Morgan Leah, had battled the Shadowen. Before that, Shea and Flick Ohms-ford had fought with Allanon against the Warlock Lord, Wil

Ohmsford had stood with Eventine Elessedil and the Elves against the Demon hordes, and Brin and Jair Ohmsford had gone in search of the Ildatch in the dark reaches of the Eastland.

But they had all been dead for many years, and the rest of the Ohmsford family had died out. Coran had told him so.

"Your magic is the legacy of your family, Bek." The Druid looked back over the railing into the gloom. "It was absorbed by Wil Ohmsford into his body hundreds of years ago when he used the Elfstones to save the lives of two women, one who became the Ellcrys, one who became his wife. His Elven blood was too thin to permit him to do so safely, and he was altered irrevocably. It didn't manifest itself in him so much as in his children, Brin and Jair, who were born with the use of magic in their voices, just as you were. It was strong in both, but particularly in the girl. Brin had the power to transform living things by singing. She could heal them or destroy them. Her power was called the wishsong."

He took a deep breath and exhaled slowly. Bek was watching him closely now. "The magic surfaced in other generations, but only sporadically. It was five hundred years before it returned in a meaningful way. This time, it appeared in the brothers Par and Coll Ohmsford, who fought with me and with the Elf Queen Wren Elessedil against the Shadowen. The magic was strong in Par Ohmsford, very powerful. He was your great-great-grandfather, Bek."

He shifted away from the railing and faced the boy anew. "I'm related to you, as well, though I wouldn't care to try to trace the lineage. We are both scions of Brin Ohmsford. But whereas you inherited her use of the wishsong, I inherited the blood trust bestowed on her by Allanon as he lay dying, the trust that foretold that one of her descendants would be the first of the new Druids. I was that descendant, though I didn't want to believe it when it was revealed to me, didn't want to accept it afterwards for a long time. I came to the Druid order reluctantly and served with constant misgiving."

His sigh was soft and wistful. "There. It's said. We are family, Bek, you and I—joined by blood as well as by magic's use." His smile was bitter. "The combination allowed me to summon you on Shatterstone when we were under attack, to connect with you through your thoughts when I could not do so with the others. It wasn't a coincidence that I called to you."

"I don't get it," Bek blurted out in confusion. "Why didn't you tell me this before? Why did you keep it a secret? It doesn't seem so bad. I'm not afraid of my magic. I can learn to use it. It can help us, can't it? Isn't that why I was asked to come? Because I have the magic? Because I'm an Ohmsford?"

The Druid shook his head. "It isn't so simple. In the first place, use of the magic carries a terrible responsibility and a very real threat to the bearer. The magic is powerful and sometimes unpredictable. Using it can be tricky. It can even be harmful, not just to others but to you, as well. Magic often reacts as it chooses and not as you intend; your attempts to control it can fail. It isn't necessarily good that you know you have it and can call it forth. Once you have unearthed its existence, it becomes a burden you cannot put down. Ever."

"But it's there nevertheless," Bek pointed out. "It isn't as if I had a choice about adopting it. Besides, you brought me on this journey to use my magic, didn't you?"

The Druid nodded. "Yes, Bek. But there is more to it than that. I brought you for the use of your magic, but I brought you for another reason, as well—a more compelling one. Your parents and your sister were the last of the Ohmsfords. There were others, distant cousins and so forth, but your father was the last direct descendant of Par Ohmsford. He married your mother and they lived in the hamlet of Jentsen Close not far from the northeast edge of the Rainbow Lake, in a part of the farming community off the Rabb Plains. They had two children, your sister and you. Your sister's name was Grianne. She was three years older than you, and signs of the wishsong's magic appeared in her very early. Your father recognized those signs and sent for me. He knew of the connection between us. I visited you when you were still a baby and your sister only four years of age. Because of my Druid experience, I was able to recognize the magic not only in your sister, but in you as well."

He paused. "Unfortunately, the Morgawr discovered the existence of this magic as well. The Morgawr has lived for a very long time, hidden away in the Wilderun. He may have been an ally of the Shadowen, but he was not one of them and was not destroyed as they were. He surfaced about fifty years ago and began to expand his influence to the Federation. He is a powerful warlock, with ties to the Eastland Mwellrets and shape-shifters. It was because of these ties that I learned about his interest in your family. I was friends with Truls Rohk by then, and several times he followed shape-shifters that had gone to your home. They didn't do anything but observe, but it was a clear warning that something wasn't right."

He stopped talking as a clutch of Rovers came down off the aft decking and moved to the forward stairway. Their work for the night was finished, and they were eager for sleep. One or two glanced over, then looked quickly away. In seconds, the Druid and the boy were alone again.

"I should have realized what was happening, but I was preoccupied with trying to form a Druid Council at Paranor." Walker shook his head. "I didn't act quickly enough. A band of Mwellrets dressed in black cloaks and led by the Morgawr killed your parents and burned your house to the ground. They made it look like an attack by Gnome raiders. Your sister hid you in a cold room off the cellar and told them you were dead when they took her. It was Grianne they wanted all along, for her magic, for the power of the wishsong. The Morgawr coveted her. His intent was to subvert her, to make her his disciple, his student in the use of her magic. He tricked her into believing that the black-cloaked Mwellrets were Druid led and influenced. I became the enemy she grew up hating. All of my efforts to change that, to rescue her, to gain her trust so that she might discover the truth, have failed."

He gestured toward the enfolding wall of mist. "Now she hunts me, Bek, somewhere out there on that other airship." He looked at the boy. "Your sister is the Ilse Witch."

They stood for a while without speaking, looking off into the void where the woman who had once been Grianne Ohmsford tracked them. The enormity of Walker's revelation settled over Bek. Was it the truth or was the Druid playing games with him here, as well? He had so many questions, but they all jumbled together and screamed at him at once. He did not know what he was supposed to do with what he had been told. He could see the possibilities, but he could not make himself consider them yet. He found himself remembering the nighttime visit of the King of the Silver River, all those months ago, and of the forms the spirit creature had taken—the girl, who was the past, and the monster, who was the present. That girl, he now understood, was his sister. That was why she had seemed so familiar to him—he still retained a memory of her child's face. The monster was what she had become, the Ilse Witch. But the future remained to be determined—by Bek, who must not shy from his search, his need to know, or what his heart compelled him to do.

The jumble of questions gave way to just one. Was it within his power to change his sister back?

"There is one last thing, Bek," Walker said suddenly. "Come with me."

He moved away from the railing toward the center of the airship, and the boy followed. Within the pilot box, black-bearded Spanner Frew faced ahead into the gloom, paying them no attention, his eyes sweeping the mist and the dark.

"Does she know I'm alive?" Bek asked quietly.

The Druid shook his head. "She believes you dead. She has no reason to believe otherwise. Truls Rohk found you in the ruins of your home three days after your sister was

stolen. He was keeping watch on his own and had seen the
Mwellrets returning through the Wolfsktaag. He was able to
find the hiding place that they had missed. You were almost
dead by then. He brought you to me, and when you were
strong enough, I took you to Coran Leah."

"Yet my sister blames you for what happened."

"She is deceived by her own bitterness and the Morgawr's
guile. His story of what happened is quite different from the
truth, but it is a story she has come to believe. Now she cloaks
herself in her magic's power and shuts out the world. She
seeks to be a fortress that no one can breach."

"Except perhaps for me? Is that why I'm here? Is that what
the King of the Silver River was showing me?"

The Druid said nothing.

They stopped before the mysterious object he had brought
aboard in secret and wrapped in chains of magic. It sat solitary and impenetrable against the foremast, a rectangular box
set on end, standing perhaps seven feet in height and three
feet across and deep. The canvas concealed all trace of what
lay beneath, revealing only size and shape. The chains glistened with the mist's damp and on closer inspection seemed
to have no beginning and no end.

Bek glanced around. The decks of the airship were deserted this night save for the helmsman and a pair of Elven
Hunters of the watch, who were clustered about the aft
railing. None of these would venture forward to take up his
position while the Druid stood talking with the boy. In the
wake of the airship's silent passing, the only movement came
from the shadows in the mist.

"No one will see what I show you now but you and me,"
the Druid said softly.

He passed his hand before the casing, and it was as if the
side they were facing melted away. Within the blackness revealed, suspended blade downward, was a sword. The sword
was slender and its metal shone a deep-bluish silver against
the surrounding dark. The handle was old and worn, but

finely wrought. Carved into its polished wooden grip was a fist that clenched and thrust aloft a burning torch.

"This is the Sword of Shannara, Bek," the Druid whispered, bending close so that his words would carry no farther than the boy's ears. "This, too, is your legacy. It is the birthright of the descendants of the Elven King Jerle Shannara, for whom this vessel is named. Only a member of the Shannara bloodline can wield this blade. Ohmsfords, who were the last of the Shannara, have carried this sword into battle against the Warlock Lord and the Shadowen. They have used it to champion the freedom of the races for more than a thousand years."

He touched Bek's shoulder lightly. "Now it is your turn."

Bek knew the stories. He knew them all, just as he knew the history of the Druids and the Wars of the Races and all the rest. No one had seen this talisman in over five hundred years, when Shea Ohmsford stood against the Warlock Lord and destroyed him—though there were rumors it had resurfaced in the battle with the Shadowen. Rumors, the Druid's words would suggest, that were true.

"The sword is a talisman for truth, Bek. It was forged to defend against lies that enslave and conceal. It is a powerful talisman, and it requires strength of will and heart to wield. It needs a bearer who will not shrink from the pain and doubt and fear that embracing the truth sometimes engenders. You are a worthy successor to those others of your family who have been called to the sword's service. You are strong and determined. Much of what I exposed you to on this voyage was meant to measure that. I will be frank with you. Without your help, without the Sword's power to aid us, we are probably lost."

He turned back to the casing and passed his hand in front of it once more. The Sword of Shannara disappeared, and the wrappings of canvas and chains were restored.

Bek continued staring at them, as if still seeing the talisman they concealed. "You're giving the Sword of Shannara to me?"

The Druid nodded.

The boy's voice was shaking as he spoke. "Walker, I don't know if I can—"

"No, Bek," the Druid interrupted him quickly, gently. "Say nothing tonight. Tomorrow is soon enough. There is much to discuss, and we will do so then. You'll have questions, and I will do my best to answer them. We will work together to prepare for what will happen when it is necessary for you to summon the sword's magic."

Bek's eyes shifted anxiously, and the Druid met the question mirrored there with a reassuring smile. "Not against your sister, though one day you might have to use it in that way. No, this first time the magic will serve another purpose. If I have read the map correctly, Bek, the Sword of Shannara is the key to our gaining entry into Ice Henge."

TWENTY-SEVEN

Come daybreak, Bek rose and went about his morning
duties as cabin boy in something of a daze, still struggling
with the previous night's revelations, when the Druid intercepted him coming out of Rue Meridian's cabin and told
him to follow. It was an hour after sunrise, and Bek had
dressed and eaten breakfast. He still had tasks to perform,
but Walker's summons didn't leave room for discussion on
the matter.

They climbed topside and walked forward to the bow
railing, very close to where they had stood the night before.
The sky around them was unchanged, gray and misted and
impenetrable. Everywhere Bek looked, right or left, up or
down, the color and light were the same. Visibility was still
limited to thirty feet or so. Those of the ship's company already on deck had the look of ghosts, ethereal and not quite
fully formed. Redden Alt Mer stood in the pilot box with Furl
Hawken, two Rovers were at work aft, braiding new ends on
the portside radian draws, and Quentin sparred with the
Elven Hunters on the foredeck under Ard Patrinell's steady
gaze. No one looked up as Bek passed or acted as if anything
about the boy had changed, even though in his mind everything had.

"To begin with, you are still Bek Rowe," Walker told
him when they were seated together on a casing filled with
light sheaths. "You are not to use the name Ohmsford. It is

too recognizable, and you don't want to draw unneeded attention to yourself."

Bek nodded. "All right."

"Also, I don't want you to tell anyone what you've told me or what you've learned from me about your magic, your history, or the Sword of Shannara. Not even Quentin. Not one word."

He waited. Bek nodded once more.

"Finally, you are not to forget that you are here to serve as my eyes and ears, to listen and keep watch. That wasn't an idle assignment, meant to give you something to do until it was time to tell you who you were. Your magic gives you powers of observation that are lacking in most. I still need you to use those talents. They are no less important now than they were before."

"I can't see that I've put them to much use so far," Bek observed. "Nothing I've told you has been particularly useful."

The Druid's ironic smile flashed momentarily and was gone. "You don't think so? Maybe you're not paying close enough attention."

"Does Ryer Ord Star see anything in her dreams that could help you? Is she keeping watch as well?"

"She does what she can. But your sight, Bek, though not a seer's, is the more valuable." He shifted so that he was leaning very close. "She dreams of outcomes before they happen, but you spy out causes while they're still seeking to create an effect. That's the difference in the magic you wield. Remember that."

Bek had no idea what Walker was talking about, but decided to mull over it another time. He nodded.

Curtains of gray mist drifted past, and the sounds of sword-play and of metal tools in use echoed eerily in the enshrouding haze. It was as if each group of men formed a separate island, and only the sounds they made connected them in any real way.

"The Sword of Shannara," Walker began quietly, "is not

like any other weapon. Or any other magic. It seeks truth where truth is concealed by deception and lies, and through revelation, it empowers. But empowerment comes at a cost. Like all Elven talismans, the sword draws its power from the wielder. Its strength, and thereby its effectiveness, depends entirely on the strength of the bearer. The stronger the bearer, the more effective the magic. But the connection between the two is established by subtle means. The Sword of Shannara relies on the bearer's willingness to shed personal deceptions, half-truths, and lies in order to see clearly the same in others."

He gave Bek a moment to digest this. "This is what will happen, Bek. When you call up the power of the sword, it will seek to reveal the larger truths that other magic and magic wielders mask. But in order to understand those larger truths, you must first accept the smaller truths about yourself. This requires sacrifice. We live our lives hiding from the things that displease and discomfort us. We reinvent ourselves and our history, constantly placing things in a light most favorable to us. It is in the nature of mankind to do this. Mostly, our deceptions are small ones. But they gather weight through numbers, and having them revealed all at once can be crushing. As well, there are larger truths that, exposed, seem more than we can bear, and so we hide them most carefully.

"After you have been confronted by these personal truths, you will be confronted by truths about those you love and care for, then of the world you know through your own experience, and finally of the deception or lie you seek to unmask. This will not be easy or pleasant. Truth will assault you as surely as an ordinary metal blade. It will have impact and cutting edges. It can kill you if you do not ward against it. Knowledge and acceptance of what is coming are your best defense. You can do what you need to do to protect yourself and adapt. Do you understand?"

Bek nodded. "I think so. But I don't know how I can prepare myself for something like this. I don't know what sorts of lies and deceptions I have concealed over the years. Am I to try to catalogue them all before using the sword?"

"No. You've said it yourself. You can't separate them out easily. Some you will have forgotten entirely. Some you will have tried to shade with a better interpretation than you should. Some you will never even have identified. What you need to do, Bek, is to understand how the sword works so that you will not be surprised by its power and will be better able to survive its demands." He paused. "Let me tell you a story."

He spent the next few minutes relating the tale of the Elven King Jerle Shannara and his confrontation with the Warlock Lord a thousand years earlier. The Sword of Shannara had been forged out of Druid fire by Bremen in the Southland city of Dechtera and carried north so that a champion could do combat with the Dark Lord and destroy him. But Bremen had misjudged the Elf King's ability to adapt to the sword's demands and not sufficiently prepared him. When Jerle Shannara called up the magic of the sword, he failed to bring sufficient strength to bear. As a result, he broke down the Dark Lord's physical form but did not destroy him completely. It would be left to his descendant, Shea Ohmsford, five hundred years later, to complete the job.

"My task with you, Bek," Walker finished, "is to make certain you do not falter as Jerle Shannara did, that once you summon the sword's magic, you employ it to the degree necessary. Your first usage of the talisman is not so demanding. It does not involve an encounter with another creature of magic that seeks to destroy you. It involves a portal that is warded by an impersonal and indiscriminate barrier. It is a good test with which to begin your training."

Bek looked down at his feet, then up into the Druid's dark eyes. "But my sister, the Ilse Witch, will be waiting to test me, as well."

"Not waiting. She knows nothing of you or the sword. But, yes, the possibility is good that you will have to face her eventually. Even so, that is not your principal concern. Your testing will come from other sources, as well. Everything connected with this expedition is shrouded in deception and lies, Bek. It might seem straightforward enough, a map and a castaway found floating on the Blue Divide, a trail to a place reached by other Elves and their ships thirty years ago before they disappeared, and the lure of a treasure beyond price. But few things are as they seem in this matter. If we are to succeed—indeed, if we are to survive—we will require the power of the Sword of Shannara to see us through. Only you can use the sword, Bek, so you must be ready to do so when the magic is needed. I bring a Druid's fire and insight to our task. Quentin brings the power of the Sword of Leah. Others bring their own gifts and experience. Perhaps we will find the missing Elfstones. But your use of the Sword of Shannara is vital and necessary to everything we attempt to do. And your training in that use begins now."

They spent the remainder of that day and much of every day after talking about the sword's magic and how it would work. Walker understood the principles, but he had never experienced the power of the sword's magic himself, so they were reduced to fencing without weapons. It wasn't so different, Bek supposed, than what Quentin did in his training with the Elven Hunters. He sparred, but the combat wasn't real. Because there was no way to call up the magic of the sword until it was actually needed, there was no way to test its effect on Bek. What Walker did mostly, besides talk about the nature of self-deception, was to teach a form of acceptance that came with finding inner peace, with going deep inside to let go of extraneous matters and concerns, and with opening up instead of closing down as a way of dealing with the things that caused pain.

It was a grueling and often frustrating exercise that sometimes left Bek more confused than when he started. Already reeling from revelations of his identity and history, the boy was staggered by the responsibility the Druid was giving him for the safety of the ship's company. But he understood the importance of that responsibility and so trained and studied hard, working to prepare himself, to become more adaptable, to be ready for what would happen when he was infused with the sword's power.

Nor did he neglect his other duties. He was still the ship's cabin boy and must continue to behave as such. The combination of time spent with the Druid talking about magic, with Redden Alt Mer in the pilot box, and with carrying out his daily chores pretty much filled up the day. He saw less and less of Quentin and Ahren Elessedil, but that saved him from having to work so hard at keeping what he knew to himself.

A few days after their encounter with the Ilse Witch, the fog dissipated, the skies cleared, and the broad expanse of the Blue Divide lay revealed once more and the Wing Riders had returned. Repairs were made to the airship, and foraging resumed with the discovery of several clusters of islands. The air became sharp and cold, and the members of the expedition wore winter coats and gloves most of the time now. Ice floes were spotted between the channels of the islands, and the skies turned gray and wintry. Days grew shorter, and the light took on a pale, thin cast that washed the earth and sky of color.

All the while, Bek wondered what lay ahead. Walker had cautioned him that everything surrounding the expedition was mired in deception and lies. If so, how much of it had the Druid uncovered? What else did he know that he was keeping secret?

Nine weeks after leaving Mephitic, with thin sheets of sleet driving out of the north on the back of a polar wind, they arrived at the cliff-walled fortress of Ice Henge, and the boy found out.

The land appeared as a low dark rumpling of the horizon's thin line and was a long time taking shape. It stretched away to either side of center for miles, sprawled like a twisted snake atop the blue-gray sea. Hours passed before they drew close enough 'to make out a wall of cliffs so sheer they dropped straight down into the ocean and so towering that their peaks disappeared into clouds of mist and gloom. Cracked and broken, the carcasses of trees bleached by the sun and stripped bare by the wind jutted out of the rock. White-and-black flashes against the gloom, seabirds screamed as they soared from hidden aeries to the waters below. Smaller islands led up to the cliffs like stepping-stones trod upon by time and weather, barren atolls offering little of shelter or sustenance, devoid of vegetation save for hardy sea grasses and wintry gray scrub.

Walker held up the airship when they were still miles away and sent the Wing Riders ahead for a quick look. They were back again very quickly. Shrikes inhabited the cliffs, and the Rocs could fly no nearer. Leaving Hunter Predd and Po Kelles on one of the larger atolls, Walker had Redden Alt Mer sail the *Jerle Shannara* right up to the landmass. A closer inspection did nothing to lessen his concerns. The cliffs formed a solid, impenetrable wall, split now and then by narrow fissures that were flooded with mist and rain and virtually impassable. As Shrikes regarded them warily from their perches, waiting to see what they would do, winds blew off the cliffs in sharp, unpredictable gusts, knocking the airship about even before it reached the wall.

Walker had them sail the coastline for a time. Caverns had been carved into the cliffs by the ocean, and clusters of rock tumbled from the heights formed odd monuments and outcroppings. Waves crashed against and retreated from the base of the cliffs, surging in and out of the caverns, washing over the rocks and debris. No passage inland revealed itself. Alt Mer refused to fly into the mist and wind that clogged the fissures; suicide, he declared, and put an end to any discussion of it. He shook his head when asked by Walker if they might fly over the mist. A thousand feet higher into thicker mist and stronger winds? Not hardly. The castaway's map revealed that this was a peninsula warded by miles of such cliffs and that the only opening lay through pillars of ice. Big Red was inclined to believe the map.

They sailed on, continuing their search, and the look of the land never changed.

Then, late in the day, the cliffs opened abruptly into a deep, broad bay that ran back through the mist and gloom to a towering range of snowcapped mountains. Through gaps in the barren peaks, glaciers wound their way down to the water's edge, massive chunks of ice, blue-green and jagged, a grinding jumble of frozen moraine that emptied into the bay in blocks so huge they formed small islands, some rising several hundred feet off the surface of the water. Within the bay the winds died, the seabirds huddled in their rookeries, and the ocean's crash faded. Only the occasional crack of the ice as it split and re-formed, chunks breaking away from the larger mass to tumble down slides and ravines, disturbed the deep stillness.

The *Jerle Shannara* sailed through the cliffs into the bay, sliding between icebergs and rock walls, listening to the eerie sound of the shifting ice, searching the gloom for passage. The opening to the bay narrowed to a channel, then opened into a second bay and continued on. The mist thickened above them, forming a roof so dense that it shut out the sun and left the light as pale and gray as the mist. Colors washed away until ice, water, mist, and gloom were all of a piece. With the deepening of the light and the fading of color came a sense of the land's presence that was inexplicably terrifying—a feeling of size and power, of a giant hidden somewhere in the gloom, crouched and waiting to spring. The sounds it emitted were of glaciers breaking apart and sliding into the bay, of fissures opening and closing, of mass shifting constantly from the pressure and cold. The men and women aboard the *Jerle Shannara* listened to it the way a traveler would listen to a storm tear at his lean-to, waiting for something to give way, to fail.

Then the channel narrowed once more, this time clogged by pillars of ice so huge they blocked the way completely, crystal towers that rose out of the bay's liquid floor like spikes. Through gaps in the pillars Bek could see a brightening of the light and a lessening of the mist, as if the weather and geography might be different on the other side. Walker, standing close, touched his shoulder and nodded. Then he turned to Redden Alt Mer and told him to hold the airship where it was.

Hovering before the pillars of ice, clustered at the railings in silent groups, the ship's company stood waiting. The cold air shimmered and seabirds glided in silence. Through the deep mist, the ice continued to rumble and crack, the reverberations distant and ominous.

Then abruptly the pillars began to shift, tilting in a series of thrusts and twists that mimicked the closing of jaws and the grinding of teeth. As the awestruck company watched, the icy towers came together in a series of grating collisions, smashing into each other with booming explosions, closing off the channel's entry and clogging all passage through. Shards of ice catapulted through the air and into the bay's waters, and new cracks opened along the huge towers as they collided then retreated, shifting leviathans hammering at each other in mindless fury. Waves surged and the bay boiled with the force of the furious movement.

Minutes later, the pillars retreated once more, backing away from each other, taking new positions, bobbing gently in the dying swells.

"That," the Druid whispered in Bek's ear, "is called the Squirm. That is what the Sword of Shannara must overcome."

On the Druid's orders, they sailed back out of the bay and down the coast to the atoll where the Wing Riders waited. It was almost dark by then, and Redden Alt Mer had his crew secure the *Jerle Shannara* for the night. Bek was still pondering the Druid's words, trying to figure out how the magic of the Sword of Shannara was supposed to find a way through those shifting icebergs, unable to see how the talisman could help. Walker had left him almost immediately to confer with the Rover Captain, and Ahren had come over to occupy his attention, so there was nothing further he could do to find out right away. Mostly, he had to trust that the Druid knew what he was talking about.

When they were anchored and had eaten dinner, Walker called his council of eight together for a final conference. This time Hunter Predd was included to bring the number to nine. They gathered in Redden Alt Mer's cabin—the Druid, the Rover Captain and his sister, Ard Patrinell and Ahren, Quentin and Bek, Ryer Ord Star, and the Wing Rider. The sky was overcast and the night so black that it was impossible to see either the ocean or the atoll to which they were anchored.

"Tomorrow we will pass through the pillars of the Squirm," Walker advised when they were all gathered and settled. "Captain Alt Mer will command from the pilot box. I will stand on the deck in front of the foremast and call out directions. Bek will help me. Everyone else will take their normal stations and stand ready. No one is to go forward until we are through—not one step beyond me."

He looked at Big Red. "Adjustments will have to be made swiftly and accurately, Captain. The ice will not forgive us our mistakes. Listen carefully to what I call out. Do exactly as I tell you. Trust my directions, even if they seem wrong. Do not try to second-guess me or anticipate my wishes. This one time, I must be in command."

He waited for the Rover to acknowledge him. Redden Alt Mer glanced at his sister, then nodded his agreement.

"Hunter Predd," Walker continued. "The Wing Riders must remain behind. The Shrikes are numerous and the winds and fog treacherous. Fly down the coast and try to find a better place than this atoll to await our return. If we can, we will come back for you or at least get word to you. But it may take time. We may be gone for as long as several months." He paused. "Maybe longer."

The grizzled rider nodded. "I know what to do."

He was saying he understood that those who passed through the pillars of Ice Henge might not be coming back. He was saying that he would wait until waiting was pointless, then try to make his way back to the Four Lands. But Bek heard something more. Hunter Predd wasn't the sort to give up easily. If those on the *Jerle Shannara* didn't make it home, then in all probability, neither would he.

If Walker had picked up on this, he gave no indication. "Ryer Ord Star has had another vision," he advised, beckoning the young woman forward.

She came reluctantly, head lowered into the silver shadow of her long hair, violet eyes directed at the floor, moving into the Druid's shadow as if only there could she be safe, so close that she was pressing up against him. Walker put his hand on her shoulder and bent down. "Tell them," he urged gently.

She took a moment before she responded, her voice high and clear. "I see three moles who seek to burrow into the earth. They carry keys to a lock. One is caught in an endless maze. Ribbons of fire trap another. Metal dogs hunt a third. All are blind and cannot see. All have lost their way and cannot find it again. But one will discover a door that leads to the past. Inside, the future waits."

There was a long silence when she was finished. Then Redden Alt Mer cleared his throat. "Kind of vague, isn't it?" he offered with a wry, apologetic smile at the seer. "What does it mean?"

"We don't know," Walker answered for her. "It might mean that one of us will find the entry into Castledown and the treasure that lies within. That would be a meeting of past and future. Whatever other purpose it serves, it gives warning of three dangers—an endless maze, ribbons of fire, and metal dogs. In some form, these are what we will face when we gain land again." He glanced at Ryer Ord Star. "Maybe by then, we will have new insights to ponder."

We can only hope, Bek thought to himself, and the discussion turned to other matters.

Bek slept poorly that night, riddled by self-doubt and misgiving. He was awake when dawn broke lead-gray and misty, the sun a red-glowing forge at the edge of the world. He stood on deck and watched the light grow from pale to somber as the sky took on a wintry cast that layered clouds and mist and water like gauze. The air was chill and smelled of the damp, and the cliffs of Ice Henge were aswirl with snowflakes and wheeling gulls. The Shrikes were up, as well, hunting the coastline, their larger forms all wings and necks, their fierce cries echoing off the rock walls.

Walker appeared and stopped long enough to place a reassuring hand on the boy's shoulder before moving on. Anchor lines were cast off, sails were unfurled, and the *Jerle Shannara* rose from its berthing and flew north. The Wing Riders left at the same time, flying south. Bek watched them go from the aft railing, solitary forms riding the air currents in a slow, steady glide, the Rocs' great wings spread to the faint winter light. In seconds they were gone, disappeared into the gloom, and Bek turned his attention to what lay ahead. Perhaps a mile offshore, they sailed up the coast making for the opening in the cliffs that led to the Squirm. Breakfast, a hearty mix of breads and cheeses washed down by cold ale, was consumed in shifts and mostly on deck. The day advanced in a slow passing of the hours and an even slower brightening of the sky. The air warmed just enough to change snowflakes to rain, and the wind picked up and began to gust in fierce giant's breaths that knocked the airship about.

Bek stood in the pilot box with Redden Alt Mer for a long time while Walker paced the decking like a ghost at haunt. The Rover Captain said almost nothing to the boy, his concentration focused on the handling of his vessel, his gaze directed ahead into the gloom. Once he caught Bek's eye and smiled briefly. "We'll be fine, Bek," he said quietly, and then looked away again.

Bek Rowe, born Bek Ohmsford, wasn't at all sure that was so, but if hope and determination counted for anything, maybe they had a chance. He was wrestling with doubts about his ability to control any sort of magic, even his mastery of the wishsong suspect. It was all too new and unfamiliar for him to have much confidence. He had experienced the magic of his voice, but in such a small way and with so little sense of control that he barely felt he understood what it could do. As for the magic of the Sword of Shannara, he had no idea what he could do with that. He could repeat everything Walker had told him about how it worked. He could intellectualize its behavior and function. He would apply all the appropriate and correct words to how it would affect him. But he could not picture it. He could not imagine how it would feel. He had no frame of reference and no sense of proportion with which to measure its power.

He did not try to deceive himself. The magic of the Sword of Shannara would be immense and overwhelming. It would engulf him like a tidal wave, and he would be fortunate to survive its crushing impact, let alone find a way to swim to its surface. All he could do was hope he would not be drowned straightaway when it swept over him. Walker had not said so, but it was there in the gaps between his words. Bek was to be tested in a way he had never imagined. Walker did not seem to think he would fail, but Walker would not be there inside him when the magic took hold.

Bek climbed down out of the pilot box after a while and went to stand at the ship's railing. Quentin came up to him, and they talked in low voices about the day and the weather, avoiding any mention of the Squirm. The Highlander was relaxed and cheerful, in typical fashion, and he made Bek feel at ease even without intending it. Wasn't this everything they had hoped for? he asked his cousin with a broad smile.

Wasn't this the adventure they had come to find? What did Bek think lay on the other side of those ice pillars? Somehow they must make certain they stayed together. Whatever happened, they must remember their promise.

It was nearing midmorning when they reached the gap in the cliffs and rode the edges of the air currents through its opening and into the silence and calm beyond. The roar of the ocean and the whistle of the wind died away, and the bay with its cliff walls and cloud ceiling enfolded them like an anxious mother would her offspring. The ship's company crowded to the railings and looked out over the gray expanse of water and ice. Floes passed beneath like massive ships launched off the glaciers, riding the currents out to sea. Ice cracked and chuttered in the silence, filling hearts with sudden moments of apprehension and eyes with bright looks of concern. Bek stood in the cold and silence like a statue, wrapped in the former's raw burn and layered in the latter's rough emptiness.

The *Jerle Shannara* passed through the outer bay and rode down the narrowing channel inland, the ceiling of mist lowering to scrape the airship's raked masts, the gloom a whisper of shadows that tricked the eyes into seeing things that weren't there. No one spoke as the airship slid past icebergs and along cliff walls, moving so slowly that it seemed almost at rest. Seabirds arced and soared about them, soundless and spectral. Bek watched them keep pace, following their progress, intrigued by their obvious interest.

Then his throat tightened and his breath exhaled in a sharp cloud as he realized they were waiting to see if there would be bones to pick once the airship reached the Squirm.

Moments later the haze cleared sufficiently that he could see the first of the ice pillars that barred their passage, towering spikes swaying hypnotically, seductively in the gloom.

"Come with me," Walker said softly, causing the boy to jump, to feel the tightening in his throat work swiftly to his chest and stomach.

So it was time. He remembered his certainty months earlier when he had agreed to come on this voyage that it would change him forever. It had done that, but not to the extent it was about to do now. He closed his eyes against a fresh wave of fear and doubt. He understood that the course of his life was already determined, but he could not quite accept it, even now. Still, he must do the best he could.

Obediently, silently, willing himself to place one foot in front of the other, Bek followed after the Druid.

TWENTY-EIGHT

Bek waited in the shadow of the chain-wrapped casing that housed the Sword of Shannara while Walker moved everyone back from the forward deck to take up positions along the aft and side railings. Redden Alt Mer occupied the pilot box with Rue Meridian. Spanner Frew stood just below, ready to leap into action if his aid was required. Furl Hawken commanded the Rover crew from the rise of the aft deck, and the Elven Hunters under Ard Patrinell clustered on both sides, safety lines firmly attached. Panax, Quentin, and Ahren Elessedil were gathered on the starboard railing just to one side of the aft mast, whispering. About *him*, Bek thought uncomfortably, but that was nonsense. Their eyes were directed toward the Squirm, and their concentration was on its movements within the ice-melt bay. Only Walker knew what he was there to do. Only Walker understood how much depended on him.

The Druid reappeared at his side. "Ready, Bek?"

Not trusting himself to speak, the boy nodded. He was not ready, of course. He would never be ready for something as frightening as this. There was no way to become ready. All he could do was trust that the Druid was right about his connection to the magic and hope that he could find a way to make himself do what was needed.

But looking at the monstrous barrier ahead, at the tons of ice and rock that rose above him, he could not imagine doing anything that would make a difference.

He breathed slowly, calming himself, waiting for something to happen. The *Jerle Shannara* advanced toward the pillars on a slow, steady course, easing up to the barrier as if seeking an invitation to enter. Walker was speaking to Redden Alt Mer, but Bek could not make himself focus on the words. His heart was hammering in his chest, and all he could hear was the sound of his breathing and the cracking of the ice as new pieces broke away.

"Now, Bek," the Druid said softly.

Walker's hand swept the air about them, and the air shimmered and turned murky with a swirling of mist and gloom. Everything behind and to either side of the boy and the Druid lost focus and faded away. All that remained was a window before them that opened on the channel and the cliffs and the ice.

As if in response, the pillars began to move.

"Hold steady, Bek," Walker urged softly, touching Bek's shoulder to reassure him, dark face close, his eyes staring out at the ice as it came together.

Like mobile teeth, the pillars tilted and clashed, grinding and crunching until shards of ice splintered and flew in all directions. The sea below boiled and crashed in waves against the base of the cliffs, spray rising in clouds to mingle with the mist. Bek flinched at the sound and the motion, hunched his shoulders in spite of himself. He could feel the ice closing about him, crushing him, reducing the airship to driftwood and the ship's company to pulp. He could feel it happening as if it really were, tearing at him in ways that turned him so cold and dead he could not bear it. He stood on the deck of the *Jerle Shannara*, washed by spray and hammered by sound, and felt as if his soul had been torn open.

Something burned before him, a beacon out of the gloom, rising like a flame into the gray haze. He stared at it in wonder, and he saw that he held in his hands the Sword of Shannara and that it was ablaze with light.

"Shades!" he hissed in disbelief.

He had no idea when Walker had given it to him, no idea how long he had been holding it. He stared at its light, transfixed, watching it surge up and down the blade in small crimson ribbons that twisted and wound about the metal. He watched as it descended into the pommel and wrapped about his hands.

Then it was rushing through him in a wave of warmth and tingling sensation, spreading all through his limbs and body. It consumed him, swallowed him, wrapped him about, and made him its own. He was captured by it, and there was a slow leavening of thought, emotion, and feeling. Everything about him began to disappear, fading away into darkness which only the sword's light illuminated. The airship, the ship's company, the gloom and mist, the ice, the cliffs, everything was gone. Bek was alone, solitary and adrift within himself, buoyed on the back of the magic that infused him.

Help me, he heard himself asking.

The images began at once, no longer of the Squirm and its crushing pillars, no longer of the world in which he lived, but of the world he had left behind, of the past. A succession of memories began to recall themselves, taking him back in time, reminding him of what had once been and now was gone. He grew younger, smaller. The memories became a rush of sudden, frightening images, rife with fury and terror, with distant cries and the labored breathing of someone who held him close before tucking him into a black, cold place. The smell and taste of smoke and soot filled his throat and nostrils, and he could feel a panic within that refused to be stilled.

Grianne! he heard himself call out.

Blackness cloaked and hooded him once more, and a new series of images began. He saw himself as a child in the care of Coran and Liria. He saw himself at play with Quentin and his friends, with his younger brothers and sisters, at his home in Leah and beyond. The scenes were dark and accusatory, memories of his growing up that he had suppressed, memories of the times in which he had lied and cheated and deceived, in which his selfishness and disregard had caused hurt and pain. Some of these scenes were familiar; some he had forgotten. The weaknesses of his life were revealed in steady procession, laid bare for him to witness. They were not terrible things taken separately, but their number increased their weight, and after a time he was crying openly and desperate for them to end.

A wind of dark haziness swept them all away and left him with a view of the Four Lands in which all that was bad and terrible about the human condition was displayed. He watched in horror as starvation, sickness, murder, and pillage decimated lives and homes and futures in a canvas so broad it seemed to stretch from horizon to horizon. Men, women and children fell victim to the weaknesses of spirit and morality that plagued mankind. All of the races were susceptible, and all participated in the savagery. There was no end to it, no lessening of it, no sense that it had ever been other than this. Bek watched it unfold in horror and profound sadness and felt it to be a part of himself. Even in his misery he could sense that this was the history of his people, that this was who he was.

Yet when it was over, he felt cleansed. With recognition came acceptance. With acceptance came forgiveness. He felt cleansed, not just of what he had contributed to the morass, but of what others had contributed as well—as if he had taken it all on his shoulders, just for a little while, and had been given back a sense of peace. He rose up within the darkness, strengthened in ways he could not define, reborn into himself with a boy's eyes, but a man's understanding.

The darkness drew back, and he stood again on the deck of the *Jerle Shannara*, arms lifted, sword outstretched. He was still masked back and sides by Walker's magic, but the way forward was clear. The Squirm had opened anew, its pillars swaying seductively, beckoning him to proceed, to come within their reach. He could feel the cold that permeated them. He could feel their crushing weight. Even the air that surrounded them was infused with their power and their unpredictability. But there was something else here as well; he felt it at once. Something man-made, something not of nature but of machines and science.

A hand reached out to him, not made of flesh and blood, but of spirit, of ether, of magic so vast and pervasive that it lay everywhere about. He shrank from it, warded himself against it by bringing the sword's light to bear, and abruptly it was gone.

Walker? he called out in confusion, but there was only silence.

Ahead, the pillars of the Squirm rocked in the ice-melt sea, and the gulls flew round and round. Bek tested the air and the temperature. He joined himself to the ice of the spikes and the rock of the cliffs. He immersed himself in their feel, in their movements, in the vibrations of sound they emitted, in the shifting of their parts. He became one with his immediate world, extending into it from where he stood, so that he could read its intention and anticipate its behavior.

"Go forward," he instructed, gesturing with the sword. The words seemed to come from someone else. "Ahead, slow."

Walker must have heard him. The *Jerle Shannara* eased cautiously toward the pillars. Like a fragile bird, it sailed within their monstrous jaws, through the misted gaps of their teeth. "Left fifteen degrees," he said, and heard Walker repeat his orders. "Ahead slow," he called. "Faster now, more speed," he instructed. The airship slid through the forest of ice, a moth into the flame, tiny and insignificant and unable to protect itself from the fire.

Then the pillars shifted anew and began to close on them. Bek was aware of it from somewhere deep inside, not just through his eyes, but through his body's connection with the sword's magic and the sword's magic with the land and air and water. Cries rose from members of the ship's company, frantic with fear. The boy heard them as he heard the crashing of waves against the cliff walls and the whisper of gull wings on the morning air. He heard them and did not respond. "Go right twenty degrees. Take shelter in that pillar's crevice." His voice was so soft it seemed a wonder to him that anyone could hear.

But, hearing the words repeated by Walker, Redden Alt Mer did as Bek instructed. He rode the *Jerle Shannara* swiftly into a split that warded her while all about the ice pillars clashed and hammered at each other, and the air turned damp with spray and the sea white with foam. The sound and the fury of it deafened and shocked, and it felt as if an avalanche were sweeping over them. In the midst of the madness, Bek ordered the airship out of its protection through a momentary gap in two of the surging towers. The ship responded as if wired to his thinking, and an instant later, a wedge of ice broke off from the pinnacle of their momentary shelter and crashed down to lodge in the crevice they had just departed.

Forward they sailed, down through the haze, through errant and sudden collisions, through the closing of icy jaws and the grinding of sharpened teeth. A tiny bit of flotsam, they weaved and dodged, barely avoiding a crushing end time after time, riding spray and wind and cold. What must have gone through the minds of his shipmates, Bek could only imagine. Later, Quentin would tell him that after the first few moments, he had been unable to see much and had not wanted to look anyway. Bek would reply that it had been like that for him as well.

"Up! Quickly! Go up!" he cried a sharp and frantic warning, and the airship rose with a sudden lurch that threw everyone to the deck. Kneeling with the sword outstretched and his legs spread for balance, Bek heard the explosion of an ice floe beneath them, and a massive piece, propelled from the water's surface like a projectile, just missed the underside of their hull before falling back into the sea.

Sword raised to the light, magic entwined with the air and

the ice and the rock, Bek shouted his instructions. Relying on instinct rather than sight, on sensation rather than thought, he responded to impulses that flashed and were gone in seconds, trusting to their ebb and flow as he guided the airship ahead. He could not explain to himself then or later what he was doing. He was reacting, and the impetus for what he did came from something both within and without that lacked definition or source, that was like the air he breathed and the cold and damp that infused it—pervasive and all-consuming. Again and again, huge shadows fell over him as the pillars of the Squirm swept by, barely missing them, rising and falling in the misty light, advancing randomly, soldiers at march through the gloom. Over and over, the monoliths collided, splintered, exploded, and turned to jagged shards. Lost within himself, wrapped within his magic, Bek felt it all and saw none of it.

Then the gloom began to brighten ahead, the haze to thin, and the sound and movement of the pillars to lessen. Still focused on the crushing weight of the ice and rock, Bek registered the change without letting it distract him. There was a sense of growing warmth, of color returning, and of smells that were of the land and not the sea. The airship surged ahead, propelled by an expectancy and hope Bek had not felt before. He lowered the Sword of Shannara in response, and his connection with the magic was broken. The warmth that infused him drew back, and the light that encircled the blade faded. Still on his knees, exhausted, he sagged to the decking. He breathed in deeply, gratefully, head lowered between his shoulders.

Walker took the Sword of Shannara from his hands and knelt beside him. "We're through, Bek. We're safe. Well done, young Ohmsford."

The boy felt the Druid's arm come about his shoulders, and then he fell away into blackness and didn't feel anything.

*   *   *

When he regained consciousness, he was lying beneath the foremast with Joad Rish bent over him. He blinked and stared down at himself for a moment, as if needing reassurance that he was still all there, then looked up at the Healer.

"How do you feel?" the Elf asked, concern mirrored in his narrow features.

Bek wanted to laugh. How could he possibly answer that question after what he'd been through? "I'm all right. A little disoriented. How long was I unconscious?"

"No more than a few minutes. Walker said you were thrown into that crate and cracked your head. Do you want to try to stand up?"

With the Healer's help, Bek climbed to his feet and looked around. The *Jerle Shannara* was under sail, moving down a broad, twisting channel through a bleak landscape of barren cliff walls and small, rocky islands. But the mist had begun to clear, and traces of blue sky shone in the bright light of an emerging sun. Trees dotted the ridgelines of the cliffs, and the glaciers and ice floes were gone.

A rush of memories crowded into Bek's mind, hard and fast and dangerous, but he blinked them away. The Squirm and its pillars of ice were gone. The Sword of Shannara was gone, as well, put back into its casing by Walker, he supposed. He shivered momentarily, thinking of all he had experienced, of the feelings generated, of the whiplash of power. The sword's magic was addictive, he realized. He didn't need more than one experience with it to know. It was terrifying and overwhelming and incredibly empowering. Just to have survived it made him feel strangely exhilarated. As if he could survive anything. As if he were invulnerable.

Quentin came up and put a hand on his shoulder, asking how he was. Bek repeated Joad Rish's story about hitting his head when the ship lurched, playing it down. Nothing much. Nothing to give a second thought to. It was such a ridiculous explanation that he felt embarrassed giving it, but he realized it seemed ridiculous only if you knew the truth. One by one, the members of the ship's company came up to him, and he repeated the story to each. Only Ahren Elessedil voiced any skepticism.

"You're not usually so clumsy, Bek," he observed with a grin. "Where were your instincts when you needed them? An Elf wouldn't have lost his footing so easily."

"Be a touch more careful next time, young hero," Little Red joked, ruffling his hair. "We can't afford to lose you."

Walker appeared momentarily, shadowed by the slight, silver-haired figure of Ryer Ord Star. Distant, he nodded to the boy without speaking, and passed on. The seer studied the boy carefully before following.

The morning had passed away into afternoon, and the landscape began to change. The sharp-edged cliffs retreated from the waterline and softened to gentle slopes. Green and lush in the sunlight, forests appeared. From where they flew, the ship's company saw rolling hills stretching into the distance for miles. The river they followed split into dozens of smaller tributaries that spiderwebbed out through the trees to form lakes, rivers, and streams. There was no sign of the ocean; the peninsula was sufficiently large that its outer shores were too distant to spy. Clouds were gathered on the horizons to either side and behind, markers of where the shoreline probably lay. Bek thought that Redden Alt Mer had been right not to try to fly over the cliffs to come inland. Even had they been able to do so, they would probably never have found this channel in the maze of rivers that surrounded it. Only by coming through the Squirm could they have known where to go.

The channel narrowed, hemmed in by old-growth spruce and cedar, the scent of the trees fragrant and lush on the warming air. The smells of the sea, of kelp and seaweed and fish, had faded. For all that remained of the coastline and its forbidding passage through the Squirm, they might have passed into another world entirely. Hawks soared overhead in slow, sweeping glides. Crows cawed raucously, their calls echoing down the defile. The *Jerle Shannara* edged ahead carefully, so close to the shore at times that its spars brushed against the tree limbs.

The river eventually ended in a bay surrounded by forest and fed by dozens of rivers and streams. A huge waterfall tumbled into its basin at one end, and a handful of smaller falls splashed over rocky precipices farther along. Birdsong filled the air, and a small herd of deer moved quickly off the water's edge on sighting their craft. The *Jerle Shannara* eased into the bay like a large sea creature that had wandered inland, and Redden Alt Mer brought her to a stop at the bay's center.

Gathered at the railings, the ship's company stared out at the destination they had traveled so far to find. It was nothing special. It might have been any number of places in the Westland, so similar did it look with its mix of conifers and hardwoods, the scent of loam on the air, and its smells of needles and green leaves.

Then Bek realized in mild shock that it didn't look or feel like winter here, even though it was the winter season. Once through the Squirm, they hadn't found anything of ice or cold or snow or bitter wind. It was as if they had somehow found their way back to midsummer.

"This isn't possible," he murmured softly, confused and wary.

He glanced quickly at those around him to see if anyone else had noticed, but no one seemed to have done so. He waited a moment, then moved over to where Walker stood, alone, below the pilot box. The Druid's eyes were leveled on the shoreline ahead, but they registered the boy's approach.

"What is it, Bek?"

Bek stood beside him uncertainly. "It's summer here, and it shouldn't be."

The Druid nodded. "It's a lot of things here it shouldn't be. Strange. Keep your eyes open."

He ordered Big Red to take the airship down to the water

and anchor her. When that was done, he sent a foraging party of Elven Hunters ashore for water, warning them that they were to stay together and in sight of the shoreline. The company would remain aboard ship tonight. A search for Castledown would begin in the morning. What was needed now was an inventory of the ship's stores, an updated damage report, an unpacking and distribution of weapons to the members of the shore party, and some dinner. The Elven Hunters under Ard Patrinell and Ahren Elessedil would accompany him on the morrow's search, along with Quentin, Bek, Panax, Ryer Ord Star, and Joad Rish. The Rovers would remain aboard ship until their return.

Before anyone could offer comment or complaint about his decision, he summoned his council of eight to a meeting in Redden Alt Mer's cabin and walked from the deck.

Quentin sidled up to Bek. "Something is up, I'll wager. Do you think the seer's had another vision?"

Bek shook his head. The only thing he knew for certain was that Redden Alt Mer, dark-browed and stiff-necked as he came down off the pilot box, was not happy.

When the eight who composed Walker's inner council were gathered belowdecks in the Rover Captain's cabin, the boy found out what it was.

"I didn't come this far to be left aboard ship while everyone else goes ashore," Big Red snapped at the Druid.

"Nor I," Rue Meridian agreed, flushed and angry. "We sailed a long way to find out what's here. You ask too much of us, Walker."

No one else spoke. They were pressed close about the Druid, gathered at the table that held the large-scale drawing of the castaway's map, all but Ryer Ord Star, who remained in the background, a part of the shadows, watching silently. The warmth of their new environment not yet absorbed into the hull, the room smelled of damp and pitch and was still infused with the feel of the ice and cold they had left on the other side of the Squirm. Bek glanced at the faces about him, surprised by the mix of expectancy and tension he found mirrored there. It had taken them a long time to reach their destination, and much of what they had bottled up inside during their voyage was coming out.

Walker's black eyes swept the room. He gestured at the map laid out before them. "How do you think the castaway who brought us the original of this map managed to get all the way from here to the coast of the Westland?"

He waited a moment, but no one answered. "It is a voyage of months, even by airship. How did the castaway manage it, already blind and voiceless and probably at least half-mad?"

"Someone helped him," Bek offered, not wanting to listen any longer to the uncomfortable silence. "Maybe the same someone who helped him escape."

The Druid nodded. "Where is that person?"

Again, silence. Bek shook his head, not eager to assume the role of designated speaker for the group.

"Dead, lost at sea during the escape, probably on the voyage back," Rue Meridian said. "What are you getting at?"

"Let's assume that is so," Walker replied. "You have had a chance to study the map at length during this voyage. Most of the writings are done not with words, but with symbols. The writings aren't of this age, but of an age thousands of years old, from a time before the Great Wars destroyed the Old World. How did our castaway learn that language?"

"Someone taught it to him," Rue Meridian answered, a thoughtful, somewhat worried look on her sun-browned face. She tossed back her long red hair impatiently. "Why would they do that?"

"Why, indeed?" Walker paused. "Let's assume that the Elven expedition that Kael Elessedil led thirty years ago reached its destination just as we have, and then something happened to it. They were all killed, all but one man, perhaps Kael Elessedil himself. Their ships were destroyed and all trace of their passage disappeared. How did they find their way here? Did they have a map, as we do? We must assume so, or how would the castaway know to draw one for us to follow? To make the copy we have, they must have followed the route we followed. They must have visited the islands of Flay Creech, Shatterstone, and Mephitic, and found the keys we found. If so, how did those keys get back to the islands from which they were taken?"

Another long silence filled the room. Booted feet shifted uncomfortably. "What are you saying, Walker?" Ard Patrinell asked.

"He's saying we've sailed into a trap," Redden Alt Mer answered softly.

Bek stared at the Rover Captain, repeating his words silently, trying to make sense of them.

"I have given this considerable thought," Walker said, folding his arm into his robes, a pensive look on his dark face. "I thought it odd that an Elf should have possession of a map marked with symbols he couldn't possibly know. I thought it convenient that the map spelled out so clearly what was needed for us to find our way here. The keys were not particularly well concealed. In fact, they were easily gained once the creatures and devices that warded them were bypassed. It struck me that whoever hid the keys was more interested in seeing if and how we managed to overcome the protectors than whether or not we found the keys. I was reminded of how hunters trap animals, laying out bait to lure them to the snare, the bait itself having no value. Hunters think of animals as cunning and wary, but not of intelligence equal to their own. Animals might mistrust a baited trap instinctively, but they would not be able to reason out its purpose. That sort of thinking seems to be at work here."

He paused and looked at Big Red. "Yes, Captain, I think it is a trap."

Redden Alt Mer nodded. "The keys are merely bait. Why?"

"Why not just provide us with a map and let us find our way here? Why bother with the keys at all?" Walker looked around the room, meeting each person's eyes in turn. "To answer that, you have to go all the way back to the first expedition. A different technique was employed to lure the Elves to this place, but the purpose was probably the same. Whoever or whatever brought us here is interested in something we have. I wasn't sure what it was at first, but I am now. It is our magic. Whatever hunts us wants our magic. It used the mystery of the first expedition's disappearance to lure us here. It knows we possess magic because it has already encountered the power of the Elfstones that Kael Elessedil carried. So it expects us to have magic, as well. Requiring us to gain possession of the three keys gave it an opportunity to measure the nature and extent of that magic. The protectors of the keys were set in place to test us. If we could not overcome them, we had no business coming here."

"If you suspected most of this before we set out, why didn't you tell us then?" Redden Alt Mer snapped, angrier than ever now. "In fact, why did you bring us here at all?"

"Don't give me too much credit for what I am presumed to have known," Walker replied quietly. "I suspected more than I knew. I intuited the possibilities, but could not be certain of their accuracy without making the journey. How could I have explained all this and made sense if I had done so without your having experienced what you have? No, Captain, it was necessary to make the voyage first. Even so, I would not have changed my decision. Whatever destroyed Kael Elessedil and his Elven Hunters seeks to do the same to us. Nor will it stop there. It is a powerful and dangerous being, and it has to be destroyed. The Elves want their Elfstones back, and I want to free the magic our adversary hoards. There are good reasons for being here, in spite of what we know, in spite of the obvious dangers. Good enough that we must accept the risks they bear."

"Easy enough for you to say, Walker," Rue Meridian observed. "You have your magic and your Druid skills to protect you. We have only our blades. Except for Quentin Leah, who has his sword, who else has magic to protect us?"

Bek braced for the response he expected Walker to give, but the Druid surprised him. "Magic is not what will save us in this matter or even what will do us the most good. Think about it. If our adversary uses a language of symbols, a language that was devised before the Great Wars by a Mankind steeped in science, then in all likelihood, it has no magic itself. It brought us here because it covets our magic. It covets what we have and it does not. Why this is so is what we must determine. But our chances of overcoming our adversary are not necessarily reliant on the use of magic."

"That is a large assumption, Druid," Little Red declared bluntly. "What of the things that warded the keys on the islands we visited? The eels might have been real enough, but what of that living jungle and that castle? Wasn't magic in play there?"

Walker nodded. "But not a magic of the sort that devised those keys. The keys are a technology from the past, one lost since the Great Wars or perhaps even before. The magic of the castle and the jungle are Faerie-induced and have been resident since the time of the Word. The eels probably mutated after the Great Wars. Our adversary did not create them, but only identified them. What's interesting is not that these traps were baited to test the strength and nature of our magic but that it was done without having to overcome the things that warded those islands. How did our adversary do that? Why didn't it try to steal their magic, as well? Why did it choose to go to so much trouble to summon us instead?"

He nodded toward Big Red. "The reason I am leaving the Rovers aboard ship instead of taking them inland with the Elven Hunters is that I think our adversary might well try to steal our ship. It knows we are here, I expect, and how we arrived. It will know as well that if it steals the *Jerle Shannara,* we will be marooned and helpless. We can't afford to let that happen. Who better to protect and defend our airship than the people who sailed and built her?"

Redden Alt Mer nodded slowly. "All right. Your argument is sound, Walker. But how will we fight this thing off if it comes after the ship? We won't have any magic to use against it, only our blades. If it's as powerful as you suggest—"

"After we go ashore tomorrow," Walker interrupted quickly, holding up his hand to silence the other, "you will take the *Jerle Shannara* out of this bay and back down the channel toward the Squirm. Then take a bearing and fly back out over the peninsula to the coast and find the Wing Riders. When you've done so, bring them back to a safe haven downriver. Map your route going out so you can find your way coming back. Have the Wing Riders fly inland over this bay and the surrounding forests every day until we signal you to take us out. If you aren't where you can be easily found, you'll be safe enough."

Big Red looked at his sister. Rue Meridian shrugged. "I don't like the idea of splitting up," he said. "I understand the reason for it, but it puts you and those with you at great risk if something goes wrong. You will be marooned if we can't find you."

Walker nodded. "Then we'll have to make sure you can."

"Or if we can't find the Wing Riders," Little Red added.

"The Wing Riders will find you. They will be looking for you, for the airship. Just be certain you map your route out and back carefully."

"I'll see that I do." Rue Meridian held his gaze.

Bek glanced from Quentin to Ahren Elessedil to Ard Patrinell and finally to the wan, youthful face of Ryer Ord Star. There was determination and acceptance on each, but the seer's face showed apprehension and conflict, as well. She knew something she was not telling them. Bek sensed it instinctively, as if he still held the Sword of Shannara and had brought its magic to bear, seeking out the truth, drawing back the veil of concealment the young woman held in place.

What was it she was hiding? Something of their fate? Something of what waited inland? Bek studied her surreptitiously. Had she told Walker everything? Or was she holding something back? He didn't have any reason to ask himself that question, no cause to believe that she would conceal anything from the Druid.

But there was something in the way she distanced herself from him, from everyone . . .

"Let's finish our preparations and have something to eat," Walker said, breaking into his thoughts. "Tomorrow we set out at sunrise."

"Good luck to you, Walker," Rue Meridian said.

He gave her a wry smile. "Good luck to us all, Little Red."

Then he gathered in his black robes and walked from the room.

TWENTY-NINE

Anchored well offshore and forty feet above the water, the company of the *Jerle Shannara* spent the night in the tree-sheltered bay. Taking no chances, Walker set a full watch—one man forward, one aft, and one in the pilot box—using Rovers so that the Elven Hunters could get a full night's sleep and be fresh for the morning's search. Even so, the Druid suspected that sleep was an elusive quantity that night. He slept little himself, and while pacing the corridors and decks he encountered, at one time or another, almost everyone else doing the same. Anticipation kept them all on edge and restless, and even the absence of wind and surf did nothing to ease their discomfort.

Dawn arrived in a flare of golden light that burst through the trees and across the horizon, brightening a clear blue sky and heralding a weather-perfect day. The members of the company were up and moving about almost instantly, grateful for any excuse to quit pretending that sleep might somehow come. Breakfast was consumed and weapons and provisions were gathered up. The search party gathered on deck in the early light, grim-faced and resolved, no one saying much, everyone waiting for the order to depart. Walker did not give it at once. He spent a long time conversing with Redden Alt Mer and Rue Meridian, then with Spanner Frew. They walked the length and breadth of the airship while they spoke, one or the other gesturing now and then at the ship or the surrounding forest. Bek watched them from where he sat cross-legged against the port railing, running through a list of what he carried, checking it off mentally against the list he had prepared last night. He bore virtually no weapons—a dagger and a sling—and he was less than comfortable with having only those for protection. But Walker had insisted they were all he would need or could carry, and no amount of protesting on his part had changed the Druid's mind.

"This would be a good day for hunting," Quentin, who was seated beside him, his gear at his feet, observed.

Bek nodded. Quentin carried a short sword at his belt, a bow and arrows over his shoulder, and the Sword of Leah strapped across his back in the Highland style. Bek supposed that if they encountered anything really dangerous, he could rely on his cousin to come to his aid.

"Do you suppose they have boar here?"

"What difference does it make?" Bek found the small talk irritating and unnecessary.

"I was just wondering." Quentin seemed unperturbed. "It just feels a little like home to me."

Ashamed of his disgruntled attitude, Bek forced a smile. "They have lots of boar here, and you couldn't track a one of them without me."

"Do tell." Quentin arched one eyebrow. "Will I see some proof of your prowess one day soon? Or will I have to go on taking your word for it for the rest of my life?"

He leaned back and stretched his arms over his head. Quentin seemed loose and easy on the outside, but Bek knew he was as anxious as the rest of them where it couldn't be seen. The banter was a time-honored way around it, a method of dealing with it that both instinctively relied on. They had used it before, on hunts where the game they tracked was dangerous, like boar or bear, and the risk of injury was severe. It moved them a step away from thinking about what might happen if something went wrong, and it helped to prevent the kind of gradual paralysis that could steal over someone like a sickness and surface when it was too late to find an antidote.

Bek glanced across the decking to where the Elven Hunters clustered around Ard Patrinell, talking in their low, soft voices as they exchanged comments and banter of their own. Ahren Elessedil stood a little apart from them, staring off into the trees, where night's shadows still folded through the gaps in thick layers and the silence was deep and steady. Nothing of his newfound maturity was in evidence this morning. He looked like a little boy, frightened and lost, stiff with recognition of what might happen to him and fighting a losing battle against the growing certainty that it would. He carried a short sword and bow and arrows, but from the look on his face he might as well have been carrying Bek's weapons.

Bek watched him a moment, thinking about how Ahren must feel, about the responsibility he bore as nominal leader of the expedition, then made a quick decision and climbed to his feet. "I'll be right back," he told Quentin.

He crossed to Ahren and greeted him with a broad grin. "Another day, another adventure," he offered brightly. "At least Ard Patrinell gave you a real sword and an ash bow."

Ahren started at the sound of Bek's voice, but managed to recover a little of his lost composure. "What do you mean?"

"Look what Walker gave me." Bek gestured at his dagger and sling. "Any small birds or squirrels that come after me, I'm ready for them."

Ahren smiled nervously. "I wish I could say the same. I can barely make my legs move. I don't know what's wrong."

"Quentin would say you haven't hunted enough wild boar. Look, I came over to ask a favor. I want you to keep this for me."

Before he could think better of it, he took off the phoenix stone and its necklace and placed them about Ahren's neck. It was an impulsive act, one he might have reconsidered if he had allowed himself time to think about it. The Elf looked down at the stone, then back at Bek questioningly.

"I'm afraid I haven't been entirely honest with you, Ahren," Bek admitted. Then he told his friend a revised version of his encounter with the King of the Silver River and the gift of the phoenix stone, leaving out the parts about his sister and the spirit creature's hints of the stone's real purpose. "So I do have a little magic after all. But I've been keeping it a secret from everyone." He shrugged. "Even Quentin doesn't know about it."

"I can't take this from you!" Ahren declared vehemently, reaching up to remove the stone and necklace.

Bek stopped him, seizing his hands. "Yes, you can. I want you to have it."

"But it isn't mine! It wasn't given to me; it was given to you! By a Faerie creature at that!" His voice softened. "It isn't right, Bek. It doesn't belong to me."

"Well, it doesn't belong to me, either. Not really. Consider it a loan. You can give it back to me later. Look, fair is fair. I have Quentin to protect me, and he has a talisman to help him do the job. You have Ard Patrinell, but he doesn't have any magic. The Elfstones might turn up along the way, but for now, you need something else. Why not take this?"

Bek could tell that the Elf wanted to accept the gift, a talisman of real magic that would give him fresh confidence and a renewed sense of purpose. Just now, Ahren needed those things more than he did. But the Elven prince was proud, and he would not take something from Bek if he thought it was a charity that would put his friend at risk.

"I can't," he repeated dully.

"Could you take it if I told you that Walker has given me another magic to use, something else with which I can protect myself?" Bek kept the truth behind the lie masked in a look of complete sincerity.

Ahren shook his head doubtfully. "What magic?"

"I can't tell you. Walker won't let me. I'm not even supposed to tell you I have the magic. Just trust me. I wouldn't give you the phoenix stone if it was the only real protection I had, would I?"

Which was true enough. The fact that he possessed the magic of the wishsong gave him some reassurance that by handing over the phoenix stone, he wasn't leaving himself entirely defenseless. Anyway, the stone hadn't been of much use to him; perhaps it would help his friend.

"Please, Ahren. Keep it. Look, if you promise to use it to help me if you see that I'm in trouble, that will be repayment enough. And I'll do the same for you with my magic. Quentin and I already have an agreement to look out for each other. You and I can have one, too."

He waited, holding Ahren's uncertain gaze. Finally, the other boy nodded. "All right. But just for a while, Bek." He ran his fingers over the stone. "It's warm, like it's heating from the inside out. And so smooth." He glanced down at it a moment, then back at Bek. "I think it really is magic. But maybe we won't have to find out. Maybe we won't have to use it at all."

Bek smiled agreeably, not believing his reassurances for a single moment. "Maybe not."

"Thanks, Bek. Thanks very much."

Bek was on his way back to Quentin when Walker stopped him amidships and turned him gently aside. "That was very foolish," he said, not unkindly. "Well intentioned, but not particularly well advised."

Bek faced the Druid squarely, the set of his jaw revealing his attitude on the matter. "Ahren has nothing with which to protect himself. No magic of his own, Walker. He is my friend, and I don't see anything wrong with giving him something that might help keep him alive."

The dark face looked away. "You weren't listening to me as closely as I hoped when I said that magic wasn't necessarily the key to survival here. Instincts and courage and a clear head are what will keep us alive."

Bek stood his ground. "Well, maybe having the phoenix

stone will help him find those particular attributes. What's bothering you, Walker?"

The Druid shook his head. "So many things I don't know where to start. But in this case, your rashness gives me pause. Giving up magic entrusted to you by the King of the Silver River may cost you more than you realize. The magic of the phoenix stone wasn't intended as a defense. The King of the Silver River would know, as I do, that you possess the magic of the wishsong. The stone is for something else, most likely something to do with your sister. Mark me well, Bek, and retrieve it as soon as you reasonably can. Promise me."

Only partially convinced, the boy nodded without enthusiasm. Too much of what the Druid had told him during their travels was suspect. This was no exception. No one could know the future or what it would require of a man. Not a spirit creature. Not even a seer like Ryer Ord Star. The best anyone could do was reveal glimpses out of context, and those could deceive.

"Meanwhile," Walker said, interrupting his thoughts, "I am giving you this to carry."

He reached beneath his black robes and produced the Sword of Shannara. It was sheathed in a soft leather scabbard, but the carving of the fist and the raised torch on the pommel were unmistakable.

Bek took it from the Druid and held it out before him, staring at it. "Do you think I will need it?"

The Druid's smile was unexpectedly bitter. "I think we will need whatever strengths we can call upon once we are off this airship. A talisman belongs in the hands of a bearer who can wield it. In the case of the Sword of Shannara, that bearer is you."

Bek thought about it for a moment and then nodded. "All right, I'll carry it. Not because I am afraid for myself, but because maybe I can be of some use to the others. That's the reason I went with Truls Rohk into the ruins on Mephitic. That's the reason I agreed to use the sword at the Squirm. I came on this journey because I believed what you told me the night we met—that I could do something to help. I still believe it. I'm a part of this company, even if I don't know for sure yet what that part might be."

Walker bent to him. "Each of us has a part to play and all of us are still discovering what that part is. None of us is superfluous. Everyone is necessary. You are right to look out for your friends."

He put his hand on the boy's shoulder. "But remember that we can do little to look out for others if we forget to look out for ourselves. In the future, don't be too quick to discount what might be required to do that. It isn't always apparent beforehand. It isn't always possible to anticipate what is needed."

Bek had the distinct impression that Walker was talking about something besides the phoenix stone. But it was clear from his words that he had no intention of saying what it was. By now, the boy was used to veiled references and hidden meanings from the Druid, so he felt no real urgency to pursue the matter. Walker would tell him when he was ready and not before.

"Ahren and I made a pact to stick together," he said instead. "So the phoenix stone won't be far away. I can get it back from him anytime I choose."

Walker straightened, a distant look in his dark eyes. "Time to be going, Bek. Whatever happens, remember what I said about the magic."

He called out sharply to those waiting and beckoned them to follow.

Redden Alt Mer brought up the anchors and eased the *Jerle Shannara* across the still waters of the bay to a broad stretch of open shoreline. Using rope ladders, the search party descended from the airship, seventeen-strong—Walker, Bek, Quentin Leah, Panax, Ryer Ord Star, Joad Rish, Ahren Elessedil, Ard Patrinell, and nine Elven Hunters. From there, they gathered up their weapons and supplies and stood together as the airship lifted off and sailed back along the channel that had brought her in. They watched until she was out of sight, then on Walker's command, they set out.

The Druid placed Ard Patrinell in charge, giving over to the Elf the responsibility for protecting the company. The Captain of the Home Guard sent a young woman named Tamis, a tracker, ahead some fifty yards to scout the way in and placed an Elven Hunter to either side to guard their flanks. The rest of the company he grouped by twos, placing Walker in the vanguard and Panax in the rear, with Elven Hunters warding them both. Quentin was given responsibility for the center of the formation and those who were not trained fighters, Joad Rish and Ryer Ord Star and Bek in particular.

Walker glanced at the boy from time to time as they proceeded, trying to take his measure, to judge how Bek felt about himself now that he knew so much more. It was difficult to do. Bek seemed to have adapted well enough to his increased responsibility for use of the magic of the wishsong and the Sword of Shannara. But Bek was a complex personality, not easily read, and it remained to be seen how he would react to the demands that his heritage might require of him down the road. As of now, he had only scratched the surface of what he could or would in all probability be asked to do. The boy simply didn't understand yet how enmeshed in all this he was and what that was likely to mean to him. Nor was there any easy or safe way to tell him.

Like it or not, Bek would grow increasingly difficult to manage. He was independent to begin with, but what control the Druid had maintained over him to date was mostly the result of what he knew that the boy didn't. Now that advantage was pretty much gone, and in the process Bek had grown distrustful of him. As matters stood, the boy was as likely to do what he felt like as what Walker suggested, and choices of that sort could prove fatal.

The Druid was reminded once again how far he had strayed

from his vow to avoid falling into a Druid's manipulative ways. He could not escape the fact that he was becoming more like Allanon with the passing of every day. All of his good intentions and promises had come to nothing. It was a sobering conclusion, and it induced a deep and profound sadness. He could argue that at least he was aware of his failings, but what good was that if he was unable to correct them? He could justify everything and still feel as if he had betrayed himself utterly.

The company pressed deeper into the woods, climbing from the bay's coastline into the surrounding hills, burrowing deeper into the sun-speckled shadows and thickening woods. The ground was rough and uneven, crisscrossed by ravines and gullies, blocked entirely in places by deadfall and heavy brush. A handful of times they found their way blocked by cuts too deep and wide to cross. Twice they encountered clumps of trees that appeared to have been dropped by a storm, twisted masses of deadwood that ran for a quarter of a mile. Each time they had to back away from one approach and try another. Each time they were forced to change direction, and with each change it grew increasingly difficult to determine exactly where they were.

Walker carried a compass he had borrowed from Redden Alt Mer, but even so it was impossible to maintain a straight line of approach. The best the Druid could manage was to plot a course from where they had come, which was of dubious value. But the day stayed bright and warm, the sun a cheerful presence in the blue sky, and the sounds of birdsong comforting and reassuring. Nothing threatened from the shadows. Nothing dangerous appeared or gave sign of its presence. Nothing appeared out of the ordinary in a forested wilderness that could easily have been their own.

Even so, Walker was wary. Despite appearances, he knew what waited for them somewhere along the way. He would have preferred to have Truls Rohk foraging ahead to ward their approach, but there was no help for that. The Elven

Hunters would have to do. They were well trained and able, but no one was as good at staying hidden as the shape-shifter. He wondered where the other was, if he had escaped detection aboard the airship of the Ilse Witch, if he was accomplishing something important. He shook his head at the thought. Whatever Truls was doing, it couldn't be as important as what he could be doing here.

Morning came and went, and still they trekked on through the forest without finding anything. The castaway's map had brought them to the bay and pointed them inland and that was as much direction as they were going to get. On the map, a dotted line led to an X that said Castledown. There was no explanation of what Castledown was. There was no description of how they might recognize it. Walker had to assume that its identity would be self-evident when they came across it. It wasn't the biggest assumption he had made in this business by any means, so he wasn't uncomfortable following it.

It was late in the afternoon when his faith was rewarded. They topped a steep rise through a heavily wooded draw and discovered all three Elven scouts clustered together waiting for them. Her pixie face solemn and expectant, Tamis pointed ahead.

It was hardly necessary for her to do so. The hillside before them fell away into a broad, deep valley that easily ran ten miles from end to end and another five across. Trees carpeted the slopes and ridges, a soft green ring in the afternoon sunlight. But across the entire valley floor, all ten miles wide and five miles deep of it, sprawled the ruins of a city. Not a city from the present, Walker realized at once. Even from where they stood, still a half mile away, that much was apparent. The buildings were low and flat, not tall like those of Eldwist had been in the land of the Stone King. Some were damaged, their surfaces cracked and broken, their edges ragged and sharp. Holes opened through walls to reveal twisted, burned-out interiors. Debris lay scattered everywhere, some of it rusted and pitted by weather, some of it overgrown with lichen and moss. There was a uniformity to the ruins that indicated clearly that no one had lived here for a very long time.

But what struck the Druid immediately about the city, even more so than its immense size, was that virtually everything was made of metal. Walls, roofs, and floors all gleamed with patches of metallic brightness. Even bits and pieces of the streets and passageways reflected the sun. As far as the eye could see, the ruins were composed of sheets and slabs and struts of metal. Scrub grasses and brush had fought their way up through gaps in the fittings like pods of sea life breaching in an open sea. Isolated groves of trees grew in tangled thickets that might have been parks, carefully tended once perhaps, gone wild now. Even in its present state, crumbling and deteriorated since the Great Wars had reduced it to an abandoned wreck, the nature of its once sleek, smooth condition was evident.

"Shades!" Panax hissed at his elbow, thinking perhaps of the ruins his people had once mined in the aftermath of the holocaust.

Walker nodded to himself. The ruins of Castledown were gigantic. He had never imagined something of this size could exist. How many people had there been in the world if this was an example of the massiveness of their cities? He knew from the Druid histories that the number had been large, much larger than now. But there had been thousands of cities then, not hundreds. How many of them had been this huge? Walker found himself suddenly overwhelmed by the images, the numbers, and the possibilities. He wondered exactly what it was they were going to find. For the first time, he found himself wondering if they were up to it.

Then it struck him suddenly that perhaps he had made an incorrect assumption. The more he stared at the ruins, the more unlikely it seemed that it had been built to house people. The look of the buildings was all wrong. Low and wide and flat, vast spaces with high windows and broad entrances, sprawling foundations with no personal spaces, they seemed better suited for something else. For warehousing, perhaps. For factories and construction yards.

For housing machines.

He glanced at those around him. All looked awestruck, staring at the city as if trying to comprehend its purpose, as if working to make it seem real. Then he noticed Ryer Ord Star. She stood apart from the others as she always did, but she was shaking, her eyes cast down and her fingers knotted tightly in the folds of her clothing. Her breath came in short, ragged gasps, and she was crying soundlessly. Walker moved next to her, placed his arm on her shoulders, and drew her slender body close.

"What's wrong?" he asked softly.

She glanced up at him momentarily, then shook her head and melted against him once more, burying her face in his robes. He held her quietly until she stilled—it took a few minutes, no more—then stepped away from her and ordered Ard Patrinell to move out.

They descended the valley slope to its floor, stopping in a wooded clearing a hundred yards back from the edge of the ruins to make camp for the night. By now the sun was brushing the valley rim west and would be down in another hour. It was too late to attempt any exploration of the city today. Walker felt confident that they had located Castledown and that what they had come to find was hidden somewhere within. How difficult it would be to uncover what he sought remained to be seen, but he preferred that their first foray be undertaken in daylight.

Alone, while the others set camp and prepared dinner, he walked to the edge of the city. He stood there in the waning light staring into the shadowed ruins, down long, broad avenues, through gaps in the metal walls, along rooflines long since reshaped by time and the ravages of a conflict he was grateful he had not been alive to see. The races of the present thought of a Druid's magic as powerful, but real power was unknown to them. Real power was born of science. He found himself wondering what it might have been like to live in those distant times, before the Old World was destroyed. How would it have felt to have power that could destroy entire cities? What sort of havoc would it play with your soul to be able to snuff out thousands of lives at a touch? It made him shiver to imagine it. It made him feel frightened and sick inside.

Perhaps that was what Ryer Ord Star was feeling. Perhaps that was why she cried.

Thinking of her triggered a memory of her vision of the islands and their protectors. It was what she had said after speaking of the keys that surfaced unexpectedly in his thoughts. He had almost forgotten it, dismissed it out of hand as obvious. *I see this in a haze of shadow that tracks you everywhere and seeks to place itself about you like a shroud.* He had believed her words referred to the Ilse Witch and her relentless pursuit of him.

But looking into the ruins of Castledown and feeling the presence of the thing that waited there like an itch against his skin, he knew he had been mistaken.

THIRTY

Morning arrived in a haze of mist and light rain. Crowded together in leaden skies, dark clouds hid the sun and foreshadowed a gloomy day. The air was windless and warm and smelled of damp earth and new leaves. Silence wrapped the world in a veil of hushed expectancy and whispered caution, and even the small comfort of yesterday's birdsong had disappeared.

In the valley's pale brume, the ruins of Castledown hunkered down in glistening, sharp-edged relief, dark metallic surfaces streaked bright green by rain-dampened lichen and moss.

Walker divided the search party into three groups. Ard Patrinell would take Ahren Elessedil, Joad Rish, and three of the nine Elven Hunters on the right flank. Quentin Leah and Panax would take another three Elven Hunters on the left. He would occupy the center with Bek, Ryer Ord Star, and the remaining three Hunters. They would enter the ruins with the center group slightly ahead of the other two, all of them spread out but in sight of one another. They would move directly through the city to its far side and then reverse their march displaced by the width of the search party. They would do this for as many times as it took to complete a sweep of the city, changing their route each time. Anything that appeared worth investigating would be given a look. If they failed to turn up what they were looking for today, they would resume their search on the morrow. It was a huge city. Even if they were quick and encountered no difficulties, it could take them more than a week.

Everyone was to stay quiet and listen carefully, he cautioned. There would be no talking. They were to watch out for one another and keep one eye on the leader of their group, taking directions from him. If something required a look, signal by hand or whistle. Stay low and use the buildings for cover. There was every reason to believe that an enemy who was on watch for intruders had laid traps throughout the city. What they had come to find would be carefully guarded.

"Which is what exactly?" Panax asked, an uneasy look in his eyes. Like the others, he was wrapped against the weather in a cloak and hood. In the misted gloom, they looked like wraiths. "What is it we've come to find, Walker?"

The Druid hesitated.

"We've come a long way not to be told now," the Dwarf pressed. Rain ran down his seamed face into his beard. "How are we supposed to find what we're looking for if we don't know what it is?"

A moment's silence followed. "Books," Walker answered softly. The silence returned and lengthened. "Of spells and magic," he added with a quick glance around. "Gathered during the time of the Old World, then lost in the Great Wars. Except that some of those spells and that magic may have been saved. Here, in Castledown. That's the treasure the map says is hidden here."

"Books," the Dwarf muttered in disbelief.

"They will be of immense value to the races, if we find them," Walker assured him. "More so than you can imagine. More so than anything else we might have set out to find. But your skepticism is not unwarranted. As far as we know, no books survived the Great Wars. They would have been one of the first things destroyed, if not by fire, then by time and weather. The writings of the Old World were lost two thousand years ago, and only our oral storytelling traditions have preserved the information they contained. Even that small knowledge was diluted and changed over time, so that much of it was rendered useless. What books we have now were assembled by the Druids during the First and Second Councils at Paranor. The Elves have some at Arborlon and the Federation some in Arishaig, but most are kept in the Druid's Keep. But they are books of this world and not the old. So if there are books here that have survived, they will have been sealed away. That they are books may not be immediately apparent. Their form may have been changed."

"If the books are numerous and have retained their original look, it will take a large building to house them," Bek offered quietly.

Walker nodded. "We begin our search with that in mind. We search for anything that might serve as a safehold, a container, or a storehouse. We might not know it when we see it. We will have to be open-minded. Remember, too, that we've come here to discover what became of Kael Elessedil's expedition and the Elfstones he carried with him."

No one said anything. After a moment, Quentin adjusted the Sword of Leah where it was strapped across his back and glanced at the sky. "Looks like the rain's letting up," he advised to no one in particular.

"Let's get on with it," Panax added with a grunt.

They set out then, crossing the open ground between the forested valley slope and the ruins, a line of dark ghosts approaching through the haze. They entered the city in three loosely knit groups set about fifty yards apart. They moved swiftly at first, finding mostly rubble amid the shells of smaller buildings that contained machines and apparatuses that sat rusted and dead. They had no idea what they were looking at for the most part, although some of the equipment had the look of weapons. A thick layer of dust had settled over everything, and there was no indication that anyone had come this way recently. Nothing had been disturbed or changed with the passing of the years. Everything was frozen in time.

Walker was aware of Ryer Ord Star pressing close to him, enough so that they were almost touching. Last night, when the others were asleep, she had come to him and told him what had frightened her so. In the hushed darkness of a moonless night, she had knelt beside him and whispered in a voice so soft that he could barely make her out.

"The ruins are the maze I saw in my vision."

He touched her thin shoulder. "Are you certain?"

Her eyes were bright and staring. "I felt the presence of the other two, as well. As I stood on the rim of the valley and looked down into the maze, I felt them. The ribbons of fire and the metal dogs. They are here, waiting for me. For all of us."

"Then we will be ready for them." She was shaking again, and he put his arm about her to keep her from her fear, which he could feel through her clothing as if it were alive. "Don't be afraid, Ryer. Your warnings keep us safe. They did so on Flay Creech, on Shatterstone, and on Mephitic. They will do so here."

But she shrank from the words. "No, Walker. What waits for us here is much bigger and stronger. It is embedded in the ruins and in the earth on which they rest. Old and hungry and evil, it waits for us. I can feel it breathing. I feel its pulse in the movement of the air and the rise and fall of the temperature. It is too much for us. Too much."

He held her quietly in the velvet darkness, trying to comfort her, listening to the sound of her breathing as it steadied and slowed. Finally, she rose and began to move away.

"I will die here, Walker," she whispered back to him.

She believed it, he knew, and perhaps she had seen something in her visions that gave her cause to do so. Perhaps she only sensed it might be so, but sometimes even that was enough to make something happen. He would watch out for her, would try to keep her from harm. It was what he would have done anyway. It was what he would do for all of them, if it was within his power. But even a Druid could do no more than try.

He glanced over his shoulder. She had dropped back to walk with Bek, keeping pace with the boy, as if finding some comfort in his silent presence. Fair enough. She could do worse than stay close to him.

He looked ahead into the gloom, into the maze of the ruins, and he could feel the seer's vision, mysterious and dark, drawing them on like bait on a hook.

Miles away, back toward the channel's headwaters, but well clear of the Squirm, Redden Alt Mer stood at the bow railing of the *Jerle Shannara* and looked off into the gloom. The weather was impossible. If anything, it was worse now than when they had sailed inland two days ago. Yesterday had started out fine, but the sunshine and clear skies had gradually given way to heavy mist and clouds on the journey downriver. They had anchored the airship several miles from the ice, safely back from the clashing pillars and the bitter cold, and had gone to sleep, hoping to continue on this morning as Walker had wanted.

But the haze was so thick now that Alt Mer could barely make out the cliffs to either side and could not see the sky overhead at all. Worse, the mist was shifting in a steady wind, swirling so badly that it cast shadows everywhere and rendered it virtually impossible to navigate safely. In these narrow confines, with treacherous peaks, glaciers, and winds all around, it would be foolhardy to attempt to venture out of the channel when they could not see where they were going. Like it or not, they would have to wait for the weather to clear, even if it meant delaying their departure a day or two.

Rue Meridian came up beside him, long red hair as darkened by the damp as his own. It wasn't raining, but a fine mist settled over them like gauze. She looked out over the railing at the fog and shook her head. "Soup."

"Soup that Mother Nature feels a need to stir," he amended

with a weary sigh. "All for the purpose of keeping us locked down for the foreseeable future, I expect."

"We could sail back up the channel and hope for a break in the clouds. Inland, it might be better."

He nodded. "It might, but the farther back up the channel we go, the harder it becomes to track our course. Better to do it from as close to the coastline as possible."

She snorted. "Have you forgotten who you have as your navigator?"

"Not likely. Anyway, a day of waiting won't hurt us. We'll lie to until tomorrow. If it doesn't clear up by then, we'll do as you say and sail back up the channel and try to find a cloud break."

Her eyes found his momentarily. "No one much cares for this sitting around, Big Red." She glanced off into the haze. "If you listen closely, you can hear those pillars clashing. You can hear the ice crack and the glaciers shift. Far away, off in the haze." She shook her head. "It's spooky."

"Don't listen, then."

She stood with him a moment longer, then moved off. He didn't care for the waiting either or their proximity to the Squirm or anything about their situation, but he knew better than to overreact. He would be patient if he must.

After a few minutes, he walked back to where Spanner Frew sat working on a diapson crystal that had been damaged in their collision with *Black Moclips*. The Rover Captain was still perplexed at the appearance of the ship. In all likelihood it meant she was being sailed by a Federation crew. That gave Alt Mer a distinct advantage with his Rover crew, but not one he was eager to test. *Black Moclips* was much bigger and stronger than the *Jerle Shannara*, and in close quarters could probably reduce it to kindling. It would be strange in any case to do battle with a ship he had flown for so long and of which he had grown so fond.

"Making any progress?" he asked the shipwright.

The big man scowled. "I'd make more if people didn't distract me with foolish questions. This is delicate work."

Alt Mer watched him for a moment. "Did you get a good look at that other airship when she rammed us?"

"As good as your own."

"Did you recognize her?"

"*Black Moclips*. Hard to mistake her. Doesn't give me a good feeling to know she's the one chasing us, but on the other hand this ship's quicker and more responsive." He paused to hold the crystal up to the pale light, squinting as he examined it. "Just keep her from getting too close to us, and we'll be fine."

The Rover Captain folded his arms within his cloak. "Can't be sure of doing anything on a hunt like this. We may have to stand and face her at some point. I don't relish that happening, I can tell you."

Spanner Frew stood up, gave the crystal a final check, then grunted in satisfaction. "Won't be a problem today, at least. Nothing can sail in this."

"Not safely, anyway," Alt Mer amended. He resumed staring out into the gloom. The wind had picked up, and the airship was rocking with its sudden gusts. The Rover Captain walked slowly across the deck, checking things in a perfunctory manner, giving himself something to do besides think about their predicament. A low whistle had begun to develop, faint and distant still, but unmistakable. He glanced in its direction, back toward the Squirm. Maybe he should move the *Jerle Shannara* farther upriver. Maybe they should find a cove in which to take shelter.

He walked the aft railing, the sound of the wind enveloping him like a shroud, strangely warm and comforting. He stopped to listen to it, amazed at its appeal. Winds of this sort were rare in a sailor's life and as out of place to this land as yesterday's weather. They belonged in another climate and another part of the world. How could glaciers and snowpacks exist in such close proximity to warm air and green trees?

His thoughts drifted, and he found himself remembering his childhood in March Brume, days he had spent on land, wandering the forests, playing with other children. Those days had been few and passed swiftly, but their memory lingered. Perhaps it was because he had spent so much of his life on the sea and in the air. Perhaps it was because he could never have them back again.

Something moved in the mist, but staring blankly at its darkening form, he could not seem to put a name to it.

To one side, a Rover slid to the decking and lay there, silent and unmoving, asleep. Redden Alt Mer stared in disbelief, then pushed away from the railing to go to him. But his legs wouldn't work, and his eyes were so heavy he could barely keep them open. All he could seem to focus on was the sound of the wind, risen to a new pitch, wrapping him about, closing him away.

Too late, he realized what was happening.

He staggered a few steps and fell to his knees. On the decks of the airship, the Rovers lay in heaps. Only Furl Hawken was still upright in the pilot box, if barely so, hanging on to the handgrips, draped over the controls.

A huge, dark shape had come alongside the *Jerle Shannara*. Redden Alt Mer heard the sound of grappling hooks locking in place and caught a glimpse of a cloaked form approaching through the mist. A face lifted out of the shadows of a hood, a young woman who looked at him with blue eyes that were as cold as glacier ice. Helpless, he stared back at her with undisguised fury.

Then everything went black.

Bek glanced over at the strained, frightened face of Ryer Ord Star and smiled reassuringly as they moved with the others of the company through the deepening gloom. The rain had turned to a fine mist. The seer blinked against the droplets that gathered on her eyelids, and brushed at her face with her sleeve. She moved closer to Bek.

The boy peered left and right to where the groups led by Quentin and Ard Patrinell navigated the misted ruins. He caught a glimpse of his cousin and the Captain of the Home Guard, but found no sign of Ahren Elessedil. The buildings were growing larger now and took longer to get around. At times the searchers were separated by walls fifty feet high and would catch only momentary glimpses of one another through sagging doors and burned-out entries. The buildings were all the same, either empty or full of rusted machinery. In some, banks of casings sat in long rows, studded with dials and tiny windows that resembled the blank, staring eyes of dead animals. In some, machines so large they dwarfed the searchers hunkered down like great beasts fallen into endless slumber. Shadows filled the open spaces, layering machines and debris alike, stretching from one building to the next, a dark spiderweb tangled through the city.

He looked again for Ahren, but everyone in the Elven Hunter group looked pretty much the same, hooded and cloaked against the damp. A sudden wave of fear and doubt washed over him. He forced his gaze back to Walker, who was striding just ahead. He was being stupid. It was probably the look on Ryer Ord Star's face that infused him with such uneasiness. It was probably the day, so dark and misted. It was probably this place, this city.

In the silence and gloom, you could imagine anything.

He thought about the books that Walker had come to find and was troubled anew. What would the people of the Old World be doing with books of spells? No real magic had been practiced in that time. Magic had died out with the Faerie world, and even the Elves, who had survived when so many other species had perished, had lost or forgotten virtually all of theirs. It was only with the emergence of the new Races and the convening of the Druids at Paranor that the process of recovering the magic had begun. Why would Walker believe that books of magic from before the Great Wars even existed?

The more he worried over the matter, the more obsessed

with it he became. Soon he found himself wondering about
the creature that had lured them here. Ostensibly to steal their
magic, it seemed—yet if it already had books of magic at
its disposal, why not use these? Surely they were written
in a language it could understand. What was it about the
magic that Walker and Quentin and he possessed that was so
much more attractive? What was it that had doomed Kael
Elessedil's expedition thirty years earlier? He could repeat everything that Walker had told him, had told them all,
and still not get past this gaping hole of logic in the Druid's
explanation.

They passed through a cluster of large empty warehouses
into a section of low, flat platforms that might have been
buildings or something else entirely. Windowless and sealed
all about, they appeared to lack any purpose. Pitted with rust
and streaked with patches of moss and lichen, they shimmered in the rain like huge ruined mirrors. Walker took a moment to study one, placing his hands on its surface, closing
his eyes in concentration. After a moment he stepped away,
shook his head at the others, and motioned for them to continue on.

The platform buildings disappeared behind them in the
mist. Ahead, a broad metal-carpeted clearing that was studded
with odd-shaped walls and partitions materialized out of the
gloom. The clearing stretched away for hundreds of yards in
all directions, and dominated the surrounding buildings by
virtue of its size alone. The walls and partitions ranged in
height from five to ten feet and ran in length anywhere from
twenty to thirty more. They were unconnected to each other,
seemingly placed at random, seemingly constructed without
purpose. They did not form rooms. They did not contain fur-
niture or even machinery. Here, unlike the surrounding warehouses, there was no rubble. Or plants, grasses, and scrub.
Everything was swept clean and smooth.

At the center of the square, barely visible through the
gloom, an obelisk rose more than a hundred feet. A single

door opened into it, massive and recessed, but the door was sealed. Above this entryway, a red light blinked on and off in steady sequence.

Walker brought them to a halt with a hand signal and stood staring into the tangle of half walls and partitions to where the obelisk sat like a watchtower, its blinking light a vigilant eye. Bek searched the ruins about them, his uneasiness newly heightened. Nothing moved. He turned back to Walker. The Druid was still studying the obelisk. It was clear that he sensed the possibility of a trap, but equally clear that he believed he must step into it.

Ryer Ord Star bent close to Bek. "It is the entrance we seek," she whispered. Her breathing was quick and anxious. "The door to the tower opens into Castledown. The keys he carries fit the door's lock."

Bek stared at her, wondering how she knew this, but she was staring at the Druid, the boy already forgotten.

Walker turned. His eyes were troubled and his face bore a resigned look. "Wait here for me." His voice was so low that Bek could barely hear him. He gestured at the Elven Hunters. "All of you."

He straightened and signaled to Quentin and Panax on his left and Ard Patrinell on his right to remain where they were.

Alone, he started toward the tower.

The Ilse Witch walked the deck of the *Jerle Shannara*, making certain all of the Rovers were asleep. One by one, she checked them, then signaled for Cree Bega to come aboard and ordered him to send one of his Mwellrets below to search for anyone she might have missed. The chosen ret disappeared down the hatchway and returned again in only moments, shaking his head.

She nodded, satisfied. It had been easier than she had thought. "Take them below and lock them in the storerooms," she ordered, dismissing Cree Bega with a gesture. "Separate them."

She walked to the pilot box and climbed up to stand next to the big Rover slumped over the controls. She stood in the box and stared out over the length and breadth of the captured airship, taking in its look and feel. A sleek and able vessel, she saw. Quicker and more maneuverable than her own. Mwellrets were swarming over the sides of *Black Moclips* to haul the sleeping Rovers belowdecks. She watched them without interest. The magic of her wishsong had overcome the Rovers before they knew what was happening. Not expecting it or able to fight it and without the Druid to ward them, they had been powerless. Her spy had provided her with a link to the *Jerle Shannara* from the beginning, and it was easy enough to get close once she was through the Squirm. Using the wishsong to put the unsuspecting crew to sleep was child's play. Transforming her magic to sound like the wind, soft and lulling and irresistible, was all it took.

Even getting past the ice pillars was not much of a challenge, although it required a little inventiveness. Choosing to avoid that approach completely, she used her magic to harness one of the Shrikes that nested on the outer cliffs, mounted it, and had it fly them over the top. Even with the heavy fog, she was able to guide *Black Moclips* without too much risk. The Shrike was a native and knew its way in and out of the mountains well. The winds were tricky, but not so much so that the airship couldn't manage them. She had no idea how Walker had managed to navigate the pillars, believing his own magic, while powerful in some ways, not sufficiently adaptable for this. Her spy hadn't been able to communicate that information. Not that it mattered. Both of them had made it through. They were still on course for their confrontation.

Except that now, for the first time, she had the upper hand. He was ashore and marooned there, even if he didn't realize it yet. Without the use of an airship, he was helpless to escape her. Sooner or later, she would track him down, either on foot

or from the air. The only question that remained to be answered was whether she would get to him before the thing
that waited in the ruins did.

Even in this, she had an advantage the Druid did not. She
knew what the thing was. Or more to the point, what it wasn't.
She had gone inside Kael Elessedil's ruined mind to discover
why he had been lost for thirty years. By doing so, she had
seen through his eyes what it was that had captured him. She
had witnessed the tearing out of his tongue and the gouging
out of his eyes. She had witnessed the uses to which he had
been put. Walker knew none of this. If he wasn't careful, he
might come to the same end. That would achieve her goal of
destroying him, but cheat her of the personal satisfaction she
would derive by seeing him die at her hands.

Yes, Walker would have to be very careful. The thing that
had lured them here was patient and its reach was long. It was
dangerous in ways she had not encountered before. So she
would have to be careful, too. But she was always careful, always on guard against the unexpected. She had trained herself to be so.

Cree Bega sidled up to her. "The little peopless are all
ssafely locked away," he hissed.

"Leave five of your rets to make sure they stay that way,"
she ordered. "Commander Kett will assign two of his crew to
watch over the ship. The rest of us will take the *Black Moclips*
after those already ashore."

I'm coming for you, Druid, she thought triumphantly. *Can
you feel me getting close?*

She climbed down from the pilot box, wrapped in grim
fury and fierce determination, and walked back through the
mist and gloom.

When the attack came, Walker was a little more than halfway between the others of the company and the obelisk, deep
inside the maze of half walls and partitions. He heard a sharp
click, like a lock opening or a trigger released, and he threw

himself down just as a slender thread of brilliant red fire
lanced overhead. Without even thinking, he turned the Druid
fire on its source and fused the tiny aperture through which
the thread had appeared.

Instantly, a dozen more threads crisscrossed the area in
which he lay, some of them burning paths across the metal
carpet, seeking him out. He rolled quickly into the shelter of a
wall and burned shut one opening after another, snuffing out
the threads, exploding apertures and entire sections of wall,
filling the hazy air with smoke and the acrid stench of
scorched metal.

Then he was on his feet and moving swiftly toward the
obelisk, sensing that whatever controlled the fire could be
found there. His robes hindered his progress, prevented him
from running, and kept him to a quick shuffle. *Ribbons of fire.*
He repeated the words as he angled his way through the
maze, ducking behind walls and through openings as the
slender threads sought him out, Ryer Ord Star's vision come
to life.

He had gotten maybe twenty yards deeper into the maze
when the walls began to move. Without warning, they started
to raise and lower, a shifting mass of metal that cut off some
approaches and opened others, whole sections materializing out of the smooth, polished floor while others disappeared. It was so disorienting and unexpected that he slowed
momentarily, and the ribbons of fire began to close on him
once more, new ones stabbing out from sections of wall
closer to where he hesitated, old ones shifting to target him.
In desperation, he threw a wide band of his own fire back at
them, knocking some askew, destroying others. He heard
shouts behind him, rising from behind a screen of smoke and
mist, from out of a well of emptiness and darkness.

"Don't come in here!" he shouted in warning, hearing the
echoes cried of his voice come back at him.

Fire lances burned in faint glimmerings through the haze,
penetrating the darkness with killing quickness. Screams

rose, and he felt his heart sink at the realization that at least some of those he led had not heard him. He started back for them, but the walls shifted anew, the fire threads barred his path, and he was forced to back away.

Get to the obelisk! he screamed at himself in the silence of his mind.

Heat radiated through his body as he turned and hurried ahead once more, sweat mingling with beads of mist on his taut face. Something moved to one side, and he caught the sound of skittering, of metal scraping metal. Fire exploded next to him, barely missing his head, and he ducked and moved faster, twisting and turning through the shifting walls, the changing maze, losing track of everything but the need to reach the obelisk. He felt a stickiness on his hand, and glanced down to find his fingers red with his blood. A fire lance had opened a gash in his arm just above his wrist.

Ignoring the wound, he glanced up to find the obelisk directly in front of him. Impulsively, he darted out from behind the wall that had sheltered him right into the path of a creeper.

For a second he was so stunned he just stopped where he was and stared, his mind a jumble of confusion. What was a creeper doing here? Wait, it wasn't a creeper at all, it just looked like one. It was spidery like a creeper, had a creeper's legs and body, but it was all metal with no fusing of flesh, no melding of animate and inanimate, of matter and material . . .

There was no more time for speculation. It reached for him, pincers extending at the end of flexible limbs, and he thrust out his arm in a warding motion and sent the Druid fire flying into it. The creeper was rocked backwards on its spindly legs and then toppled. It lay writhing, no longer able to rise, thrashing as it melted and burned. Walker raced past. It was constructed entirely of metal, just as he'd thought. He caught a glimpse of another, then two more, three, four; they were all around, coming toward him.

Metal dogs!

All of the components of Ryer Ord Star's vision had come

together—the maze, the ribbons of fire, and the metal dogs—
pieces of a nightmare that would consume them if he couldn't
find a way to stop it. He sidestepped another fire lance,
dashed across an opening between several shifting walls, and
leapt onto the threshold of the doorway to the obelisk.

Behind him, there was chaos. He could hear shouts and
screams, the rasp of metal on metal, the steady hiss of fire
threads, and the boom of explosions. He could see the distinctive flash of Quentin Leah's blade. He could smell the
magic and taste the smoke. The entire company was under attack, and he was doing nothing to help them.

Quickly! Get into the tower!

He spied the slots for the keys in a raised metal surface
to one side of the door. Swiftly he produced the keys from
his robes and inserted them into the thin, flat openings. The
keys slid into place easily, a bank of lights flashed in the
black metal surface of the wall, and the door eased aside to
give him entry. He stepped through quickly, the sounds of the
pursuing creepers spurring him on, and the door closed behind him.

He stood blinded by the blackness for a moment and
waited for his vision to return. He saw the lights first, some
steady and unchanging, some blinking on and off, some
green, some red, some yellow. There were hundreds of them,
ahead somewhere, tiny beacons glowing in the dark. When he
could make out the surfaces of floor and walls and ceiling
sufficiently to find his way, he started toward them. The controls to the fire threads and the creepers would be there. This
was a kingdom of machines, and the machines in this tower
would control the machines in the maze. Shut down the one,
and you shut down the others.

It was his last thought before the floor opened beneath him,
and he tumbled away into space.

THIRTY-ONE

Rue Meridian woke when her head banged against the wall of the storeroom in the forward hold. She tried to roll away and found herself pinned to the floor by a heavy weight. The weight turned out to be Furl Hawken, who was still unconscious, his bulk sprawled across her torso. She could hear the wind howling like a scorched cat and feel the pitch and roll of the ship. A storm was in progress, and a bad one at that. With every fresh gust and new jolt she was thrown headfirst back toward the offending wall.

Squirming and wriggling, she worked herself free of Hawk and pushed herself into a sitting position, her back to the bulkhead. For a moment she couldn't remember what had happened, then couldn't figure out how. What was she doing down here, belowdecks? She had been working with another Rover on setting a fresh radian draw, tightening it down, when that wind had come up, soft and lulling, singing to her like her mother once had.

And put her to sleep, she thought ruefully, beginning to see exactly what had happened.

She climbed to her feet and staggered across the room through the lurching of the ship to the door. She tried the handle. Locked. No surprise there. She grimaced and exhaled sharply. The Rovers were all prisoners or dead, overpowered in all likelihood by the Ilse Witch. Somehow she had gotten to them when they weren't expecting it, put them to sleep, and locked them below. Or worse, it wasn't the Ilse Witch at all, but the thing that Walker had gone inland to find. Or was it worse, the one rather than the other? She rubbed her head where it had banged against the wall, wondering how many jolts it had taken to wake her. Too many, she decided, feeling an ache work its way through her skull and down into her neck.

She glanced around the room. It was empty except for Hawk and herself. The others were somewhere else. There were crates of supplies stacked against the walls, but they contained light sheaths, radian draws, parse tubes, ropes, and the like. No heavy clubs or axes. No sharp objects or keen blades to rely on. No weapons of any kind.

She looked down hopefully for her sword and throwing knives, even though she knew her weapons belt was gone. She reached into her boot. The dagger she hid there was gone, as well. Whoever put her here was smart enough to search her before locking her in. Hawk's weapons would have been taken, too. Escaping confinement was not going to be easy.

But it would, of course, be possible.

Little Red never once stopped to think otherwise. It wasn't in her nature to do so. She did not panic and she did not despair. She was a Rover, and she had been taught from a very early age that Rovers had to look out for themselves, that no one else was going to do it for them. She was locked in the hold of her own ship, and it was up to her to get free. She already knew she was going to do that. Someone had made a big mistake in assuming she wasn't. Someone was going to pay for putting her here.

A sudden violent pitch of the airship sent her staggering to one side, and she was barely able to keep her feet while righting herself. Something bad was happening topside, and she had to get up there quickly to find out what it was. It didn't feel as if the people who had locked her in had any idea what they were doing with the ship. If there was a storm in progress, it would take accomplished sailors to see the *Jerle Shannara* safely through. She thought briefly of the Squirm's grinding pillars, of the sheer cliffs surrounding them, and of their proximity to both, and she felt a tug of concern deep in her stomach.

She worked her way over to Furl Hawken and began to shake him. "Wake up, Hawk!" She kept her voice low enough that anyone standing outside the door wouldn't hear. Not that there was much chance with the storm howling all about them. "Hawk!" She slapped his face. "Wake up!"

His eyes fluttered and he grunted like a bull. Slowly he rolled onto his side, clasping his head, muttering to himself. Then he sat up, running his big hands through his tangled blond hair and beard. "What hit me? I can feel it all the way down to my teeth!"

The airship did a quick pitch and roll, causing him to brace himself hurriedly with his hands. "Shades!"

"Get up," she ordered, pulling at him. "We've been drugged and locked up, and the ship's in the hands of incompetents. Let's do something about it."

He lumbered to his feet, steadying himself by leaning on her shoulder as the ship shook with the force of the wind. "Where's Big Red?"

"Can't say for sure. He's not here, anyway." She hadn't allowed herself to think what might have happened to her brother. Locked in another storeroom, probably aft of this one, she told herself. They'd probably been separated to render them more manageable. Alive, though. She wouldn't consider the alternative.

She moved back over to the door and stood with her ear pressed against the wood, listening. All she could hear was the howl of the wind, the singing of the draws, and the rattle of something not properly tied down. She sat with her back to the wall and pulled off her boot. Inside the heel, tucked into the leather, was a metal hook.

"I see they didn't get quite everything," Hawk chuckled, coming over to stand next to her.

She pulled on her boot and stood up. "Did they miss anything you were carrying?" she asked.

He reached under his left arm, found a small opening in the seam of his stiff leather vest, and removed a long, slender blade. "Could be." He grinned. "Enough to get us close to some real weapons, if we're lucky."

"We're Rovers, Hawk," she said, bending to the lock in the door. "We make our own luck."

Kneeling with one leg braced against the door, she inserted the pick into the lock and began to work it around. The lock was new and its workings easily tapped. It gave in less than a minute, the latch snapping open as she pulled down on the handle, the door giving way. She cracked it and looked out into the passageway. Shadows cast by oil lamps and ropes hung from pegs in the walls flickered and danced with the rolling of the ship. At the passageway's forward end, a bulky form braced against the shipwalls and stared up the ladder at the hatchway.

Rue Meridian ducked back inside the storeroom and eased the door closed again. "One guard, a big guy. I can't tell who or what he is. We have to get past him, though. Do you want to handle him or shall I?"

Furl Hawken tightened his grip on the knife. "I'll deal with him, Little Red. You get to the others."

They stared at each other in the dim light, breathing quickly, faces flushed and anxious. "Be careful, Hawk," she told him.

They went out the door on cat's paws, sliding silently into the shadowed hallway. Furl Hawken glanced back at her, then started toward the guard. The *Jerle Shannara* continued to shake and sway in the grip of the storm, the wind howling so fiercely that the guard seemed unable to think of anything else. A crash jarred the decking, something falling from a height, a loosened spar probably. The guard stared upward, frozen in place. Rue Meridian glanced at the doors of the storerooms closest, two only. The smaller held their water and ale in large casks. There was no extra room for prisoners in there. The other contained foodstuffs. That was a possibility, but the larger holds lay farther aft.

Another few steps, Rue Meridian was thinking, watching Hawk's cautious progress, when the hatchway opened, and a rain-drenched figure started down the stairs.

He caught sight of the Rovers immediately, screamed a warning to the guard with his back turned, and bolted up the ladder. The guard wheeled at once toward Furl Hawken, a wicked-looking short sword in one clawed hand. Hawk closed with him at once, and Rue Meridian could hear the impact of their collision. She caught a glimpse of the guard's reptilian face, scaled and glistening with rain that had washed down the hatch. *A Mwellret!* The other man, by the look of his uniform, was a Federation soldier. She felt a cold sinking in the pit of her stomach. She and Hawk were no match for Mwellrets. She had to stop the fleeing soldier from giving warning to whatever others there were.

Impulsively, she went after him, leaping past Hawk and the Mwellret. Bounding up the ladder through the hatchway, she charged onto the open deck into the teeth of the storm, the wind whipping so wildly that it threatened to tear her clothes from her body, the rain drenching her in seconds. The ship wheeled and twisted in the storm's grip, its light sheaths down, its draws gathered in, stripped bare as she should be in this weather, but for some reason drifting in powerless confusion. Rue Meridian took in everything in a heartbeat as she raced after the soldier. She caught up with him amidships, just below the pilot box, where a second soldier struggled with the airship's steering, and she threw herself on his back. Locked together, they rolled across the deck and into the foremast. The soldier was so desperate to escape, he didn't even think to draw his weapons. She did so for him, yanking loose the long knife he wore at his belt and plunging it into his chest as he thrashed beneath her.

Leaving him sprawled out and dying on the deck, she

sprang back to her feet. The Federation soldier in the pilot box was screaming for help, but there was nothing she could do about that. If she killed him, the ship would be completely out of control. The wind was obscuring his cries, so perhaps no one would hear. She started aft. Without a safety line to tether her, she was forced to creep ahead, bent low to the deck, taking handholds wherever she could find them, slipping and sliding on the rain-soaked wood. Through clouds of mist and sheets of rain, she glimpsed the rugged gray walls of the channel's cliffs, rising through the mist. Somewhere not too distant, she could hear the pillars of the Squirm clash hungrily.

She came upon another of the Mwellrets almost immediately. It emerged from the gloom of the aft mast carrying a coil of rope. It was staggering and stumbling with the movements of the airship, but it threw down the rope, drew out a long knife, and came for her at once. She dodged away from it. The Mwellret was much stronger than she was; if it got hold of her, she would not get free unless she killed it, and she had no reason to expect she could manage that. But there was nowhere for her to go. She scrambled for the starboard railing, then turned to face it. It charged after her recklessly, and she waited for its momentum to carry it close, dropped into a crouch, and whipped her legs into its heavy boots, causing it to lose its balance. It staggered past her, fighting to stay upright against the pitch and roll of the ship, slammed into the railing, toppled over the side, and was gone.

That was easy, she thought giddily, suppressing a ridiculous urge to laugh. *Bring on another!*

She had just regained her feet when her wish was granted. Two more of the creatures appeared through the aft hatchway and started toward her.

Shades! She stood her ground in the swirl of wind and rain, trying desperately to think what to do. She had only her long knife, a poor weapon to keep two Mwellrets at bay under any circumstances. She edged along the railing, trying to gain some time, to think of a way to get past them and down the hatchway to where she believed Big Red and the others were imprisoned. But the Mwellrets had already guessed her intention and were spreading out to cut off any attempt she might make to get past them.

An instant later, a wild-eyed Furl Hawken emerged from the forward hatch, covered in blood and shouting like a madman. With a Mwellret's short sword in one hand and his dagger in the other, he charged bowlegged and crouched at Little Red's attackers. They turned instinctively to defend themselves, but they were too slow and too unsteady. The burly Rover slammed into the closest and sent it sprawling, then catapulted into the second, plunging his dagger into the cloaked body over and over while the Mwellret roared.

Rue Meridian broke at once for the hatchway. Hawk had bought her the precious seconds she needed. Leaping heedlessly across debris and through slicks, she gained the aft hatch—only to have yet another of the Mwellrets heave through the opening to greet her.

This time, she had no chance to escape. It was on top of her almost instantly, its broad sword swinging at her head. She slipped trying to avoid the blow and went down, flailing helplessly. But a sudden lurch of the airship saved her, and the Mwellret's blow went wide, the blade burying itself in the wood of the deck. She rolled to her feet as the Mwellret struggled to free its weapon, and slammed her long knife into its side. The Mwellret jerked away with a hiss, released its grip on the sword, and fastened its clawed hands about her neck. Down they went in a heap, and Rue Meridian could feel her head begin to swim. She tried to yank free the knife for another blow, but it was caught in the Mwellret's leather clothing. She kicked and struggled against the tightening hands, hammered at the muscular body with her fists, and fought like a trapped moor cat. Nothing worked to free her. Spots danced before her eyes, and her strength began to ebb.

She could feel the Mwellret's breath on her face and smell its stench.

Groping desperately for a weapon, she found the pick she had stuck in her pocket after she'd left the storeroom. Yanking it out, she jammed it into her attacker's hooded eye.

The Mwellret reared back in pain and surprise, releasing its grip on her throat. She twisted clear instantly, scrambling away as her adversary thrashed about on the decking, its hands clawing at its bloodied eye. Using both hands and what remained of her fading strength, she worked free the Mwellret's embedded sword and jammed it all the way through the writhing body.

Drenched in blood and rain, tangled knots of her long red hair plastered against her face, she dropped to her knees, gasping for air. Rain beat down ferociously, the wind howled and gusted, and the airship twisted and lurched as if alive. Little Red felt the decking shudder and creak beneath her, as if everything was coming apart.

A booming crash brought her head up with a jerk. The lower aft spar had broken loose and fallen on top of the pilot box. The Federation soldier who had been struggling with the steering lay crushed and dying in a mass of splintered wood and bent metal. The *Jerle Shannara* was flying out of control.

Then she saw Furl Hawken. Almost buried by broken parts and debris, he lay atop one Mwellret and close beside another, bleeding from a dozen wounds, his face a mask of blood. A long knife was buried in his back and a dagger in his side. His short sword was still clutched in one hand. He was staring right at her, blue eyes open and fixed. He seemed to be looking past her to something she could not see.

She choked back a sob as tears filled her eyes and her throat tightened in a knot. *Hawk! No!* She pushed herself to her feet and started toward him, already knowing she was too late, but refusing to believe it. Staggering against the force of the wind and the lurching of the airship, she shook her head and began to cry, unable to help herself, unable to stop.

Then the Mwellret that lay next to the dead man turned slowly to face her. Blood streaked its reptilian face and cloaked body, and its eyes were dazed and furious. Lurching to its feet, it yanked the long knife from Hawk's back and started toward her.

She retreated slowly, realizing she had no weapon with which to defend herself. When she stumbled over the Mwellret she had killed, her hand brushed against the sword that jutted from its body. Turning, she pulled the blade free and faced her opponent.

"Come get me, ret!" she taunted through anger and tears and a terrible sadness.

The Mwellret said nothing, approaching cautiously, warily through the haze. Rue Meridian dropped into a crouch, working to keep her balance, to steady herself against the rolling of the airship. She found herself wishing she had her throwing knives. Perhaps she could have killed the Mwellret before it reached her if she did. But the sword would have to do. Both hands gripped the pommel as she held the blade stretched out before her. There was no time to find the others and no one else to turn to for help. There was only her. If she died, they were all lost. Given the condition of the ship, they might all be lost anyway.

Like Hawk.

The Mwellret was on top of her before she realized it, a huge dark shadow. It had masked its approach with a hissing sound that was so hypnotic and distracting that for a few precious seconds she had lost all sense of her danger. It was only her tears that saved her. Hands still clasped about the sword's handle, she wiped at them with her sleeve, saw the Mwellret right in front of her, and swung the weapon without thinking. The blade slipped under the Mwellret's raised arm and bit deeply into its side. Blood spurted, and the creature staggered into her, striking at her chest with the long knife. She deflected the blow, but the blade ripped down her arm and into her thigh. She cried out, seizing the Mwellret's arm and pinning it against her body, fighting the shock that threatened to paralyze her.

Locked together, they surged across the decking, each fighting to upend the other, to gain a killing hold. The contest was equal; the Mwellret was stronger, but it was badly injured and weakened from loss of blood. Unable to find anything better, it used its claws as a weapon, shredding Ruc Mcridian's cloak and tunic and finally her skin. She shrieked in pain and fury as the claws tore at her, then threw herself backwards in an effort to break free. Rover and Mwellret careened into the masthead and went down. As they did, the latter's grip loosened, and Little Red kicked free. But the Mwellret did not lose contact with her entirely, its clawed fingers grasping one leg as she tried to crawl clear. She kicked at the creature with her other leg, her boot heel slamming into its head. Twisting and rolling, they slid toward the railing, picking up speed as the airship gave a violent lurch. A broken spar slowed their skid, then gave way before their combined weight.

In a knot of arms and legs and broken wood, they slammed into the railing. Already weakened by earlier damage, the balusters splintered and gave way before the impact. The Rover girl saw the opening appear and twisted frantically to avoid it. She was too slow. In the space of a heartbeat, Rue Meridian and the Mwellret slid through the gap and disappeared over the side.

Unmanned and out of control, its decks littered with bodies and debris, the *Jerle Shannara* wheeled slowly about and began to move downriver toward the grinding pillars of the Squirm.

THIRTY-TWO

Bek was standing right next to Ryer Ord Star when the attack on Walker began, so close that he could hear her sudden intake of breath as the first fire thread lanced out at the Druid. The seer staggered, a high keening sound escaping her lips, and then she bolted into the maze. The boy, stunned by the unexpectedness of her action, stood rooted in place, and it was one of the three Elven Hunters who gave chase. The other two grabbed Bek's arms and pulled him back from the battleground as he struggled to break free of them. Walker was down, bolts of magic flying from his fingers in response to the attack, burning into the walls and partitions from which the fire threads burst. To either side of the boy, members of the flanking parties charged into the maze in support of the Druid, swords drawn, shouting out their battle cries.

Then the fire threads lanced from the walls through which they rushed, too, cutting into their unprotected bodies, slicing them apart. In horror, Bek watched one Elf disintegrate in a cross-hatching of threads, body parts and blood flying everywhere. Screams rent the misted air, mingling with smoke and the acrid stench of burning flesh. As the fire began to seek them out, trailing lines of red death, the Druid's would-be rescuers flattened themselves against the metal floor of the maze and crawled swiftly into the protection of its closest walls. Bek saw one of the threads clip Ryer Ord Star, spinning her into a wall where she collapsed in a heap. The Elf who chased her was cut in half a dozen yards away.

Walker had regained his feet and was calling back to them, but his words were lost in the tumult. Without waiting for their response, he started ahead, a wraithlike figure in the gloom, his arm extended before him like a shield, swinging right and left to counterattack the fire threads with his magic as he fought his way toward the obelisk.

Bek exhaled sharply, a wave of despair sweeping through him, and turned to the Elves who held his arms. He was surprised to see that one was the tracker Tamis. "We have to go to him!" he snapped at her in frustration, renewing his struggle to break free.

"He told us to stay where we are, Bek," she replied calmly, gray eyes sweeping the haze as she spoke. "It's death to go in there."

A scraping of metal on metal drew their attention to their left. From the low flat buildings they had passed coming in, a cluster of spidery forms skittered into view. Crooked-legged and squat, they spread out behind what remained of the flanking party led by Quentin and Panax.

"Creepers," Tamis said softly.

Bek went cold. Ordinary men didn't stand a chance against creepers. Even Quentin, with the magic of his sword, would be hard-pressed to stop so many. An endless maze, ribbons of fire, and now metal dogs—Ryer Ord Star's horrific vision had come to pass.

"We're getting out of here," Tamis announced, pulling him back in the direction from which they had come.

"Wait!" He brought her up short with a jerk of his arm. He pointed into the maze. Ryer Ord Star was trying to rise, dragging herself to her knees. He looked at Tamis pleadingly. "We can't just leave her! We have to try to help!"

Driven by a sudden wind, the taste and smell acrid, smoke roiled past them, and ash-clouded mist swept into their faces.

The tracker stared at him a moment, then released his arm, leaving him in the grip of her companion. "Wait here."

She sprinted into the maze without hesitating, the fire threads chasing after her, trying to cut her off, burning across the metal carpet in pursuit. Twice she went down in a long slide that took her under the threads, and once she barely cleared the edge of a wall before the fire scorched its smooth surface. Ahead, Ryer Ord Star was on her hands and knees, head bent, long silver hair hanging like a curtain across her face. Blood streaked one arm, soaking into the torn fabric of her tunic.

To Bek's right, more creepers had emerged from the gloom and were descending on Ard Patrinell's group.

Tamis reached Ryer Ord Star in a flying leap that sent both of them sprawling out of the sweeping path of a fire thread. Dragging the seer to her feet, the tracker led her back through the maze, running crouched along walls and across open spaces as the threads burned all around them.

They aren't going to make it, Bek thought. *It's too far! The fire is everywhere!*

He looked for Walker, but the Druid had disappeared. The boy hadn't seen what had happened to him, where he had gone, even if he had managed to reach the obelisk. The center of the maze was choked with mist and smoke-shrouded forms and sudden bursts of the red fire. To his left, Quentin was under attack, the blue fire of the Sword of Leah flashing bravely, the sound of his battle cry lifting out of the haze. To his right, the creepers were spreading out through the maze in search of Ard Patrinell, Ahren Elessedil, and the remainder of the Elven Hunters.

A trap, a trap, it was all a trap! The boy's throat burned with anger and frustration, his mind awash with thoughts of missed chances and bad decisions.

Tamis burst through the smoke and out of the spiderweb of killing red fire, dragging Ryer Ord Star in her wake. "Go, go, go!" she screamed at the waiting Bek and his companion, and in a knot they charged back through the ruins.

Quentin! Bek cried out in the silence of his mind, glancing helplessly over his shoulder.

They had gone less than a hundred feet when a pair of creepers intercepted them. The metal beasts appeared to have been waiting for anyone who made it this far, emerging from behind one of the low buildings, metal limbs scraping and clanking as they blocked the way forward. Tamis and her companion leapt instantly to the defense of the boy and the seer. The creepers attacked at once, moving so fast that they were on top of the Elven Hunters before they could defend themselves. Tamis dodged her attacker, but the other Elven Hunter was less fortunate. The creeper bowled him over, pinned him to the ground, reached down with one pincer while the Elf thrashed helplessly, and tore off his head.

Bek watched it happen as if it were a dream, each movement of Elf and creeper clearly visible and endlessly long, as if both were weighted and chained by time. He crouched with Ryer Ord Star held protectively in his arms, his mind telling him to do something, anything, to help because help was needed and there was no one else. Frozen in place by his horror and indecision, he watched glimmerings of light flash off the edges of the pincers as they descended, the frantic movements of the Elf's arms and legs as he struggled to break free, and the gouts of blood spurt from the severed neck.

Something inside him snapped in that instant, and forgetting everything but the now-overpowering impulse to respond to what he had witnessed, he screamed. A dam broke, and rage, despair, and frustration that he could no longer contain flooded through him, releasing his magic in a torrent, giving it life and power, lending it the strength of iron, honing it to the sharpness of knives. It tore from him in a rush and it ripped through the creepers as if they were made of paper, shredding them instantly and reducing them to scrap.

He was on his feet now, wheeling in a miasma of invincibility, everything forgotten but the euphoria he felt as the power of his magic swept through him. Another of the creepers appeared ahead, and he savaged it with the same ruthless determination—his voice seizing it, lifting it, and tearing it apart. He sent the pieces whirling into space. He scattered them to the wind like leaves and cried out in triumph.

Then something clutched at his leg, drawing him back from the brink of wildness into which he had allowed himself to wander. His voice went silent, its echoes singing in his ears, its images flashing through his mind like living things. Ryer Ord Star was grasping at him with her fingers crooked like claws, her bloodshot eyes gazing up at him in horror and disbelief.

"No, Bek, no!" she was crying out over and over, as if she had been doing so for a long time, as if she had been seeking to reach him through stone walls and he had not heard.

He stared down at her stricken face without comprehension, wondering at the pain and despair he found there. He had saved them, hadn't he? He had found another use for his magic, one that he had not even suspected. He had tapped into power that transcended even that of the Sword of Leah— perhaps even that of Walker himself. What was so wrong with what he had done? What, that made her so distraught?

Tamis was at his side, reaching down for the seer and pulling her back to her feet, her young face grim and bloodstreaked. "Run, don't look back!" she commanded at Bek, shoving Ryer Ord Star into his arms.

But he did look. He couldn't help himself. What he saw was nightmarish. The maze was alive with creepers and threads of red fire. Ryer Ord Star's vision had engulfed them all. His eyes stung with tears. Nothing human could live in there. Screams rose out of the gloom, and explosions rent the air with wicked flashes of light. What had become of Ard Patrinell and Ahren and Panax? What about Quentin? He remembered their promise, brothers in arms, each to look out for the other. Shades, what had become of that?

"Run, I said!" Kreshen screamed in his ear.

He did so then, charging through the gloom with Ryer Ord Star hanging off one arm as she struggled to keep up. She was keening again, a high soft wail of despair, and it was all he could do to keep from trying to silence her. Once, he glanced over, thinking to stop her. She ran with her eyes closed, her head thrown back, and a look of such anguish on her face that he let her be.

Shards of bright magic flickered in his eyes, hauntings of the legacy he had uncovered and embraced, whispers of a power released. Too big a legacy, perhaps. Too much power. A yearning for more speared through him, an unmistakable need to experience anew the feelings it had released. He gasped at the intensity of it, breathing quickly and rapidly, his face flushed, his body singing.

More, he kept thinking as he fled, was necessary. Much more, before he would be satisfied.

Moments later, the chaos of the maze behind them, the screams and flashes of fire fading, they disappeared into the gloom and the mist.

They ran for a long time, all the way back through the ruins and into the forest beyond before Tamis brought them to a halt in a shadowed stand of hardwoods. With the damp and the mist all about, they crouched in the silence of the trees as the sound of their heartbeats hammered in their ears. Bek bent over, gasping for air, his hands on his knees. Beside him, Ryer Ord Star still keened softly, staring off into space as if seeing far beyond where they huddled.

"So cold and dark, metal bands on my body, emptiness all around," she murmured, lost in some inner struggle, not aware of anything or anyone about her. "Something is here, watching me . . ."

"Ryer Ord Star," he whispered roughly, bending close to her.

"There, where the darkness gathers deepest, just beyond . . ."

"Can you hear me?" he snapped.

She jerked as if she had been struck, and her hands reached out, grasping at the air. "Walker! Wait for me!"

Then she went perfectly still. A strange calm descended on her, a blanket of serenity. She sank back on her heels, kneeling in the gloom, hands folded into her robes, body straight. Her eyes stared off into space.

"What's wrong with her?" Tamis asked, bending down beside Bek.

He shook his head. "I don't know."

He passed his hand in front of her eyes. She neither blinked nor evidenced any recognition of him. He whispered her name, touched her face, and then shook her roughly. She made no response.

The tracker and the boy stared at each other helplessly. Tamis sighed. "I've no cure for this. What about you, Bek? You seem to be full of surprises. Got one to deal with this?"

He shook his head. "I don't think so."

She brushed at her short dark hair, and her gray eyes stared at him. "Well, don't be too quick to make up your mind about it. What happened back there with those creepers suggests you've got something more going for you than the average cabin boy." She paused. "Magic of some sort, wasn't it?"

He nodded wearily. What was the point of hiding it now? "I'm just finding out about it myself. On Mephitic, I was the one who found the key. That was the first time I used it. But I didn't know it could do this." He gestured back toward the ruins, toward the creepers he had destroyed. "Maybe Walker knew and kept it a secret. I think Walker knows a lot of things about me that he's keeping secret."

Tamis sat back on her heels and shook her head. "Druids." She looked off into the trees. "I wonder if he's still alive."

"I wonder if any of them are still alive." Bek's voice broke, and he swallowed hard against what he was feeling.

The tracker stood up slowly. "There's only one way to find

out. It's getting dark. I can move about more easily once the light's gone. But you'll have to stay here with her, if I do." She nodded toward Ryer Ord Star. "Are you up to it?"

He nodded. "But I'd rather go with you."

Tamis shrugged. "After seeing what you did to those creepers, I'd rather that, too. But I don't think we can leave her alone like this."

"No," he agreed.

"I'll be back as quick as I can." She straightened and pointed left. "I'll skirt through the trees and come at the ruins from another direction. You wait here. If anyone got out, they'll likely come back this way and you should see them. But be careful you know who it is before you give yourself away."

She studied him a moment, then leaned close. "Don't be afraid to use that newfound magic if you're in danger, all right?"

"I won't."

She gave him a quick smile and melted into the trees.

It grew dark in a hurry after that, the last of the daylight fading into shadow until the woods were enveloped by the night. Clouds and mist masked the sky, and it began to rain again. Bek moved Ryer Ord Star back under the canopy of an old shagbark hickory, out of the weather. She let herself be led and resettled without any form of acknowledgment, gone so far away from him that he might as well not have been there for all the difference it made. Yet it did make a difference, he told himself. Without him, she was at the mercy of whatever found her. She could not defend herself or even flee. She was completely helpless.

He wondered why she had rendered herself so vulnerable, what had happened to make her decide it was necessary. It was a conscious act, he believed. It had something to do with Walker, because everything she did had something to do with the Druid. Was she linked to him now, just as Bek had been linked to him those few moments on Shatterstone? But this was continuing for so much longer. She hadn't spoken or reacted to anything in several hours.

He studied her for a time, then lost interest. He watched the trail instead, hoping to see someone from the company emerge from the gloom. They couldn't all be dead, he told himself. Not all of them. Not Quentin. Not with the Sword of Leah to protect him. Bitterness flooded through him, and he exhaled sharply. Who was he kidding? He had seen enough of the fire threads and the creepers to know that it would take an army of Elven Hunters to get free of those ruins. Even a Druid's magic might not be enough.

He leaned back against the hickory and felt the flat surface of the Sword of Shannara push against his back. He had forgotten it was even there. In the scramble to escape the fire threads and the creepers, he hadn't even thought to use it as a weapon—though what sort of weapon would it have made? Its magic didn't seem like it would have been of much use. Truth? What good was truth against fire and iron? As a fighting weapon, it might have served a purpose, but not against something like what they'd found back there in the ruins. He shook his head. The most powerful magic in the world, Walker had told him, and he had no use for it. The magic of his voice was the better weapon by far. If he could just figure out the things it could do and then bring it under a little better control . . .

He left the thought unfinished, aware of doubts and misgivings he could not put a name to. There was danger in the use of his voice, something nebulous, but unmistakable. The magic was too powerful, too uncertain. He didn't trust it. It was enticingly seductive, and he sensed something deceitful in its lure. Anything that created such euphoria and felt so addictive would have consequences. He was not yet certain he understood what those consequences were.

It was growing cold, and he wished he still had his cloak, but he had lost it in the flight here. He looked at Ryer Ord

Star, then moved over to tuck her robes closer about her. She was shivering, though clearly unaware of it, and he put his arms around her and held her against him for warmth. What would they do if Tamis found no one else alive? What if the tracker herself failed to return? Bek closed his eyes against his doubts and fears. It did no good to dwell on them. There was nothing he could do to change things. All he could do was to make the best of the situation, bleak as it was.

He must have dozed for a while, exhausted from the day's events, because the next thing he remembered was waking to the sounds of someone's approach. Yet it wasn't so much the sounds of approach that alerted him as it was his sense of the other's nearness. He lifted his head from the crook of Ryer Ord Star's shoulder and blinked at the darkness. Nothing moved, but something was there, still too far away to see, but coming directly toward them.

And not from the direction of the ruins, but from the direction of the airship.

Bek straightened, eased himself away from the seer, and came to his feet, listening. The night was silent save for the soft patter of a slow rain on the forest canopy. Bek reached back for the Sword of Shannara, then took his hand away. Instead, he moved to one side, deeper into the shadows. He could feel the other's presence as if it were an aura of heat or light. He could feel it as he could the skin of his own body.

A cloaked figure materialized in front of him, appearing all at once, wraithlike. The figure was small and slight and not physically imposing, and the boy could not identify it from its look. It approached without slowing, robed and hooded, a mystery waiting to be uncovered. Bek watched in fascination, unable to decide what to do.

An arm lifted within the robes and stretched out toward Ryer Ord Star. "Tell me what has happened," a woman said, her voice soft but commanding. "Why are you here? You were instructed—"

Then she saw Bek. It must have startled her, because she

stiffened and her arm dropped away abruptly. Something in her carriage changed, and it seemed to him that she was unsettled by his unexpected presence.

"Who are you?" she asked.

There was no friendliness in her voice, no hint of the softness that had been there only seconds before. She had changed in the blink of an eye, and he did not think he was the better off for it. But he heard something familiar in her voice, too, something that connected them so strongly he could not miss it. He stared at her, sudden recognition flooding through him.

"Who are you?" she repeated.

He knew her now, and the certainty of it left him breathless. Years dropped away, shed like rainwater from his skin, and a kaleidoscope of patchwork memories returned. Most he had forgotten until his use of the Sword of Shannara had caused them to resurface. They were of her, holding him close as she ran through smoke and fire, through screams and shouts. They were of her, tucking him away in a dark, close place, hiding him from the death that was all around them. They were of her, a child herself, long ago, in a place and time he could only barely remember.

"Grianne," he answered, speaking her name aloud for the first time since infancy. "It's me, Grianne. It's your brother."

Here ends Book One of *The Voyage of the* Jerle Shannara. Book Two, *Antrax,* will reveal the secrets of Castledown and its magic as the Druid Walker and his companions confront the mysterious creature that wards both.

What will happen next?
Please turn the page
for a sneak preview
of the next book—

The Voyage of the Jerle Shannara:
Antrax

available everywhere.

ONE

Grianne Ohmsford was six years old on the last day of her childhood. She was small for her age and lacked unusual strength of body or extraordinary life experience and was not therefore particularly well prepared for growing up all at once. She had lived the whole of her life on the eastern fringes of the Rabb Plains, a sheltered child in a sheltered home, the eldest of two born to Araden and Biornlief Ohmsford, he a scribe and teacher, she a housewife. People came and went from their home as if it were an inn, students of her father, clients drawing on the benefit of his skills, travelers from all over the Four Lands. But she herself had never been anywhere and was only just beginning to understand how much of the world she knew nothing about when everything she did know was taken from her.

While she was unremarkable in appearance and there was nothing about her on the surface of things that would suggest she could survive any sort of life-altering trauma, the truth of the matter was that she was strong and able in unexpected ways. Some of this showed in her startling blue eyes, which pinned you with their directness and pierced you through to your soul. Strangers who made the mistake of staring into them found themselves glancing quickly away. She did not speak to these men and women or seem to take anything away from her encounters, but she left them with a sense of having given something up anyway. Wandering her home and yard, long dark hair hanging loose, a waif seemingly at a loss for something to do or somewhere to go, or just sitting alone in a corner while the adults talked among themselves, she claimed her own space and kept it inviolate.

She was tough-minded, as well, a stubborn and intractable child who once her mind was set on something refused to let it be changed. For a time her parents could do so by virtue of their relationship and the usual threats and enticements, but eventually they found themselves incapable of influencing her. She seemed to find her identity in making a stand on matters, by holding forth in challenge and accepting whatever came her way as a result. Frequently it was a stern lecture and banishment to her room, but often it was simply denial of something others thought would benefit her. Whatever the case, she did not seem to mind the consequences and was more apt to be bothered by capitulation to their wishes.

But at the core of everything was her heritage, which manifested itself in ways that hadn't been apparent for generations. She knew early on that she was not like her parents or their friends or anyone else she knew. She was a throwback to the most famous members of her family—to Brin and Jair and Par and Coll Ohmsford, to whom she could directly trace her ancestry. Her parents explained it to her early on, almost as soon as her talent revealed itself. She was born with the magic of the wishsong, a latent power that surfaced in the Ohmsford family bloodline only once in every four or five generations. Wish for it, sing for it, and it would come to pass. Anything was possible. The wishsong hadn't been present in an Ohmsford in her parents' lifetimes, and so neither of them had any firsthand experience with how it worked. But they knew the stories, had been told them repeatedly by their own parents, the tales of the magic carried down from the time of the great Queen Wren, another of their ancestors. So they knew enough to recognize what it meant when their child could bend the stalks of flowers and turn aside an angry dog simply by singing.

Her use of the wishsong was rudimentary and undisciplined at first, and she did not understand that it was special. In her child's mind, it seemed reasonable that everyone would possess it. Her parents worked to help her realize its worth, to harness its power, and to learn to keep it secret from others. Grianne was a smart girl, and she understood quickly what it meant to have something others would covet or fear if they knew she possessed it. She listened to her parents about this, although she paid less attention to their warnings about the ways it should be used and the purposes to which it should be put. She knew enough to show them what they expected of her and to hide from them what they did not.

So on the last day of her childhood she had already come to terms with having use of the magic. She had constructed defenses to its demands and subterfuges to her parents' refusals to let her fully test its limits. Wrapped in the armor of her strong-minded determination and stubborn insistence, she had built a fortress in which she wielded the wishsong with a sense of impunity. Her child's world was already more complex and devious than that of many adults, and she was learning the importance of never giving away everything of who and what she was. It was her gift of magic and her understanding of its workings that saved her.

At the same time, and through no fault of her own, it was what doomed her parents and younger brother.

She knew there was something wrong with her child's world some weeks before that last day. It manifested itself in small ways, things that her parents and others could not readily detect. There were oddities in the air—smells and tastes and sounds that whispered of a hidden presence and dark emotions. She caught glimpses of shadows on the vibrations of her voice that returned to her when she used the magic of her song. She felt changes in heat and cold that came only when she was threatened, except that always before she could trace their source and this time she could not. Once or twice, she sensed the closeness of dark-cloaked forms, perhaps the shape-shifters she had found out on several occasions before, always hidden and out of reach, but there nevertheless.

She said nothing to her parents of these things because she had no solid evidence of them and only suspicion on which to buttress her complaints. Even so, she kept close watch. Her home was at the edge of a grove of maple trees and looked out across the flat, green threshold of the Rabb all the way to the foothills of the Dragon's Teeth. While nothing could approach out of the west without being visible from a long way off, forests and hills shielded the other three quadrants. She scouted them from time to time, a precaution undertaken to give her a sense of security. But whatever watched was careful, and she never found it out. It hid from her, avoided her, moved away when she approached, and always returned. She could feel its eyes on her even as she looked for it. It was clever and skilled; it was accustomed to staying hidden when others would find it out.

She should have been afraid, but she had not been raised with fear and had no reason to appreciate its uses. For her, fear was an annoyance she sought to banish and did not heed. She asked her father finally if there was anyone who would wish to hurt her, or him, or her mother or brother, but he only smiled and said they had nothing anyone would want that would provide reason for harm. He said it in a calm, assured way, a teacher imparting knowledge to a student, and she did not believe he could be wrong.

When the black-cloaked figures finally came, they did so just before dawn, when the light was so pale and thin that it barely etched the edges of the shadows. They killed the dog, old Bark, when he wandered out for a look, an act that demonstrated unmistakably the nature of their dark intent. She was awake by then, alerted by some inner voice tied to her magic, hurrying through the rooms of her home on cat's paws, searching for the danger that was already at the door. Her family was alone that morning, all of the travelers either come and gone or still on their way, and there was no one to stand with them in the face of their peril.

Grianne never hesitated when she caught sight of the shadowy forms sliding past the windows. She sensed the presence of danger all around, a circle of iron blades closing with inexorable purpose. She yelled for her father and ran back to her bedroom, where her brother lay sleeping. She snatched him up without a word, hugging him to her. Soft and warm, he was barely two years old. She carried him from the room and down into the earthen cellar where perishable food-stuffs were kept. Above, her parents sought to cover her flight. The sounds of breaking glass and splintering wood erupted, and she could hear her father's angry shouts and oaths. He was a brave man, and he would stand and fight. But it would not be enough; she sensed that much already. She released a catch and pulled back the shelving section that hid the entrance to the cramped storm shelter they had never used. She placed her sleeping brother on a pallet inside. She stared down at him for a moment, at his tiny face and balled fists, at his sleeping form, hearing the shouts and oaths over-head turn to screams of pain and anguish, aware of tears flooding her eyes.

Black smoke was seeping through the floorboards when she slipped from the shelter and sealed the entry behind her. She heard the crackle of flames consuming wood. Her parents gone, the intruders would come for her, but she would be quicker and more clever than they expected. She would escape them, and once she was safely away, outside in the pale dawn light, she would run the five miles to the next closest home and return with help for her brother.

She heard the black-cloaked forms searching for her as she hurried along a short passageway to a cellar door that led directly outside. Outside, the door was concealed by bushes and seldom used; it was not likely they would think to find her there. If they did, they would be sorry. She already knew the sort of damage the wishsong could cause. She was a child, but she was not helpless. She blinked away her tears and set her jaw. They would find that out one day. They would find that out when she hurt them the same way they were hurting her.

Then she was through the door and outside in the brightening dawn light, crouched in the bushes. Smoke swirled about her in dark clouds, and she felt the heat of the fire as it climbed the walls of her home. Everything was being taken from her, she thought in despair. Everything that mattered.

A sudden movement to one side drew her attention. When she turned to look, a hand wrapped in a foul-smelling cloth closed over her face and sent her spiraling downward into blackness.

When she awoke, she was bound, gagged, and blindfolded, and she could not tell where she was or who held her captive or even if it was day or night. She was carried over a thick shoulder like a sack of wheat, but her captors did not speak. There were more than one; she could hear their footsteps, heavy and certain. She could hear their breathing. She thought about her home and parents. She thought about her brother. The tears came anew, and she began to sob. She had failed them all.

She was carried for a long time, then laid upon the ground and left alone. She squirmed in an effort to free herself, but the bonds were too tightly knotted. She was hungry and thirsty, and a cold desperation was creeping through her. There could be only one reason she had been taken captive, one reason she was needed when her parents and brother were not. Her wishsong. She was alive and they were dead because of her legacy. She was the one with the magic. She was the one who was special. Special enough that her family was killed so that she could be stolen away. Special enough to cause everything she loved and cared for to be taken from her.

There was a commotion not long after that, sudden and unexpected, filled with new sounds of battle and angry cries.

They seemed to be coming from all around her. Then she was snatched from the ground and carried off, leaving the sounds behind. The one who carried her now cradled her while running, holding her close, as if to soothe her fear and desperation. She curled into her rescuer's arms, burrowed as if stricken, for such was the depth of her need.

When they were alone in a silent place, the bonds and gag and blindfold were removed. She sat up and found herself facing a big man wrapped in black robes, a man who was not entirely human, his face scaly and mottled like a snake's, his fingers ending in claws, and his eyes lidless slits. She caught her breath and shrank from him, but he did not move away in response.

"You are safe now, little one," he whispered. "Safe from those who would harm you, from the Dark Uncle and his kind."

She did not know whom he was talking about. She looked around guardedly. They were crouched in a forest, the trees stark sentinels on all sides, their branches confining amid a sea of sunshine that dappled the woodland earth like gold dust. There was no one else around, and nothing of what she saw looked familiar.

"There is no reason to be afraid of me," the other said. "Are you frightened by how I look?"

She nodded warily, swallowing against the dryness in her throat.

He handed her a water skin, and she drank gratefully. "Do not be afraid. I am of mixed breed, both Man and Mwellret, little one. I look scary, but I am your friend. I was the one who saved you from those others. From the Dark Uncle and his shape-shifters."

That was twice he had mentioned the Dark Uncle. "Who is he?" she asked. "Is he the one who hurt us?"

"He is a Druid. Walker is his name. He is the one who attacked your home and killed your parents and your brother."

The reptilian eyes fixed on her. "Think back. You will remember seeing his face."

To her surprise, she did. She saw it clearly, a glimpse of it as it passed a window in the thin dawn light, dusky skin and black beard, eyes so piercing they stripped you bare, dark brow creased with frown lines. She saw him, knew him for her enemy, and felt a rage of such intensity she thought she might burn from the inside out.

Then she was crying, thinking of her parents and her brother, of her home and her lost world. The man across from her drew her gently into his arms and held her close.

"You cannot go back," he told her. "They will be searching for you. They will never give up while they think you are alive."

She nodded into his shoulder. "I hate them," she said in a thin, sharp wail.

"Yes, I know," he whispered. "You are right to hate them." His rough, guttural voice tightened. "But listen to me, little one. I am the Morgawr. I am your father and mother now. I am your family. I will help you to find a way to gain revenge for what has been taken from you. I will teach you to ward yourself against everything that might hurt you. I will teach you to be strong."

He whisked her away, lifting her as if she weighed nothing, and carried her deeper into the woods to where a giant bird waited. He called the bird a Shrike, and she flew on its back with him to another part of the Four Lands, one dark and solitary and empty of sound and life. He cared for her as he said he would, trained her in mind and body, and kept her safe. He told her more of the Druid Walker, of his scheming and his hunger for power, of his long-sought goal of dominance over all the Races in all the lands. He showed her images of the Druid and his black-cloaked servants, and he kept her anger fired and alive within her child's breast.

"Never forget what he has stolen from you," he would repeat. "Never forget what you are owed for his betrayal."

After a time he began to teach her to use the wishsong as a weapon against which no one could stand—not once she had mastered it and brought it under her control, not once she had made it so much a part of her that its use seemed second nature. He taught her that even a slight change in pitch or tone could alter health to sickness and life to death. A Druid had such power, he told her. The Druid Walker in particular. She must learn to be a match for him. She must learn to use her magic to overcome his.

After a while she thought no longer of her parents and her brother, whom she knew to be dead and lost to her forever; they were no more than bones buried in the earth, a part of a past forever lost, of a childhood erased in a single day. She gave herself over to her new life and to her mentor, her teacher, and her friend. The Morgawr was all those while she grew through adolescence, all those and much more. He was the shaper of her thinking and the navigator of her life. He was the inspiration for her magic's purpose and the keeper of her dreams of righting the wrongs she had suffered.

He called her his little Ilse Witch, and she took the name for her own. She buried her given name with her past, and she never used it again.

The adventure continues in

The Voyage of the Jerle Shannara: Antrax

As the crew aboard the airship *Jerle Shannara* is attacked by evil forces, the Druid's protégé Bek Rowe and his companions are pursued by the mysterious Ilse Witch. Meanwhile, Boh is alone, caught in a dark maze beneath the ruined city of Castledown, stalked by a hungry, unseen enemy.

For there is something alive in Castledown. Something not human. Something old beyond reckoning that covets the magic of Druids, elves, even the Ilse Witch. Something that hunts men for its own designs: Antrax. It is a spirit that commands ancient technologies and mechanical monsters, feeds off enchantment, and traps the souls of men.

Published by Del Rey Books.
Available in bookstores everywhere.

Discover the secrets behind one of the greatest fantasy epics of our time

THE WORLD OF SHANNARA

The beloved Shannara series by #1 *New York Times* bestselling author Terry Brooks is universally acclaimed as a towering achievement, an unquestioned masterpiece in fantasy literature. Now, for the first time, all the wonders of Shannara have been gathered into one single, indispensable volume in which Terry Brooks shares candid views on his creation. Lavishly illustrated with full-color paintings and black-and-white drawings, this comprehensive guide ventures behind the scenes to explore the history, the people, the places, the major events, and of course the magic, of one of the world's greatest fantasy epics.

Written by Terry Brooks and Teresa Patterson Art by David Cherry

Published by Del Rey Books. Available in bookstores everywhere.

Visit www.delreydigital.com— the portal to all the information and resources available from Del Rey Online.

- Read sample chapters of every new book, special features on selected authors and books, news and announcements, readers' reviews, browse Del Rey's complete online catalog and more.

- Sign up for the Del Rey Internet Newsletter (DRIN), a free monthly publication e-mailed to subscribers, featuring descriptions of new and upcoming books, essays and interviews with authors and editors, announcements and news, special promotional offers, signing/convention calendar for our authors and editors, and much more.

To subscribe to the DRIN: send a blank e-mail to join-ibd-dist@list.randomhouse.com or you can sign up at www.delreydigital.com

The DRIN is also available at no charge for your PDA devices—go to www.randomhouse.com/partners/avantgo for more information, or visit www.avantgo.com and search for the Books@Random channel.

Questions? E-mail us at delrey@randomhouse.com

 www.delreydigital.com

Look for Terry Brooks' bestselling epic trilogy of good vs. evil!

—————◆◆◆—————

RUNNING WITH THE DEMON

Sinnissippi Park, in Hopewell, Illinois, has long hidden a mysterious evil. But now the malevolent creatures that normally skulk in the shadows of the park grow bolder. The brewing conflict draws John Ross to Hopewell. A Knight of the Word, Ross is plagued by nightmares that tell him someone evil is coming to unleash an ancient horror upon the world. Caught between them is fourteen-year-old Nest Freemark, who senses that something is terribly wrong but has not yet learned to wield her budding powers. These two souls will discover what survives when hope and innocence are shattered forever.

"FABULOUS. . A breathtaking run of near-catastrophes and revelations. . .His fans should embrace it as eagerly as they have *The Sword of Shannara*."

—*Publishers Weekly* (starred review)

A KNIGHT OF THE WORD

Fallen Knight John Ross makes a tempting prize for the Void, which could bend the Knight's magic to its own evil ends. Once the demons on Ross's trail track him to Seattle, neither he nor anyone close to him will be safe. His only hope is Nest Freemark, now a college student. Nest must restore Ross's faith, or his life—and hers—will be forfeit . . .

"SUPERIOR TO ANYTHING BEING WRITTEN IN THE GENRE . . . Terry Brooks is one of a handful of fantasy writers whose work consistently meets the highest literary standards."
—*Rocky Mountain News*

———◆———

ANGEL FIRE EAST

Knight John Ross has learned of the birth of a gypsy morph, a magical, rare, and very dangerous creature. If he can discover its secret, the morph could be an invaluable weapon against the Void. But the Void, too, knows the value of the morph, and will not rest until the creature has been corrupted—or destroyed. Desperate, Ross returns to Hopewell, Illinois, home of Nest Freemark. Together they face an ancient evil beyond anything they have ever encountered, for a demon of ruthless intelligence and feral cunning awaits them in Hopewell . . .

Brooks has a "way of casting spells—transporting his readers into plausible realms where sorcery is alive. . . . Magical."
—*The Seattle Times*